Reader, I Murdered Him

Jen Green, editor

Reader, I Murdered Him
Original Crime Stories by Women

With an Introduction by Alison Hennegan

St. Martin's Press
New York

Library of Congress Cataloging-in-Publication Data

Reader, I murdered him / edited by Jen Green : introduction by Alison
    Hennegan.
            p.   cm.
        ISBN 0-312-03415-6
        1. Detective and mystery stories, English—Women authors.
    2. Crime and criminals—Fiction. 3. Women—Fiction. I. Green,
    Jen.

    PR1309.D4R4   1989   89-35076
                                                            CIP

First published in Great Britain by The Women's Press Limited.
First U.S. Edition
10 9 8 7 6 5 4 3 2 1

Contents

ALISON HENNEGAN

Introduction

Time was when writers of detective fiction consented to be bound by a firm set of rules. Members seeking admission to the Detection Club (established in 1930) were asked:

> Do you promise that your Detectives shall well and truly detect the Crimes presented to them, using those wits which it may please you to bestow upon them and not placing reliance upon nor making use of Divine Revelation, Feminine Intuition, Mumbo Jumbo, Jiggery-Pokery, Coincidence or the Act of God? Do you solemnly swear never to conceal a Vital Clue from the Reader? Do you promise to observe a seemly moderation in the use of Gangs, Conspiracies, Death-Rays, Ghosts, Hypnotism, Trap-Doors, Chinamen, Super-Criminals and Lunatics, and utterly and forever to forswear Mysterious Poisons unknown to Science?

Penalties for defaulters were severe. The oath, often administered by the formidable Dorothy Sayers who had had a hand in its composition, is both serious and self-mocking. It acknowledges the writer's contract with the reader whilst making fun of clichés of plot and solution already firmly embedded in the genre by the later 1920s. Indeed, the capacity to make fun of itself was already one, if only one, of the characteristics of detective fiction.

Writers in the Golden Age of the 1930s could look back upon almost a century of a rich and tremendously diverse tradition of fiction primarily concerned with the motivation and detection of crime. Not all of it was instantly recognisable as detective fiction; much of it seemed far too grand for that. Nevertheless in the short stories of Edgar Allan Poe and the novels of Wilkie Collins and Sheridan Le Fanu, in works such as Bulwer-Lytton's *Eugene Aram*, George Eliot's *Felix Holt the Radical*, Victor Hugo's *Les Misérables*, Dickens's *Bleak House* and the unfinished *Edwin Drood*, later writers could discover familiar preoccupations with the nature of guilt and justice, could watch those earlier authors wrestle with the technical problems of leaving clues, laying false trails, building suspense and engineering satisfying denouements and retribution.

From the 1860s onwards less grand authors, many of them now completely forgotten, produced the novels and short stories which helped to establish a recognisable new genre. Several decades before Sherlock Holmes's first appearance in 1887, authors such as 'Anonyma', Andrew Forrester and Harry Rockwood had been writing not only of detectives but of women detectives. Throughout the 1890s and early years of this century increasing numbers of authors experimented with the new form. The prolific Baroness Orczy, creator of the Scarlet Pimpernel, also found time to chronicle the exploits of *Lady Molly of Scotland Yard* (1910). By the 1920s the detective story was firmly established as one of the most popular branches of fiction. The critic Q.D. Leavis felt nothing but contempt, anger and more than a little fear at the spate of books written to meet a seemingly insatiable appetite in the decade which followed the Great War. In *Fiction and the Reading Public* (1932) she noted with anxious distaste that 'schoolboys, scientific men, clergymen, lawyers and business men generally' were amongst the keenest readers of detective stories. Moreover, to her horror, at least one writer of detective novels believed he was read 'more by the upper classes than the lower classes and by men more than women'. For Queenie Leavis (who in 1936 was to launch a vicious attack on Dorothy Sayers and *Gaudy Night* in the pages of *Scrutiny*) detective fiction was essentially frivolous, time-wasting and pernicious. The majority of those who read – and wrote – it were people 'who in the last century would have been the guardians of the public conscience in the matter of mental self-indulgence'. In the degenerate present, however, 'there is no [self-]restriction now even among the professionally cultured'.

It was a curious attack coming from one who believed so passionately in the moral basis of literature. For although it was true that one particular, and very popular, type of detective story consisted of little more than an ingenious puzzle, on a par with a crossword, the breaking of a cipher or an exercise in pure logic, there had from the earliest days been an alternative type of tale intent on exploring the psychology of motive, the roots of crime and the curiously complex relations between pursuer and pursued. Holmes's own character is compounded of teasing moral ambiguities endlessly disturbing to a Watson who prefers his ethics and heroes clean-cut. In 1905, when G.K. Chesterton made his first foray into detective fiction with a collection of short stories called *The Club of Queer Trades*, he was already incorporating literary parody, social satire and his own brand of moral commentary. Six years later he was making triumphant use of his favourite and best didactic tool, paradox, in the first of the Father Brown stories where a shrewd and saintly detective priest constantly upends cherished assumptions about sin, crime and justice.

From the beginning detective fiction has shown a remarkable capacity to incorporate, adapt and transform elements borrowed from other genres, and women quickly established themselves amongst its finest practitioners. Hardly surprising in a branch of fiction so deeply concerned with the making and breaking of social codes, the apportionment of guilt and blame and the processes of judgement and punishment. For most of our history laws have been made, enforced and interpreted by male legislatures, Home Secretaries, legal officers, police forces, barristers, juries, judges and courts of appeal. Even today the legal profession, in all its many ramifications, remains largely male. If it's true that there's one law for the rich and one for the poor, how very much truer it is that all too often there has been one law for men and another for women. Women have always had bitter cause to distrust high-sounding abstractions, such as Justice. They have learned from experience that needs, emotions, decisions, and deeds found commendable in men are often judged heinous in women. The accused's gender rather than her innocence or guilt can determine a jury's verdict.

Moreover the law often fails to acknowledge that some of the crimes most often enacted against women are criminal: rape within marriage, for example, is, legally, no crime. Legal theory likes to distinguish between sin and crime, loves to explain that whilst some deeds are both sinful and criminal (murder for instance), others which are simply sinful (avarice, say, or pride) fall, and fall rightly, outside the law. Such helpful distinctions notwithstanding, the fact remains that many an accused woman has been found guilty for her sins, not her crimes. Mrs Maybrick[1] was probably not a poisoner but was most definitely an adulteress, as was Edith Thompson[2] who neither killed nor helped to kill the husband for whose murder she was hanged.

For many women crime writers and their characters, Natural Justice replaces the endlessly unsatisfying, because unjust, workings of the official judicial system. But their natural justice is far removed from Hollywood's recent visions of the mad, self-appointed crusading male who machine-guns his way through the urban jungle, possessed by a personal mission of revenge. Traditionally the women have rarely been motivated by retribution. Their concerns are to render the malefactor harmless, to remove the burden of unjust suspicion from the innocent, to set the record straight and to ensure that the final price is paid by the guilty rather than by luckless relations and friends caught up in crime or evil. Where punishment is official it is usually enacted after the book's end. More often than not, punishment comes informally, by suicide, by fatal disease, by accident, or by a judicious, rather than judicial, murder disguised as accident.

If all that sounds too close to a detective writer's version of Oscar Wilde's dictum 'The good ended happily and the bad unhappily. That is what fiction means', then it's only fair to add that many women authors have kicked against the code, impatient with its dishonest comforts. It's true, for instance, that Agatha Christie never describes the convicted murderer awaiting execution. Dorothy Sayers, however, in *Busman's Honeymoon* (1937), shows Harriet Vane's and Lord Peter Wimsey's new marriage all but destroyed by Wimsey's anguish as he awaits the hanging of the man he has brought 'to justice'. Josephine Tey's *Miss Pym Disposes* (1946) ends with an innocent woman planning a lifetime of expiation for the murder which someone else committed, without her knowledge, on her behalf. And Margaret Yorke, who contributes to this volume her own exploration of natural justice, created in *No Medals for the Major* a haunting and deeply distressing novel in which a small community imposes its own savage punishment upon an innocent and vulnerable man quite wrongly suspected of child murder.

Regardless of the frequent conflicts between the relative merits of the official judicial system and natural justice women, in life and fiction, often chose the latter because they were excluded from the former. Women detectives, independent and often professional, had flourished in fiction for several decades before British police forces consented to employ a tiny number of women in their criminal investigations departments. In real life, women and official detection were kept firmly apart. In fiction 'Anonyma's' Lady Detective, Mrs Paschal, was already at work by 1861, joined three years later by Andrew Forrester's unnamed Female Detective. On the other side of the Atlantic, Harry Rockwood's *Clarice Dyke* (married, unfortunately) had already earned a reprint by 1883. And, in fiction at least, many a grudgingly grateful policeman recognised that without female assistance he'd be hopelessly and humiliatingly defeated. Both Agatha Christie's Sir Henry Clitheroe and Dorothy Sayers's Lord Peter Wimsey hit upon a truth that was to become one of the most dearly cherished clichés of detective fiction, and one that was to give rise to some of its most memorable protagonists. Both Sir Henry and Lord Peter gazed at the potential detective power of England's womanhood and saw a grievously under-used resource.

Not, let it be said, *all* English womanhood. Some women are more grievously under-used than others, especially those who are widowed or unmarried, intelligent, alert and spirited, divinely endowed with insatiable curiosity and most conveniently free from encumbrances – husbands, children, employers – who drain strength, restrict mobility and hinder detection. Throughout the 1920s and '30s England's 'superfluous' post-war women were eagerly snatched up by novelists who had work for them to do. Christie's Miss Marple is indubitably the best known but Sayers' Miss Climpson, Patricia Wentworth's Miss Silver and Gladys's Mitchell's Dame Beatrice Lestrange Bradley are honourable associates. In America Stuart Palmer's astringently idiosyncratic Hildegarde Withers, a retired schoolteacher hopelessly wooed by Inspector Oscar Piper, extended the tradition. After the Second World War writers such as Nancy Spain and Joyce Porter, mavericks both, extended it yet further with the creation of their principally comic characters, Miriam Birdseye and The Honourable Constance Ethel Morrison-Burke ('the Hon Con' to her friends).

It is a tradition which has proved remarkably resilient. Always implicitly, often explicitly, it has consistently rejected insulting judgements traditionally passed upon 'redundant' women – the widowed, the single, the middle-aged, the elderly and the physically frail – from whose numbers so many highly successful fictional female detectives are drawn. It is, moreover, a tradition which has always implicitly questioned the effectiveness of conventional law enforcement. Exclusion is a two-way process and those who exclude are themselves excluded. Predominantly male police forces, rooted in a sexual division of labour, eventually isolate their members from knowledge and understanding of the larger, sexually mixed world in which they are to operate. The sexual double standard is not only unjust; it is also inefficient. Conversely the many handicaps experienced by the amateur female detective are constantly offset by her access to the privileged information available only in a world of women. The sexual double standard remains rooted in injustice but can be turned to her advantage.

Many fictional female detectives have in fact worked with the police: so, for example, Miss Marple is in touch with the admiring Sir Henry and the altogether less admiring Inspector Crisp; Miss Silver enjoys a curiously semi-detached working relationship with Inspector Frank Abbott; Dame Beatrice, a doctor of medicine and a psychiatrist, has official connections with the Home Office. Such collaborations are obviously beneficial for the woman detective, but they are also useful for the novelist. A story which incorporates two different types of detection – the powerful weight of the official state investigation and the individualistic amateur enquiry – can provide the opportunity to explore differing conceptions of evil, morality, crime, decency, truth and justice. The public morality decreed by the state is constantly at odds with the private morality of its citizens. Officially, the police view is the state's; often the amateur detective upholds a more ambiguous, less rigidly defined position.

Miss Marple and Miss Silver, both highly moral characters with an apparent respect for the men who uphold the dignity of the state and its institutions, might well be shocked to hear themselves described as morally ambiguous. Nevertheless both of them retain a stubborn core of independent moral judgement and Miss Marple consistently and explicitly expounds her belief that men and women experience and inhabit worlds made different by their gender and, to a large extent, shape for themselves different moral universes. In part Miss Marple's position echoes a long established and frequently expressed belief that all women are at heart law-breakers – uncowed by the Law, unwilling to accept its authority, unconvinced of its relevance, wisdom or justice. It is a belief that has often been misogynistically employed, offered as 'proof' that women constitute an inherent danger to the stability of the body politic and must therefore be excluded from and coerced by its legal processes. But it is also a belief which will bear a feminist interpretation in which women, seeing themselves ignored, traduced or discriminated against by the Law they have not made and do not administer, withhold their deepest moral and emotional allegiance from it.

Miss Marple may, at first sight, seem an unexpected repre-sentative of feminist views, though both she and her creator are far more complex characters than many critics allow. Other characters and novelists, however, have since the 1920s explicitly employed feminist perspectives in novels of crime and detection, even if the feminism has sometimes been as idiosyncratic as the authors (Dorothy Sayers and Gladys Mitchell both come to mind . . .).

Over recent years fiction's traditional division between usually male police officers who are necessarily professional and private detectives who are frequently amateur and often female has been breaking down. In films, in television programmes and in books the number of women police officers engaged in criminal investi-gation has been steadily increasing. But the newcomers have not ousted the female amateurs. Nine of the stories included in this collection have characters actively engaged in detection: only one of them (Detective Sergeant Maggie Staniforth in Val McDermid's 'A Wife in a Million') is a police officer.

In the sixteen stories gathered here we can recognise many of the elements which, over the years, have helped to make women's crime and detective fiction so vigorous and so versatile.

Crime is not synonymous with murder. Nonetheless, more than three quarters of these stories are concerned with violent death. Five place it in its traditional setting – the family. Traditional, that is, in Britain. In life, as in fiction, domestic murder has long been seen by other nations as a peculiarly British vice, as has the passionate and remarkably informed interest in murder found amongst so many Britons (although Susan Dunlap and Sara

Paretsky, two Americans who contribute here their own domestic murders, may well feel that the country which produced Lizzie Borden needs no lessons from Britain). Observers have been eager to suggest reasons for our curious national obsession. Murder happens most often when there is no other way out. The overpowering need for Respectability which, until so recently, gripped Britons of almost all classes, closed so many other escape routes. The stigma, or sheer expense and difficulty, of divorce welded together dangerously ill-matched partners. Inequities built into the laws governing marriage, property and inheritance not only kept women financially dependent but also allowed husbands to use physical restraints to imprison wives in the marital home. Truly troublesome spouses could be permanently confined, and many were, in private asylums. When the Law refuses its protection, desperate women must seek other remedies. Murder is one. For unmarried women, also, the demands of Respectability could prove impossible. The sexual double standard, with its relentless emphasis on female chastity, could turn a delightful male lover into a liability too dangerous to leave alive, as Madeleine Smith[3] discovered in Edinburgh in 1857. Only the Scottish verdict of 'not proven' saved her from the gallows.

It's true that over the years the worst of the laws discriminating against women have been removed but plenty of sanctioned injustices remain. And although Mrs Grundy no longer holds unquestioned sway, her rule has lasted much longer than we sometimes care to admit. Ruth Rendell, writing as Barbara Vine, created her magnificent recent novel, *The Dark-Adapted Eye*, in part to demonstrate that the social laws which governed the 1950s may be more alien to us now than those of previous centuries. Families today can often sustain blows to pride and reputation which might have led to murder in earlier times when concern for the Family Name frequently outweighed concern for family members. But, whatever the changes in the larger world, the family, by virtue of its tightly enclosed, inward-looking nature, remains a place of tension, secrecy and danger, ambivalent in its attitudes to the world outside, half yearning for its larger freedoms, half resentful of its intrusions. That remains true even when our definition of 'family' is extended to include communal households and lesbian partnerships (as in Diane Biondo's 'Something to Cry About', Val McDermid's 'A Wife in a Million' and Penny Sumner's 'Caroline').

The subject matter of much crime fiction is inherently disturbing – murderous emotions, the menace of physical and psychological violence, the battle for personal survival when security and sanity are under attack. Little wonder that writers have so often turned to comedy, either to distance themselves and their readers from the horrors they have conjured up or to make affectionate fun of a genre so utterly dependent on our strange attachment to the terrifying. Few authors have insisted on the comical aspects of murder so spiritedly as Pamela Branch who, throughout the 1950s, created a remarkable series of novels whose heroes and heroines were, every last one of them, fully accredited murderers who, for a consideration, were prepared to transmit their valuable skills. Her Murder Club formed, in effect, an oddly distorted mirror-image of the real life Detection Club, each bound by elaborate rules and punctiliously observed ritual. The comic tradition is ably represented in this collection by Susan Dunlap's 'A Burning Issue', by Jane Burke's 'The Permanent Personal Secretary' and by Sara Paretsky's 'A Taste of Life' whose briskly matter-of-fact narrative tells a tale in which the balance between horror, pathos and comedy is deftly held. And when Barbara Wilson in 'Murder at the International Feminist Bookfair' pokes reasonably gentle fun at certain aspects of feminist publishing, she continues a long tradition in which crime writers have bitten the hands that fed them. Parodies, of individual writers and of the genre, are almost as old as crime fiction itself. Few attain the impudent brilliance of E.C. Bentley's 'Greedy Night' (no prizes for guessing which book it parodies) and few, like Marion Mainwaring's *Murder in Pastiche*, sustain the joke throughout a whole novel, but the tradition lives on.

The horror and violence of murder are immediately apparent. But not all violence, not all murder, indeed, is physical. (Sara Paretsky's 'A Taste of Life' is as much concerned with something which our forebears would unembarrassedly have called 'soul-murder' as it is with physical dissolution.) Violence done to the emotions can destroy as thoroughly as a blow; faith, love and trust can be murdered as well as people. New light shed upon past events can alter our present relationship to everything, including the dead. Our present is the product of our past and when that past is suddenly transformed by new and often unwelcome knowledge our present must change too. Many crime writers have returned again and again to explore the explosive power of the past, as Sue Ward does in this collection with 'Teddy'.

Sue Ward's detectives (both outwardly unremarkable middle-aged women who cause younger, more self-consciously sophisticated observers mild amusement) proceed to gather their evidence painstakingly and methodically. Quite right, too. Did not the Detection Club itself have harsh things to say to those authors who relied upon 'feminine intuition'? Yet despite the strictures of the Detection Club intuitions have always played an important part in detective fiction. Around the turn of the century a number of writers (Grant Allen and Baroness Orczy amongst them) claimed that women's intuitive skills made them the best detectives. Subsequent authors have continued to debate the matter. In Christie's novels Hercule Poirot and Ariadne Oliver (a detective writer based in part on Christie herself) maintain an amicable disagreement on the subject. Mrs Oliver believes passionately in her feminine intuition. Poirot doubts that she, or any other woman, possesses it. But even he is prepared to acknowledge that 'intuition' may be the conscious product of subconscious observation.

Others would go further and argue that those who observe from the sidelines, from a position of exclusion or subordination, see more, see differently and see different things. Servants, for example, are the people best placed to know whether their employers are genuinely courteous, generous and just. They see, literally and metaphorically, aspects of character which may be concealed from their employers' peers. And subordinate, and therefore vulnerable, groups (such as women) must do more than listen to other people's words. They need to pay attention to body language, vocal inflections, facial expressions, inconsistencies in conduct, changing moods, discrepancies between words and deeds. From this mass of minutiae comes the information on which vitally important judgements may be based. These tiny details constitute evidence of character and intention.

But will a policeman recognise such 'evidence' if you take it to him? What *is* evidence? What constitutes proof? Nowadays forensic scientists are called in to help determine innocence and guilt. Just a few centuries ago, when science and magic were still friendly members of the same family, a magician might have been called as an expert witness. Even in our own fiercely empiricist age the police have been known to use – and use successfully – the skills of mediums and clairvoyants. The lines between the material, the paranormal and the supernatural are not, it seems, as rigidly drawn as we might wish to believe. In earlier fiction there is often a considerable overlap between stories of ghosts, mystery and detection. In 'Thinking of Evans' Lucy Anne Watt draws on all those elements and combines them in a remarkable and unusual tale.

For Queenie Leavis it was the escapist element of popular fiction, including detective fiction, which worried her most. To her it appeared to offer endless opportunities of evading responsibility and neglecting necessary but demanding duties. Yet one of the most striking aspects of women's crime writing is the range of social and moral issues it has addressed. At any point where specifically female needs and experience run counter to man-made laws and systems, you will find a woman crime novelist examining that conflict. Over the decades authors have built novels around abortion, rape, incest, marital violence, illegitimacy, voyeurism, sexual intimidation, medical mismanagement of pregnancy, birth and menopause, homophobia. . . . The list could legitimately be even longer. And, needless to say, they have not neglected other, more general threats: pollution, radiation, increasing surveillance, political corruption, the growth of fascism, the dangers of multinationals. Again, the list is hopelessly incomplete. Women crime writers, far from shunning unpleasant realities, constantly confront them. Crime fiction, as is the case with so much women's writing, is an adjunct to life, not an evasion of it.

Notes

Some readers may wish to know more about those women I have mentioned who, in real life, stood trial for murder. All of them have been much discussed in print, but the following books are particularly useful or interesting:
1.   Mrs Maybrick, accused of poisoning her husband and found guilty in 1889, was sentenced to death but at the last minute

was reprieved. She served fifteen years of a life sentence. See *The Trial of Mrs Maybrick* edited by H. B. Irving (Notable British Trials Series, William Hodge, Edinburgh and London, 1912); *Victorian Murderesses* by Mary S. Hartman (Robson Books, London, 1977 hardback, 1985 paperback).

2. *The Trial of Frederick Bywaters and Edith Thompson* edited by Filson Young (Notable British Trials Series, William Hodge, Edinburgh and London, 1923); *Criminal Justice: The True Story of Edith Thompson* by René Weis (Hamish Hamilton, London, 1988): a new study, drawing on Home Office papers originally embargoed until the year 2000 but made available early to the author; *Messalina of the Suburbs* by E. M. Delafield (Hutchinson, London, 1923): a novel based on the murder; *A Pin To See the Peep-Show* by F. Tennyson Jesse (London, 1934, reissued in Virago Modern Classics, 1979): a novel, closely based on fact.

3. *The Trial of Madeleine Smith* edited by F. Tennyson Jesse (Notable British Trials Series, William Hodge, Edinburgh and London, 1927); *Madeleine Smith: A Famous Victorian Murder Trial* by Henry Blyth (Duckworth, London, 1975); *Victorian Murderesses*, op. cit.

SUSAN DUNLAP

A Burning Issue

I am not thorough.

I don't explore every minute detail, every aspect and angle of a subject. Only fanatics do that. But there is a basic amount of preparation required of any adult who seeks to live in relative comfort, without being pummelled by recurrent blows of humiliation. And that preparation is what I fail to do.

It is not that I am unaware of this fault. *Au contraire.* Rarely does a day pass without it being thrust to my attention. There are the small annoyances; grocery lists I tell myself I needn't write down; recipes I skim, only to discover, as my guest sits angrily getting looped in the living room, that the last words are 'bake in hot oven (what other kind is there?) for ninety minutes'.

Or the time, as a surprise for Andrew, I painted the house. Anyone, I told myself, can paint a house. I do, after all, have two weeks, and it's not a mansion. This time I did not neglect the instructions on the can. I read them. What I did not do was ask if any preparation was necessary. 'Everybody knows you need to scrape off the old paint first,' Andrew told me later. Almost everybody. I had the second coat halfway on before I realised the house looked like a mint-green moonscape. But all was not lost. The day I finished, it poured. As Andrew said, 'You don't use water-based paint outside.'

I could go on, but you get the picture. I've often puzzled as to what causes this failing of mine. Is it laziness? Not entirely. Or a short attention span? Perhaps. 'You don't prepare thoroughly,' Andrew has told me again and again. 'Why can't you force yourself?'

That, I don't know. I start to read directions, plodding through word by word, giving time for each phrase to sink into my mind, like a galaxy being swallowed by a black hole. But after two or three paragraphs I'm mouthing hollow words and thinking of Nepal, or field goals, or whatever. And I'm assuring myself that I know enough already that this brief review will stimulate my memory and bring all the details within easy calling range.

In fairness to Andrew, he has accepted my failing. And well he should, since my decision to marry him was one of its more devastating examples.

I met him while planning a series of Man-in-the-Street interviews in Duluth. (Easy, I thought. People love to hold forth on their opinions. Not standing on a Duluth street corner in February they don't.) Amongst the shivering pasty male bodies of Minnesota's northernmost major city, Andrew Greer beamed like a beacon of health. Lightly tanned, lightly muscled, with bright blue eyes that promised unending depths, he could discuss the Packers or Virginia Woolf; he could find a Japanese restaurant open at midnight; he could manoeuvre his Porsche through the toboggan run of Duluth streets at sixty miles per hour and then talk his way out of the ticket he so deserved. And, most important, my failing, which had enraged so many, amused him.

And so six weeks later (what could I possibly discover in a year that I hadn't found out already?) I married him.

We spent a year in Duluth; bought a Belgian sheepdog to lie around the hearth and protect us. ('Belgian sheepdogs are always on the move,' I read later, as Smokey paced through the apartment.) I left the interviewing job (abruptly) and had a brief stint as an administrative assistant, and an even briefer one as a new accounts person in a now defunct bank. And in January Andrew came home aglow. He was being transferred to Atlanta.

I packed our furniture (which is now somewhere near Seattle, I imagine. There was some paragraph about labelling in the moving contract . . .) and we headed south.

It was in Atlanta that I painted the house. And it was in Atlanta that I discovered what I had overlooked in Andrew. For all his interest in literature and sports, his acumen in business, he had one passion that I had ignored. The hints were always there. I could have picked them up. A thorough person would have.

Above all else, Andrew loved sunbathing. Not going to the lake, not swimming, not waterskiing. Sunbathing. He loved the activity (or lack of it) of sitting in the sun with an aluminium reflector propped beneath his chin.

Each day he rushed home at lunch for half an hour's exposure. He oiled his body with his own specifically created castor oil blend, moved the reflector into place, and settled back as Smokey paced from the living room to him and back.

And the weekends were worse – he had all day. He lay there, not reading, no music, begrudging conversation as if the effervescence of words would blotch his tan.

I thought it would pass. I thought he would reach a desirable shade of brown and stop. I thought the threat of skin cancer would deter him. (Castor oil blocks the ultraviolet rays, he told me.) I coaxed, I nagged, I watched as the body that had once been the toast (no pun intended) of Duluth was repeatedly coated with castor oil and cooked till it resembled a rare steak left on the counter overnight.

On the infrequent occasions Andrew left the house before dark, people stared. They moved away, as they might do in proximity of a red leper. But Andrew was oblivious.

Vainly, I tempted him with Braves tickets, symphony seats, the *Complete Works* of Virginia Woolf (in fifty-eight volumes).

In March the days were lengthening. Andrew's firm moved him 'out of the public eye'. I suggested a psychiatrist (but, of course, they see patients in daylight hours).

By April his firm had encouraged him to work at home. Delighted, Andrew bent over his desk from sunset till midnight, and stumbled exhausted into bed. By nine each morning he was in the sun. The only time he spoke to me was when it rained.

In desperation, I invited the psychiatrist to dinner for an informal go at Andrew. (That was the two-hour late meal, and he the looped shrink.)

Finally, I suggested divorce. I almost filed before my lawyer insisted I read the Georgia statutes, this time carefully. It is *not* a community property state, far from it. And as Andrew pointed out, I was unlikely to be able to support myself.

So the only way left was to kill him. After all, it would matter little to him. If he'd led a good enough life, he would pass on to a place closer to the sun. If not, he could hold his reflector near the fire.

For once, I researched painstakingly, lurking near the poisonous substance books in the public library, checking and rechecking. I found that phenol and its derivatives cause sweating, thirst, cyanosis (a blue colouring of the skin that would hardly be visible on Andrew's well-tanned hide), rapid breathing, coma, and death – all with a fatal dose of two grams. Mixed thickly with Andrew's castor-oil blend, I could use five times that and be assured he would rub it over his body in hourly ministrations before the symptoms were serious enough to interfere with his regimen. If he got his usual nine a.m. start Saturday morning, he would be red over brown over blue, and very dead by sundown.

I hesitated. I'm really not a killer at heart. I hated to think of him in pain. But, given his habit, Andrew was slowly killing himself now. And one day's pain was preferable to the lingering effects of skin cancer.

I poured the phenol into Andrew's castor oil blend, patted Smokey as he paced by, and tossed the used phenol container into the boot of the car as I left.

I don't know where I drove. (I thought I knew where I was going. I thought I wouldn't need a map.) Doubtless I was still in the city limits as Andrew applied the first lethal coating and lifted his reflector into place.

It was warm for April; ninety degrees by noon. I rolled down the window and kept driving. If I'd thought to check on gas stations I wouldn't have run out of gas. If I'd thought to bring my AAA Card, I wouldn't have had to hitch a ride into the nearest hamlet.

It was still light and well over a hundred degrees when I pulled up in front of the house. Andrew's contorted body would be sprawled beside his deck chair. I hoped Smokey hadn't made too much fuss.

Cautiously I opened the door. Warily I walked through the living room, as if the ghost of Andrew's reddened corpse were waiting to spring out.

I heard a sound in the study and moved toward it. Andrew sat at his desk.

He looked awful, but not more so than usual.

I ran back to the car and grabbed the phenol container out of the boot. It was too hot to hold. I dropped it, picked up an oil rag, and tried again.

Slowly I read the instructions and the warning: 'If applied to skin can cause sweating, thirst, cyanosis, rapid breathing, coma and death.' I read on. 'Treatments' (a section, for obvious reasons, I had omitted.) 'Remove by washing skin with water. To dissolve phenol, or retard absorption, mix with castor oil.'

I slumped into the back seat. The sun beat down. Why wasn't I more thorough? Glaring at the phenol container, I read the last line on the label: 'Caution. Phenol is explosive when exposed to heat or oxidising agents.'

I dropped the oil rag. But, of course, it was too late.

DIANE BIONDO

Something to Cry About

There they were again. The screams. She rolled on her side and pulled the clock to her face. Three a.m. Right on time. Sometimes they came at midnight, sometimes at two or five or all those times, but always she could rely on being woken at three by that piercing painful holler.

It penetrated the thin walls easily. As if seeking her out, the screams moved about her bedroom, settled on the dresser, the rocker, then the bed itself, chasing her under the cover. Three minutes past three. Helpless, all he could do was scream, on and on, shriller and louder as hunger gave way to panic.

Becky sat up. He was getting himself in a right state. 'He'll have the hiccups and won't be able to breathe in a minute,' she said aloud. His small red face would be contorted. He'd be crying real tears by now, and his fists, like Becky's, would be clenched in rage at having been made to wait so long for relief.

What was it about the three a.m. feed? Why didn't they go to him? Six minutes past. If only they would pick him up! How could they sleep through the sound of it?

She got out of bed and put on her dressing gown. She kept the room dark so she wouldn't have to see herself doing it. Later, in the morning, she could pretend she had dreamt it. Otherwise, how could she explain to herself that she had sat up at three in the morning, dressing gown open at the top, touching and feeling her breasts? How could she be anything but mad if she believed the pinching of her nipples was the hard sucking of a baby's mouth and not the pulling touch of her own fingers? It wasn't that she believed he was with her, not really. It was just that they took so long and left her so much time to imagine she could do it herself.

Go to him. Lift him gingerly from the cot supporting the back of his neck. Rest his head in the bend of her arm. Carry him to the chair. Open the dressing gown. Quiet the hunger. Rock.

The trouble was, once he had actually stopped crying when she opened her gown to him. Was this coincidence? At one time she believed in accidents, but now it made her wonder. Why did silence fall that moment she felt the round little mouth close on her nipple? Why did the two of them arrive home to the same house on the same day from the same hospital? Should she call it coincidence that the day she learned she was unable to have children, a brand new baby moved in next door?

Ten past three. 'There, it's all right,' she whispered, 'Shhh. Dinner's here.' Suddenly it was quiet. She stopped rocking, her eyes wide open. There! It had happened again! What did it mean when it happened twice? She quickly covered her breasts and climbed into bed. She couldn't hear a sound.

The telephone woke her the next day. She groaned and put the pillow over her head. The phone continued to ring. She went and got it, crawled back into bed and picked the receiver up.

'Didn't wake you, did I, Becks?'

'Hello, Chris.'

'Now before you go getting funny 'cause I woke you up, I'm just ringing to say: a, it's twelve o'clock midday and b, I'm coming round.'

'Chris, I'm all right. Really.'

'Who said you weren't all right?' As it happens, I've got some work to do in your area, so I thought I'd do your front door lock, as I'm going to be around, you know, sort of by coincidence.'

'I don't believe in coincidence.' But she was thinking of how they had returned home within minutes of each other. She had just put her bag down and was retrieving the post from their shared front hall, when the door had clicked. She tried to get away, but there it was, the blue bundle, held slightly away from the neighbour's body as if being presented. It was no coincidence that there was no way round it, and that, faced with the baby, she had to say it. Congratulations. Her tongue might bleed on the word, but she didn't have to look. She tucked her chin in and retreated.

'Well, you've got to believe in something,' Chris was saying. 'And it's not God and not work, so what then? A chance meeting of two fine friends.'

'It's not chance if you ring me first.' Becky picked up a hand mirror and looked at herself. Her dark hair had an unwashed shine to it. The longer strands were curling in different directions. Her heart-shaped face was very white, and a sleep line creased her left cheek. She shook her head and turned the mirror over. 'Don't make a special trip for me,' she said.

'I wouldn't act out of obligation, Becks, you know me better than that!'

Chris hung up. Becky rested the phone on her shoulder and listened to the sound of the dead line. It wasn't pleasant like music or unnerving like screams. It was a nothingness sound, a dull humming noise without pitch, tone or variation. She lay very still and listened to its flatness go on and on. She liked it because it sounded like how she felt inside.

Chris let herself in and shouted at her. 'Are you still in bed, I thought you said you were all right?' She went into the kitchen, unpacking a carrier as she went. 'I'll put the kettle on. Cheese on toast, okay?' she called.

Becky got out of bed and went to the wall. She pressed her cheek to it, but all she could hear was the dead telephone line. She looked to see that she'd hung it up. She had.

'Becky,' Chris was behind her. 'What are you doing?'

'I'm listening for the baby.'

'Why?'

'I can't stop thinking about him. I think he's –' She stopped.

'Let me make you some lunch. Come on, Becky, here!' Chris tossed her a T-shirt. 'Put this on.' Becky half-smiled and got dressed. 'Whew, that's a relief. Now what's happening with the flat you and Sandy are renting? Council finish the floors yet?' Becky shook her head. 'Why don't you move in anyway, it's yours, isn't it? No point in waiting for a few tiles to be laid.' Becky moved past her into the kitchen. Chris followed. 'Or what about staying at Sandy's until the flat's ready? You know you can stay with me. I reckon there'd be some hurt feelings, but still. Anything's better than staying here.'

Becky sighed and sat down at the table. 'I live here,' she said.

'I know you live here, Becks, but it's not for the best, is it? It's not doing your head much good listening to that baby cry all night!'

'Well I can't move out just because there's an infant next door. I can't duck behind a tree everytime I see a pram coming, can I?'

'No, but you're just out of hospital and you should be resting and not having to listen to that shit!' Chris was rubbing her palms up and down the front of her legs, something she did when she was agitated. Some of the dirt from her work overalls came off on to the floor.

'It's not shit, Chris,' Becky said patiently. 'It's a baby crying for food. We all did it.'

'Okay, it's not shit. It's just normal everyday neighbourlike sounds. But' – she couldn't refrain from making her point – 'that doesn't mean you have to be tortured by them. It's not fair.'

'Fair!' Becky blew out her cheeks. 'Please don't talk about fair!' She got up, but didn't know where to go. The small kitchen looked as if it wouldn't contain her. She looked at Chris as if she might spit. Now we are getting somewhere, Chris thought. She preferred the abuse that accompanied Becky's anger. It was lethargy that defeated her.

'Why don't you talk to me,' Chris said. 'That's what I'm here for.'

'I thought you were doing the lock on my door.' Becky's face relaxed.

'I am. In a minute.' Chris settled herself in a chair.

'This baby next door,' Becky began, 'is connected to me in some way. Please don't laugh, I couldn't bear it –'

There was a knock on the kitchen door and Sandy came in. 'Just thought I'd see if you needed anything?'

Sandy was the largest of the three women, almost five foot ten and big-boned, but she had a way of shrinking herself by speaking softly and sitting down whenever possible.

'Chris,' she went on pleasantly, 'I see you're wearing work clothes. Could this be connected to work in any way?'

'Funny you should say that, Sandy.'

'Nothing to do with fixing the front door by any chance? I didn't even use my key, I just blew on it and it opened.'

'Be sure to take this, then.' Chris passed her a new spare key. 'No more blowing down doors after today!'

Chris had her feet on another chair and her hands folded across her stomach. Sandy eyed her sceptically. 'Anyway, it doesn't matter if you don't get to it, does it, Becky? We'll be moving soon.' She smiled at Becky. Becky smiled back, but sidestepped Sandy's hug by going for the teapot.

'You must've heard the kettle click off,' Becky said. She put everything out on the table and sat down. She pushed the hair back from her face and continued. 'Actually, it's good timing, Sandy, because me and Chris were just starting to talk about babies.' Sandy sunk into a chair and quickly looked at the floor.

'What we were saying before you came in was, I was saying to Chris, this baby is connected to me in some way. Every morning at three he wakes up. He cries and cries. They don't hear him. Three minutes, five minutes, can you imagine sleeping through those screams? They do. After a few minutes, I can't bear it, I get up. I sit in my chair and I – talk to him. Not out loud or anything, but in my mind. I calm him and then – well, you know I'm not spiritual or anything, but he stops. This process takes about ten minutes.' Becky looked intently at Chris who was rubbing her overalls and then to Sandy who met her gaze but was silent. 'Can't you think of anything to say?' she asked.

'It's not good for you to be here.' Sandy reached out and tried to take her hand, but Becky pulled away.

'In stereo!' She motioned to the two women opposite her. 'Where do you suggest I go? Is there a place in the world where babies don't get born?'

'Why don't we move into the flat?' Sandy had trouble finding her voice. 'Or you could stay at my place . . .'

Becky took a deep breath and said, 'Sandy, I don't want us to live together.' Sandy's mouth dropped open. Chris said, 'I'll go do some work,' and left. Sandy took out a tissue and blew her nose.

'Please don't cry,' Becky pleaded. 'Please, Sandy, didn't I say I only wanted to live together if I had a baby?'

'You shouldn't have agreed to the flat –'

'I thought I'd be pregnant by the time our names came up.'

'You agreed to live there with me –'

'*If* I got pregnant –'

'Did I agree to that?'

'I said it'd be great to live there if I had a baby. An extra room, it's economical, a good arrangement for the three of us. But it won't be three now.'

'We can have a room each, there'll be plenty of space. What have we got to lose?'

'If I move out of here and it doesn't work, I've lost my flat. My independence. That's all I've got now. My independence – it's the consolation prize for infertility. I can't give up the consolation prize!'

'You don't want me for myself. If I'm not part of your nuclear family, I'm redundant.'

'I still want you, Sandy. I just don't want to give up my flat.'

'And what about him next door then?' She leaned forward on the table and suddenly seemed her full height. 'How long will you listen to his screams, get up with him, time his feeds, talk to him through the wall –'

'Leave me alone, will you?' Becky tried to get away.

Sandy grabbed her arm. 'I'm worried for you. How long will you pretend he's yours?'

Becky pushed aside a chair and faced her lover. 'Until he is.'

Essentials for the trip would be bought beforehand. Nappies, obviously. A plastic bottle. Formula. She was going to have a problem with nappies labelled according to weight since she had never seen him properly. She would have to guess. What would he eat? She had no idea. What if he refused it, holding out for the breast? If he was starving, he would eat it eventually, wouldn't he? She decided to go to Boots straight away.

Chris was working in the front hall. Sandy had left in a huff. What should she tell Sandy and Chris? She considered inviting them. The journey would certainly be easier and more enjoyable if they came along. They could swap round the driving while she fed him. But they wouldn't agree to it. They'd try to stop her and she wasn't strong enough to carry through against their resistance. No, it was best for the two of them to travel alone. He'd have to lie on some blankets on the floor in the back seat. Blankets were just the sort of thing she'd be likely to forget. She rushed into the bedroom and pulled two old rugs down from a shelf. She spotted her suitcase and snatched that down as well. Why not throw a few things together now? She stopped and listened for Chris. The shrill noise of the drill assured her she was still occupied, so she packed, all the while composing a mental list of what the baby would need from the chemist.

Sandy walked from room to room surveying the emptiness. Each room had been freshly plastered and painted. They'd agreed on brilliant white – it would lend the rooms added dimension and depth. And it seemed to be true, leaning against one wall, that the opposite wall was very far away and space was everywhere, emphasising her aloneness. She moved across the cold concrete floors and into the kitchen. She opened the fridge door and looked inside. Of course it was empty. She opened the newly installed wooden cupboards and left them open. She dropped the oven door and left it hanging, opened the doors under the sink. Everywhere was empty, not a household item to be seen anywhere. Clean, shining surfaces, fresh brilliant white paint they'd agreed could easily be changed if they fancied colours later on. What did Becky say was her reason for not wanting to move in? Sandy left everything open and empty and went into the bedroom. Independence. The consolation prize, she'd called it. Sandy lay on the floor where she imagined the double bed would have gone. If Becky had a baby, she would always be answerable to Baby's needs, bound to the clockwork of Baby's routine. She'd be more or less housebound, at least in the early months. Only in these restricted circumstances was she willing to live with Sandy. Why was Sandy good enough to share her restrictions, but not good enough to share her freedom? By grouping them together like that, Becky was suggesting Sandy would inhibit Becky's movements as much as a baby would. Where did Becky want to go, untied to Baby and unnoticed by Sandy? Perhaps Becky was slowly withdrawing from the relationship. Maybe she wanted another lover now, one who was not so fond of children. Perhaps in the wake of her failure to conceive a child, Becky was inventing a new plan – a plan that did not include Sandy.

She wished for the anger that follows rejection, but all she could feel was sorrow and fear, crawling up her back like the cold from the concrete. She should have stayed and tried to reason with her. It truly was not good for Becky to stay where she was, regardless of Sandy's desires. All that business about calming the baby through the wall! She certainly wasn't in a rational frame of mind. It was selfish and cowardly to leave in a huff, thinking only of how Becky's disappointment had affected her. No doubt Becky was considering leaving her right now. Sandy sat up and decided to go back. But what would she say? All the words, apologies and sympathy in the world wouldn't change things. Nonetheless, she should apologise for pressurising Becky at a time when she needed help and support.

But at the door of the bedroom that would have been for the baby, she stopped. The last time they were here they verbally designed and furnished the room. Against her better judgment, Sandy went into the room to see whether or not the news had erased what their imaginations had created. She cried when she saw it was still there, the small white square room full of toys and books, the walls lined with cartoon posters and rainbow friezes. She was finally angry. Why did her mind insist on doing that? If the room had really been full of the clutter she envisaged, then she could unload the cardboard boxes and pack them full of belongings to be stored away. But how could she pack away what did not exist? How could they be expected to properly mourn someone for whom they had no memories? It was a cruel trick – that they should have lost the child they loved before they'd had a chance to meet.

It was no wonder Becky was behaving like she was! She felt a sticky grey shadow of madness folding over her own brain, and to think that on top of everything, she was about to lose Becky because she couldn't help her. In a flash she saw that it wasn't help or support Becky needed – she needed what she wanted, a baby. Standing in the centre of the would-be nursery, Sandy resolved to get her one.

Chris was just pausing to smoke a cigarette when the neighbour came out of her flat. Chris had only seen her at a distance and thought she always looked rather glamorous, but today she looked like somebody else. Her hair was a mousey colour and there was lots of it, all back-combed and tied up in a large orange flowered scarf. She wore a loose black T-shirt, a short black skirt and a pair of pink slippers with a hole in the toe. Chris thought her face looked too white to be healthy and her lip too puffy to be normal, but she didn't like to stare so she half smiled and turned her back. To her surprise, the neighbour touched her shoulder and whispered, 'I see you're doing a lock for your friend. Do you reckon you could put one on my door today?'

'Today?' Chris repeated.

'I can pay you what you ask . . .' She kept her voice low.

'It's not that.' Chris thought she should whisper as well. 'It's the time, really.'

'If I give you this now,' she removed some notes from a small purse, 'You could buy it before the shops shut and put it in, say in a couple of hours.'

Not being one who enjoyed hurrying, Chris looked doubtful. 'I haven't finished the one I'm doing,' she said.

The neighbour moved a bit further from her door while making sure it was still open. 'Don't mind me asking, but you don't go with men, do you?'

Chris blushed bright red. 'Sorry?' she said.

'I'll be honest with you,' she hurried on, 'I want to put my husband out.' Chris tried to look casual and nodded. 'He'll be waking up soon. He does shift work. When he leaves, I want you to put the new lock in. Can you help me?'

Despite her embarrassment, the neighbour's pleading blue eyes touched Chris' soft spot. She took the money and agreed.

'Thanks a lot,' the neighbour said, 'We've been rowing over the baby.' She looked as if she would disappear inside but instead stepped forward. 'I feel sorry for a baby with a dad like him. The man's not right – well, you can see that for yourself, can't you?' She pointed to her swollen mouth. 'Evil, that is. Anyway, thanks again.' She touched Chris' shoulder once more, smiled and went inside.

Chris shook her head and looked at her watch. Becky must have gone a long way for that pint of milk. She went inside and put the kettle on. She wondered if she should worry about what was taking her so long. She wasn't a worrier by nature, but perhaps this explained why her gas and electricity were off more than they were on. Just then Becky came in and before she could stop herself, Chris said, 'Where have you been?'

'Don't talk to me like that,' Becky took her coat off. 'We're not lovers any more, you know.'

'Oh, Becky,' Chris made her voice high and sweet, 'please tell me what took you so long?' Becky gave her a filthy look. 'Becky, don't look at me with such love in your eyes. It makes me think you regret the day you let me go.'

'I wasn't aware that day had come. Don't you have work to get on with?' Becky suddenly started searching the kitchen.

'What are you looking for? Listen,' Chris lowered her voice, 'I just spoke to your neighbour. Becky, why are you opening and slamming the cupboards?'

'I'm looking for the hot water bottle!' Becky's face was pinched

with worry. 'Maybe it's in the bathroom . . .' She rushed off.
Chris followed her. 'Are you cold?' she asked, leaning against
the door. Becky stopped shoving towels around and sat on the
edge of the bath. Chris took this to mean the hunt was off and
Becky was ready to listen, so she went on, 'Your neighbour wants
me to fit a lock for her today.'

'Today is almost over. I thought you had another job in the
area?'

'They cancelled. Anyway, I have to get to the shop before it
closes.' Chris moved to go.

'Hang on! Why do you have to do it today?'

'Never let it be said I haven't done my bit for the emancipation
of women. She wants to lock her husband out.'

'Oh, my God.' Becky took a deep breath.

'What's wrong with that?' Chris raised her eyebrows.

'What's she want to lock him out for?'

'She says he's "evil". I think they're rowing over the baby.'

Becky's knuckles were white from gripping the edge of the bath.
Sandy was right, you could blow on the old locks and get in. But
how would she manage if there was a new lock on the door? She
felt a stabbing desire to consult Sandy, but fought against it. She
could never explain how she'd gone to Boots and joined the queue
with two mothers also buying baby's things. Only they'd had
babies with them, attached to their breasts by little blue denim or
corduroy sacks with shoulder straps. Did they look at her with
curiosity, or did she imagine that they wondered where her infant
was? Because she was tense and the queue moved so slowly, she
said to the woman ahead of her, 'I'm doing some shopping for my
sister.' And bounced the armful of nappies to prove it. The woman
smiled and said, 'Mmm, it's hard to get out when they're so tiny,
isn't it? You need all the help you can get.' The woman ahead of
her joined in. 'What I wouldn't give for my sister's help!' she said.
'What I wouldn't give for me husband's!' the first woman said, and
they laughed at their shared joke. 'If I could just get a night's
sleep,' continued the second woman. She had her hand on the
baby's bottom and she bounced it up and down. 'Just one night's
sleep, I'd be happy.'

How could she explain to Sandy how the two of them started
talking and laughing together as if she weren't there? One of them
wanted one night's sleep, the other wanted to go to the pub but she

was breastfeeding and naturally the smoky atmosphere wasn't good for the baby. One of them agreed with the other how true it was you just could *not* be prepared for the pain when it comes out, and no, there was no way, no matter how many of your friends and sisters and sisters-in-law had had babies, that you could know what a responsibility it was going to be. How could she explain to Sandy that her anger made the shop swim and was murderous?

She knew she wanted Sandy with her, but she could not speak about what had happened in Boots or what she planned to do that morning. Words would make her into a pathetic monster and that wasn't fair. Her actions came from a place where there were no words, a place empty of explanations and justifications, a place fierce and raw in its desire. She knew without thinking, that speaking about it would render the whole thing impossible.

'I don't see why you have to do it the *minute* she asks you.' Becky tried to keep her voice down. 'Another day's not going to make a difference.'

'I know. But as I'm here, and she's in trouble . . . '

'One lock a week isn't enough work for you now?' She tried to make it sound like a joke but failed.

'What's wrong, Becky?'

'You hadn't even finished my door yet . . . '

'I'll just go and get the lock before the shop closes. Then I'll come right back and finish it –'

'You won't finish it, will you? You never finish anything you start.'

'Come to the shop with me,' Chris' voice was still level, 'and tell me why you're cross.'

'I can't come to the shop with you, can I? I can't come because we can't lock up the flat because you haven't finished the lock.'

'What is this about?' Chris knelt down on the bathroom mat.

'You'd rather help her than help me.'

'Of course I'll help you, Becky, trust me.'

'I can't trust anybody who works for a woman who doesn't even know how to feed a baby.'

'Why don't you like her?' Chris held on to Becky's knees.

'Why don't I like her?' Becky laughed. 'Because she's going to be one of those mothers I can't bear! You see it all the time, on the streets, in the shops, it drives me mad! The child is crying and the mother *smacks* it to make it *stop*! "Now there's something to cry about," she says. When I see that I want to go over there. I want to take the child away from the mother. Then I'll say, "Now *there's* something to cry about!" '

Chris sat back on her heels and stared at Becky as if she'd seen her for the first time. Frightened by the look on Chris' face, Becky pushed past her, knocking her off balance. Chris rolled on her side, got to her feet grumbling and went after Becky who had slammed her way into the bedroom.

'Why don't you like her, really?' she demanded.

'Go away!' Becky turned her back.

'Why don't you want me to put the lock in?'

'For God's sake, be quiet!' Becky cried. 'She'll hear us!'

'Why can't she hear us? Why –'

Becky lunged at Chris and grabbed her arm. 'Please don't let her hear us,' she whispered desperately.

Chris pulled Becky to the bed and sat down beside her. Lowering her voice as far as it would go, she said, 'Are you planning on taking that baby?'

Immediately Becky grabbed Chris' hand and said, 'Make me a key then!' Chris pulled away a little, but Becky held on. 'I'll be safer with a key.'

'Oh, Becky,' Chris said.

'You said I could trust you.'

'I know, but this?'

'I'm trusting you. Help me, Chris.'

'I don't want you to get caught!'

'Then make me a key and I'll get in and out in under a minute.' She shook Chris by the arm. 'I'll do it whether you help me or not. Will you? Tell me quickly, yes or no?'

'All right. Yes. Bloody hell.' She looked away.

'When you come in, put it under the pillow so we don't have to talk about it again.' And then she let go of Chris' hand and looked past her.

Chris stood up. Becky leaned back on her bed and covered her eyes with her arm. 'I better go before it's too late,' Chris said, but she lingered by the door. 'Becky?' Becky didn't move. 'I know you're listening, so I'll say it. For all I care, this woman next door can give us this one and have another. What I hope is that it makes you happy. I want it to be worth it.' Becky took her arm away from her face and sat up. Her eyes were so cold Chris couldn't meet their gaze. 'Under the pillow,' Chris said. 'If you need it.' As Becky stared in her direction, Chris hurried away.

She had just under ten minutes to get him out if she went in at three a.m. She wouldn't need longer than that. She knew the layout of the flat as it was a conversion and the same as Becky's. If, for the last three weeks, they had slept through the crying for ten minutes, was it possible they might sleep through the night if the cries were removed before they had a chance to be disturbed by them? Sandy thought it was more likely that their internal clocks were in better working order than their conscious minds and, come ten past three, screams or no screams, they would wake up and hear the silence. She threw her jumper over her head. When they did, she and the baby would be on their way to their new home.

She parked the car around the corner from Becky's and checked her watch. Ten to three. Swiftly and quietly, she got out of the car and began walking. She felt in her pocket for the small screwdriver. At exactly three she would slip it into the door. It wouldn't need more than a few pokes. The baby would just be starting to fuss. She'd wrap him in his blanket, pick him up and go. Once outside, she would run back to the car and get in. She was confident this would take less than ten minutes. She'd drive straight to the new flat where they would wait until it was late enough to ring Becky. In the morning, Becky would come and together they would forge a plan of escape.

She rounded the corner to Becky's street and checked her watch, five to. She walked faster. All she could hear was the sound of her own breathing. She felt again for the screwdriver. She went silently to the front door. Except for a faint shadow the streetlight cast over her, it was very dark. She used her old key to get through the first entrance. She stopped in the hallway and listened carefully. Not a sound. She checked her watch. One minute to go. She listened again, this time by Becky's door. For a second she worried that Becky, and not the neighbour, would discover her. What would she say? That she couldn't sleep and she'd come to apologise? Dressed in black from head to toe, wearing gloves when it wasn't winter and carrying a screwdriver? Never mind. Becky wouldn't guess her intention, she'd have to believe her. She removed a tiny bottle of whisky from her pocket, emptied it into her mouth, swished it around and swallowed. If she happened to be caught by the neighbour, her plan was to be drunk and have entered the wrong flat.

It was three o'clock. Time to go in. She took out the screwdriver. She slipped it into the keyhole. It made a clicking noise. She squinted and tried to focus, but it was too dark to see clearly. She touched the door handle and then her heart jumped in her chest. Someone had put in a new lock! She tried the screwdriver again, but the old lock used to move in the door and this one was firmly fitted. Damn Chris! Why did she think it was Chris? She checked her watch. Two minutes past three. Was there another way in? Through the baby's window? It was too dangerous. Someone would call the police if they saw her climbing in, and how would she get the baby out if she was unfamiliar with the way the front door locked? She had an idea to try Becky's key, just on the off chance. She was about to slip it in when she realised the baby wasn't crying. It was three minutes past. Hadn't Becky said he always had a three o'clock feed? He cries for ten minutes, she'd said, and then they pick him up. But there was no sound. It was so dark and so quiet! Sandy tried not to panic, but sweat was forming on her upper lip and under her arms and her feet were rooted to the floor. She knew she had to make a decision but her head was fuzzy with fear. She knew if she didn't act at once, her chance would be lost for ever because something awful would happen. And then it did. The woman next door screamed.

Instinctively, Sandy slid her new key into Becky's door and slipped inside. She tore off the gloves and stuck them with the screwdriver into the pocket of a coat hanging near by. She held her breath, waited for the lights to go on. The woman next door was sobbing. 'Becky?' she called out hoarsely, moving into the kitchen. With shaking hands, she reached for the light. She saw the note before the room was lit. 'Becky?' she cried, running to the bedroom and flinging open the door. The bed was made and the room was tidy. Sandy grabbed at the drawers. Some of them were empty. She looked in the wardrobe. The suitcase was gone. She could hear the sirens now, screaming their way towards her. She ran back to the kitchen and snatched up the note. The entrance door opened and slammed. She stuffed the paper in her jeans without reading it. The woman met the police in the hall. 'He's gone!' Sandy heard her wail, 'my baby's gone!'

She heard the crackling of police radios and male voices

mumbling. 'No, not the door, it's the window!' The entrance door
opened again. A loud male voice said, 'Mrs Wallace, I'm Inspector
Keneally.' Mrs Wallace screamed, 'If you're the bloody inspector,
can you stop this wanker cop playing with my front door? I'm
telling you they got out through the window!' Sandy rubbed her
arms to keep from shaking. The door to Mrs Wallace's flat opened
and closed. Interminable minutes passed as she paced, waiting for
the knock. 'Can you tell me what time it was when you last saw
your husband?' she heard the inspector ask. It wouldn't be long
before they made the rounds, asking the routine questions, 'Did you
hear anything unusual?' They would come in, and then, slowly, it
would dawn on them, no Becky, no clothes, no suitcase . . .

The flashing lights from the police cars shone through the thin
curtains. In the darkened living room, they reflected arcs of colour
against the far wall like disco strobes, round and round. Sandy
went to the window and looked out. Despite the time, a sizeable
crowd had gathered, most of them standing about unashamedly in
dressing gowns and slippers. That's how she spotted Chris. She
was wearing jeans, a jacket and a cap. Sandy dropped the curtain
and leaned back against the wall. Why was Chris outside? Had
Becky told Chris of her plan but not Sandy? She pushed this
thought from her mind. It was no time to be feeling jealous.

Outside, a door slammed. Sandy jumped. The voices and radios
came nearer. Sandy clenched her fists. Her teeth were chattering.
'Don't worry, we'll find him, Mrs Wallace.' The entrance door
closed. Sandy hid behind the curtain and watched as Mrs Wallace
was helped into a police car. Eventually the lights moved off the
wall and they were gone. Sandy took a deep breath. She couldn't
believe her luck. She could get out of there tonight and not be
around if they came back for questioning. So Becky hadn't been
deterred by the new lock. She'd gone straight to the window. But if
Chris had been in on it, had she agreed to put the lock in for the
neighbour, and if so, why? Maybe someone else had put the lock
in. She went to the window again. Chris was doing her Humphrey
Bogart imitation, standing under a streetlight smoking a cigarette,
no doubt waiting for the all-clear signal. Sandy lifted her hand.
Chris dropped her fag and came up. Sandy let her in. They moved
silently into the kitchen. Chris sat down, hands deep in her jeans
pockets.

Sandy spoke first. 'Did you know?' Chris nodded. 'Oh, why am

I so stupid?' Sandy moaned. 'She told me straight to my face and I missed it. I asked her how long she was going to pretend he was hers and she said "until he is". I just carried on like that was normal behaviour!'

'Don't beat yourself up, Sandy. You were upset about the flat thing.'

'I know, but I shouldn't have left her today! Chris, why didn't she include me? Do you think she was afraid for me or did she want to split up?'

'She loves you, Sandy.'

'Do you know what I was going to do to prove I love her? *That*. What she did! I came here to do it *for* her, but can you believe she beat me to it? Isn't it just like Becky to meet her own needs before you even have the chance to try!'

'You came here to take the baby?' Chris gasped.

'But I couldn't get in! The lock was changed. What a pathetic criminal! I don't know where Becky found the courage to go through the window.'

'What makes you think she went through the window?' Chris sat up straight.

'I heard her next door. She said they got out through the window.'

'Bloody hell!' Chris jumped out of her chair and dashed to the bedroom, Sandy close behind her. Chris dived at the pillow and tore it away from the bed. There, on the sheet, was the key to Mrs Wallace's flat.

'What the hell is that?' Sandy breathed, standing behind Chris.

Chris looked at Sandy with an expression that was wide and open and a bit mad. 'Why didn't she use the key?' she whispered.

'The key?' Sandy echoed.

Chris gripped Sandy's arm and pulled her to sit on the edge of the bed, the same spot where she and Becky had sat twelve hours before. 'When I was doing Becky's lock today,' she explained, 'the woman next door asked me to do a lock for her. I told Becky about it and she went mad. She'd been planning to get in tonight using a screwdriver. I think she was panicked she wouldn't be able to get in. She asked me to help her. It seemed a small way to give her some protection. But it's still here. Why would she choose to get in through the window?'

'Maybe she didn't go through the window,' Sandy said.

'Then how did she get him out?'
'Maybe she didn't take him.'
'Who took him then?'
'Who was Mrs Wallace locking out?'
Chris frowned impatiently. 'That doesn't help us with where Becky is.'
'Maybe she explains in the note,' Sandy said quietly.
'In the note!' Chris shrieked. 'Did she leave us a note?'
'I don't know if she left *us* a note, but she left *a* note on the kitchen table.'
'Please read the note,' Chris said more kindly.
'I stuck it in my pocket when the cops came. I was afraid it might be incriminating.' Slowly Sandy took the wrinkled paper from her pocket and unfolded it. 'The first bit's to me,' she said. Reluctantly, Chris leaned away from the paper.

Dear Sandy,
    I'm sorry for the pain I caused you. Please bear with me. I want us to be together. Do you believe me? I'm taking a short break, but when I get back, we have lots to talk about. I can start by explaining my note to Chris, written below.

All my love, Becky x

'All right?' Chris asked.
'Yes.' Sandy smiled at her and handed her the note.
'Read it with me.' Chris smiled back. Together they read,

Dear Chris,
    When you said she could give us this one and have another, I felt sick and ashamed. Hearing you say that made the reality of what I was planning come crashing in on me. I thought when the crunch comes I can't do that to her, because I know how the loss feels. To intentionally make someone feel like this is evil. I say leave the evil to the men.

See you soon, love, Becky

PS The key is under the pillow.
    I didn't need it after all.

AMANDA CROSS

The Disappearance of
Great Aunt Flavia

Great Aunt Flavia was the only member of Kate Fansler's family of the older generation to whom Kate would give the time of day. 'Even a minute is too precious to waste on Fanslers,' she used to say. 'Some people spend time with other people just because they're family, but I spend time only with those who move me forward into experience, not backward into memory or resentment or weary tolerance.'

'You've got it down pat,' I said. 'You must have rehearsed it. You better watch out or you'll start sounding pompous.'

' "Authoritative" is the word you want. "Bossy" if you insist, but not, I beg you, Leighton, pompous. As you will realise before long,' Kate said, 'when you decide to have nothing to do with your family, you have to have the reasons down pat; you have to live with them safely accepted by your unconscious. Otherwise you're more in family company than if you saw your family weekly. How did we get on that dreary subject?'

'It's Great Aunt Flavia,' I said. Kate sometimes calls her Great Aunt Flavia because my cousin Leo and I do. Otherwise she calls her Flavia, and with great affection. Great Aunt Flavia is, properly speaking, neither an aunt nor a Fansler except by marriage (his second) to one of Kate's uncles. The Fanslers were, until Kate came along, unremittingly masculine. Kate has three much older brothers; Kate's father had three brothers. One of these, left a widower, married the much younger Flavia who, Kate conjectured, had tired of chastity and decided to try another mode. She had produced, at the latest possible moment, a son, Martin, and as her husband slipped into senility she embraced eccentricity or what the Fanslers called plain dottiness. Leo and I tended to find Great Aunt Flavia a bit much until Kate told us to see Lily Tomlin as a bag lady in touch with people from outer space. 'Great Aunt Flavia to a T,' Kate said, 'in spirit if not literal fact. She has too much money to be a bag lady, but I'm sure she comes as close as her income allows.' The Fanslers are very rich and very dull; Kate thought it to Great Aunt Flavia's eternal credit that as a Fansler, becoming the first had not entailed becoming the second.

'What's happened to Great Aunt Flavia?' Kate asked.

'The family fears she intends to kill herself,' I said. 'They thought you might rally round.' Kate's family does not usually call upon her for assistance of any sort; doubtless they felt, in this case, that one prodigal could help another.

'How characteristic of them,' Kate said. 'They have considered her nothing but a nuisance and a burden, but when she decides to take control of her life, they interfere because she isn't playing by their rule book. Flavia is seventy-five if she's a day; she ought to know whether she wants to live or not. Why in the world did she confide in them about her plans?'

'She didn't. She made the mistake of consulting her lawyer about bequests and such. He sneaked to one of your brothers, or maybe a wife. Great Aunt Flavia is furious.'

'As well she might be. Can't she just tell them to buzz off?'

'Of course. But Daddy, knowing I like you or, as he puts it, allow you undue influence over me, thought I might talk you into talking Great Aunt Flavia out of doing anything drastic. Between us, I don't know if he's worried about her or her money; most of it's in trust for her son, of course, but Great Aunt Flavia has a good bit of her own, and under Fansler surveillance, it has grown and ought not to be allowed to wander off unattended. To do them justice, they may even be feeling a pang of guilt: they've never really treated Great Aunt Flavia well. Anyway, it was thought that you would sneer at Daddy but listen to me. You have to give him credit for that much intelligence.'

'Are you suggesting that I call up Great Aunt Flavia and ask her intentions, counselling caution?'

'Something like that.'

'Well,' Kate said, 'I may call her; I was about to anyway. But I don't promise a thing. Not a thing. And you can tell that to your daddy. Kate dislikes all her brothers, but my father most of all, since he is the youngest and should know better.

'Thank you, dear,' Flavia said. 'You do know how to give one a proper tea unlaced with nostalgia. Do you think we might move on to something a bit more fortified?' Kate, grinning, offered her a Scotch and soda, taking one herself. They were used to toasting each other. 'None better, damn few as good,' Great Aunt Flavia liked to say, not just repeating herself, but admitting a tradition and an alliance.

'They've put you on to me, haven't they?' Flavia, once fortified, asked.

'Yes,' Kate said. 'But I refused. It did remind me, though, that I'd been missing you. One of the defects of liking the young is that one is always the oldest person in the room. You make a welcome change.'

'I know what you mean. And that's especially hard for the likes of you and me who grew up used to being the youngest. Have you ever seen a movie called *It's a Wonderful Life*, with James Stewart, at Christmas?'

'Not that I can remember,' Kate said. 'Have you taken to watching old movies?'

'I've taken to watching television. Gives you an idea of what's going on, what people believe in. I think it's frightful, but I can't keep myself from watching.'

Kate was delighted. Great Aunt Flavia had never even owned a television set. She, Kate, did not watch much television, but she hoped, at Flavia's age, to become more open-minded. It was vital to acquire new habits in old age, boldly countering old prejudices, Kate said.

'In this movie,' Flavia explained, 'James Stewart plays a man who decides to jump into the river. The reasons aren't important, except that he considers his life a failure. He isn't old enough for such a decision, of course, he has little children, but no one who doesn't play a villain or a doctor can be old in movies. Things only happen to the young, even inappropriate things. One has to overlook it, in the name of sex. Anyway, he is rescued by an angel.'

'An angel?' Kate asked.

'Yes. He's male and timid and not quite successful, and he sets out to prove to James Stewart how much poorer everyone would be had he never lived. We learn that his wife without him would have become a spinster in glasses working in a library (a fate of hideous proportions, needless to say, despite the fact that she is played by a gorgeous actress who would have had no trouble joining a well-paying high class bordello); that some druggist would have killed someone with the wrong prescription; that the bad man, Lionel Barrymore (who *is* allowed to be old) would have taken over the town – you get the picture.'

'It's clear enough,' Kate said, 'and sounds a very good reason not to watch television.'

'Well, it was originally a movie, but they show it every Christmas. I've studied it carefully, and have decided that it is garbage in at least three different ways, but what really struck home, *despite* the movie, was the simple truth that because you've mattered in life doesn't mean you can go on mattering. James Stewart has friends who pay his bills, and little children, and a luscious spouse, but his past – anyone's past – is hardly the point. It's what you have now that makes you decide whether or not to jump into the river in winter, figuratively speaking.'

'I quite agree,' Kate said. 'There is only the present.'

'Thank God,' Flavia said, holding out her glass. 'Someone who understands.'

'Which is not to say,' Kate said, handing it back to her refilled, 'that I necessarily agree with your view of your present. I might agree, but I need to be persuaded. Try me.'

'I started talking to people about giving away my money, for scholarships, guaranteeing college to poor children who finish high school, that sort of thing. I soon discovered that while I was eagerly courted by those in charge of scholarships and such, it was my money they wanted, I was just a means of getting it, I didn't matter. I know I can trust you not to deny so obvious an observation.'

'You can. But there's always the matter of deciding where to give it. Only you can do that.'

'I have. Spent quite a time at it. I can leave all my money.'

'And then not have any more to live on?'

'Not even that. The income from the trust fund that is mine for life and then will go to Martin is more than ample.'

'Yes,' Kate said. 'I see.'

'You're such a comfort to me, dear,' Flavia said. 'You see things.'

'I can't help feeling, all the same, that you haven't taken advantage of your age and station in life.'

'Meaning?'

'Meaning you have enough money and are invisible. Have you thought where that could lead?'

'Invisible?' Flavia looked at her hand as though expecting to find it gone.

'I mean, when a woman is old, no one sees her unless she comes attached to money or some other sort of power that brings her momentarily into focus. So you must hold on to your money to become visible when you choose. It will, all in good time, get to the right causes. Meanwhile, why not have on your magic cap, be invisible, discover things?'

'I see what you mean. You mean like Agatha Christie's Miss Marple; pussy-foot around. Notice people when they don't notice you. See what's going on. Be clever.'

'Exactly,' Kate said. 'Too few people take advantage of the fun of being old; they're always trying to pass for young.'

'I'll have another watercress sandwich,' Flavia said. 'It's almost dinner time; this will save me having to think about eating.' She already had a far-away look in her eye.

Some considerable time later, I had to tell Kate that the family was again worried about Great Aunt Flavia. 'Worried' was a nice word in the circumstances; they were hysterical.

'It's Great Aunt Flavia,' I said when I had got Kate on the phone. 'She's disappeared.'

'Disappeared!' Kate all but shouted.

'In the South,' I said.

'The South,' Kate said, softer this time.

I really was annoyed with her. 'If you're just going to keep repeating everything I say, it will not help Flavia.'

'I suppose she was visiting Georgiana,' Kate said.

'You guessed right. Georgiana was quite upset on the telephone, I understand. She called Larry, you not being available.' Larry is Kate's brother, not my father, probably the stuffiest of the brothers, which is a little like saying that one elephant is bigger than another.

'When did Flavia disappear?'

'Several days ago. Georgiana, being Southern, wanted to

wait a while before causing a fuss.'

'What was she waiting for?' Kate shouted, but I had already
decided to hang up and go see Kate in person. She tended to repeat
herself more on the phone than when face to face. I knew she could
call Georgiana, and I wanted to be with Kate when she decided
what to do, to keep informed and be part of the action. Kate never
means to overlook me, but she tends to get involved and forget to
tell me things.

Georgiana Montgomery had been to Bryn Mawr with Flavia at
a time when few women went to college – so Great Aunt Flavia
always told us – and nice young ladies from the South never went
to college, and certainly never to a Northern college. But
Georgiana's mother, who was from the North, expected her
daughter to do great things, to challenge Southern ladyhood. So
much for parental expectations: the nearest Georgiana came in her
youth to challenging anything was in befriending Flavia. They
were Freshman roommates by college fiat, and roommates after
that by choice. Georgiana returned South after graduation,
married a proper Southern gentleman who died twenty years later
leaving her a childless and (one supposed) rich widow. All
Georgiana would ever tell Flavia was that she was 'comfortable'.

But Great Aunt Flavia must have had more of an effect on
Georgiana than anyone realised, because bit by bit she began to
work for civil rights for blacks who, Flavia said, were called
coloured people in those days, and by civil rights Georgiana meant
the whole bag: votes, education, desegregation all along the line.
Georgiana kept her local friends because she was from an
important family, had married into an important family, and was
a fine person, and because (Kate guessed) she stuck to civil rights,
and never went in for any other fancy ideas, like the Equal Rights
Amendment, or sexual liberation, or divorce, or the idea that
man's lot wasn't just as hard as women's. She wanted the coloured
people to have their fair rights, and apart from that, she led the life
of a Southern lady.

Flavia visited Georgiana for a month every spring, both before
Flavia's husband died and after. Flavia used to say life took on a
new prospect in the South, where one lived in an orderly, gracious
fashion, inhaling the scent of magnolias or verbena or whatever
they grow in the South, having lemonade on the porch, paying
calls on Georgiana's friends and having them to dinner. Most of

the civil rights business was done by Georgiana on the telephone, and intruded little into their daily routine. They went their separate ways in the morning, had their lunch, separately or together, in one of the nice restaurants in town (Georgiana said preparing lunch was just too much for her housekeeper) and met in the late afternoon for tea or, more likely, lemonade. Flavia said it was a most relaxing life, for one month a year.

By the time I got to Kate's she had reached Georgiana on the telephone, was obviously listening to some long explanation and motioned me to sit down and keep quiet. Unobserved I would have picked up an extension and listened in, but Kate thought eavesdropping on telephone calls in the order of poisoning wells (it poisoned trust) so I waited for her to hang up and start telling me what was going on.

As it turned out, there wasn't much to tell. The last time Georgiana saw Flavia, they had had dinner with some friends, and sat around together for a while talking of this and that. Then Flavia and Georgiana had gone to bed; a perfectly ordinary evening. Georgiana always breakfasted in her room and stayed there throughout the morning attending to business. Flavia had breakfast in the breakfast room – nothing in the least unusual. When Georgiana came downstairs preparatory to going out to lunch, she learned that Flavia had already left for her own luncheon engagement. From which Flavia never returned.

'That's the last anybody heard from her?' I asked. 'How many days ago?'

'Three days ago, four if we count today,' Kate said. 'Georgiana heard from Flavia once, on the evening of the day she didn't return. She sounded rather breathless, and simply said: "Don't worry about me if you don't see me for a while. I'm just away for a few days. I can't call because they'll probably listen in on your telephone. Don't worry." Georgiana insists that was the whole and exact message, and I've never seen any reason to doubt what Georgiana says.'

'What are you going to do?' I asked Kate.

'I'm going there, of course,' Kate said. 'I have a horrible feeling I'm responsible for all this.' I knew Kate wouldn't let me come, and she didn't, but she did promise to call me every evening from a phone booth, in case Georgiana's telephone was tapped.

'You're kidding,' I said.

'Leighton,' Kate said sternly, while throwing things into a flight bag (Kate is not one of your neat packers) 'if you don't think we live in a total surveillance society, you had better wake up. Have you any idea the watch that can be kept on people?' she added darkly. 'Please try to be home each day at six in the evening.' And with that she was gone.

Kate went right to Georgiana's from the airport and heard the whole story again while drinking lemonade on the porch. Georgiana said she had informed the police about Flavia's disappearance, and they had made all the usual enquiries – the morgue, hospitals, vagrants, reports of old ladies hanging around bus and train stations or airports – all to no avail. 'No avail,' Georgiana repeated, sighing. She had always feared Flavia would do something impulsive and foolish, and clearly Flavia had gone and done it.

'Was there anything unusual about her this time?' Kate asked Georgiana. 'Was she different than on her previous visits?'

'Yes and no,' Georgiana said, in her slow, Southern way. Kate had long ago discovered that Southerners do not think as slowly as they talk, but Northerners have to train themselves not to snatch the end of sentences out of the mouths of their Southern friends. 'Flavia seemed more, you might say *purposeful*, than I remembered her. She asked more questions, and read the papers more intensely. She even seemed more interested in my Merryfields day. Before, she always refused to go with me, saying she saw enough old folks without looking for them.'

'Merryfields?' Kate asked.

'The old people's home, nursing home really, but we don't like to call it that. For old folks who can't care for themselves and haven't any family hereabouts. It's a nice place, for a place like that. Not like the nursing homes I read about in New York.'

Kate merely nodded. The last thing she wanted at the moment was to get Georgiana started on the merits of the South and the horrors of New York, not what Kate thought of as a productive conversation at the best of times. 'Flavia seemed more interested in – er – Merryfields this time?'

'Much more interested. She surprised me right at first by offering to come with me for my weekly visit when I hadn't even asked her – she'd always refused and I thought the question of her coming was moot. Then she asked all sorts of questions about it, and talked to many of the women patients. There are many more women patients than men, as you might expect. She even wanted to stay on when I was ready to go. I was quite concerned. "You aren't thinking you might end up in a place like that, I hope, Flavia," I said, "because I wouldn't allow it. You'd make your home right here with me," I said.'

'And what did she say to that?' Kate asked when Georgiana's pause was longer than could be accounted for by the speech habits of the South.

'She said: "You're a dear, Georgiana, and you know there's always a place for you in New York with me, if the situations should be reversed." Now that's about as likely as a blizzard in Alabama, but I appreciated the thought. Anyway, she wasn't looking at Merryfields in a personal way, so I paid the matter no more mind. When Flavia's here she always goes her own way until tea time, and I was glad she seemed occupied and busy. Mostly when she visited she read a whole lot, but this time she seemed to spend hours in the town noticing things. I took that as a good sign; lack of interest is bad in the old. I was glad not to have to worry about Flavia on that score. I couldn't have known, could I, that she would disappear and worry me just when I was easy in my mind?'

Kate nodded her understanding of Georgiana's worry. 'Do you think I ought to consult the family lawyer, Matthew Finley?' Georgiana asked Kate after a time. 'He's the son of our old family lawyer, and his granddaddy was Papa's lawyer before that. He's young, but he understands how to deal with the world and with old folks like me. Maybe he could give us some good advice.'

'We ought to keep him in reserve, anyway,' Kate said. 'In case we actually have some facts to deal with. Meantime, I think I'll just poke around a little on my own. Try not to worry too much; the old saw about no news being good news was invented for situations just like this. Besides, I can't imagine Flavia doing anything foolish, not really.'

'That's the difference between us,' Georgiana said. 'I can.'

Kate stayed several days with Georgiana hoping for a sign from Great Aunt Flavia, but there wasn't the breath of a sign. Kate called me each day at six from a phone booth as she had promised, but she had nothing to report. The police, egged on by Georgiana's influential friends and relations, had stepped up their search, but they found nothing. Kate was ready to retreat back to the North, since there seemed little anyone could do down there among the magnolias or verbena or whatever it is, when the most extraordinary story appeared in the papers with the sudden force of a powerful explosion. The minister of one of the most successful of the fundamentalist churches, who had collected millions of dollars in the service of God at His explicit direction, was photographed entering a motel in Georgiana's town with a prostitute. There was no question of the woman's profession, nor of her understanding of her client's intentions as they entered the motel. By that evening, the minister himself was on television – most of his congregation were reached in this way – pleading for forgiveness of his sin, and promising to reform. Kate, for reasons she could not explain to herself let alone to Georgiana, decided to stay on for a bit.

When she called me that evening, she said she was talking from Georgiana's phone, since there wasn't any more anyone could learn by listening in. At Kate's insistence, Georgiana had called Matthew Finley, the family lawyer, and urged him in her gentle but firm manner to discover from the newspaper that had first printed the picture where they had got it. Georgiana told Finley she would wait by her phone for an answer, but could not give a reason. She made it clear, however, that her future legal business depended on prompt action: this disappearance of Flavia had gone on long enough, and if Kate thought this information would hasten Flavia's return, she, Georgiana, would supply it.

Finley stopped asking questions, and went to work. He rang back with the information in a remarkably short time. Kate, listening to Georgiana receive it on the telephone, fought the impulse to grab the receiver from her gentle hands.

'I don't know what you expected, my dear,' Georgiana said when she had hung up after thanking Finley in her deliberate way, 'but the photograph was dropped off at the paper anonymously; that is, it was left at the reception desk, and no one remembers who left it. It was marked 'urgent', but bore no message other than the name of the minister in the picture.'

'An invisible person left it. Didn't they check out the picture?'

'I was just coming to that, dear,' Georgiana mildly said, while Kate wondered if stressful impatience could shorten one's life by decades, as seemed likely. 'The newspaper sent out an "investigative reporter",' Georgiana ever so lightly emphasised the phrase, 'and he found the – er – woman in the picture. She admitted readily enough that it was indeed she, and that the man with her was indeed the minister, whose photograph the reporter showed her. She had not known who her "client" was, but this was not the first time she had "serviced" him. Poor Matthew Finley was quite embarrassed at having to report this unseemly business. When they had verified all this, the newspaper people decided to print the picture.'

'The rest is history,' Kate said. 'Georgiana, may I stay on a day or two more. I think I may be able to find Flavia. But I'm going to have to visit your old people's home, Merryland, as soon as possible.'

'Merryfields, dear. We'll go this very minute, if you'll just let me get ready. Surely you don't think one of those old people did Flavia in?'

'I think they did the naughty minister in, but time will tell.'

'If you want any information from the old people, Kate,' Georgiana said, pausing on the staircase, 'perhaps you had better let me try to elicit it. Your rather, well, *Northern* manner might just confuse them, and take more time in the end. Besides, they know me. Now what is it you're trying to discover?' Kate, who could not but see the force of Georgiana's words, had to consent, but she wondered if she would survive waiting for Georgiana to return with her information. I told Kate later that now, at last, she knew how *I* felt when she left me so cruelly suspended in the course of investigations.

Georgiana allowed Kate to go with her to Merryfields, but not to accompany her upstairs on her visits to the old people. 'You'll just upset them; even if you don't speak (and we know how unlikely that is, dear) just the presence of a stranger may very well put them off their stride. Now you just sit in the waiting room and *wait*.' No one but Georgiana could have got away with it.

But when she came down again a considerable time later, it was clear that she thought she had got what Kate wanted. And Kate, when she heard it, thought so too. 'Though what this has to do with Flavia's disappearance, I cannot imagine,' Georgiana announced in the face of Kate's excitement.

Georgiana reported that the dear old ladies had told her *all* about the visits of her dear friend from the North: Flavia. They tended to wander and to repeat themselves, but there was no doubt the conversation had certainly turned to the Divine Church of the Air, which they watched assiduously. Surely, they told Flavia, their dear Minister was talking to each of them personally, because he had read their letters, had answered them personally, and was grateful that their contributions, slight as they were, were helping to spread the word of God and lead others to be born again to Christ. Each lady had shown Flavia her letters, typed of course but addressed to her personally, with the minister's promise to pray for her with special fervour and by name. Each old person, however deserted in this world, was not forgotten by God or by His minister on earth and the Divine Church of the Airwaves. The ladies had even trusted Georgiana with a few of their letters, which Georgiana produced.

'How much money did they send?' Kate asked. Of course, Georgiana didn't like to ask the *exact* amount, but it had been as much as the poor dears could afford. They didn't have much left over after paying for their care: just a little for personal use, most of which they were honoured to give to the dear Minister.

'Flavia must have felt like throwing up,' Kate said without thinking. Georgiana, firm in her breeding, ignored this. Kate saw her into her car, and left, saying she would return soon, and assuring Georgiana that Flavia too would soon be back.

'But how did you know where to look?' I asked Kate when she had returned to New York, bringing Flavia with her. Flavia had thought she owed it to Georgiana to stay on a few days, but Kate wouldn't hear of it. 'You can never be as invisible as all that, not in Georgiana's house,' Kate said, and to this they all had to agree.

'I began with camera stores,' Kate said. 'Flavia hadn't taken one down with her, so she had to have acquired one. Oddly enough, the only place an old lady is noticeable is in a camera store, particularly if she asks for a special kind of camera to do a special kind of thing, money no object. There were three large camera stores in town, and Flavia turned out to have got her camera in the third, naturally. The young man at the counter remembered her perfectly: Northern, perky, knew exactly what she wanted. He tried to fob her off with an instamatic, but she wanted a camera with a photo lens and great clarity of focus: that wasn't the way she put it of course; she said she wanted to take pictures from a distance and have them come out well. The man sold her an expensive camera with a telephoto lens and fully expected to have it back on his hands the following day, but he never saw her again. Asked to describe her, he said that she looked like any other old lady, neat, grandmotherly but firm. She paid with cash, which surprised him, but she explained that she was too old to learn to use credit cards. Kate smiled at this, since she had often seen Flavia use credit cards in restaurants and comment on their usefulness: so much easier to figure out the tip. Flavia had been covering her tracks.

Finding Flavia herself was a little harder, but not much. She had stolen one of Georgiana's credit cards and one of her suitcases, and simply checked into the town's largest hotel as Georgiana. Naturally, the police didn't think of that. They had checked hotel registrations, looking for Flavia's name, or at least an obviously phony name. They had interviewed the help in all the hotels, but there were far too many old ladies to make further investigation practical. None of them, in any case, were reported as looking the least bit 'lost'. When Kate finally tracked Flavia down, she was relieved, but also frightened. 'I fear for my life,' she said, 'which is rather silly since I had been thinking of flinging it away. That Divine Church has lost millions of dollars because of me, and they may decide not to leave vengeance to the Lord.' Kate agreed.

When we were all discussing it later in Kate's apartment, armed with fortified refreshment, Great Aunt Flavia was full of praise for Kate for finding her and especially for realising that she had been responsible for the photograph. 'You recognised your advice about invisibility, didn't you, dear?' she said. 'How right you were. I loitered around that motel for days, and no one even saw me. People are afraid to speak to old ladies for fear they won't stop talking, and they aren't afraid we're going to be burglars or gunmen. It worked like a charm.'

'That's all very well,' Kate said, keeping a firm grip on Flavia's exuberance, 'but how did you know he would show up, with or without a prostitute?'

'I saw him with her on the street, and I followed him. They were in a car, but I recognised him when they stopped for a light. They turned into the motel a few yards further on. I suppose he thought he was safely distant from his usual stamping grounds. They didn't even glance at me when they went into the motel, intent upon what seemed a familiar routine. So I waited until they came out, just to see where they would go. I had called a taxi, and when it came I waited in it, with the meter going, until the Divine Church and his companion emerged. Then I said: "Follow that car." I think if I'm ever asked, I'll say that was the high point of my life. After that I bought the camera.' Flavia took a long sip of her Scotch and soda.

'How could you be sure the woman was a prostitute?'

'He dropped her off, so I saw where she lived. I asked a man working in her building if he knew her name, because I thought she might be the daughter of a dear friend, but I hadn't really seen her very clearly. The man said he thought I must be mistaken, since she wasn't the sort of woman a lady like myself would know. "Do you mean she's a fallen woman?" I asked him in my most elegant way.'

'Flavia, you didn't,' Kate said.

'I did, and very convincingly too. He told me you might put it that way. So I went off and bought a camera. Fortunately, I didn't have to wait long to get my picture; he was clearly in town for several days. But after I got the picture back and sent it to the newspaper, I thought I'd better hide out. I didn't want to bring any danger on poor Georgiana. I just went right on being invisible in that hotel until you found me. I'm glad you did, Kate; I was getting very tired of that life.'

'What set you off on this adventure,' I asked, 'apart from the thrills of being invisible?' I glared at Kate.

'Hypocrisy and greed, dear. I can't bear people ranting on about sin and old values and being born again, when they're just trying to make money like any insider trader on Wall Street. And then, to take money from those poor old ladies, and pretend you are writing personal letters, when it's all done with computers. Taking advantage of loneliness: I was shocked, really shocked. I thought if the old ladies all over the country knew what sort of man he was, they might think again before sending him money. Really I was just lucky that he picked that place to sin in. Or do you think the Lord was getting tired of him?'

'Well, you certainly started a huge scandal. It may be in the news for weeks.'

'I hope it will all have died down by next spring when it's time for my visit to Georgiana,' Great Aunt Flavia said.

LUCY ANNE WATT

Thinking of Evans

The night they took Teresa Dark the wind came in from the east, bending the pines as if they were saplings, and roaring through the forestry land like a soul in torment. The wind that night spoke in many voices, among which I could distinguish, as clear as if someone were speaking to me, there in the room where the fire sometimes leapt, sometimes guttered, the incontrovertible voice of portent.

Looking back, I realise that even that voice may have more than one meaning: that it may be a portent at the same time both for good and bad, or that what it predicts may change, according to the development of a situation. In the same way, what I am about to say may seem to you a terrible story; but you must understand that I have tried to find the reason for that little bit of good which came out of the bad, and still, to my mind, despite the pain to some, survives it. I have tried to find the true explanation, and whether it is to your taste is neither here nor there. Also, I have shouldered the bulk of the responsibility for what I have found; that is the least, in the circumstances, I feel I can do.

But to go back to that night, the night in the year of the comet, when I sat on over the fire nursing the starved coals and listening to the wind brutishly overcoming the resistance of branch and tile: I knew, not this time through divination, but with the ordinary knowledge of country people who, year after year, must put the same two and two together, that that night something other than wood would be bent and broken. I was in the same position as all of our community, at the receiving end of events which I tried, with perhaps a little more skill than most, to juxtapose and interpret. Some do it in one way; and I, as I will explain, in mine.

But that night. Usually, when there's a death in such weather, it's to do with labour. A woman loses heart in a gale, and a child can be easily frightened out of its breath, before the habit's established. Though, as no baby was expected that month (the nearest was Rose Neath, and she wasn't due for three) I thought it would be poor Jenet Cousins who was breathing her last. She was a poor thin thing anyway, and while no one has any business to die in her forties, we all knew she would, that was why they had brought her back, installed her in the best room at home.

So I concentrated, that night, sympathetically, on Jenet: indeed, it seemed as if all the elements – the wind, whistling spongily down the chimney, the great gib of the roof-beam stirring in the more explosive blasts, the long capillaries of laburnum gasping at the window – entered in, attempting together and separately to imitate the suffocating commotion, the in-out, partial, inadequate filling of Jenet's tubercular lungs.

'Not long now, Jenet,' I said, and sent her my good wishes which I am sure are just as efficacious as prayers.

And only when the storm had reached its pitch and begun to die, did I reckon her struggle over enough for me to go round, secure the house, and make my way, with a good conscience, to bed, for I had done what I could.

But as it turned out, it wasn't Jenet at all. This shows, you see, how wrong you can be. I hadn't been able to see it wasn't Jenet. I walked out under a lighter sky, but with the wind blowing sharply, and debris, branches and leaves, making a chaos of the road, and thought only to hear of her last moments. But that was the night (so, in a manner of speaking, they were eager to relate at the shop) when the fates, who are answerable to no one, missed Jenet and took Teresa Dark.

Teresa: half English like myself. Good-looking, strong-willed, twenty-four, as healthy as a girl should be who only paints her skin and nails, and sometimes some parts of her hair, and commits no other travesties. Jenet Cousins was still alive, in the house two down from the post-office and general, breathing in her insufficient, gurgling way. But Teresa Dark was dead: dead in a ditch, with her prized long hair strangely cropped off close to the skull, and her blouse torn open to show the knife through her heart.

Dai Thomas found her, on his way home from we all knew

where. And though he'd got blood on his hands and shirt from his efforts to revive her, we all knew it wasn't him: Dai couldn't kill, and would never be so quick, efficient. Besides, the look on her face, they all said, was surprise rather than shock; and if it had been Dai, stabbing her face to face, it would have been more than surprise – wouldn't it?

But then, shock: shock is reserved for a stranger, the unknown assassin, the man in the mask. That Teresa registered only surprise indicated she must have known the man in some way, known him enough to be, of all things, just surprised, not really believing in what he meant to do; for there was not, so it later came out, one trace of flesh or blood on her long tapering nails.

Teresa's surprise, Teresa's passivity, and that it should be Teresa at all, that this should happen here. This is what our small neighbourhood talked about mournfully, quietly, incessantly that Tuesday, Black Tuesday, in the aftermath of the storm.

To say that we were shocked (and Teresa's family far more than that) doesn't express it quite. We were (as a body) outraged: outraged in our blood, in the core of our unity as people who shared the same valley, the same land, same chapel and shop and, in some cases, same name, same genes. We were silently, unassuageably angry, that this spoliation, this violation, this unparalleled act of theft had been visited on us.

And even I couldn't understand – could throw no light on it at all. There seemed to be some inexplicable malignancy present, which having touched us, seemed like a cancer to multiply spores, so that our sense of horror and shock, if anything, only increased as the weeks passed and the police, despite their diligence, got nowhere near to solving the crime.

The police in fact brought a menace of their own – as if we were not already tense and alert enough, waking at night at the slightest sound, magnifying the merest undersides of facts. Their dark suits soon colonised our locality, moving silently and seriously about, not speaking unless it was to ask questions, and bringing a blot on each house they entered.

Or we saw them as we drove in and out of our homes, moving furtively in the lanes, or waiting for hours on the verges, hoping perhaps that a murderer in his manner of passing is as distinguishable as an erring motorist, and might be apprehended in nothing more difficult than a chase.

Sometimes the men of the place vanished to the police station in the town some twenty miles away. On these occasions, the women of the family shut their mouths, no one issued out until the man returned exhausted, battered, but at least partially cleared. Sometimes the men came back triumphant that despite the interrogator's exertions, their stories and alibis had not been broken. But in a sense, they also seemed ashamed that they personally had not been able to clear up the mystery.

It was not a case of being scapegoats only. It was a case of responsibility and pride. If we had been another community in another place, I suppose someone, sooner or later, would have babbled fictitiously of guilt. As if was, no man among us would confess about Teresa. Despite their shame generally about this burden, they could no more posture than they could self-sacrifice. And, so it was claimed – mostly by wives – they did not lie.

A strange situation, gripping but divisive, and one that was as yet barely understood as, on a clearer but watery day, the wind still not quite dead, we buried Teresa.

The police had held her body for twenty days in the mortuary, from which her mother had returned with lugubrious tales of the star-shaped wound, the roughly chopped line like a necklace cut about her throat. Otherwise, not a mark nor sign of struggle. And so it was as a virgin, an innocent (which was, at least, the public truth) we buried Teresa Dark in the graveyard which runs on direct to the forest and the beginning of the ascent to the mountains behind.

All of us went, though I stood on the edge of the crowd, not liking the way they do it here, and being, anyway, only an acquaintance of the family. And while the interminable process went on, I let my eyes wander from the sombre crowd, over the grass with its light dusting of spring flowers, to the rising fields with their studs of buttercups. At the edge of these, the dark cultivated pines swarmed up the sides of the mountain, lying like a frown on the edge of our space, a foreboding, a heavy, smudged duplication of the malaise festering in our midst.

I remember that day as I looked at the pines, feeling terribly oppressed, not so much by what had happened, but because there is really nothing more terrible than knowing, in a way that poisons all your relationships, that the murderer is most likely one of your acquaintances; is probably one of your friends. And that, if evil has exploded once, it is very likely to happen again.

All the men I suspected were there that day. I watched them covertly, but they all acted sadly, considerately, just as you would expect, and not one stepped out of line. They held their hats mournfully in their hands, their heads were bowed, and when it was all over they took the arms of their wives and escorted them to their homes or their cars. Llewelyn, who had no wife, was there with tears on his cheeks, I had seen them, and his old dog.

There were altogether four suspects in my eyes, and while we waited for the priest to finish his intoning, I went through their cases again, cases compiled as I sat night after night over the fire, throwing on the dead hairs from my comb, hearing them snap, smelling that acrid aroma, and trying to imagine the kind of man who would want Teresa's hair, even after he had taken her life. Would want it, even, at the cost of her life.

The way I saw it, there were four who might have given something to get Teresa's blood on their fingers, or, if you ignore the bizzare circumstances and repercussions, to possess her, albeit briefly.

Besides, you could argue that circumstances always become bizarre in a panic, and certainly no one could say for sure when it was the hair was taken, before or after the crime, an afterthought or as the motive itself. We only had the evidence with its ambiguous meaning, and that was all I had to draw on as I walked, or drove, slowly round the neighbourhood in the days that followed, always having to be circumspect, because of the police. It was that on which I leant in my nightly consultations with the charts of stars, trying to find some reason, some cause such as violent planetary conjunctions, for that action; and a possible date for the sequence.

We all expected another occurrence; we all knew we were not in the clear, and for that reason I felt bound to compete with the official investigators; it was a matter of urgency. Of course, I could not divulge my suspicions, I could not go to them and say: 'Look, this is what I suspect.' On the whole the police do not want advice, and least of all do they want it from a lonely woman of whom it would be said, in other times and other places, that she was nothing more nor less than – well, I will not name it, I dislike the term, but you will guess.

So I worked on my case in secret, watching my suspects as much as I could, at night straining the stars for clues. I watched them that day at the graveyard, still no nearer the heart of the mystery. And when they had all gone, and the gravediggers were piling the soil on top of poor Teresa, I got into my car, and drove round the neighbourhood, round all the outlying farms, and on to the villages, hunting and assimilating.

I had no experience in such cases: crime is not my forte. On reflection, I went about it in the wrong way, and that is what nearly made me fatally wrong. Even though I had narrowed the field down, I was depending too much on that shallow evidence and the riddle of the stars, when I should have used other skills, and not minded if people divined what I did.

For as the healer must lay hands on one who suffers, so should I have laid my hand on each of the men I suspected, and looked into the undeceiving map, the constellation of colours, flecks and concentric rims in the eyes. There is no one whose eyes, if read aright, can deceive everyone all of the time; there will always be those moments of inattention, of unguarded confrontation, a drawing back of shutters, through which the alert expert can slip.

Reading eyes is an exquisite art, but an important one. What they, and the face, have to say tallies with the nature of serious crime. Just one small, unshielded moment can give the murderer away – whatever he may afterwards swear. It's the moment when horror and guilt, and possibly additional hunger, blaze in a face, blaze in a dark, insistent way, though the eyes, quickly glazing, deny all knowledge, and the mouth repeats its lie.

But, initially, being without experience, I ignored all this. I preferred my usual methods. And so it was that the weeks went past, and the grass greened on Teresa's grave, and the trees began to flicker with new leaf, and neither I nor the police were any nearer identifying the culprit. They had, I think, grown bored with the case, though they still stopped me sometimes on the road, to ask where I went.

'Eggs,' I said on that particular day, some six weeks after Teresa's death – the tension, I might say, no less in the neighbourhood: we were learning what tremendous staying power lies in unsolved crimes. 'Groceries, food.'

They let me pass, and, to be honest, I was not really thinking of that business as I drove in to Evans' farm for the eggs. Because of his chapel three times a week, I had long crossed Evans off my list. I would have said that influence was in him like a good strong tea, it would not turn against him, it was his taste, his habit. He was, we all said, an exemplary, honest man, if lonely now his sister was gone, with nothing but that stubborn farm, a few beasts, and an ageing dog for company.

I had been there often, once a week, since Teresa went, and on each occasion found him just the same – only shocked as we all were, and saddened. And for that reason, and for his equilibrium, I crossed him from my list. I was thinking not of Teresa, nor of the unknown felon, but actually what I would make tonight with the eggs, when I set the tray he had brought at my feet, hunted in my bag, and gave him two pound coins.

And it was then, you see – though you might think this is exceptional, even fabricated, but it is true – it was only then, after knowing him all those years, that I read his eyes aright. His limpid blue eyes, flecked daily with blood (for he drinks) which, at that moment of meeting mine as I gave him the two coins, had forgotten to hold a curtain, the opaque curtain of common usage, across their brilliance.

And so his eyes, Evans' sharp blue eyes, meeting mine, condemned him. The sweat broke out instantly in his palm, before I even knew of what he was condemned, as my fingers, touching his, withdrew from the coins I left there. I was in the process of saying something ordinary, such as 'I'm afraid I haven't got the exact money, Hugh' and I just managed to finish – but with difficulty, on account of the way he was still looking, staring, at me, as if I had walked naked into a room, and he had been forced to reassess someone he was used to seeing in quite a different way.

There I was, in a moment of naked honesty, revealed not only as someone who could see through him almost down to the pit of his soul, but who herself had a kind of vulnerability, a dark side she was always careful to conceal. That, in a sense, was the nakedness, which made that moment of recognition intensely potent, electrical. In the moment of withdrawing my fingers, I shivered, genuinely chill in the May air, while his eyes, having realised their mistake, having held me for that moment, dropped to his feet. I knew that when I met them again they would be different. He wasn't stupid. They would be just the same old mild eyes of Hugh.

'I'll get some change, then,' he said quietly, turned and walked with his usual even pace, shoulders slightly rounded, across the yard.

But the yard had been altered because of that moment. The sun, dipping again beneath the scudding clouds, had cast it into shadow, and ominous dullness massed where previously I had seen only an ordinary place, bound by neglected sheds and pens. On the far side the house, with its heavy grey stone, dark paint and lightless windows, looking as unwelcoming as the bare top of the mountain, or the naked slate-grey outcrops which littered its sides.

It seemed in that long darkness made by the sun, which highlighted the neglect of the place, that any amount of evil could happen here, that it was not possible to be light and happy in such a place. I remembered Evans' mother as she appeared in chapel on Sundays, a grim woman saddened by the burden of the farm, thinned by the cancer which took years to kill her. I could picture her thinness, her despair, as growing directly from daily concourse with such a place.

Even the pigs in the pen in the corner, which drew my attention by their noise, appeared capable of ill-doing. They were rooting about in a hopeless fashion in the dirt, which looked quite barren, though I could see that someone had been raking it up, it had been recently disturbed. As I watched, the boar made a desultory attempt to mount a sow. He failed and wandered off without trying again. All this only contributed to the deep sense of wrongness, of displacement, of tragedy, which entered into me as I stood, the eggs at my feet, waiting for Evans to return.

He took maybe six or seven minutes, six fatal minutes during which I became convinced in a series of visions or insights, that rapid blend of razor-sharp perception and strong intuition which is no more magical than radio waves or a TV signal, but enough to canonise a saint. Became convinced not only of what Evans had done, his deeds crying out to me from under the earth of the pig-pen, but of what he planned yet to do. I who had fumbled about blindly for so long, could smell not only the scent of Teresa, but the fresh blood of unidentifiable others; I could hear them crying out, though their words were not yet clear.

Standing there, listening and trying to resolve the rapid, not yet wholly translatable images, I became convinced of Evans' guilt.

Convinced, as if the earth had been rolled back and I had seen his victims and the shades of his victims to be, laid out, as if in daylight, in their beds. I saw them and understood suddenly, as if a screen had rolled back on the concept of murder, on their suffering and mixed emotions, and on the tragic beauty of their bodies as he placed them there. There was even triumph in the way they called out to me, an undertone of triumph amongst the pain and anger; and another note, I thought, of sisterhood, insistence.

All this was emerging swiftly, wave on wave, though largely confused. I stood in the yard, as someone apart from time, listening to the urgent signals which came to me as easily as if a woman, or women, had shouted, clinging to the gates of the ancient pen. I listened and was both terrified and moved, in the six or seven minutes of Evans' absence, during which a great deal was imparted to me. Knowledge which would have shocked others, which may shock you, but which to me, when I had thought about it, proved to be only part of the great cycle of things which must be done to honour our pact with this planet, and the forces which guide it and rule. Though a part of me was worried and grieved by what I had missed for so long (no one wants to feel they have failed in their skill) in the main I accepted that all this insight had remained hidden for good reason. And it was for the same reason that it was suddenly vouchsafed.

While Evans was gone it seemed that I was standing in another sort of timescale altogether, in which those visions began to converge from surrealism through naked fascination, into the horror of ritual murder. This horror was just beginning to impress itself on me, to make itself plain, swim from unfocus to focus – when Evans emerged from the house.

Instantly, as if they were obedient dogs, these signals broke up and fled, like shadow from sun or optimism from rain, deserting the yard altogether, and leaving me for the time being stunned, uncertain whether I had been in a dream or a trance, or what. Uncertain of everything, except that grave wrongdoing had been perpetrated in Evans' place, had been finished just yards from where I stood.

'Here's your thirty pence.' Evans slid the coins into my hand, his eyes returned to their ordinary, defensive blue. Moments before, my head still reeling, our eyes had met and mine had steadily signalled to him that I knew – exactly what, I wasn't sure – but I

knew that Evans was implicated in the crime that cost us Teresa.
He hadn't flinched when I looked like that – just stared evenly
back.

'You'll be going straight home?' His hand went to his pocket,
and jiggled some loose change up and down.

I looked past him to the pig-pen, where the straw was clean over
the raked earth, and the pigs, their smell coming to me now
stronger than anything, obliterating the smell of blood, shifted and
circled hopelessly. I let him register my look before I answered.

'No – not yet. I've a call or two to make. Calor gas, and a sack of
coal: I'm right out.'

'Yes, you wouldn't think it, would you? This cold, for May.'

Evans steered me firmly by the elbow away from the pig-pen
towards the car. It was as if we were not talking of the weather at
all, but of other things for which there are hardly words. I could
not help wondering where he had got his knowledge, how he had
understood what to do, or if it was entirely the force of instinct.

When I had settled the tray of eggs and was sliding into the
driver's seat, he said, as he held on to the top of the door, keeping
himself between it and me, 'You're still casting horoscopes for
people?'

'Oh – once in a while.'

Since I could do nothing else, I looked up into his face as he
continued to hold the door. In the shadow made partly by the lack
of sun and partly by his downcast features, I saw his eyes glittering
with dark glaze, as over a bog. Glittering with the old loneliness,
hurt and pride, the old ancient unhappiness, stemming from
almost forgotten traditions, the war of the mind with the brute,
frightened animal in all, the war of the first man with the man he
had become, ambivalence, polarity of custom and need. It was as if
I looked directly down through the tunnel of his vision, to the soul
of a man not at peace with this world; a lonely, primitive man,
uncauterised by love.

And as our eyes met for the second time in unguarded honesty, I
seemed to see, as if projected on his cornea, a microscopic image, a
series of images, in which I saw him, at the end of those deliberate,
unrepeatable actions, lift each woman's head in sequence with
unsurpassable tenderness, as one would a child, settling it to sleep.
I saw him, in each image, in each instance, do it and all that came
after, not with violence, but with love.

I saw him looking down at the moist barrow of earth, the white lily within. Then I saw her head, their heads, turn, the eyes flicker open, the lips part and move without sound as the gentle rain of earth fell from the spade upon them. I could not hear their primal, horrified scream, I could hear no sound except the sound of the earth falling down over their faces, and then his grief, his tears.

And I wanted to say, thinking of Teresa's cropped head, of all their cropped heads, 'What did you do with the hair, Evans?'

But he spoke first, still looking down as he held the car door, but with the images gone, his eyes completely in shadow. 'You must come up, one evening, Angharad, and do my stars. I'd like to see how you do it.' That was all – Evans wasn't one to say much.

'You will though, won't you?' he said, still holding the car door, for such a long time that it seemed he wasn't going to let me go at all.

'If you like,' I said, at last, not bringing much enthusiasm to my voice.

'Yes. You'll come – won't you.' Only with that statement did he let go and step back, so that I was able to fasten and lock the door.

I wound the window down and replied – it was pure inspiration, I didn't know then exactly what I meant – 'Yes. And anyway, I'll be back next week, as usual, for the eggs.'

He watched me, his look unflinching, as I drove off, my palms hot, my skin cold, my heart beating hard.

That night, another night of strong wind, I sat up and began to piece it all out. As I have said, I have some skill, though not enough to change circumstances, work wonders. But as I pondered what I had experienced that afternoon, I became convinced that my vision, my intuition, was right: that Evans had killed, that there was a killer in Evans, who had acted long before the occasion of Teresa Dark. There was something, more than one thing, buried in that pig-pen: the girls, or women, who had cried out, not only in their pain, anger and frustration, but to warn me, I believed.

What other man but Evans, I asked, would be so lonely as to kill; would believe, in his complex Methodist blood, a blood which had been farming this valley for centuries, that in the end there was no other expression for his loneliness, his potential to love? A man who does not know how to court women, and he did not, must use violence in the end, or abstain, as Hugh Evans evidently, having lived always with women, could not.

Or so I reasoned, counting down the years since his mother and sister died from those slow cancers, and finding that twelve years is enough to make a man turn deeply inwards, like a dammed stream which, swelling, breaks new boundaries in its old course. What has logic, I asked, or our nice rules, to do with the great hurt, the emptiness, festering in a man whom no one since his mother and sister, those two grim women, had loved?

Then, as I pieced those bits of jigsaw together, it was easy to interpret the events: to see how, as he laid each girl in her moist barrow, gently as a new wife in her bed, he felt, and felt he was expressing, tremendous tenderness, tremendous love. I see him, at the end of that unique process, sprinkling the earth on the white lilies of their bodies, sprinkling it as roses on a bier, heaping, patting it as thoughtfully as one would a quilt or a pillow, about one who is asleep.

I think of him holding their long hair in his hands, the tears raining down his rough but not bad-looking face, of his redoubled loneliness, being left when they were gone. How it was certainly only loneliness that brought out the wilder, more desperate man in Evans, the man who, to save his own life, to save his mind, and to bring himself in his pinched circumstances a little love, must turn to the old rituals, the slaughter of innocents, to appease the gods.

And what if a man must kill what he most loves – must, in the situation where he feels it kinder to kill than let live? Wasn't Abraham himself prepared to do it? Wasn't . . .

But when I got this far, I realised the one point I hadn't covered, the flaw in the picture I had presented to myself – that look that Evans and I had exchanged just before he gave me the three coins. That look, a meeting of equally affirmative eyes, had in it the nature of a bargain, a bargain whose terms were set by Evans, to which I could only concede.

I knew what it meant, though I suppose the terms might have been put differently. He knew what I had guessed, and that I was not afraid to show that I had guessed. And with that understanding, he was daring me to tell, to implicate him on no evidence at all; and if I did, the dark steady promise in his eyes told me, then he would act swiftly. Thinking over it, I had no doubt that, if I put one foot wrong, I would be the next on Evans' list.

Strangely, this perception, as I have pieced it out, does not frighten me. In one way I feel safe, not only because, if Evans makes no more blunders, I have no reason to tell, but also because I am just not the kind of woman for Evans' plans. I know who they are – drifters, hitch-hikers, girls who disappear from motorways and cafés, their absence unnoticed for months, their last whereabouts never exactly known. What perfect targets they must seem to Evans: brave lives requiring (in his view) the utmost bravery at the end.

Teresa Dark was like that; living as she wanted, disdainer of timetables and rules, she might have seemed to play right into his hands. Though had it not been for Evans' mistake, I might never have found what he did – found it out in a way that will not be believed by some, as there is nothing rational or concrete in my methods. But it is these same methods I now use to hold him at bay.

The method surely works, for weeks have passed smoothly and uneventfully since that catalytic afternoon when I went to get the eggs – weeks during which I have been back regularly every six or seven days, to Evans' farm, to get more. He greets me, noncommittally, as usual, and, as usual, I wait in the yard to get change. I wait and watch the pigs, and listen to the siren-song of my sisters who call to me from their rumpled earth.

I have a long way to go in gaining Evans' confidence, but I will do it. His blue eyes still confront me with their usual reserve, as we stop to talk, longer and longer, in the sun, both of us enjoying a kinship in our mutual solitude. Sometimes, he speaks of my coming to read his horoscope – only speaks; but I will come, and spend the evening there.

This visit, or maybe several, will be necessary, if I am to establish the proof I so desperately need. I know I am not capable of the travesty of raking them up from their beds. But I must, if only to satisfy myself, find the hair of those girls and women, the hair cropped from each skull, including Teresa's. I only want to see, and feel certain that I am right; I only want to touch those lost riches.

I know exactly where to look, the two places which my concentration has revealed to me. The first is the chest on the landing where, in the third drawer, among the lavender scents of his mother's linen, are coiled multi-coloured locks, auburn, raven and gold, their tresses pressed and sweetened by the sheets, already tangled by his hands. The other is under his pillow, where, nightly, I know he keeps, so as to dream of her, the waist-length abundance of Teresa Dark.

But this occasion, my coming to the house, when on some pretext I will steal upstairs, is a long way off. We still only talk, out there in the sun in his yard, talk of ordinary, uninteresting things, while clearly I hear my prone sisters singing. All the time, though, we are making progress; I feel myself inching into his confidence, I have even, once or twice, made him laugh.

The day will come. And meanwhile, I am sure that, so long as I maintain silence, Evans will keep to his bargain: he will not harm me, nor anyone else from this neighbourhood. Besides, if I wanted to tell, who would listen to my story, or credit it for one instant? The police have all withdrawn back to the town, leaving Teresa's file open, naturally.

There is really no one of authority or of a persuadable nature about, no one with enough imagination to credit my convictions – no one whose tongue at one time or another hasn't turned against me. There are those who would really love to use these mad-cap theories to endorse my reputation, my bad name. Anyway, I like the secret, the fine power balance between myself and Evans; I like the challenge of the last bit of information I must find.

How to do it, and what I will do then, I often plan, as I drive home from his farm through the lush narrow hedgerows. Or sometimes on the way down as I look out, occasionally stopping completely to stare at the mountains and fields spread in the sun's chequerboard, I find myself thinking, not of plans, nor of consequences, but only of Evans.

BARBARA WILSON

Murder at the International
Feminist Bookfair

'Dee!' I called to the woman in the peg-board exhibit stand, the small freckled woman with a round green cap who was staring a little woefully around her at unopened cardboard boxes.

'Cassandra Reilly, my girl!' She fell into my arms. 'It's been years.'

'Was it Manila or Auckland?'

'Manila,' she said. 'I missed Auckland. And now here we are at Vladivostok. Who could have imagined it?'

'Thank goodness for *glasnost*.' I began to help her unpack the boxes. 'Still just doing Canadian authors?'

'It's all you can get money for,' she said. 'Though of course as a loyal Canadian I'm convinced our writers *are* the best.' She taped up a photograph of Serena Wood, Coastal Editions star author. Back in the 1970s she had written a book on log cabin building for women, and it was still selling. 'I thought they might be interested in this in Siberia,' Dee said hopefully. 'That's around here some place, isn't it?'

'Further south, I think,' I said, shivering slightly.

'How about you?' Dee asked. 'Still doing Spanish translation? Still living in London? I don't know how you stand the place.'

'Oh, it's all right,' I said. 'I'm hardly ever there, anyway. I just came back from six months in Buenos Aires.' I swung my briefcase for her to see. It was packed with manuscripts and books that I hoped to foist on reluctant publishers. 'I'm on a translation panel tomorrow. One of my authors, Luisa Alvarez, is here. She's a depressed Uruguayan, very famous. Actually I have to meet her now. Can we get together for lunch tomorrow?'

'Great.'

The fair began with a flourish of speeches in Russian, English and Japanese, with simultaneous translation into French, Spanish, Catalan and Serbo-Croatian. I looked around for a couple of hours and chatted to friends and acquaintances, then I made my way over to Dee's stand, which now had, like all the others, a number and a printed title. CAOSTAL EDITIONS. Well, it was close.

When I arrived a tall woman in a black skirt, black leather jacket, black scarf, black boots and black hat was haranguing Dee in an upper-class British accent.

'But my books do *extremely* well in England,' she was saying. 'My last novel was about a woman who left her husband for another woman, and it received *very* good reviews in the *Observer* and *The Times*.' She pulled a clipping from her Filofax and read, ' "Mrs Horsey-Smythe treats this subject subtly and maturely, with none of the po-faced humourlessness characteristic of the so-called lesbian-novel." So, you see, there's no *reason* why it shouldn't do well in America, my agent doesn't understand why . . .'

'I'm sure your book is just wonderful,' said Dee insincerely, 'but, as I've been trying to tell you, I'm not an American publisher. Oh, Cassandra, hello!' She looked relieved to see me. 'This is Felicity Horsey-Smythe. Cassandra Reilly. Cassandra lives in London too. Peckham or someplace, isn't it?'

Felicity gave me a smile the shape of a fingernail clipping and, pretending to see a dear friend across the hall, escaped.

'Don't say Peckham in public,' I warned her. 'Anyway, I moved. To East Dulwich.'

But Dee wasn't really listening. 'Do you think I'm going to have to spend the rest of my life explaining to people that Canada is not a state of America? It even happened when the fair was held in Montreal. The woman's fucking English – didn't she learn any geography?'

'Probably not in ballet school or wherever she went,' I comforted Dee. 'Can you leave your stand or should I get some food and bring it back?'

'Let's get out of here,' she said. 'The public doesn't come till two. I'm going to need all my strength to deal with the Rooskies.'

'Has it been hard getting here?' I said. 'These things are so easy for me. I just fly in and fly out.'

'It gets harder every year to leave Vancouver,' Dee said. 'I'm not sure I'm cut out to be a jet-setting feminist.'

'What? And miss out on all the gossip?' We went past the British women's presses and I waved to a friend of mine at Sheba. 'That's what these things are really about. Remember a few years ago?'

Dee's blue eyes began to sparkle. 'The showdown between the Northern and Southern hemispherists?'

'Or Oslo in 1986?'

'It stayed light too late was the problem. It went to people's heads.'

We laughed. 'What about this year?' I asked. 'Heard anything scandalous yet?'

Dee thought. 'Well. You-know-who is here from Germany again . . . and . . . Oh, I know. Lulu Britten's got a stand.'

'Lulu Britten?'

'The editor of *Trash Out*.'

'Oh, really,' I said. 'That should provoke a few fireworks.'

As an American resident in London I was usually a little behind the times, but even I'd heard of the New York-based *Trash Out: a Journal for Contentious Feminists*. It was a forty-page monthly, stapled, on newsprint, with a glossy cover usually featuring someone in the women's community. A feminist version of the *Sun* or the *New York Post*, it usually focused on one outstanding feminist a month for general trashing. Gloria, Rita Mae, Lily, Martina had all been among the first faces to appear on the cover. Inside was a lengthy (negative) assessment of their writing, performance and lifestyle, spiced with innuendo and rude remarks from unnamed sources. CIA connections, drinking and drug bouts, hysterical displays of temper, peculiar sexual tastes and, most of all, the hypocrisy of their moral public pronouncements contrasted with their sordid personal lives. It was hot and it was nasty. But that wasn't all.

In addition to the 'profiles' of infamous feminists, *Trash Out* also offered blow-by-blow accounts of women's conferences rather in the manner of *off our backs*. The difference was that what went on during the panels and plenaries was rarely reported while the cruel remarks and furious dissensions behind stage were given the full treatment. The journal also had a lengthy review section where critics slandered and dismissed feminist authors, musicians and artists.

Since feminism is in many ways a literary movement, it wasn't surprising that *Trash Out* concentrated on well-known authors, nor that it had been able to exploit a market hungry for the low-down on mentors who had gotten too famous. The journal gave a voice to critics who were tired of being forced to at least appear to be giving a balanced assessment of writers' work and allowed the personal life of the writer to come in for as much dirt as possible. Yet the profiles, conference reports and reviews were only part of *Trash Out*'s appeal. Many of its readers couldn't have cared less why such and such famous authors fell out, or why a certain author was no longer publishing with a certain press. What the average reader looked forward to every month was the letters section where any feminist could write and complain about her sisters.

Once we had 'criticism/self-criticism', the Maoist-inspired exchange that used to come at the end of bruising political meetings. The 'Trash Box' section of *Trash Out* was a little like that – but without the self-criticism. Women wrote in to detail the wrongs that had been done to them by ex-lovers, by political enemies, by feminist publishers, recording companies, theatres and galleries, and by their mothers and former best friends. In her editorials Lulu justified this massive mud-slinging (and counter mud-slinging, because almost everybody wanted to reply) as 'cathartic'. 'For too long,' she wrote, 'we have been silenced by the false claims of sisterhood. We cannot live in the rarefied air of feminist solidarity. Our divisions are too deep to be mended, too harsh to be smoothed over. Only by speaking of our differences can we move forward . . .'

I said to Dee, 'Do you think Lulu is here gathering dirt on the bookfair for the journal?'

'No doubt. We'd better lie low,' she laughed.

'Oh, we're too insignificant for her. She's never trashed anyone outside America, has she?'

'Margaret Atwood. Though possibly she thought she was American,' said Dee. 'Maybe I should stick her on Felicity Horsey-Smythe. After all, there is a certain prestige attached to being on the cover of *Trash Out*. It means you're important enough to criticise.'

'It's funny, now I think about it,' I said. 'Not only has the journal never had a non-American woman on the cover, it's never had a woman of colour. Either Lulu has decided that women of colour are off bounds or else she's racist enough not to think they're important enough to trash.'

'Maybe she's planning to remedy that. Look over there.' Dee pointed across the central courtyard where a couple of black women stood talking. Close enough to overhear, but not to be obvious, was a chunky white woman with glasses and a funny kind of topknot. She was swathed in as many scarves as a fortune teller and her long multi-coloured skirt reached her ankles. She was sucking on the tip of a pen and regarding the two women avidly.

'The woman on the right is Simone Jefferson,' said Dee, 'and Madame Zelda over there is Lulu.'

'So you think Simone's her next victim?' It would make sense. With a brilliant first novel and a book of essays just out this year Simone was already being compared to Alice Walker. She looked very young next to the older woman, a writer I recognised from Nigeria. 'Do you think we should warn her?'

'Just a word maybe,' said Dee. 'Not that Lulu lets much of anything get in her way. She went to law school and knows the libel laws backwards and forwards.'

The cafeteria was serving some kind of goulash. In front of us a woman named Darcy Joanne from a feminist press in Santa Cruz, California, was making a big deal about vegetarian food to the woman behind the counter.

'Macro-bi-otic,' she repeated. 'You know – tofu? Tempe? Nori? What about just some brown rice and broccoli?'

The thickset Russian woman stared at her and continued to hold out the goulash.

With a sigh Darcy took it. 'Nobody thinks about the culinary aspects of where we hold these things,' she complained to us. 'God, remember Oslo? Twenty bucks for a seafood salad that turned out to be covered with artificial crabmeat.' Without a change in her voice she went on. 'These Russians. Have you met that poet Olga Stanislavkigyovitch or something? She's been pestering me all morning to publish a book of her poems.'

'No,' said Dee feelingly. 'But I had some French deconstructionist yammering away at me for an hour about translating her book.'

'Honestly,' said Darcy, moving away to join a group from the States. 'Everybody knows translations don't sell.'

Later that day, after I'd spent an exhausting hour on the translation panel defending a sister translator's right to have translated the place names in a German novel, and an even more punishing hour meeting with Luisa the depressed Uruguayan about why her British publishers were refusing to take her latest novel (¿ What do they mean, not enough local colour? It's a book from the heart, a prize-winning novel. ¡ It's not a travel guide!'), I stopped by Dee's stand to see how she was getting on. A very attractive young Russian woman was making her case to Dee: '*Glasnost* is a farce. Everyone knows that. This fair is just another propaganda tactic. None of the real feminist or dissident writers are being allowed to participate. There is still repression, censorship, no possibility of emigration for dissidents or Jews. I say that in my poems and that is why my poems cannot be published here in the Soviet Union. They must be translated and published in English!'

'I can see your point,' Dee said. 'I really can. Really. But I'm only supposed to be publishing Canadian authors. I have enough trouble just publishing women. Oh look, here's Cassandra. She's a translator. Maybe she has some ideas.'

I glared at Dee, but actually, I did have some ideas – and some contacts in London and New York. After I'd written out a few addresses for Olga, I mentioned that she might want to keep a slightly lower profile. Just in case there were . . . you know . . .

'I am not afraid,' said Olga. 'I must say now what I think. It is my opportunity.'

'Maybe she should go talk to Lulu if she wants publicity,' said Dee. 'She could write the first feminist letter trashing out the KGB.'

'Who is this Lulu?' Olga demanded.

'Over there, but I was just . . . joking,' she added, as Olga raced off. 'Well, at least she's a good self-promoter.'

The fair was by now packed with Soviet visitors, but there weren't many around Dee's stand. 'They don't want to build log cabins?' I asked.

'I don't have enough lesbian books,' Dee said glumly. 'Look over there – Naiad press is doing landslide business. Beebo

Brinker's never been on sale in the Soviet Union before.'

'Is that what's causing the commotion?' I asked. 'Is Ann Bannon making a personal appearance or what?'

'There's too many people to see,' said Dee, straining. 'But it doesn't seem to be coming from that direction.'

The pushing grew stronger as people attempted to see what was happening, the muttering louder. Unfortunately, whatever message was being passed through the crowd was in Russian, so we were as much in the dark as ever. Suddenly we heard a siren outside and then a phalanx of men and women in white rushed in with a stretcher. As the crowd parted it was just possible, if we stood on the chairs in Dee's stand, to see where they were headed.

Stand 103, the sign read. TRESH OOT. A few minutes later the stretcher went by again. And Olga was on it.

That night in the Vladivostok People's Hotel Dee and I tried to make some sense of what had happened. According to Felicity Horsey-Smythe, who, with Lulu, was the nearest witness, Olga had been standing there talking to the editor of *Trash Out*. The next moment she had collapsed writhing to the floor and was dead within seconds. No one had seen anything untoward or threatening. There wasn't a mark on her. She'd simply gasped as if she couldn't breathe, clutched her throat, spasmed a few times, and gone down.

'And we laughed about the KGB,' Dee moaned. 'Did you see how fast those security men were on the scene? They got her out of there in no time. Oh yeah, they pretended to ask people what had happened, but that was just a ploy. They murdered her because she was a dissident!'

'Rubbish,' I said. 'They'd be far more likely to arrest her and throw her in prison than to murder her in the middle of an international bookfair. That sort of thing doesn't look very good.'

But Dee refused to see that. 'I think they should stop the bookfair. I want to go home. It's too scary.'

I ignored her wails. 'Don't you think it's a strange coincidence that Olga keeled over right in front of Lulu's stand? It might make you think that . . .'

'Think what?' Dee was looking for bugging devices under the night table, in the closet. Soon her paranoia would have her taking the telephone apart, and turning up the radio while we talked.

'Let's get out of here,' I said.

Felicity Horsey-Smythe was in a room down the corridor. When we knocked and entered she was on the phone trying to get through to her agent in London. 'That's Philip Foxton-ffoulkes,' she was shouting to the operator, 'ffoulkes, not Vooks. What do you mean he won't accept the charges?' She slammed down the receiver and said to us, 'They're hopeless down there in reception. This is the eighth time I've tried to reach him today.'

'Felicity,' I said. 'Do you remember what Olga was doing just before she died?'

'Oh, please let's not go into that. I've spent the last two hours with a Russian detective and my nerves are absolutely shattered. Olga wasn't doing anything. She was just standing there writing down something for Lulu, some address or something.'

'Maybe Olga was trying to pass her a message and they had to kill her,' suggested Dee.

'Nonsense,' I said. A sudden memory of Lulu standing in the courtyard listening to Simone and sucking on her pen came back to me. I said casually, 'So whose pen was it anyway?'

'What do you mean? Well, Lulu's, I suppose. Yes, she picked up a pen lying on the stand table.'

I tossed Felicity a pen from my pocket. 'Could you just show me how Olga was standing, what she was doing?'

'Oh really,' Felicity said. But she stood up and, holding the pen, she touched it thoughtfully to her mouth. 'I told you, she was just standing there, thinking.'

'Oh well,' I said. 'Thanks anyway.' I nodded to Dee and we left.

Out in the corridor I could hardly contain my excitement. 'That's it, don't you see?'

'What? Felicity said Olga wasn't doing anything.'

'She *was* doing something. She touched the pen to her mouth and the pen had poison on its tip.'

'Oh my God.' Dee leaned against the corridor wall. 'Then Lulu poisoned Olga. But why? Is Lulu a KGB agent?'

I shook my head impatiently. 'It's more likely that Lulu was the target. Someone knew about Lulu's habit of sucking her pens and substituted one with poison for an ordinary one. Olga was killed by mistake. The poison was really meant for Lulu!'

Dee stared at me. 'Do you think we should tell her?'

'I think she may know. Did you see her face when they were taking Olga's body away?'
'But who could have wanted to kill Lulu?'
'That's the trouble. There are probably dozens.'
'But only some of them are here at the fair.'

Half an hour later we'd come up with a list of five names. Four of them had been featured on *Trash Out* covers in the past year. They were:
   1. Jean Winthrup, a veterinarian who had written a popular book on lesbian sexuality and who had become a sort of sexual pundit/entertainer. An article in *Trash Out* had revealed that Jean's personal sexual habits weren't all that normal (she could only do it in a large kitty litter box) and had quoted a number of ex-lovers.
   2. Monica Samson, a feminist poet who had won all sorts of major awards and who taught at Yale. *Trash Out* had exposed her work as unoriginal and accused her of plagiarism. The anonymous piece, possibly written by her rival Lois MacGuire, claimed that one of Monica's most famous books had whole lines lifted from an obscure Swedish woman poet of the nineteenth century.
   3. Davis McKee, an influential feminist linguist/philosopher who had given lesbianism a whole new vocabulary of invented words. Detractors said she was like a kid who'd gone crazy with Pig Latin; admirers carried her dictionary around like the Bible. *Trash Out* had unleashed a scathing account of her financial holdings in South African companies.
   4. Casey Walters, a prolific anthologist. For the past ten years Casey had put together anthologies of poetry and prose on every conceivable subject that had to do with women. The *Trash Out* feature had parodied her by including 'excerpts' from a supposed new anthology, *Feminist Chimpanzee Stories*, and its companion volume *Women and Parakeets: An Anthology*.

The fifth suspect, as yet unprofiled in *Trash Out*, was Simone Jefferson.
   'I'd say she's the most likely,' I said, 'because she hasn't been trashed yet.'
   'But we don't know for sure that Lulu was planning to trash her,' Dee said.

I looked at my watch. 'It's only half past ten. Why don't we pay a visit to Lulu?'

There were voices in Lulu's room, but they stopped when we knocked. 'Come in,' said Lulu, a little unsteadily.

She and Felicity Horsey-Smythe were sitting rather close together on the single bed with glasses in their hands. A half-empty bottle of vodka stood on the night table beside them.

Dee and I perched on the armchair and declined to share the vodka.

Felicity said, 'Lulu and I were just talking about what happened today.'

'It was a real shock,' Lulu said. She sounded pretty drunk. Her topknot was slightly askew and her scarves twisted and jumbled around her thick neck. 'Olga was a nice kid. She was going to write an article on Raisa Gorbachev for the next issue of *Trash Out.*'

'I told Lulu that it would be more understandable if somebody had maybe been trying to kill *her.*' Felicity laughed shrilly and took another gulp of vodka.

'Why do you say that?' I asked innocently. 'To me it would seem just the opposite. If someone killed Lulu if would mean they were probably on the cover of *Trash Out.* Then it would be purely a question of narrowing the suspects down. Why would anyone famous take a chance like that?'

'They probably would if they thought they could get away with it,' Lulu muttered, pouring herself another drink. 'I've had death threats, you know.'

'Who here would you think most likely?' Dee asked. 'I mean if we pretended it was you, not Olga, who was the target.'

A strange look passed over Lulu's face. 'I've been wondering that myself. I have lots of enemies here.'

'You should have thought about this when you started your journal.' Felicity giggled. She'd taken off her hat and her streaked blonde hair stood up wildly.

'I did think about it.' Lulu moroseness seemed to be growing in direct proportion to Felicity's vodka-induced gaiety. 'But I wanted to go ahead – it was something I'd thought of for a long time: investigating the fault lines in certain women's strength, exposing the pretensions and predilections behind the famous masks. A lot of people have said that wasn't fair, that these women didn't become famous on purpose, that it was their work that was important, not their personalities. I say that's garbage. No one becomes famous without wanting on some level to be famous. None of the women who's been on the cover is famous for her ideas alone. She's partly famous because she's got charisma or a beautiful face or because she's got ins with the right people or she's outrageous. She's famous precisely because she's a hypocrite, espousing one thing publicly, another privately, writing books or making speeches about feminism and sisterhood and screwing over any individual woman who stands in her way. To me that's not feminism and women deserve to know what their heroines are really like.'

'But what about Simone Jefferson?' Dee broke in, perhaps unwisely. 'I've met her and she's really nice.'

'What about Simone?' Lulu said. 'She's never been on the cover.'

Felicity leapt in. 'Well then, according to your theory, Cassandra, *she'd* be a good suspect, just because she wouldn't be suspected.'

'She'd only be a good suspect if Lulu was planning to put her on the cover. But you're not, are you, Lulu?'

Lulu said nothing. She emptied her glass and stared very hard at the opposite wall. Finally she muttered, 'I've got to get some sleep.'

Dee and I stood up obediently. Felicity stayed right where she was.

'Well,' said Dee, when we were back out in the corridor. 'I thought Mrs Horsey-Smythe was married.'

'I'm sure she's just researching her next lesbian novel,' I said comfortingly.

The next morning at breakfast we happened to stand behind Darcy Joanne again. She was asking for scrambled tofu and herb tea. 'Well then, what about yogurt? What about all those Ukrainians who live to be 105 and only eat yogurt?'

Sighing, she took her plate of fried eggs and said, 'Really incredible what happened yesterday, don't you think? I'm thinking of bringing out Olga's poems. They'd probably sell really well now.'

'That's morbid,' said Dee.

'That's publishing,' Darcy replied. 'You don't have to think about that stuff up in Canada. We do.'

'Doesn't it seem odd that it happened in front of Lulu's stand?' I asked.

'Yeah,' said Darcy. 'If I didn't know better, I'd say Lulu had engineered it for publicity. She's in real financial trouble, that's the rumour. I don't know how she could afford to come here.'

'But I thought *Trash Out* was a huge success.'

'It had a novelty value,' Darcy said. 'But that's worn off. People are saying that it sounds the same every month. And nobody but feminists are interested in the dirt on other feminists. But Lulu put a lot of money into it. I guess her loans are probably coming due. Cash-flow problems, that's the polite term for imminent bankruptcy.' And Darcy drifted off to join her Californian friends.

'Yeah, I know she has me in mind for her cover,' said Simone, almost in resignation. We'd caught up with her in the courtyard outside the exhibit hall. 'But what can you do? Better Lulu trashing me out than Ishmael Reed. At least Lulu doesn't pretend to be the voice of injured black manhood.'

'But what can she dig up on you?' Dee asked. I wanted to warn her that this was a potential murderer we were dealing with, but Dee rushed on. 'I *love* your work. And your life has seemed so straightforward. I mean, at least in that article I read in *Time* magazine. You went to college, graduate school, published a novel, that's all.'

Simone smiled. 'Nobody's life is that straightforward. Everybody does little deals, makes little trade-offs, has skeletons in the closet. Mine are no worse than anyone else's but I have them. For instance, I'm a lesbian, but I'm not out to a lot of people, and I don't write about lesbian characters. That's how I want it at the moment, that's how I can do my best work at the moment. But Lulu's bound to make that the focus. I'm angry, but I'm prepared. People have said worse things about me. I've got a thick skin.'

Simone's face was a calm mask. I couldn't really tell what she was feeling and thinking.

'It's terrible about Olga, isn't it?' I said.

But Simone just nodded.

'Either Simone's a psychopathic liar or we've got the wrong suspect. And she didn't look upset about Olga at all.'

Dee and I were at her stand, surrounded by hordes of Russians.

If anything, Olga's death had increased the attendance, and there was an especially large crowd around TRESH OOT. 'Maybe we should give up,' said Dee. 'The Soviets probably killed Olga. And if they didn't they'll have to figure out who did.' 'Rubbish,' I said. 'What does the KGB know about feminism? They have no idea it's a greater threat to world stability than capitalism. No, there must be a connection somewhere – to the idea that Simone is somehow involved and the rumour that Lulu's losing money on *Trash Out*.'

Fifteen minutes later I had broken into Lulu's room at the Vladivostok People's Hotel. I realised how little I knew about her as I leafed though a box of back issues of *Trash Out* and rooted in a suitcase full of scarves and black underwear. There must be a clue here somewhere, but I was damned if I knew what it was or where to find it.

I heard footsteps in the corridor and hastily crawled under the bed. While I held my breath the footsteps continued down the hall and disappeared. I scrambled out again. But my eye had been caught by a crumpled piece of paper in between the bed and the night stand. It looked as if it had been thrown there in a fit of anger. I smoothed it out and read:

POISON PEN

Some authors are sensitive about their secrets. I found that out the hard way during the most recent international feminist bookfair in Vladivostok when Simone Jefferson tried to poison me with a quantity of strychnine placed on the tip of my pen. Like many people Simone had noticed that I'm in the habit of sucking my pen when I'm thinking. So she substituted one that had poison in order to shut me up. The only reason I'm here today is that there was only enough of the substance to make me really ill, not enough to kill me. Otherwise I would have been murdered in cold blood in the very midst of the bookfair, while selling this journal.

Lulu went on to detail the means by which Simone was caught. The bottle of rat poison in her hotel room. Her fingerprints on the pen. 'All because,' Lulu wrote, 'Simone was afraid I was going to finally expose the secret she'd hidden for so long. Her lesbianism.'

Again I heard footsteps in the corridor, but this time I wasn't fast enough. I was on my hands and knees by the bed when Lulu came in. She immediately spotted the paper in my hand.

'I didn't mean to kill Olga,' she said, edging towards me while she kept the door well blocked. 'Nobody can accuse me of premeditated murder. That editorial is proof. The poison was meant for me. That's not a crime, is it?'

'No,' I said. 'Not if you really meant to commit suicide. But you miscalculated the dose, you only thought you'd get ill and that Simone would be blamed. It was a big risk to take, Lulu. And Olga took the consequences.'

I couldn't see a way around her body toward the door.

'No one's going to know,' she said, coming closer to me. 'I've still got some strychnine here and, as we both know, it doesn't take much.'

'I've always thought,' I said calmly, 'that all those scarves were a big fashion mistake.' I grabbed the ends of one of them and started twisting.

The door behind her burst open.

'KGB!' said Felicity Horsey-Smythe playfully, and then gasped. 'Oh my, Cassandra dear, whatever are you doing to poor Lulu? She looks as if she can't breathe very well like that.'

'Be a good girl, Felicity,' I said, still keeping a firm grip on Lulu, 'and call the police, dear.'

A half hour later Simone had retrieved the bottle of rat poison Lulu had planted in her room and we'd presented it together with Lulu's editorial to the Soviet police. I had no idea what would happen to Lulu now; whether she'd be tried and punished, sent to Siberia or locked up in the Lubyanka. Whatever her punishment, I suspected it would be milder than what some of Lulu's victims would have meted out if they'd had the chance.

Still, I suppose some good did come out of it all. Felicity Horsey-Smythe had a wonderful subject for her next novel and Darcy Joanne said she'd publish it in the States. They signed a contract at Vladivostok airport and agreed to move quickly on the project. They did want, after all, to get the book out in time for the next international feminist bookfair.

'Tierra del Fuego!' said Dee when I told her. 'I can hardly wait!'

MILLIE MURRAY

A Blessing in Disguise

Out of every tragedy must come some good. Is so mi granny always tell me when something bad happen: 'Wilima, don't worry yurself, in a lickle time you will see a blessing come out of dis situation.' Every time mi think of mi granny, mi think of mi niece Celeste. Mi remember telling her de same thing when her husband died and her friend Florica turn mad: 'Celeste, even though de situation is bad, a blessing is soon to come,' and yu know it was true!

When mi sister Lilith went back to Jamaica fi live out de rest fi her days, Celeste came fi live with me. She was training fi be dancer. Every day she would exercise before she went fi college and after she had spent all day dere, she would still come home and practise.
    'Celeste, yu will wear yurself out, chile?'
    She would say between breaths, 'No I won't, Auntie, practice makes perfect.'
    What could mi say to dat?
    We were very happy living together, mi and Celeste. She hardly made any mess, she never did go out to disco and mi never hear her talk bout any bwoyfriend. Mi was glad in a way, because mi know how man can stop a woman from looking out fi herself. Hmm, is so dem call love.

Mi did have fi give up mi cooking job because fi mi age, it nearly bruck mi heart, so all mi could do was cook at home. Celeste did love mi cooking but every minute she a 'check her diet'! Hmm. On Sundays mi love fi cook up a big big dinner: rice and peas, chicken or beef and some curry goat, some sweet potato roast up tender, corn and green beans, and even Irish baked potato. Yes mi dear, all dat fi one meal. Den bout a hour after mi would bring out some Gizadas with thick thick coconut pon de top and each piece mi bite come in like a slice of heaven. Then mi have to loosen mi skirt band til most of de time mi start fi wear mi broad-cut summer frock.

'Auntie, you shouldn't eat so much, it's not good for your heart!'

Mi just smile, she was so concern fi mi! 'Dat's all right dear, God looks after his own.' All Celeste do is nibble!

De only person Celeste had as a visitor was Florica. She call her her friend. Mi wasn't so sure. She had some long long fingernail that come in like claw. Mi granny always sey, 'Wilima, any ooman dat have long long fingernail, nar trust dem, especially with yur man!'

Celeste was kindness itself. Just looking at her, with her fine bones and her honey coloured skin shine up like mi coffee table, make mi heart swell with pride.

Mi house was in a very quiet area, and from de time mi did hear sey de street call Proverbs, mi did purchase de house. It had three bedrooms. Mi did have de front one, which could hold all mi things dem; a very large wardrobe which go from one corner to de next, a big big bed mi could bounce around in and still have room! Mi dressing table stretch from under one window to de next, yes it was a big room. Celeste bedroom was next door. Her room was half de size of mi own. She had a small wardrobe and single bed and one little chest of drawers she use as dressing table. De next room could just about hold mi. By de time mi stretch out mi hand so, and turn, de room full up. Now Celeste use dat room to do her exercise, it was just enough fi lift up her leg and spin round!

'Celeste, mi wish mi have more money so dat mi could build up extension on de back of de house, so yu could have a big big room fi sleep in and a next one fi dance in.'

Celeste would come and hug mi up, she was a good gal! 'Auntie, it's okay. My room is fine, it's big enough for me. Anyway, one day I'll be making enough money so that we can live in a bigger house with lots and lots of room,' she would say, kissing mi on mi head top.

'Oh, chile, where yu getting all dat kinda money from ee?' mi just laugh.

'Well, when I become a famous dancer, I'll be able to make lots of money.'

Mi smile. 'But tell mi, Celeste, yu not going fi dance all yur life, so yu have to start make some soon.' Mi just a jest, but Celeste turn serious pon mi.

'Auntie, I intend to dance for the rest of my life, and that's how I'll make my living and furthermore, nothing or no one will stop me and if they try, I'll kill them.' She get on de floor and do some exercise.

Yu know, life is funny. De way Celeste so thin it come in like she weak, dat's how people see her, but dat lickle girl have determination enough fi lift up de island of Jamaica outa de sea, with one hand. Hmm!

It was late spring, nearly summer, all de flowers dem a bloom, de grass look green and early morning de bird dem a sing out dem heart, right outside mi bedroom window, so mi get up early. When mi think back to dis particular time mi have fi blame miself somehow. Mi know dat sound hard, but mi did encourage Celeste. Yu see, mi love picknee. Mi never did get round fi have any miself, due to de fact of one wutless man mi did have fi run from, and so from dat mi did not want no more man! So, as mi was saying, whenever mi see picknee mi feel funny inside, no matter if mi out a street, or in de shops. So one morning when mi get up early and watch de television, mi see Lady Di have one lickle picknee bwoy, mi feel sad.

'Oh, look at de lickle picknee bwoy Lady Di have, look how she look at him,' mi sigh.

Celeste finish her exercise and a eat her bran (de bran taste awful - it come in like punishment to eat it). 'Auntie, be patient, I'll have so many children one day you'll probably get fed up babysitting.'

Mi smile. 'Oh, no, darlin, mi love picknee. Yu could all have ten or even twenty, bring dem all to yur Auntie Wilima.' Mi well serious.

Celeste would laugh. 'Auntie, ten or twenty – I'd have no energy left to dance!'

Now, dat Florica start come to de house often. Mi granny sey people dat come to yur house often, a look fi something. Mi granny right. Florica come fi take Celeste out disco and party, but from de way she dress up fi kill, mi can see she a look man. But

still, yu have fi understand dat mi mind was not so good at de time
– it was full of picknee.

So Celeste start go out one time, two time, it come in regular dat
she is out dancing every week. Mi never did mind, mi love fi see her
dress up and enjoy herself.

Summer come. For a English summer it was very hot. All day
long mi drinking ice water and just a take it easy. One Wednesday
evening Celeste sey, 'Auntie sit down, I have something to tell
you.' So mi sit down. 'Well, I've been meaning to tell you this for a
while, but I wasn't sure myself, but, I think I am now. You see, I've
met a young man . . .'

'Yes, yu have? Oh, mi so happy,' mi did ball out, mi so glad.

'Auntie wait, let me finish.' She was laughing. 'His name is
Lowell, he's sooo handsome, he's a jeweller . . .'

'Him have money den . . .' Mi grin mi teeth.

'Auntie, don't be so materialistic, I'm not even sure, anyway,
well, perhaps he might be . . .'

Mi start squealing. All mi could think bout was – picknee.

'All right, Auntie, seeing how you're not going to let me finish,
I've invited him here for dinner on Friday.'

'Yes, tell him fi come.' Mi start fi plan out one big dinner fi cook
him.

All Thursday mi looking in shop window at perambulator.

Mi start fi cook early Friday morning. Mi remember what mi
granny say: 'Wilima, de sure way fi secure yur husband, is put
plenty pepper in de meat, and plenty sugar pon de sweet.' Mi cut
up some extra pepper in de meat pot, and shake in some black
pepper seed on de fish – mi was making Solomon Gundy. Mi make
one everlastingly big carrot cake, and pour some sweet, sweet
syrup pon de top. Hmm, hmm.

Well by de time mi spin round and finish cook and dress up,
Lowell come. At first mi wasn't too too sure whether dis bwoy was
de right one fi mi niece. Him hair shave clean off with one thin line
down de side fi him head. Him did have on one leather suit, de
trousers so tight mi was surprise when mi hear him voice so low.
Him did have one thick gold chain round him neck, it come in like
toilet chain, and one big big gold ring on him finger, how him lift
up him hand mi don't know. But him did smell sweet, and when
him shake mi hand, mi find him own more soft dan mine own! But
she seem so happy, and de way him did eat like hog, mi was

frightened dat de fish bone was going fi cut him palate. Mi never see him take out any bone out fi him mout, so mi suppose him did swallow dem. Him was a strong bwoy, because mi put so much pepper in de food, mi could just about eat it, in between two glass of ice water. Him have two large piece of carrot cake and lots of de sweet syrup, and him never once belch!

It was a nice dinner and all him could sey was, 'Auntie Wilima, that was fantastic. I'm surprised you haven't got a hundred men banging on your door. You're brilliant!' Mi just smile. Mi could see him did have manners and would treat Celeste and dem picknee good.

De only problem dat did hang over de whole evening was dat Florica did come. From mi understanding of de situation, she invite herself. Mi couldn't sey a thing until after dey both gone – which again mi never did think sey it was good fi Lowell fi drop home Florica. Mi start wash de dishes and Celeste was drying dem.

'Celeste, who invite Florica?'

'Oh, she just came along, she didn't have anything planned for the night.'

'So hmm, so she have bwoyfriend?'

'No, not really. She used to like Lowell quite a lot, but he was only prepared just to be friends with her, and now he loves me, she said she's happy he didn't have a girl that she didn't know. She's a good friend, Auntie.'

'Hmm, so mi see.'

All through de summer Lowell was always at de house. Him would drive up in one big red car, Celeste sey it was a Mercedes – mi never know about car. Mi just know him did drop mi to church one day and de way him a drive mi knew sey mi would be seeing mi Saviour soon.

As fi de gal Florica, she come to de house every living day. Mi never know how de young lovin couple put up with her, dem never have lickle time to demself. It start make mi think, what does dis gal want? Yu know, mi is a person who no like mystery. Mi like plain fact. Even when mi go school, if teacher say one thing, mi have fi question why and where and what. Mi granny say, 'Wilima, don't trouble trouble, till trouble trouble yu.' But mi never could help it, mi have fi know. Sometimes de way mi see people carry on, mi could all write one book.

Autumn come. All de leaves dem drop off right outside mi doorstep. Every day mi a sweep – come in like mi is street sweeper! Now dat de birds dem don't sing outside mi window, mi never get up so early.

It was a Saturday morning when Celeste burst into mi bedroom and jump pon mi bed, nearly bust de springs. 'Auntie, auntie, look!' She push some paper right under mi nose.

'How yu expect mi fi read dis, pass mi eyeglass!' But de way she a bounce and a carry on, mi could only read de top of de letter: 'Royal School of Ballet'.

'I've done it, I've done it, I'm in,' she bawl out loud.

'What yu sey?'

'Auntie, I've been accepted at the Royal School of Ballet, and I'm to start next autumn.'

'Yes, is so de letter sey. Oh mi dear, mi so happy fi yu.' Mi kiss and hug her.

By de time mi reach downstairs, Celeste is on de phone telling all de world she get in.

'Remember fi call yu mother, chile.'

She put her hand over de moutpiece. 'I've done it already,' she smile. Mi start fi fret bout how much de bill will be?

When Celeste come off de phone she was a lickle upset because something Florica sey to her. She did not want fi tell mi, but mi get it out of her. Imagine – Madam Florica tell Celeste sey she only get accept because dey want a 'token black'! Mi never know what she seying or meaning, mi just tell Celeste don't pay her no mind.

Anyhow dat evening Lowell come smelling sweet as usual. All him do is grin and sey, 'I'm right proud of you, babes. I knew you could do it!'

Him ask fi speak to mi. Yu know mi know what he was going to ask mi, mi could feel it in mi bones.

'Eh, Aunt Wilima, Celeste and I would like to get married.' Mi coulda cry.

'Oh yes!' Dat all mi could sey.

Yu know, it's not every man dese days dat want fi get married, and fi come and ask de family fi permission is such good manners, mi think to miself dat Celeste really marry a gentleman. But still yu know dis Florica business unsettle mi. She still a hang bout – so mi did encourage dem fi get married as soon as possible. Dem did – within a month. Mi sister never come to England – dey were having dem honeymoon in Jamaica. At de wedding it was mostly de young people dem and family. It was mi parson who marry dem. Celeste look so beautiful and fresh, mi eye did run water, and de bridesmaids come in like angels. Lowell have on one suit dat did cost so much mi coulda build up mi extension, and Madam Florica have on one tight up dress mi start fi wonder how she manage fi breathe.

De reception was nice. Mi alone did all de cooking, and every last crumb did get eat off, none did leave. De sound system play some nice music; mi did get fed up with de reggae beat, but de young people dem like it. Lowell father was de Master of Ceremony, de man can chat! And every time him sey a few words him have fi drink a gallon of rum. By de time dem get to de final toast, de man could barely stand up. But all in all, everybody did enjoy demself.

Well de only sad thing at dat time was mi would now have fi live back by miself. Mi would really miss Celeste. She was moving into Lowell house in one posh district. De house was nice and big, it did have four good good size bedroom. It was only join up with one house next door, and it did have a verandah with big flowers pot on de ledge, running underneath de upstairs window.

When de young lovin couple was on honeymoon, mi was given de key fi check out de house all over, so dat if tief did come, mi would know what dem take – right. All over de house was one bouncy bouncy carpet, it come in like trampoline. In de front room was black leather furniture, mi woulda prefer a red flowers one instead, but de young people have different taste. De television was big like a cinema screen, mi enjoy watching mi favourite daytime programme.

Upstairs was beautiful, all de bedroom except fi one was de same size as mi own! In de young lovin couple bedroom was one everlastingly big kingsize bed! Dat was all. It did have one white silk bedspread. De bed was firm, just right fi mi back.

De bathroom make mi sigh. It was pink and white and yu have fi step up to de bath and den down into de bath tub. All de taps and things in gold. Mi dear, dem coulda invite Prince Charles and Lady Di fi de weekend and feel no shame.

Time wait fi no man. Before mi know it de young lovin couple back! And winter nearly end. Celeste was teaching dancing and arrowbactics or something. She was getting herself ready fi go a ballet school. Mi did still wish fi picknee.

Mi love fi visit Celeste, her cooking not too bad, Lowell eat off everything anyway. But yu know, when mi did look at mi niece at dat time, her eye don't look so happy.

'Everything all right?'

'Yes, Auntie, no problems, everything's fine!' she sey.

Mi notice dat Florica would not come to de house when Lowell not dere. Mi never like mystery.

Lowell did purchase a new car. All him talk bout was dis car.

'Oh man, this car is wicked. It's like a plane on wheels.'

De car was de same red, it never look no different to mi.

Madam Florica could not stop talk bout it too: 'Oh Celeste, it's out of this world, you can't feel any bumps in the road, and as for speed, it's faster than electricity. It's wild!' She smile.

Celeste just smile back.

Mi was vex. Mi want fi know how Madam Florica know so much bout de car fi tell Celeste all bout it – when Lowell was Celeste husband?

Anyhow, all good things come to an end, mi dear. One evening mi just a relax in front of de television when de telephone ring. Mi nearly jump outa mi skin. 'Who coulda call mi now, ee?' From de time de man on de telephone sey, 'Doctor Jenkins from sucha such hospital', mi know something bad happen. It was Celeste and her husband involve inna one accident.

When mi first see Celeste wrap up in de bed in one metal contraption, with drip in her arm and plaster on her leg, and bandage tie up her head, mi heart just feel like it coulda leap out of mi body.

'Celeste, Celeste, can yu hear me?'

Nothing. She never even open her eye.

'Celeste, Celeste, poor baby.' Mi feel eye water run down mi face.

'Auntie.' Dat was all mi hear at first. 'Auntie, is it really you?'

'Yes, baby, hush now.' Mi so please she can talk.

'It's okay, Auntie, I'm just tired. Can I have a sip of water, please?' Mi hold up her head and give her de water.

'Thank you, Auntie. Where's Lowell?'

'Him okay, Celeste. Celeste, what did happen?' Mi did have to know.

'Well, Auntie, as it's summertime I thought a day in the country would be nice . . . I wasn't sure where to go, so my friend Gemma has a friend, whose friend . . .' – she get breathless, but from all dis friend business, mi know sey dat it not good – '. . . told me about this place called Beachy Head. How beautiful it was, with lots of hills and valleys, how wild blackberries and all different kind of things grew there . . . how it was a good place to go and relax.' She tired, but Celeste still struggle fi finish tell mi.

'I really wanted Lowell to go because he works so hard in the shop.' Mi give her some more water. 'So we set off in the car. I sat in the back seat because I wanted to sleep, so Florica sat in the front.' `

'Whaat!' mi shout. Mi did forget where mi was. 'How come Florica with yu both?'

'Well, Auntie, Florica wasn't doing anything that day, so Lowell asked her to come along.'

Dis really upset mi now mi know Madam Florica was dere. 'Anyhow, carry on, baby,' mi say.

'Lowell and Florica were . . . laughing and playing games.'

'How can yu play game and drive car?' mi ask Celeste.

'Auntie, I don't really know, you see I had fallen asleep, and when I woke up that's what they were doing. And then . . .' she nearly cry and mi feel so sad.

'It all right, Celeste, yu just sleep now.'

'But, but, Auntie, it was so terrible, all I can remember is the car going so fast, and Lowell was shouting that he couldn't control the wheel, and then we came off the road . . . suddenly, we were heading for an enormous tree. I started screaming and, and . . .' She crying real hard now. Mi start bawling too.

'Never mind, baby, mi have fi thank de Lawd yu is alive.' Eye water blind mi.

Mi so happy when Celeste come home, but it hurt mi fi see her inna wheelchair and now she not able fi go a ballet school. She hardly talk, just sit and stare. De hospital doctor sey dat Celeste spine bruise up so bad dem not sure how she going fi come out, and she have parralisis in her leg dem.

'We are uncertain as to whether she will ever gain full control of the use of her legs,' sey de doctor.

'But tell me something, doctor, how can yu sey dat, yu never know. Celeste was a ballet dancer and she need her leg dem, ee?'

'Well I'm sorry, but I can't be more specific. In such cases the permanence of the damage can only be determined in the course of time.' So Celeste might never walk again.

But what nearly kill mi was all dat Lowell do was lick him head, him did all right and Madam Florica bruck her fingernail – dat was it!

Mi dear, mi did feel so murderous.

Mi try fi get to Celeste house every day, especially when mi hear sey Madam Florica did move in fi nurse Celeste. What she know bout nurse? In de day time dey both working, mi sit with Celeste.

One time mi did go a bathroom and Madam Florica room door open. Mi nearly fall down in shock at all de things she have pack in her room. Now Celeste tell mi dat Florica earn only a lickle money a week time, so how she manage fi buy all dese things? She never have bwoyfriend, and her mother and father nar rich, so how? Hmm, hmm.

What a way she have so much shoes! De box dem did pile up in one corner! When mi open de wardrobe and see so much clothes, mi have fi hang on to de door, mi feel so weak. She have one long long fancy fur coat, mi could not believe it. She have so much perfume bottle on de dressing table it come in like Boots de chemist!

Bwoy! Mi could not think straight. As mi walk downstairs mi wonder fi know if Celeste see all dat Florica have in her room. What a outrageous situation!

Mi did spend one Saturday evening with de lovin young couple and Madam Florica. Mi was surprise fi see one everlastingly gi-normous diamond ring, big like a duck egg, dat not even Elizabeth Taylor could wear, pon de wutless gal finger! Dis situation is very grave.

Mi did have fi ask Celeste later – after mi calm down – bout Florica and her room.

'Celeste, as mi walk pass Florica room, mi couldn't help notice dat she have how much clothes and shoes in her room, where she get dem from, ee?'

'Well, she says that she saves all her money, and then goes out on shopping sprees.'

'Hmm. But dat fur coat alone must take her all year fi save up and buy!'

Now even mi start lose lickle weight through de fretting. All dis things come in like a real mystery, but mi remember mi granny and she sey, 'Wilima, all dat glitter is not gold.' Mi granny so wise.

Christmas come round again so quick. Celeste no better, she just sit quiet in de wheelchair. All mi find miself a do is shop, soak some fruit fi bake cake, and go see Celeste. Coming from market one day, mi did feel fi see Celeste. Mi did still have de key, so mi let miself though de door. Mi rest mi bag down (dem still heavy even though mi only shopping fi one!). Mi call out; mi coulda hear some boom booming noise, and palam-pam music a beat out.

Mi slowly open up de front room door, Celeste was sitting in de armchair breathing hard, de wheelchair was on de other side of de room by de music system. Sweat was running down her face, and her chest justa heave in and out like when used she to do exercise. Her eye dem shining bright. De music was so loud – mi turn it off and put mi bag just inside de room.

'Celeste, yu all right?'

She sound breathless. 'Yes, Auntie, the music soothes me.'

'But – but it so loud?'

She smoothe down her hair. 'Eh, it's better for me when it's loud.'

Mi sigh. 'All right, be careful yu don't burst out yur eardrum. Want some tea?'

'Oh, yes please, Auntie!' She smile.

As mi come back with de tea, mi see Celeste reading de newspaper mi did bring with mi. But wait a minute, de wheelchair too far fi Celeste fi use, so mi wonder how she manage fi get it? But den mi have to ask miself if it was dere mi did leave de newspaper? But no, mi sure mi did leave it pon top of de television, and wait, how she get de packet of mint mi leave dere too? Hmm.

'Auntie, you really shouldn't carry those heavy shopping bags. Look, next time you come to see me straight from the market, get a cab and I'll pay for it.'

Mi nearly choke on de tea. 'Ee ee, all right, dear.' Mi shock. 'Ee Celeste, how you know sey mi bag dem heavy?' mi ask.

She never even look up from de newspaper. 'Oh, Auntie, I can see from the way you were carrying them that they're heavy.' Den she smile at me. Mi just smile back.

Mi think now is de time fi ask Celeste if she woulda do a

lickle part-time work fi occupy her day.

'Well not really, and it's not as though we need the money. Lowell is worth quite a bit, what with the house and the shop and its contents – must be worth about half a million, Auntie.'

Mi could not believe dat dis young man coulda value so much. 'But dat is so much money, yu sure him worth it?'

'Well, from what I've seen of his policies, yes, I'm sure of the amount, but is he worth it . . .' De telephone ring. It just come in mi mind what mi granny would sey, 'De fish slip through de net!'

It funny, yu know, mi granny woulda see all what from what was going on. 'Wilima, what go round must come round,' mi coulda hear her sey it even now.

It did take half de year fi build up extension at de back of mi house. Every day see mi sweeping and dusting, but mi do have fi sey, de workmen did a good job. It did cost so much money but Celeste insist sey she will pay for everything.

Even de attic make into a next room. Now we live in a four bedroom mansion – imagine mi lickle house come out so big! It make it seem like a palace! But den, with mi, Celeste, her second husband and family living here, we need all de room possible. She look so fit and well now it hard fi mi fi even imagine how thin and sick she did look in de wheelchair all dat time ago.

'Celeste, mi can't stop look at you and thank de Lawd dat yu is now safe and well. Even de doctors have fi sey dat it a miracle how yu overcome de parralasis so well.' Celeste just smile.

'Oh, but Auntie, I do have you to thank for being so patient with me.'

'Dat a nothing chile, fi mi would do it fi stranger, how much more mi do it fi mi kin!'

'Auntie, that's a beautiful shawl you're crocheting, I'm so grateful to you.' Celeste rub her belly with her two picknee in it. 'You've crocheted so many things for me, you can stop when you like.'

'No, mi darlin. I like fi do it, especially fi mi grandpicknee dem.' Well, dem would be as good as grandpicknee, and mi will have dem all to miself when she go back fi take her dance class dem! When mi look at de picture fi Celeste and Nathan on dem wedding day, mi hardly think bout Lowell and Florica.

Yes dem did certainly find what dem was looking for.

Mi remember de day Celeste did tell me bout de whole situation
as clear as water. At first she never sey a word, but mi have fi keep
pushing her, cos it was pon her mind. Mi know what mi granny
would sey: 'Goat mout have fi open fi fill him belly.' 'Celeste,' I sey
to her, 'come tell yur auntie now.'

According to her, on dat fateful day, Lowell did promise fi take
her out fi a drive. But him car did have some problem, so him
decide fi fix it. All morning him busy fixing de car outside de
garage. Celeste was sitting in de wheelchair upstairs on de
verandah above de garage. Bout lunchtime Florica came back
from de shop inna taxi. Celeste hear Florica coo: 'Lowell, poor
thing, having to work on your car! Listen, I'll give you a hand.'

Now mi want fi know, how dis girl know bout car, come like she
know about everything!

And Celeste sey, dat from de time Florica start help Lowell, no
work get done. Dem justa fool round and laugh and stupidness.
Celeste sey she wheel forward, lean over de verandah and shout
out, 'Lowell, are you nearly finished, remember our drive out.'

'Babes,' him sey, 'Somehow I don't think we'll be going today, I
won't be able to have the car done in time. Maybe tomorrow.'

Madam Florica shout out, 'Why don't you water the flowers,
Celeste, that'll give you something to do.' She grin.

So Celeste sey, 'That's a good idea, Florica.'

Celeste hear Florica tell Lowell how she is going fi make lunch.
'I won't be a minute, darling.'

But stop! How can she call Lowell 'darling'! Celeste mout dry
up and she stop talk, but in de end mi squeeze it out of her.

Poor Celeste was trying fi look bout de flowers and up till now
she can't work out how it happen, because de flowers pot so heavy,
but it seem de next thing she know, de flowers pot on de verandah
ledge fall down right where Lowell was fixing de car, and him get
lick on him head top! Him fall down and not get up. By de time
ambulance come and dey get him to hospital him dead. And by de
time de police and everybody come Celeste in shock, she can't talk.
Florica a bawl and scream, it come in like she turn mad. Yu see, she
start lie bout how she see Celeste standing up, and how she musta
pick up de heavy flowers pot and fling down on Lowell! Well dat is
impossible, because Celeste could not stand, much less pick up
heavy flowers pot and walk! Anyhow, Florica could not stop
making noise, but everybody know how much she like fi chat

foolishness, so de doctor advise her fi go on a holiday fi rest. And yu know, she must have had one holiday in a far place, cos we nar see her to dis day, praise de Lawd!

And yu know, it truly amazing: after one lickle while Celeste did meet up with Nathan, such a nice man, and before mi could blink mi eye, dem married!

When mi think back to how mi granny have answer to every living thing, it come in like a Solomon wisdom she did have. Yu know de shock fi Lowell death make Celeste walk – yes, life is funny. It was truly a blessing in disguise! Hmm, hmm, and as mi granny would sey, 'Today fi mi, tomorrow fi yu', and yu know – she right.

VAL McDERMID

A Wife in a Million

The woman strolled through the supermarket, choosing a few items for her basket. As she reached the display of sauces and pickles, a muscle in her jaw tightened. She looked round, willing herself to appear casual. No one watched. Swiftly she took a jar of tomato pickle from her large leather handbag and placed it on the shelf. She moved on to the frozen meat section.

A few minutes later, she passed down the same aisle and paused. She repeated the exercise, this time adding two more jars to the shelf. As she walked on to the checkout, she felt tension slide from her body, leaving her light-headed.

She stood in the queue, anonymous among the morning's shoppers, another neat woman in a well-cut winter coat, a faint smile on her face, and a strangely unfocused look in her pale blue eyes.

Sarah Graham was sprawled on the sofa reading the Situations Vacant in the *Burnalder Evening News* when she heard the car pull up in the drive. Sighing, she dropped the paper and went through to the kitchen. By the time she had pulled the cork from a bottle of elderflower wine and poured two glasses the front door had opened and closed. Sarah stood, glasses in hand, facing the kitchen door.

Detective Sergeant Maggie Staniforth came into the kitchen, took the proffered glass and kissed Sarah perfunctorily. She walked into the living room and slumped in a chair, calling over her shoulder, 'And what kind of day have you had?'

Sarah followed her through and shrugged. 'Another shitty day in paradise. You don't want to hear my catalogue of boredom.'

'It doesn't bore me. It reminds me that there's life outside crime.'

'I got up about nine, by which time you'd no doubt arrested half a dozen villains. I whizzed through the *Guardian* job ads, and went down the library to check out the other papers. After lunch I cleaned the bedroom, did a bit of ironing and polished the dining room table. Then down to the newsagents for the evening paper. A thrill a minute. And you? Solved the crime of the century?'

Maggie winced. 'Nothing so exciting. Bit of breaking and entering, bit of paperwork on the rape case at the blues club. It's due in court next week.'

'At least you get paid for it.'

'Something will come up soon, love.'

'And meanwhile I go on being your kept woman.'

Maggie said nothing. There was nothing to say. The two of them had been together since they fell head over heels in love at university eleven years before. Things had been fine while they were both concentrating on climbing their career ladders. But Sarah's career in personnel management had hit a brick wall when the company which employed her had collapsed nine months previously. That crisis had opened a wound in their relationship that was rapidly festering. Now Maggie was often afraid to speak for fear of provoking another bitter exchange. She drank her wine in silence.

'No titbits to amuse me, then?' Sarah demanded. 'No funny little tales from the underbelly?'

'One thing that might interest you,' Maggie said tentatively. 'Notice a story in the *News* last night about a woman taken to the General with suspected food poisoning?'

'I saw it. I read every inch of that paper. It fills an hour.'

'She's just died. And there have been two other families affected. The funny thing is they can't track down a common source. Jim Bryant from casualty was telling me about it.'

Sarah pulled a face. 'Sure you can face my spaghetti carbonara tonight?'

The telephone cut across Maggie's smile. She quickly crossed the room and picked it up on the third ring. 'D S Staniforth speaking . . . Hi, Bill.' She listened intently. 'Good God!' she breathed. 'I'll be with you in ten minutes. Okay.' She stood holding the phone. 'Sarah, that woman I told you about. It wasn't

food poisoning. It was a massive dose of arsenic, and two of the other so-called food poisoning cases have died. They suspect arsenic there too. I'm meeting Bill at the hospital.'
'You'd better move, then. Shall I save you some food?'
'No point. And don't wait up, I'll be late.' Maggie crossed to her and gave her a brief hug. She hurried out of the room. Seconds later, the front door slammed.

The fluorescent strips made the kitchen look bright but cold. The woman opened one of the fitted cupboards and took a jar of greyish-white powder from the very back of the shelf.

She picked up a filleting knife whose edge was honed to a wicked sharpness. She slid it delicately under the flap of a cardboard pack of blancmange powder. She did the same to five other packets. Then she carefully opened the inner paper envelopes. Into each she mixed a tablespoonful of the powder from the jar.

Under the light, the grey strands in her auburn hair glinted. Painstakingly, she folded the inner packets closed again and with a drop of glue she resealed the cardboard packages. She put them all in a shopping bag and carried it into the rear porch.

She replaced the jar in the cupboard and went through to the living room where the television blared. She looked strangely triumphant.

It was after three when Maggie Staniforth closed the front door behind her. As she hung up her sheepskin, she noticed lines of strain round her eyes in the hall mirror. Sarah appeared in the kitchen doorway. 'I know you're probably too tired to feel hungry, but I've made some soup if you want it,' she said.
'You shouldn't have stayed up. It's late.'
'I've got nothing else to do. After all, there's plenty of opportunity for me to catch up on my sleep.'

Please God, not now, thought Maggie. As if the job isn't hard enough without coming home to hassles from Sarah.

But she was proved wrong. Sarah smiled and said, 'Do you want some grub?'
'That depends.'
'On what?'
'Whether there's Higham's Continental Tomato Pickle in it.'
Sarah looked bewildered. Maggie went on, 'It seems that three

people have died from arsenic administered in Higham's Continental Tomato Pickle bought from Fastfare Supermarket.'
'You're joking!'
'Wish I was.' Maggie went through to the kitchen. She poured herself a glass of orange juice as Sarah served up a steaming bowl of lentil soup with a pile of buttered brown bread. Maggie sat down and tucked in, giving her lover a disjointed summary as she ate.
'Victim number one: May Scott, fifty-seven, widow, lived up Warburton Road. Numbers two and three: Gary Andrews, fifteen, and his brother Kevin, thirteen, from Priory Farm Estate. Their father is seriously ill. So are two others now, Thomas and Louise Forrester of Bryony Grange. No connection between them except that they all ate pickle from jars bought on the same day at Fastfare.
'Could be someone playing at extortion – you know, pay me a million pounds or I'll do it again. Could be someone with a grudge against Fastfare. Ditto against Higham's. So you can bet your sweet life we're going to be hammered into the ground on this one. Already we're getting flak.'
Maggie finished her meal. Her head dropped into her hands.
'What a bitch of a job.'
'Better than no job at all.'
'Is it?'
'You should know better than to ask.'
Maggie sighed. 'Take me to bed, Sarah. Let me forget about the battlefield for a few hours, eh?'

Piped music lulled the shoppers at Pinkertons Hypermarket into a drugged acquisitiveness. The woman pushing the trolley was deaf to its bland presence. When she reached the shelf with the blancmange display, she stopped and checked that the coast was clear.
She swiftly put three packs on the shelf and moved away. A few minutes later she returned and studied several instant cake mixes as she waited for the aisle to clear. Then she completed her mission and finished her shopping in a leisurely fashion.
At the checkout, she brightly chatted to the bored teenager who rang up her purchases automatically. Then she left, gently humming the song that flowed from the shop's speakers.

*

Three days later, Maggie Staniforth burst into her living room in the middle of the afternoon to find Sarah typing a job application. 'Red alert, love,' she announced. 'I'm only home to have a quick bath and change my things. Any chance of a sandwich?'

'I was beginning to wonder if you still lived here,' Sarah muttered darkly. 'If you were having an affair, at least I'd know how to fight back.'

'Not now, love, please.'

'Do you want something hot? Soup? Omelette?'

'Soup, please. And a toasted cheese sandwich.'

'Coming up. What's the panic this time?'

Maggie's eyes clouded. 'Our homicidal maniac has struck again. Eight people on the critical list at the General. This time the arsenic was in Garratt's Blancmange from Pinkertons Hypermarket. Bill's doing a television appeal right now asking for people to bring in any packets bought there this week.'

'Different manufacturer, different supermarket. Sounds like a crazy rather than a grudge, doesn't it?'

'And that makes it impossible to predict. Anyway, I'm going for that bath now. I'll be down in fifteen minutes.' Maggie stopped in the kitchen doorway. 'I'm not being funny, Sarah, don't do any shopping in the supermarkets. Butchers, greengrocers, okay. But no self-service, prepackaged food. Please.'

Sarah nodded. She had never seen Maggie afraid in eight years in the force and the sight did nothing to lift her depressed spirits.

This time it was jars of mincemeat. Even the Salvation Army band playing carols outside Nationwide Stores failed to make the woman pause in her mission. Her shopping bag held six jars laced with deadly white powder when she entered the supermarket.

When she left, there were none. She dropped 50p in the collecting tin as she passed the band because they were playing her favourite carol, 'In the Bleak Midwinter'. She walked slowly back to the car park, not pausing to look at the shop-window Christmas displays. She wasn't anticipating a merry Christmas.

Sarah walked back from the newsagent's with the evening paper, reading the front page as she went. The Burnalder Poisoner was front page news everywhere by now, but the stories in the local paper seemed to carry an extra edge of fear. They were thorough in their coverage, tracing any possible commercial connection between the three giant food companies that produced the contaminated food. They also speculated on the possible reasons for the week-long gaps between outbreaks. And they laid out in stark detail the drastic effect the poisoning was having on the finances of the food processing companies.

The latest killer was Univex mincemeat. Sarah shivered as she read of the latest three deaths, bringing the toll to twelve. As she turned the corner, she saw Maggie's car in the drive and increased her pace. A grim idea had taken root in her brain as she read the long report.

While she was hanging up her jacket, Maggie called from the kitchen. Sarah walked slowly through to find her tucking into a plate of eggs and bacon, but without her usual large dollop of tomato ketchup. There were dark circles beneath her eyes and the skin round them was grey and stretched. She had not slept at home for two nights. The job had never made such demands on her before. Sarah found a moment to wonder if the atmosphere between them was partly responsible for Maggie's total commitment to this desperate search.

'How is it going?' she asked anxiously.

'It's not,' said Maggie. 'Virtually nothing to go on. No link that we can find. It's not as if we even have leads to chase up. I came home for a break because we were just sitting staring at each other, wondering what to do next. Short of searching everyone who goes into the supermarkets, what can we do? And those bloody reporters seem to have taken up residence in the station. We're being leaned on from all directions. We've got to crack this one or we'll be crucified.'

Sarah sat down. 'I've been thinking about this. The grudge theory has broken down because you can't find a link between the companies, am I right?'

'Yes.'

'Have you thought about the effect unemployment has on crime?'

'Burglary, shoplifting, mugging, vandalism, yes. But surely not mass poisoning, love.'

'There's so much bitterness there, Maggie. So much hatred. I've often felt like murdering those incompetent tossers who destroyed Liddell's and threw me on the scrap-heap. Did you think about people who'd been given the boot?'

'We did think about it. But only a handful of people have ever worked for all three companies. None of them have any reason to hold a grudge. And none of them have any connection with Burnalder.'

"There's another aspect though, Maggie. It only hit me when I read the paper tonight. The *News* has a big piece about the parent companies who make the three products. Now, I'd swear that each one of those companies has advertised in the last couple of months for management executives. I know, I applied for two of the jobs. I didn't even get interviewed because I've got no experience in the food industry, only in plastics. There must be other people in the same boat, maybe less stable than I am.'

'My God!' Maggie breathed. She pushed her plate away. The colour had returned to her cheeks and she seemed to have found fresh energy. She got up and hugged Sarah fiercely. 'You've given us the first positive lead in this whole bloody case. You're a genius!'

'I hope you'll remember that when they give you your inspector's job.'

Maggie grinned on her way out the door. 'I owe you one. I'll see you later.'

As the front door slammed, Sarah said ironically, 'I hope it's not too late already, babe.'

Detective Inspector Bill Nicholson had worked with Maggie Staniforth for two years. His initial distrust of her gender had been broken down by her sheer grasp of the job. Now he was wont to describe her as 'a bloody good copper in spite of being a woman' as if this were a discovery uniquely his, and a direct product of working for him. As she unfolded Sarah's hunch, backed by photostats of newspaper advertisements culled from the local paper's files, he realised for the first time she was probably going to leapfrog him on the career ladder before too long. He didn't like the idea, but he wasn't prepared to let that stand between him and a job of work.

They started on the long haul of speaking directly to the personnel officers of the three companies. It meant quartering the country and they knew they were working against the clock. Back at Burnalder, a team of detectives was phoning companies who had advertised similar vacancies, asking for lists of applicants. The lumbering machinery of the law was in gear.

On the evening of the second day, an exhausted Maggie arrived home. Six hundred and thirty-seven miles of driving had taken their toll and she looked ten years older. Sarah helped her out of her coat and poured her a stiff drink in silence.

'You were right,' Maggie sighed. 'We've got the name and address of a man who has been rejected by all three after the first interview. We're moving in on him tonight. If he sticks to his pattern, he'll be aiming to strike again tomorrow. So with luck, it'll be a red-handed job.' She sounded grim and distant. 'What a bloody waste. Twelve lives because he can't get a bloody job.'

'I can understand it,' Sarah said abruptly, and went through to the kitchen.

Maggie stared after her, shocked but comprehending. She felt again the low rumble of anger deep inside her against a system that set her to catch the people it had so often made its victims. If only Sarah had not lost her well-paid job then Maggie knew she would have left the force by now, but they needed her salary to keep their heads above water. The job itself was dirty enough; but the added pain of keeping her relationship with Sarah constantly under wraps was finally becoming more than she could comfortably bear. Sarah wasn't the only one whose choices had been drastically pruned by her unemployment.

By nine fifty-five a dozen detectives were stationed around a neat detached house in a quiet suburban street. In the garden a For Sale sign sprouted among the rose bushes. Lights burned in the kitchen and living room.

In the car, Bill made a final check to his search warrant. Then, after a last word over the walkie-talkie, he and Maggie walked up the drive. 'It's up to you now,' he said, and rang the doorbell. It was answered by a tall, bluff man in his mid forties. There were lines of strain round his eyes and his clothes hung loosely, as if he had recently lost weight.

'Yes?' he asked in a pleasant, gentle voice.

'Mr Derek Millfield?' Maggie demanded.

'That's me. How can I help you?'

'We are police officers, Mr Millfield. We'd like to have a word with you, if you don't mind.'

He looked puzzled. 'By all means. But I don't see what . . .' His voice tailed off. 'You'd better come in, I suppose.'

They entered the house and Millfield showed them into a surprisingly large living room. It was tastefully and expensively furnished. A woman sat watching the television.

'My wife Shula,' he explained. 'Shula, these are policemen – I mean officers, sorry, miss.'

Shula Millfield stood up and faced them. 'You've come for me then,' she said.

It was hard to say who looked most surprised. Then suddenly she was laughing, crying and screaming, all at once.

Maggie stretched out on the sofa. 'It was horrific. She must have been living on a knife edge for weeks before she finally flipped. He's been out of work for seven months. They've had to take their kids out of public school, had to sell a car, sell their possessions. He obviously had no idea what she was up to. I can't believe anyone would just go berserk like that. All for the sake of a nice middle-class lifestyle.

'There's no doubt about it, by the way. Her fingerprints are all over the jar of arsenic. She stole the jar a month ago. She worked part-time in the pharmacy at the cottage hospital in Kingcaple. They didn't notice the loss, God knows how.'

'What will happen to her?' Sarah asked coolly.

'She'll be tried, if she's fit to plead. But I doubt if she will be. I'm afraid it will be the locked ward for life.' When she looked up, Maggie saw there were tears on Sarah's cheeks. She immediately got up and put her arm round her. 'Hey, don't cry, love. Please.'

'I can't help it, Maggie. You see, I know how she feels. I know that utter lack of all hope. I know that hatred, that sense of frustration and futility. There's nothing you can do to take that away.

'What you have to live with, Detective Sergeant Staniforth, is that it could have been me. It could so easily have been me.'

REBECCA O'ROURKE

Standing Witness

It would be about five a.m., I'm not sure exactly. Woken suddenly by pandemonium it's not the first thing you think of. There was noise everywhere: shouting in the street, my bell, all the bells in the house going; feet on the stairs and running outside.

I don't react well in a crisis, didn't then. Sat bolt upright in my bed, furious. That bloody alarm again, I thought, reaching for the phone, before I realised it couldn't be that. Where I work, you see, we have this alarm, need it for the insurance. But this was wrong: no phone, no nice man saying, 'Hello, this is Securicor Cranley here. I'm afraid your alarm's gone off.'

This was jangling, insistent noise and the reflection of coloured lights flashing on the ceiling. So I'm out of bed, over at the window and I can see it's almost light when it suddenly hits me what I'm looking at. And do you know the first thing I think, well it's a terrible thought really. I think, I'm glad my cat stayed in last night. Because I'm fond of that cat. I've been through a lot with him and I know it's a crime that people think more of their pets than they do of the people around them, but have you ever wondered why that is? Anyway, the cat. That is my first thought. Because he's usually out at night, but last night when he wouldn't go, I didn't make him. I wanted something to cuddle. He's better than the pillow, purrs and is warm and alive and sometimes you need that. Looking out of my window, I think, that would scare him, that would, if it hasn't already killed him.

The place is swarming with police, running up and down, in and out of everyone's drive, ringing doorbells, shouting out to one another. They look really rattled. And I like that. It makes me smile, just for a moment. Because then I notice that all these police running crazy outside my house have come from the cars and transit vans zigzagged across the road as if they'd practised it for weeks. Then I see the ambulance and it sort of sobers me up. I think, Christ; open the window, stick my head out and shout down, 'What's going on?' to the helmetless policeman stood on my doorstep.

But he doesn't even look up. He's got a witness now, the bells have gone quiet. Someone else from the house, a woman. We say hello on the stairs, that kind of thing. He's saying, 'I'll have to take a statement,' they talk and then he goes away. Just a few seconds later I watch her run out towards him. She's wearing slippers and a blue and white dressing gown and looks funny outside like that. Very prim she is, very proper. Not the sort to run around in the early hours, dressed any sort of a way. He doesn't realise she's there at first but the other coppers do and they move towards her, as if to make her stop. And she does, puts her hand to her face, very still and quiet, as if she might scream. Looks very forlorn as the kindly, balding policeman reaches her. I hear him say, 'Perhaps we'd better talk inside. Can I come in and I'll make you some tea.' And I think, I'm glad that's not me.

I suppose I should've realised then what had happened. But I wasn't on the ball exactly, just relieved I wasn't the one entertaining the police, but sort of upset and rejected all at the same time too. Mind you, I've had an awful lot of practice at that. So I did what I always do: trotted off to the kitchen to make myself a cup of tea. Strong and hot and fresh, just how I like it. Taking the tea through and getting back into bed, I just couldn't pretend I was that tired. I couldn't get my mind off what was going on outside, so I went over to the window to watch.

It was getting light enough now to see more clearly. A car facing the wrong way parked practically under my window. There's three plain-clothes men standing in the middle of the road, one of them says: 'But that's the least of our worries that is, right at the bottom of the agenda, it is.' I watch him, I'm going to call him the mister from now on.

That's what adults, men, were called when I was a kid. The mister. There's a mister at the door. And we were slapped down when we said it. I think it sounded too like the master for their liking. I was sent home from school day after day for refusing to call the teacher sir. Mum and Dad backed me up. He's a man like any other, they'd say, there's no reason to call him sir. And it dragged on. Ended up with us all down at school in Sister Frances' office. Mr Collins, the sir in question, the lot of us. Won that one, never did call him sir. But the reputation dogged us, the 'What could you expect from a family like that?' People who felt sorry for the children, until they met us.

Right now, though, I'm thinking how they're like actors holding forth on a stage. High above them, I can see almost everything, but they can't see me. I like the idea of spying on the police, catching them unawares, as it were. So I sit and watch. I wonder why they're there, behaving as they do, but you know, I can come up with any number of explanations. None of them right, of course. I wonder whether they get away with so much they shouldn't just because their work is a mystery? We're too surprised when we see any of what they're up to, to ask them to account for it, we just think well, this all looks very strange to me but they must know what they're doing.

The ambulance is there for a long time, I can't think why. I mean, I know it must've been an accident, happens all the time. It's a bad road, cars go too fast, including the police. They take short cuts, sirens screaming past double-parked cars. Hardly surprising that they kill the odd pedestrian here and there. They're on a kind of piece work after all, aren't they? Getting points for convictions, it's numbers that count. Obviously they're going to cut corners, anyone would.

But as road accidents go, this one seems to rate a lot of attention, and that ambulance's odd. I thought they ran around with stretchers. The last accident I saw they had the red blankets out in no time. But this one just waits there with its engine running and the driver hunched over his wheel, the way you do in a traffic jam you know is going to take hours to clear.

And I can't see anybody needing attention. I wonder where the other car is and what it hit. This one's in the wrong position to have come adrift after hitting the bollards in the centre of the road and looks neatly parked, just the door to the driver's side open. But, looking closer, I see what shook that woman. The front tyre down, resting in a pool of something, a glistening liquid. I turn cold, suddenly and unpleasantly. The ambulance is obviously waiting for the car to be moved so they can free the body pinned there.

A cyclist, I know it. And in my panic, the panic of knowing so many cyclists, of trusting my own body to such a slight structure and the often absent good will and sense of motorists, I can't see that there isn't a bike. Quickly, I calm down, and see there is no body there either. That stain, it could be oil, or rain. It doesn't have to be blood, I tell myself. But if it isn't, then why is the ambulance still waiting, why are the police there at all?

They take everything very leisurely, as if there is no urgency. The mister signals one of the uniformed police over, who then walks over to the ambulance and speaks to the driver, who drives off. The uniformed police are very young, there are two women. They are all fascinated by the car, manage to pass by and peer in every once in a while. Plain nosey, the police are. No respecters of privacy. Then this young fella, he takes a big roll like a giant bandage out of his car, and starts winding it round the trees and the lamp posts and it's as if he's wrapping everything up. I giggle at that, wonder if it's what they mean when they talk about getting things wrapped up.

He winds his ribbon until he's made a neat little square around the car. He blocks out all the entrances from the flats on to the street, closes off all the approach roads. It's funny really, it's just cloth, but as soon as anything comes up to it they turn away. That's the point about the police. Because it's them behind that paltry bit of cloth, you stop. They don't even have to tell you what to do, you just do it all by yourself.

Something seems about to happen. The mister talks into his radio every so often, carrying it around with him like a baby's security blanket. There is a calm air to him, though. Of them all, he seems to treat everything as if it was normal procedure. Looks as if he spends all his time standing in this particular street, at this strange time of the morning. His matter of fact way of organising everything and everybody, well, it has a kindliness to it. He looks almost avuncular, careful of other people, considerate. But then when he stops to think and looks up, it's as if he looks straight at me and his face is a shock. Could've come straight out of a comic, the cartoon leader of a Nazi crack command. A mean man, for all that concern. But then, look at the kind of job he does. Look what's normal for him. I'm thinking this a great adventure, something to tell my friends about. For him, for all of them, it's just routine. Except, as I am beginning to gather, this is a little bit out of the ordinary. Something for them to eat out on in this one too.

He says to one of the others, 'He's on his way, we'll get moving now.' Then a car draws up, a stranger carrying a bag gets out and joins them. The stranger clambers inside the mystery car; its headlights are still on and the street lamp is flickering on and off. So I'm thinking how tricky the light is rather than about what they're doing. From inside the car there's a sort of brief flashing, then the man climbs out and speaks to the mister.

They continue standing there, as if the stranger just confirmed something they already know. While they wait I idle away the time trying to sort out what's happening. I decide the car's been stolen for joy-riding, there's been a chase and now they are sorting out who owns it. Perhaps somebody was badly hurt, killed even; the car is evidence. And I imagine too, that all of that, all the arresting and protesting and taking away of the sick and the dead, happened while I was still asleep. And it makes me shiver, that you can be asleep with people dying around you, their lives changing. You wake up and there they are, laid out in the morgue or sitting in a cell, looking at three years minimum. Sobering.

If I think of the people I knew who've died, most of them did so in that odd nowhere time: two, three, four in the morning. I remember the last time I really was called out to the alarm, cycling back just as it shifted from dark to light. It was beautiful. Hackney Downs covered in this deep purple light, and the trees looking very still and silent. I'd shaken off my irritability at being woken up, I was enjoying it. Loved being the only one out there, making my bike go faster and faster, letting it glide down the paths. There was no fear, not a thought in my mind, just sheer pleasure. Suddenly I wasn't alone. I'd seen the ambulance, looked up to the flat with its light on and my mood had changed. I'd felt like an intruder into someone else's tragedy, guilty. As if by forgetting the world for a moment, I'd been the one to let this person go. Which is a funny thought, really, that it was trouble, because it could easily have been a woman going into labour.

Down below, the stranger leaves and the uniformed police are busy writing things on clip boards. Each car must make its own report. They walk around, make notes and sketch in the position of the car, the route it must've taken. It reminds me of riders walking the course at the Grand National. Now the mister takes a large brown book out and writes in it. It's the sort of book I drool after. Cloth bound, thick, with card covers. A solid sort of book, the kind that gets discovered after you die and lets the world know what you really thought. I'm surprised by it, really. Recall how much of a policeman's lot involves the written word. They have the same tools of the trade as writers. The pencil and the notebook, the observant eye. The same ability to detach themselves from what they see and simply record and place it. And just like we have our rough notebooks and our best, so do they. I don't like to think there are things I have in common with the police. The mister keeps the book tucked under his arm, it is precious to him. I imagine it contains all his crimes, all his works. He starts at the beginning and works through until he's finished and then he starts a new one. Just like me.

I wonder whether they can leave if their shifts finish while they are here. It must be getting on for six now. The mister's going to see it through. There's a flurry of activity and the atmosphere tenses up. Three men arrive with the uniformed police. They leave two by the corner and take one over to the car. It's not clear whether they are under arrest or not. It shocks me to see they aren't young, aren't the tearaway youths I have so far imagined as the drivers of this car.

They have to support this man, he can't stand by himself. It isn't that he's drunk. At the open door of the car, he looks in then sags. The policemen hold him up and steer him away. His friends watch everything. The police don't seem to take any notice of them and suddenly they are not there any more. The mister is in the middle of the road, taking those little steps you try and warm up with. He's talking into the radio, I hear him say: 'We have identification.' He repeats a name, gives alternative surnames. Suddenly I realise it's not just an academic question of this name or that. There must be a body down there. A real person, with a real name and everything that goes with it. And because they need to name him, because it's urgent and they can't ask him, it suddenly dawns on me that he might be dead.

Dead, out there, in that car, on this street. Dead. And I think, the bastards, bringing that fella out here, putting him through that. And I wonder how they knew where to get hold of them. If they didn't know who he was, how would they know who to bring to identify him? If the car wasn't stolen, they'd know who it belonged to. That's how they pin us down these days. How many people do you know without a driving licence? Not many, is it?

They don't need to issue us with pass cards, we've done it for them, again.

I'm still trying to work out the crime, because the very presence of the police makes me believe there must be one. Guilt by association. I think maybe these men did something together; stole the car, chased through streets. Who knows? And he was the one who didn't get away. The three of them legging off, their mate stuck back there and they don't realise until it's too late. The car crashed, he was driving, badly hurt. So badly hurt he dies. But it's every man for himself, isn't it? They'd wonder why the police brought them back to the scene of their escape, why they aren't going straight to the station to be cautioned and charged and all the rest of it. But my version doesn't really make sense. I can't work it out, so I go and make some more tea. I think about taking some out for the police. Very, very briefly. I'm reminded of the soldiers first going into Belfast, how it wasn't uncommon to see them sitting on garden walls with trays of tea and cake.

I came back to the window. It takes a long time to fully register. I stare and stare at the car and there's a shape, a shadow, and ever so slowly I see a person there. Except I don't think of it as a person; I think of it as a body. A body isn't a person. Bodies are dead. Dead people. There is a dead body in a car outside my house. I say that to myself a few times. There is a dead body in a car . . . I can see that the head tilts back and doesn't move. I keep expecting it to, always do when someone's died. It's the stillness of death that frightens, not quite trusting it. Like those games you play as children, statues. Someone always gives in, it never does last for ever. But death does.

When my dad died we weren't sure quite when it happened. It's not as if the one minute you're alive and the next you're not. There's this point after you're dead, too, when all the air goes out of the body in a great noisy rush. It made me jump. Like when I was a kid and he'd play Billy Lion with me. He'd hide under the bedclothes, all quiet and still. I had to pretend I felt safe, then he'd come roaring out at me. Just a game. When he died I couldn't wait to get out of the room, I had this pact with myself that I wouldn't stay there after he'd died. Just as I turned my back, slithering across the polished floor and wondering if I was going to fall, there was this great whooshing noise, then nothing. No Billy Lion, no arms coming out to hold and tickle and trap. No Daddy.

I never did go back to look at him. The next day we had to pick up the death certificate and all his things. As we came away they were collecting bodies from the morgue. One went off in a proper coffin, straight to a funeral I expect, and one went off in a big metal container in the unmarked van with no windows.

My brother was angry, thinking someone had paid out for a proper coffin. Anyway, the door was open while the men collected the bodies and I could see in. I made a point of looking, if you must know. I saw these shapes, wrapped in sheets with the corners tucked up around their heads. They looked very contented, very still, but so tightly wrapped, as if making sure they couldn't move.

It's strange to realise there's a body feet away from you. I'd been watching it for hours, absorbed by the police, engrossed by them. And I felt bad about this body, as if I should have known it was there all the time. Stupid of me, but I felt like those people who go on expeditions to disasters. But it isn't the body that interests me. It's the balletic routines of the police. I want to be reassured that if I ever end up like that, there'll be people who know what they're doing. That's what worries me about death, you know, not knowing. Logically, if there isn't a mind, then I won't even register that I don't know things any more. It will be like before I was born. But that's not enough for me.

It's almost like sex, that point where nothing holds; where you can't speak or move or do anything. Rare it is, but what we strive for, I think. Forget all this emotion, all this love and romance; what matters is abandon. Getting beyond the letting go that is still watching yourself do it, loving yourself doing it, aware of someone else there too. Getting to where there is nothing in the world but you and that part of you, that part of her, which soaks up all the world, is all the world. Those parts together and nothing, and everything, all at the same time. When you come back, you worry that one day you'll just stay there. Death's too like that for my liking.

It reminds me, seeing him. The arch of his neck, head tilted back to the sky. I've seen that before. Not very nice, is it? Sitting thinking about sex, with a man dead outside your door. But it isn't very nice for me, thinking about sex at all, if you're interested. No reason why you should be. It isn't easy for me, not with the dying and all. I can't do it any more. And I miss it, I really feel it. Like a hollowing out, starting between my legs and working its way up through my core. As if I'm curling in at the edges, keeping something in and something out. As if a part of me is withering, drying out and flaking away. As if I have a part that I can't use any more.

And it's not just a part for this and a part for that, it's not that separate, really. More like a shadow across all of me, layers stripping off. It surprises me, looking in mirrors, that there isn't a great space there, a tangible emptiness, because that's what I feel I'm carrying around. It hurts. There's nothing there and it hurts.

The lighter it gets out there, the more clearly I can see what's going on. There are more people around now and the police stop anybody from getting too close. Except me. I'm tempted to take a picture. Later I won't believe this and nobody else will either. A picture will prove it happened. I'm thinking about this because a police photographer has set up his tripod and is taking shots from all angles. He works methodically, right around the car. Snap, snap, snap. Then he moves towards the open door and photographs inside. Click, click, click.

There is a lot of debate as he reaches the other side of the car: should he open the door or not? The mister comes over to speak to him, then he packs his equipment up and waits on the wall. Nothing else happens until two men arrive in an unmarked car. They carry a small bag and swiftly set to work, dusting and fiddling about with the car. Then they open it up and the photographer finishes off.

They are taking a break down below. The mister has found a café and organised tea. It's like he's playing daddy at Christmas or something, the eagerness with which they all pick out their cups. They saunter about, relaxing. Three or four of the youngest ones stand over at the car to drink theirs. I wonder where we get this notion that the raw recruit excuses himself, blanches at the sight of the body and throws up neatly over a garden wall. Not from life, that's for sure. Maybe we just need to believe that the police are going to register some kind of emotion about it all. Well, curiosity is an emotion, I suppose. I can't blame them for that, I feel it myself. There is something compulsive about this. I didn't ask to be woken up like that, but I have been and now I don't want to miss any of it.

Once tea is over, things speed up. They are preparing evidence. Everything down there is evidence of a kind, for somebody. Only a matter of selection and interpretation, there are no absolutes. Another car draws up, another two men get out. They aren't like the mister, these two. Nasty pieces of work. Not the kind of men you'd want to run into on a dark night, on any kind of a night.

They walk over to the mister, who takes them to the car and they poke their heads inside, first the one then the other. One is carrying a big bag and both have white gloves on, like magicians or surgeons. Then they set to work. All sorts of things from the bag are arranged on the wall near the car, everything to hand. Watching them is like watching the star turn. We all bend forward with them, waiting. And there are revelations. The clear, early morning light spotlights them.

One of the men reaches in to the car, takes something out and passes it back to his assistant. He puts it into a plastic bag, seals and labels it before putting it into the case. It looks heavy, the way things do sometimes, and it looks dark. I can't see exactly where he got it from. Next he reaches into the car again and this time pulls up the man's sweater. Oatmeal coloured, it is. A nice jumper, cosy. The kind your mother might knit for you. There's a smear of blood on the car seat, and the body is half in the driver's seat, leaning over to the other side. There's no blood on the jumper; being so pale a colour, it would show. That's odd, because when he rolls back the jumper there is this ragged hole in the man. They all react to that, like he's just pulled a rabbit out of a hat or produced a string of silk scarves.

He pulls the jumper down and they all move off to talk. It reminds me of being in hospital, the procession of men who trail from bed to bed, lift up your clothes, poke and prod before retiring to discuss you. The next thing they do is wrap the man's hands in plastic bags. A gesture carried out countless times before, well rehearsed. They prop the arms against themselves, rest the floppy hands on their shoulders and slip the bags over. They have one each and finish at exactly the same time.

It seems like the whole world is watching these two. Each time the magician does something they take off a pair of gloves. The gloves gather pinky stains. I know it's blood, but it looks too innocent, too pretty really. His assistant peels back the gloves for him, takes the used pair and puts them in a plastic bag. As each layer comes off, there's another one underneath. It's like Russian dolls. All prepared he is, and I wonder, how does he know how many gloves to put on? I wonder too, do these get thrown away now or taken somewhere and washed? I know that if they do, it'll be women doing the washing. It always is.

The magician rolls back the jumper, scrapes something up and puts it into a little glass jar which his assistant screws the top on to and labels. It's a ritual, this. The one who scrapes and pokes and searches the body, getting his hands dirty, his gloves bloody, and the one ready to wrap, parcel, label. With those gloves, they start to look like clowns. I expect them to have put red plastic blobs on to the end of their noses when they emerge suddenly from inside the car. I expect something to register on their faces. But their masks never slip, never change. Just a sly smile from the magician as he steals this or that from the body. It takes a long time. They work very slowly and carefully. They take traces, clues from the man. A series of signs to be reassembled at some later date, at which he will not be present. Their account will reconstruct his death for him. They gather what they need with the minimum of contact. I wonder, is this deliberate, and is it so as not to disturb anything or do they have a revulsion to dead flesh? I wonder what it would be like to be married to one of them, to have one for a father. To be touched by hands that spend their days measuring the damage done by the world and its people. Like being married to a butcher, I expect, only much, much worse.

Finally, all is collected, all is packed away. The last pair of pink gloves comes off, the bag is closed and the men stand to one side, their performances finished, waiting for applause.

You have to give them credit for organisation. I never noticed that van draw up, but there it is. A big black transit van with no windows, and now they're bringing the coffin over. It looks enormous, wobbles as they carry it. It fastens like a box, a slip over lid. They rest it on the pavement and one of the men unfolds a big sheet of plastic. They line the coffin with this while the magician moves in for the last time. It is he and his assistant who guide the corpse in.

He doesn't come out easily. You can see where the phrase about dead weight comes from. The magician says: 'Give us a hand with that end, will you?' He's holding the shoulders, everything sagging down, until a couple of uniformed men grab hold. He has the man by the scruff, pulling his clothes which bunch up in his grasp, and they tug and tug. When the body comes clear, they roll it into the sheet and I see the mass of blood all down the trousers. As they get the body clear of the car it crumples. I see the men's knees give, then brace as they wrestle it on to the sheet and into the coffin. Four of them carry it to the van which leaves immediately.

The car's a mess. I don't expect the stains will ever come out. Odd, all the hours I've been looking and all I saw was that small smear of blood on the driver's seat. There is something very touching about the casual fall of his jacket on the back seat. I could see him tossing it there as he got in the car, expecting to put it on again some time. The magician is pulling pieces of paper out of the car, one is torn in two and when he finds the other half he calls the mister over. For some reason then, I suddenly remember Ann. The terrible shock of her death, that terrible death.

This would have happened to her. She would've been left like that, on the pavement or in the car, wherever she actually was, however it actually happened. And she would've been just as dead, her bloody body crumpled like this. The street sealed off, the crowds and photos, the comings and goings. I start to cry then, for the awful loneliness of it. Nobody to hold her hand, just like there'd been nobody to hold his. A terrible thing, to die like that, for anybody.

This isn't an accident, this death. This is murder, and all the indignity of it, all the routine, just a job of work; all the chat and laughter from those policemen, all that drinking of tea and gawping, all that happened to her too. I want to stop looking now, I want not to have seen any of it in the first place. I want to try and forget Ann died like this, out on the streets, violently. I wonder, did he know his killer too?

But now something else has arrived, a large pick-up truck. It's nearly over and I have to see it through.

The driver brings the truck up close to the car, locks the jack and swings the hoist out. There are four clamps and he walks around the car, dumping them down at each wheel. He hesitates at the wheel resting in the pool of blood, but the mister waves him on. He just sort of kicks that clamp over. It falls in the blood.

I begin to get dressed, I have a train to catch. I want it all gone before I leave, but it just isn't possible. By the time I am out of the house, the car is swinging up above the pavement, the driver guiding it on to the truck. I hurry past, feeling the eyes of the police on me. They aren't that interested, just wave me on.

It is after midnight when I get home, so I get a taxi. The driver pulls up just a little way past my house, right there. Right where it had been. I don't want to get out of the cab, feel foolish, unable to say anything. He is impatient; I take a long time to pay him before I jump out, over the edge of the broken pavement. Jumping the cracks, I think to myself, and would laugh out loud, except none of this is a laughing matter.

The events described in this story are true; they occurred approximately a month after *Jumping the Cracks*, my first novel, was published. The book opens with a dead body, in a car, in a street not unlike my own.

ABBY BARDI

Death by Water

I was moving through the water, a movement as natural to me as breathing. Much of the coral was dead, killed by the runoff of pesticides on to the reef, but here and there patches of it still lived, clusters of gently pulsing, fleshy plant around which hovered schools of tiny purple fish. Parrot fish shot past, their iridescent bodies streaks against the water. The water itself enveloping me was a very pale blue, as warm as a bath. I floated, suspended in time, the sun beating down on my back. I was in another world, silent except for the sound of my breathing through the snorkel, a world warm and soothing and luminous.

Then I saw it. At the edge of my vision, on the ocean floor, next to a craggy volcanic-looking rock, actually dead coral. Something long and pale, a heap of something, almost like a pile of old laundry, blueish white, filmy as if seen through a soft-focus lens. I swam closer. The sandy bottom of the ocean began to drop off and the water grew slightly colder. Fish scattered. I was directly above it now, my shadow falling where it lay. I still couldn't make out what it was. I drew my head out of the water, took a good breath, and dived.

The water was colder near the bottom. I glanced warily at the rock beside me: it was full of crevices. Anything could be hiding there – eels, venomous fish, deadly sea snakes. A rock like that was full of secrets.

I drew closer to the mysterious object. Because of its strange position, I was nearly to the ocean floor before I realised what it was: a dead body.

I was sitting on the sand wrapped in an old blanket somebody,

Lilah maybe, had found me. The sand was peculiar, little bits of coral, the bones of thousands of years of dead sea creatures ground to a coarse white powder. The sand was warm but I was shivering uncontrollably. To my right, Lilah and Ben stood talking to an Okinawan policeman. I couldn't understand anything they were saying but they kept pointing to it, the body, which lay covered in an old blanket on the sand halfway between me and them.

Someone, Ben and some of the others I guess, had hauled it out of the water and dragged it up on the sand after I had run on to the beach, choking and crying hysterically and then being dramatically sick right at Ben's feet – in my panic to get back to shore I had swallowed a lot of sea water. Ben was the sort of person who immediately took charge in a crisis; he seemed in his element now, chattering animatedly away in Japanese, apparently having some kind of argument with the policeman. There was evidently some question about what should be done with the body.

Burial customs were different in this part of the world. The Okinawans placed their dead in vast concrete burial vaults; cities of them clung to every hillside on the main island. After several years, the eldest member of the family would take the corpse to the seaside and scrape the flesh from the bones, letting the wind take it to sea. Or so I had been told. This custom appealed to me because it manifestly illustrated that here was a culture that knew how to deal with death, to grasp it with both hands. In their homes the Okinawans built a shrine to their departed where they remained real, as real as you or I.

Of course, there would be a problem with this body. All sorts of diplomatic rigmarole. By this time I had figured out that the body was Lindsay's, and that even in death, he had diplomatic status.

I had met Lindsay fairly recently, although I had known of him practically from the moment I stepped off the plane six months ago and into the airless humidity, the constant smell of fish and sewage. It had been January, the rainy season, and there had been nothing to do but drink warm sake with the convivial local expatriates. Being a *gaijin* – a foreigner – as well as an American qualified one for instant membership in various subcultures. I fell in with Catherine – pronounced in the French way, for she was French, traced her roots back to some ancient fallen dynasty – almost immediately. She had described Lindsay to me in glowing terms, as if to suggest, I thought, that I should somehow pursue him. After all, he was single, unlike just about everyone else in Catherine's circle. Catherine herself was married to an Air Force pilot whom she had met in Vietnam, where she had been a photojournalist and he had flown B-52s. 'You will like Lindsay,' she said, sucking smoke from a Gitane into her nostrils and blowing it from her mouth, shaking her mane of dark brown hair. A small gold heart dangled at the base of her throat. 'Leen-zee', she called him.

I was single, I had to keep reminding myself of that. My husband of five years had one day, nearly a year before, simply cleaned out the money from our bank accounts and disappeared. He had later sent me papers for divorce which I, of course, had signed. What else was there to do, I had asked Catherine rhetorically. She had nodded, one of those inscrutable Continental nods which seem to bespeak great depths of understanding. And so, I was explaining to her, I had accepted this job for a year, to travel around Asia teaching English on American military bases. It was the closest thing I could find to the foreign legion. I was still numb, and at first I wasn't the least bit interested in Lindsay.

It was at Ben and Lilah's that I finally met him. It was a small dinner party: Catherine and her husband George were, I was sure, responsible for my invitation. The American Consul, Bernard Secrest, was there with his wife Alice. Bernard Secrest had introduced me to his assistant: 'This is Lindsay Taylor, or is it Taylor Lindsay, I always forget?' Lindsay smiled at me with resignation, as if he had heard this gag before but didn't mind humouring Bernard. We shook hands. Catherine was right, he was good-looking, though in a way I didn't much care for, a preppy way. His light brown hair was very straight and very shiny, brushed carelessly off his face, and his nose and cheekbones were prominent. Almond-shaped green eyes, almost like cats' eyes, beneath heavy brows. A tanned face. He was wearing a button-down shirt and khaki trousers which he had undoubtedly mail-ordered from L.L. Bean. I looked at his mouth: a full, almost petulant lower lip. I felt a sudden urge to bite it. This feeling shocked me because although I wasn't consciously attracted to Lindsay, beneath the surface I supposed that something very different was going on in my mind – if it was my mind at all. It had been a very long time since I had looked at a man at a party and felt that.

'Come outside,' he said. A very definite thrill ran through me in spite of myself. We went through the kitchen, where an old Okinawan man stood filleting a parrot fish, and into a small back garden. He walked over to a small pond, and I followed him. The pond was filled with carp. He threw something into the water, a piece of cracker I guess, and the fish all surged to the surface, a seething orange mass, writhing and snapping. I shivered: it was cold enough outside to require a sweater, which I hadn't brought. The moon was full and very low in the sky, huge and yellow. Lindsay opened up a black case he had been carrying and pulled out a cigarette. He lit it, took a long drag, and offered it to me. I sniffed the air. 'Pot,' I said, taken aback.

'Diplomatic pouch,' he said, grinning.

Carefully, I held the joint between my thumb and forefinger and took a hit. 'Jesus,' I said, exhaling. 'That takes me right back.'

'You looked like you needed some.'

'It shows?'

'Just a little.' He took the joint back from me and put his lips to it. The ember at the end of it glowed brighter and then faded. 'What are you doing here?' he asked suddenly.

'God,' I said, unnerved by his directness. 'I don't know.'

'No,' he said in a softer voice, 'I don't mean the party. Okinawa.'

'I teach English.'

'You're kidding!' He jerked his hand away from his mouth, expelling smoke animatedly. 'I was an English major. You teach high school?'

'College.'

'*Incroyable*! You like T.S. Eliot?'

'Of course.'

He recited a passage about Phlebas the Phoenician with which I was not, I confess, overly familiar. Then he asked me what I was teaching.

'Right now? "Women and Literature". We're reading the Brontës, Woolf, Charlotte Perkins Gilman, Kate Chopin . . .'

'Yes,' he said, frowning. He handed me the joint and I obligingly took a hit. He looked at me, narrowing his eyes. 'What do you think, are men and women different?'

'Are men and women different?'

'An echo?'

I giggled. I am not the sort of person who giggles. 'You mean are men and women – different?'

'Why have a course devoted to women? That's what I mean.'

'That's what you mean?' I inhaled some smoke, but as I started laughing inanely again it burst from my lungs into the night air. 'I don't know.' I tried to think. 'I guess because women see things differently from men.'

'Ah, but do they? That's what I want to know. I want to know,' he said, locking eyes with me, 'what you see that I don't see.'

'Well, women are traditionally held to be more intuitive, of course. But are we? I don't know. For a long time I believed that men and women were only superficially different, that the biological differences didn't matter. But recently it has seemed to me that we are worlds apart, that men are totally alien beings –' To my horror, I felt my eyes fill with tears. Lindsay put his hand on my shoulder and said nothing. 'Sorry,' I said. 'Divorce.'

'Ah. Recent?'

'Recent enough.'

'Oh, there you are,' said Lilah, coming out into the garden through a sliding door. 'Dinner.' She vanished back into the house.

Lindsay handed me his handkerchief, probably also from L.L. Bean; I wiped my eyes and handed it back. 'I've heard it said of men,' I said, 'that when they go to a party, they can tell you the exact number of people in the room, but they can't tell if someone has been crying.'

He held the sliding door to the living room open for me and as I passed through it I could hear his voice behind me: 'I can always tell,' he said.

Dinner was extremely formal by island standards, and I found it difficult to hold up my end of the conversation with George, Catherine's husband, who was seated on my right. I had to admit that I found him incredibly dull, despite the fact that pilots were supposed to be so dashing. They looked amazing in their olive green flight suits, but in civilian clothes George was terribly drab and ordinary, blond and colourless, a total contrast to Catherine who sat, dark and animated, across from us.

Lilah and Ben sat at opposite ends of the long table, Lilah in a long lavender caftan, Ben in a polo sweater and plaid trousers. Ben was an architect who had come after the war as an adviser, helping to rebuild the island which had been completely flattened in five days. Thousands of people had been killed, trapped in caves, or committed suicide, flinging themselves from cliffs. It was said that since then the island had been full of ghosts; the G I's reported constant supernatural occurrences, instances of E S P, premonition. It was hard to imagine that there had ever been a war there, it was now so thoroughly populated and so cheerful, but memories lurked beneath the surface, people on the street with horrible scars or missing limbs; monuments to the war, to dead schoolgirls, in public places; and, I noticed for the first time that night (or maybe it was the pot) a feeling in the air, an electrical throb, a constant hum. The old psychobabble term 'vibrations' came into my head – something always vibrated like supernatural music. One evening I had wandered through the winding streets on foot, up and down hills, trying to find the source of some music I heard playing the Okinawan pentatonic scale on the samisen, a banjo-like instrument covered in snakeskin. Yet as I approached the sound some trick of perception would throw it behind me, from some other hill: I never found it.

In addition to Catherine and George, Bernard and Alice Secrest, there was another couple at the table (Lindsay and I had clearly been invited as a pair. I had probably been the only unattached female available). They were Sid and Shirley Neumann. Sid was a civilian contractor with the military. I had the impression that he sold weapons. Shirley didn't seem to do much of anything. She played a lot of tennis and worked out with weights, and as a result had a lithe, wiry body though she was in her early forties, a good ten years older than Lindsay or I. I had no idea how old Catherine was. She could have been any age. Shirley also seemed to spend a lot of time shopping; in our brief conversation before dinner she had told me the best places to buy china, silk, fish, and bootleg computers. Women like Shirley made me feel uncomfortable; though she was perceptibly muscular she was also tremendously feminine – long red fingernails, immaculate permed hair, expensive perfume, a beautiful, simple dress and pearls. This is why he left me, I found myself thinking – this is what a woman is supposed to look like. Detachedly, I seemed to see myself sitting there in a plain brown cotton dress, my hair frizzing uncontrollably from the constant humidity, unadorned by scent, polish, or jewellery. I looked up and found Lindsay smiling at me from across the table. I wondered what he thought a woman should look like.

The dinner conversation orbited for the most part around international business and politics; shopping (best suits: Hong Kong; cheapest leather: Korea); and food (the freshest sushi, the crispest tempura, the rarest kobe beef). Toward the end of the evening, however, the discussion turned to Lindsay's question to me earlier: were men and women different? 'Women spend more money,' Sid said predictably. Shirley laughed airily and without mirth. 'Women are moodier,' George said, looking at Catherine. She lit a Gitane and blew smoke across the table toward him. '*Les femmes*,' she said in her low, dark voice, 'have many secrets.' 'That's right,' I said, though I can't imagine what possessed me – probably the pot. 'I mean,' I continued, 'there's the basic anatomical difference. With men everything is just there, for all to see, plain as day, the shortest distance between two points – whereas with women everything is dark, hidden, a space to be explored, full of secret places . . . ' My voice trailed off as I became aware that the table had suddenly gone silent and that everyone was staring at me.

'I'll call you,' Lindsay assured me as we said goodbye at the door.

I got into my Toyota and drove back to my room on base. I got out my copy of 'The Waste Land' and thumbed it till I found the part that Lindsay had quoted to me. It was from the section entitled 'Death by Water'.

He never called me. Now, four months later, he was dead.

I had been looking forward to the boat trip. When Catherine had invited me, I had snapped at the invitation even though, I later reflected, perhaps she had meant it casually, or not at all. I had run into her in the Officers' Wives Club Gift Shop, where she sometimes worked. She was standing behind the jewellery counter with both hands held out in front of her. They were full of pearls. We had exchanged pleasantries – I had not seen her in a while – and she told me I looked pale. I told her I hadn't been to the beach, though now that the rainy season had ended I was hoping to. 'Haven't Lilah and Ben told you about the boat trip?' she asked, making a tsk-ing sound with her tongue. 'You must come. This Sunday. We go to a small island just off the coast, Ike-shima. There is a small cove, blue water, walls of coral on each side. You would love it.' She shook her head, her voice thick with regret that I hadn't been asked.

She gave me directions to the port, which was a small village on the other side of the main island, drawing me a small map on the back of a sales receipt. I started to leave; then I turned back and asked nonchalantly, I thought, 'Will Lindsay be there?'

Her dark eyes widened, and she laughed deep in her throat. 'Leen-zee will be there. We will all be there.'

It was still very early morning as I drove in the general direction of the port. Despite the map Catherine's directions were extremely vague, which was typical not of her but of the island. There were no street signs except the occasional one in kanji, so people always directed one to landmarks like Shell stations or pink stucco buildings. The trouble was that there were so many Shell stations, so many pink stucco buildings, that following directions took on a nightmarish quality as I wondered, was it this Shell station, or did she mean that one? Catherine had told me to look for a large red sign that said 'Ice'. I circled the area a few times but could not find the sign.

Eventually I turned left at a huge gnarled tree with a large red sign in kanji and found myself winding down tiny streets into a small fishing village with a tiny harbour filled with fishing boats of various sizes. I pulled up to the concrete waterfront and saw everyone standing next to a fairly large though somewhat dilapidated boat: Lilah, Ben, Bernard and Alice Secrest, Shirley and Sid Neumann, Catherine, a few people I didn't recognise. No sign of Lindsay.

As I headed toward the dock from my parked car, a gold Toyota pulled up. A hand waved at me through the sunroof. Through the dark windows I could just barely see him. Hopping out of his car, he strode over to me with his hand extended, smiling. 'Long time no see,' he said. 'I didn't know you were coming. I've been meaning to call you since that night at Lilah's but I've been so very –'

'Me too.' We shook hands. I tried to study his face but I couldn't see his eyes; he was wearing very dark sunglasses, the kind pilots wear.

'Let's get the show on the road,' Ben shouted to us from the pier. We walked quickly to the front of the boat. People were slinging masses of scuba gear, picnic baskets, coolers, life jackets, into the boat. Gingerly I stepped on to the prow. A strong swimmer, I have always been comfortable in water, but there is something about boats that makes me nervous, the way they skim the water's surface, indifferent to the depths they skate over. I turned around and grasped Lindsay's hand. His palm was sweating, and as I looked at him I saw that he was more nervous than I was, but as we stood on the deck and got our balance, it seemed to pass.

We squeezed past the rail; a glum-looking Okinawan man with a rag tied around his head who was, it turned out, our pilot, stood in our way. A group of gaijins sat at the stern of the boat on benches, surrounded by piles of accessories. Catherine came up to us smiling and greeted me with uncharacteristic warmth, kissing both cheeks. She said hello to Lindsay. From behind her, Shirley Neumann waved a well-manicured hand. Both she and Catherine had already changed into their bikinis; both had taut, brown stomachs and long legs. I felt a sudden crisis of confidence. How could I take off my jeans? My legs were pasty white with pockets of cellulite, my knees little islands of bone beneath the pudgy flesh of my thighs; my stomach would remain somewhat flat if I held it in all day and did not allow any food whatsoever to pass my lips. I glanced over at Lindsay. He was smiling at me with what I took to be encouragement. Even now, I like to think that he had heard my thoughts and that he was willing to accept me the way that I was, the way that I am.

I sat down next to Shirley. 'It's going to be a hot one,' she said. 'Lucky we're getting away. This little island we're going to is a lot cooler.'

'Coolest island,' I said without thinking.

'Ike-shima,' Lindsay said, sitting down on Shirley's other side. She didn't look at him. 'Small, uninhabited island. The Marines call it the Blue Lagoon. Easily accessible by boat. Good for diving.'

'Are you going diving?' I asked.

'Not me. No, actually, I don't swim very well, in fact I've only learned how quite recently. A little snorkelling is all I can manage.'

'I love snorkelling!' I exclaimed.

'You've been?'

'Just once, in Acapulco, when I was a teenager. It was, oh, maybe my favourite thing, maybe the most beautiful thing ever. I love the way the whole world opens up, the underwater world. It's the real world, don't you think? After all, seven-eighths of the world is water and yet we think of this, above the water, as reality.'

'How arrogant of us,' he said, laughing with? at? me.

'It is.' I laughed too to indicate that I wasn't serious. He had taken his sunglasses off and was looking at me. Between us sat Shirley, not saying a word, languidly crossing and uncrossing her legs. At that moment her husband Sid came up on deck and stopped in the doorway. I followed his eyes. He was staring next to me, but not at Shirley – he was staring at Lindsay. Sid was a heavy-set man, though not fat, and his eyes were like cold blue marbles glistening from his reddish face. As I watched him, I felt my stomach lurch. This was a familiar sensation to me, the sensation I always got when I felt something I didn't want to feel, discovered something I didn't want to know. As I watched Sid Neumann watching Lindsay from across the deck, I knew instantly that although they hadn't said a word to each other since we'd sat down, Lindsay and Shirley were having an affair.

I excused myself and went to sit at the front of the boat. As we pulled away from the dock I watched the clusters of small, square, tiled houses turn to brown flecks against the lush dark green of the hillside. I took off my jeans and sat there watching the water turn from a light aqua to deeper blue. I lay down in the sun and fell asleep.

'You're missing the best part,' Lindsay's voice awakened me. I opened my eyes and saw that the boat was just pulling into a small cove, steering carefully between two walls of coral rock and a large rock in the centre. The water was the deepest blue I had ever seen, encircled like a pool by the edges of rock.

'It's paradise.'

'Hey, don't say that. You know what happened there.' His eyes were covered by the sunglasses again but I could see a smile crinkle their corners. He stood up, offered me a hand, and helped me to my feet as the boat stopped about six feet from the shore. 'He can't get any closer,' Lindsay said apologetically. 'We have to toss everything over the side and then swim for it. It's not very deep.'

I looked over the side at the water. It was as transparent as air, and the sand on the ocean floor was perfectly visible, refracted as if by a lens into clarity. 'Oh look, a shell.'

'Oh my. Haven't you had the Air Force briefing on marine life? You haven't? My dear, that is a cone shell, and it's deadly poison. Just last year, an Okinawan shell collector found one and put it very carefully into his backpack. As he walked, the creature inside the shell reached out and stung him.'

'What happened?'

'Died instantly,' Lindsay said cheerfully. 'And then there are the poisonous sea snakes –'

'Don't tell me,' I said. 'I don't want to know.'

Catherine and I sat on the sand, dripping wet. I had gone out snorkelling with her and she had shown me all the best spots, live coral, schools of yellow and black angel fish, enormous toast-coloured starfish (crown of thorns, she told me, *très dangereuse*). It had been years since I had swum so much, and I felt totally invigorated, though just a little tired – she had led me out a bit further than I felt comfortable going.

Catherine shook her head so that her hair fell around her shoulders. 'Isn't this marvellous! I could live here for ever.' Her right hand grasped the small gold heart around her neck. 'That is where I belong,' she said, waving her left hand toward the cliff above the beach. Thick, fleshy leaves and desiccated vines spilled down from it. 'Like, what was her name, the girlfriend of Tarzan?'

'Her name was Catherine, wasn't it?' asked Lindsay, sitting down between us, equidistant from us both. He said to her while looking at me, 'You wouldn't want to live in that jungle – too many snakes.'

'The habu? Don't be absurd, Leen-zee. I am like the mongoose. I will bite off their heads. I have my own kind of venom.'

'Quite,' Lindsay said diplomatically. For the first time since he had sat down, he looked at her. He had the same look on his face I had noticed as we had boarded the boat: his usual buoyant confidence and what can only be called *joie de vivre* seemed to have suddenly fled, drained away. She looked back at him, her hand still clutching the gold heart, and suddenly I began to sense that feeling again in my stomach, the feeling of knowing what I didn't want to know. 'Can I get you ladies something to eat?' he asked, recovering his composure.

'Nothing for me,' I said, pulling in my abdominal muscles, which I kept forgetting to do.

'Catherine?'

'Nothing for me either, thank you. Nothing at all.'

'Excuse me, then.' As he got to his feet, Catherine watched him through the thick brown fringe of her eyelashes. As he walked away, she unclenched her fist.

I was sitting next to Bernard and Alice Secrest at a picnic table beneath the thatched roof of a small shelter at the top of the beach. They were sharing an apple so large that they had sliced it up like a loaf of bread and were spreading runny brie on it. 'Where on earth did you find brie?' I asked them.

'It's just Kraft,' Alice said apologetically. She was small with grey hair, and was wrapped in an enormous beach coat as if to ward off any trace of the sun. She spread some brie on a slice of apple and offered it to me. I was about to decline but as I looked down the beach, I saw Lindsay sitting next to Catherine on her straw mat, deep in conversation.

'I haven't had brie in six months,' I told Alice, reaching for the slice of apple and taking a bite. 'It tastes heavenly.' Painstakingly, she explained to me the whereabouts of a small gourmet food store, but I was only half listening, my eyes resting a few degrees to her right so that it looked like I was watching her face and listening to her – I nodded periodically – though I was in fact looking at Lindsay. Finally she paused for breath. 'Thank you,' I said. 'And these apples – they're so enormous.'

'They're from the mainland,' Bernard said. 'The Japanese encase them in plastic when they're quite small, which causes them to grow much larger than normal. They're a bit grotesque, don't you think?'

On an enormous beach towel a few yards from Catherine, Shirley Neumann was lying in the sun. Her husband had gone scuba diving with George and a few other men. 'Don't any of the women ever scuba dive?' I asked Bernard.

'No, they wait on the shore, like the wives of Odysseus and his mariners.'

'More like sirens, some of them,' Alice said, turning around and glancing significantly at Shirley, then over at Lindsay. Then she turned and exchanged looks with Bernard; this was evidently something they had discussed.

As if sensing that he was being watched, Lindsay glanced up at us. He stood up, brushed sand from his legs, and walked up to our shelter. 'Staying out of the sun, are you?'

'It's very strong,' I said. 'I'm afraid I'm just not used to it.'

'You're very fair, aren't you,' he said.

'Yes, if that's a nice way of saying that I go lobster-red if I'm out too long.'

'Lindsay says everything in a nice way,' Alice said, smiling up at him fondly. I assumed this fondness was maternal. 'He's a natural diplomat, isn't he, Bernard?'

'Don't tell him that, Alice, he'll be after my job next.'

Lindsay smiled at them indulgently. He had certainly heard this interchange before. He sat down next to Alice and picked up a piece of apple.

'Why come to the beach at all if you're going to hide in here?' It was Shirley, who had wandered languidly over from her towel. In the shadow of the shelter her brown skin looked like leather. She sat down next to me, directly across from Lindsay. 'What do you think, am I getting too much sun?'

Lindsay reached across the table and pressed her upper arm with his thumb, making an oval white mark into which colour gradually returned. 'Maybe a bit,' he said.

'You've got to be careful, Shirley,' Alice said. 'Those ultraviolet rays are dangerous.'

'Everything wonderful is just a bit dangerous, isn't it?' Shirley said, smiling enigmatically.

'Oh Leen-zee!' Catherine's voice drifted up to us. She was standing at the water's edge holding a snorkel and a mask. 'Are you coming?'

'I promised Catherine I'd come in snorkelling with her. She said she'd show me the best spots.'

Shirley laughed, a sudden, harsh sound.

Lindsay looked at her, then at me. 'What do you think, then? Are men and women different?' He was smiling, but his eyes were serious.

'Hurry up, Leen-zee, I'm going now.'

'You'd better go,' Shirley said, still laughing. 'It isn't polite to keep Catherine waiting.'

'What do you think, Lindsay?' I asked.

'I think maybe women have their own language. Men like to call it innuendo, but it's something more than that.' He stood up and began walking backwards toward Catherine. 'We'll talk about it when I get back.'

'Love goes out your door and innuendo,' said Bernard.

The Okinawan policeman was making enquiries among us. Ben and Lilah accompanied him as he circled the beach, questioning each one of us. While Ben and Lilah interpreted, I explained to him how I had found the body. He wanted me to swim back out and show him exactly where it had been, but Ben and Lilah vetoed this. He barked something at me and his tone stung me, as if I'd been struck. 'He wants to know,' Lilah said gently, 'why you went that far out. He wants to know why you didn't notice the sign against the big rock that says "No Swimming".'

'It's in kanji,' I said tonelessly. 'I don't read kanji.' The fact was that it was a spot Catherine had taken me to, but there was no point in saying that.

Abruptly finished with me, he turned to Catherine, who was sitting in the sand about three yards from them. Her cheeks were flaming, but she seemed outwardly composed. I heard all her answers: evidently, she had gone out with Lindsay to the big rock. Then they had come back in, but as they reached the shore he said he wanted to go back out. Catherine had been too tired to swim any more, so she had let him go back out alone. 'But he wasn't a strong swimmer,' Lilah said. 'You shouldn't have let him.'

'I didn't realise that,' Catherine said. 'He seemed to swim very well.'

The Okinawan policeman said something. 'He wants to know why you took him out to the big rock,' Ben said, 'when the sign there said "No Swimming".'

Catherine looked into Ben's eyes. 'I don't read kanji.'

I sat down on the sand next to Catherine, just out of earshot of the others. 'How did you do it? Did you hold his head under water? I'm sure there must have been a struggle. He had too much energy to go without a fight.' I picked up Catherine's wrist; angry red marks encircled it like a bracelet.

She snatched it away. 'I don't know what you are talking about.'

'You took him out to that spot because you knew it was

dangerous; there was a current, it was far enough offshore that we couldn't see you from the beach. You were probably hoping that when the body surfaced it would be swept out into the Pacific, maybe end up at the bottom of the Ryukyu Trench, fourteen thousand feet down. You didn't think I would find it so quickly, did you? You thought that by the time the body was found, it would have suffered a sea change, Lindsay's eyes turned to pearls, Lindsay's bones turned to coral –'

'Stop it!' Catherine said in a harsh whisper. 'You're mad!'

'You couldn't bear it when he dumped you and took up with Shirley,' I said in a soothing voice. I looked at her and saw that I had struck a nerve. A wave seemed to wash over her, pain perhaps, but she said nothing.

'You were lying when you told the policeman you didn't read kanji. You told me to turn left at the sign that said "Ice". But it didn't say "Ice" in English – it was in kanji. You read kanji perfectly well. I'm sure George will verify it.' I pointed to her husband, who was just emerging from the water in a black body-suit and scuba gear, looking like some horrible sea creature. 'What the hell is that?' I could hear him say. 'It looks like a goddam dead body or something.'

At the sight of George, Catherine seemed to close up.

'You shouldn't have done it,' I said. 'You can't possess people that way. You thought you could own him in death, but you can't. I own him. For the rest of my life when I sleep, I'll be dreaming of Lindsay, deep below the water's surface, I'll dream over and over again that I see him there, resting against the coral, not dead but dreaming, rich and strange, rich and strange . . .'

Catherine's hand went to her throat, reaching for her necklace, which was gone.

Anyone looking at the beach from above on the cliff would have seen an odd tableau: just beyond Catherine and me, Shirley Neumann face down on a beach towel, sobbing; Sid Neumann and George a few yards from the body, staring at it with a kind of grim satisfaction; Ben and Lilah flitting about the beach, Ben trying to manage the crisis, Lilah trying to console everyone; Bernard and Alice Secrest, in each other's arms beneath the thatched roof of the shelter; Catherine and me, silent, on the sand. In the centre, the Okinawan policeman crouched over the body, examining it, prying open and drawing from within its fist a small gold heart.

PENNY SUMNER

Caroline

'And what did Principal have to say then?'
'That she knew she didn't need to tell me to be discreet.' I reach
for the coffee pot.
'Patronising bitch.'
'And that she had no doubts that it was an accident, but she'd
like to make sure.'
'She's scared it's suicide. That would make two in five years –
almost an epidemic.' Ursula props her chin on her hand and I
follow her gaze out to the roses. A pair of frayed cotton gloves sit
in the middle of the table and I know that as soon as I leave she'll
put them on and go back out into the garden.
'And you?'
'Me?' I'm suddenly exhausted.
'Do *you* think it was suicide?'
'I don't know. The police are treating it as an accident.'
'But?'
The first sip of coffee is hot and strong. 'Principal says Caroline
wasn't the sort you'd expect to find clambering around the
scaffolding in the middle of the night.'
'Not even if she was drunk?'
I smile as she looks all innocence. 'Have you ever found me
climbing out of a window when I've had a few too many?'
She smiles back. 'I seer.. to remember you climbing *in* one,
Marjorie.'
'Your bedroom, my love, was on the ground floor. And I wasn't
really drunk, only pretending.'
'You know, that's the first time you've confessed in thirty
years.'

Not really drunk, just drunk enough to attempt the unthinkable. Is that what Caroline had been attempting last night, the unthinkable? I cycle back the long way, along the towpath. I tell myself it's because I'm too tired to take on the morning traffic, but the truth is I want to put the whole business off as long as possible. A fifty-year-old woman cycles along the river bank one fine spring morning and a twenty-three-year-old one plummets to her death in the middle of the night. I find no logic, no pattern, in that.

From the outside you wouldn't know anything had happened. A large Victorian house in north Oxford, the police car, ambulance and reporters all gone. Almost yesterday's news. Principal has given me a set of keys but by ringing the bell I'll save myself from having to search for someone to show me around.

'Yes?'

I'm in luck, it's the scout. 'I'm Dr Stevenson – you must be Mrs Thomas?'

Stepping past her into the entrance hall I take in the polished parquet floor and the oak table, this morning's mail out in neat piles: I can't see any for Caroline. I'm conscious of Mrs Thomas taking me in at the same time and I wonder idly what her response will be. Bewilderment, dislike, curiosity? Aah, contempt. As I turn I can see it in her blue eyes and the rising pink of her cheeks. 'Queer,' she's thinking to herself. She turns away and vigorously strikes out with a duster at a non-existent cobweb.

'Principal rang half an hour ago. She said you had your own keys.'

'Yes,' with a bland smile. 'Could you take me up to Caroline's room?'

'I've already been up the stairs twice this morning.'

'Working here must keep you very fit.'

The walls have been done in magnolia and the carpet's a deep chocolate, the Bursar's idea of good taste combined with sound housekeeping.

'You don't do the whole house by yourself?' I call after her.

She pauses briefly on the landing to catch her breath, which allows me to do the same. 'Mrs Ingham and I do it together but she's on holiday this week.'

'Is it usually you or Mrs Ingham who does the top floor?'

'She couldn't carry a bloody vacuum cleaner three flights with her bad back!'

'So you must have known Caroline fairly well?' I have to start somewhere.

'Can't say I know any of them. I'm just here to clean up the mess.'

'What do you think she was doing out on the scaffolding? Does it surprise you?'

'She was drunk, wasn't she?'

'Did Caroline often drink a lot?'

She stops abruptly outside number 19. 'I never saw her drunk but I wouldn't, would I? I'm only here in the mornings. Sometimes she left her bin outside so I wouldn't disturb her, but I didn't always know if that was because she'd had too much the night before or because she had someone in there. And no,' she looks me up and down, 'nothing here surprises me. It's like working in a brothel and a lunatic asylum all at once.'

The room doesn't tell me much, except that Caroline wasn't short of money. There's a stereo with enormous speakers, a television with a video; the wardrobe's full of clothes which look expensive, though the labels mean nothing to me these days. A sly voice somewhere in the back of my head whispers that I could ask Ursula about the dresses and for the hundredth time this week I tell myself I'm becoming mean in my old age. Dragging Mrs Thomas all the way up here was unnecessary too; at less than £2 an hour she has every right to be sour with the world.

I have a strange *déjà vu* about this room. When I was a student I certainly didn't have money, but I did have the framed photos and the frilled cushions. Ten years later my own students' rooms were heavy with political posters and the smell of incense and marijuana; and ten years after that my brightest finalist had green hair and safety pins through her earlobes. Today, however, they turn up neatly groomed and worried about careers and I'm unhappily reminded of my own fraught adolescence.

The papers on the desk all appear to be research notes, nothing that looks suicidal. Either Caroline or Mrs Thomas dusted regularly. She didn't water her pot-plants enough.

I wander out into the hall; half an hour to go before I start talking to the rest of the household – they've all been asked to be available from eleven o'clock onwards. The attic was converted a couple of years ago and there are three largish bedrooms as well as a shower, a bathroom and two loos. There's a door at the end with a sign reading 'Bloomsbury' and I push it open on to a small kitchen with a sink of dirty mugs. Some things don't change after all. I automatically fill the sink and squirt in some green liquid; I may as well talk to people in here.

'So you didn't see Caroline after she got back from the party?' After a morning's interviewing I've drawn a complete blank on this. I smile encouragingly at Celia but she vigorously shakes her head.

'No, Rod and I were in bed by then.' Surely I'm not expected to be shocked? Maybe it's shocking for every generation at twenty-one. Maybe, with the advent of AIDS, it really is this time round.

'And you're sure she wasn't upset when you saw her before dinner?'

'Positive. She was peeved, yes, but not upset. You see she always had back-up disks.'

'Which she kept in a locker at College . . .'

'That's right – in case the house burned down or something. We all used to tease her about it!' Her eyes are suddenly large; the fact that one of her housemates really is dead is only just dawning on her.

'Paul and Zoë have said she told them she was going to collect the disks after the party.'

'Yes, I heard her saying that as I walked past here to the shower. That was the last time I saw her.' I ignore the fact that Celia's grey eyes are about to brim over; it's been a long morning.

'People at the party say she left around eleven-thirty. It would have taken her maybe twenty minutes to go to her locker and cycle back here. You were asleep by then?'

'No.' She's forgotten that I'm supposed to be scandalised. 'I wasn't asleep but I didn't hear a thing.'

The last one I speak to is Caroline's neighbour from number 20, a tall, dark-haired girl who's very obviously been crying.

'Rachel?'

She blinks at me and I shrug helplessly in the direction of the kettle. 'I'm desperate for a cup of coffee, do you have any?'

'Yes, yes of course.'

As she takes one of the clean mugs from the rack I catch a flash of yellow through the window. It's Ursula, moving slowly along the fence line. What can she be up to?

'Milk, Dr Stevenson?'

'Thank you.' I smile gratefully as she puts the mug down, then gesture to a chair. This shouldn't take long.

'Right. As you know I'm here because the Principal wants to know exactly what happened last night. It was a dreadful accident and we must make sure nothing like it ever happens again.' Damn, Ursula's disappeared. 'You all got a note from the Dean, didn't you, warning people to keep away from the scaffolding?'

'Yes. At the beginning of term.'

'And did you ever see anyone climbing around on it? I'm not asking you to inform on anyone, but as this is a postgraduate house we don't always keep a close eye on what's going on.' The yellow silk shirt's back in view; she's leaning over something.

'I'm sure no one ever climbed it.'

One of the lads has already confessed to climbing it for a bet. He was in his own words 'completely starkers' at the time but maybe she doesn't know about that.

'When did you last see Caroline, Rachel?'

She falters. 'In here, at about seven o'clock last night.'

'And was she upset about anything?'

She shakes her head and I realise that if her face wasn't swollen and red there are angles at which it would be beautiful.

'Did she say anything to you about some disks?'

'Disks?'

'Yes, for her thesis. A couple of the others have said she'd been using one of the machine downstairs: she took a break and when she got back her disks were gone.'

Sean, who confessed to climbing the scaffolding, also kindly explained about disks. I've heard people talking about computers and word processors in the Senior Common Room, but I've never used one myself.

'Oh yes. She said someone must have taken them by mistake.'

'And that she was going to collect her spare disks after the party?'

'She didn't mention that, she just talked about what she was planning to wear . . .'

'At the party she apparently had a few drinks. Did she drink a lot, Rachel?'

Five minutes later I've finished. The picture I get from Rachel is the same as from the others. Sometimes Caroline had quite a lot to drink but she'd never done anything like climb out of a window. No, she didn't seem depressed about anything. No, she wasn't on drugs. Yes, her thesis was going well. No, she'd never said anything about family problems. No, she didn't have a steady boyfriend, she went out with a few people but nothing serious. Yes, she was very friendly and everyone liked her.

'They didn't all like her.' Ursula's brought a basket from the car, and out of it produces a thermos and ham sandwiches. We're sitting under a magnificent copper beech at the end of the garden and from here Caroline's attic window doesn't look far enough from the ground . . .
   'What do you mean?' I lift a corner of bread and check for mustard.
   'What I said. She had a reputation for being all out for herself. A cold fish.'
   I look up. 'I didn't know you'd come across her . . . why didn't you say?' Please Ursula, no games today.
   'Never met the girl, the scout told me.'
   'Mrs Thomas?'
   'Mmm. She came out and chatted while I was picking flowers. Surely you've talked to her, Marjorie, she's the first person you should have interrogated!'
   'Mrs Thomas wasn't very forthcoming with me.'
   She trails a frond across my face. 'Oh dear, you always find blondes difficult, don't you? Will you be much longer?'
   'I don't think so. I'll have another look at Caroline's room, and then I'm coming home to catch up on some sleep.'
   'Your verdict?'
   I shrug. 'She fell to her death while under the influence.'
   'You're sure she fell then, and that she wasn't pushed?'
   'I'm looking for the possibility of suicide, my love, not murder.'

I've talked to her friends, looked through her books and her photo album, but I still have no real feel of what Caroline was like. Blondes: Ursula's right. I look back through the most recent photos where she's tanned and elegant in a one-piece swimsuit, blue eyes confident from under the swept-up hair. She was well-off and strikingly attractive and the news that there was some ill-feeling doesn't really surprise me; nor does it surprise me that I didn't pick up on it this morning. The girl was only a few hours dead and her death threatens them all – mortality's not supposed to assert itself so early.

Putting the album back down I re-read the note that's come from her supervisor. Caroline, she says, was an excellent student. Her thesis on Woolf was near completion, an article had already been accepted for publication. She had everything to live for.

I play with one of the biros from a pretty, handleless mug on the desk. Another thing to note, she didn't chew her pens. And that, I have to admit ruefully, is about the level of my investigative skills. The most useful thing I can do is come back tomorrow and pack her belongings ready for her parents. They haven't been located yet; according to Principal the father's in New York on a business trip and the mother and a younger sister are on a yacht on the Mediterranean.

'Bloomsbury acted as a hot-house . . .' I run my eye down the page. Caroline or a quotation? It seems to be her. Neat pages, no doodles: the bits that are quoted are all followed by titles and page numbers in parentheses. There's a red card-file labelled in silver felt-tip 'To Be Read', and another blue one bearing the message 'Completed'. She'd obviously felt she had everything under control. It had taken me a lot longer to finish my thesis – but then, I remind myself, I'd been desperate with love at the time. I'd climbed through Ursula's window on the night after I'd finished finals and in the morning she'd told me I'd have to go away to do my postgraduate degree, it wouldn't be fair on either of us if I stayed. She was just thirty then and I'd fallen in love with her three years before, during my first week in college. I'd seen her walking across the quad from my window; two weeks later I'd discovered she taught Anglo-Saxon and had begged, unsuccessfully, to be allowed to change from Classics. While I was doing my Ph.D. we'd met in London every weekend; and when I eventually got a job back in Oxford we'd set up house together.

I flip through some of the cards in the blue file. Then, as I push the drawer back in, a corner of white card shows from where it's been pushed underneath. Absent-mindedly I pull it out: in the same silver ink are the words 'HA! HA!' And underneath someone else has scrawled in red, 'YOU FUCKING COW. MAYBE NOW YOU'VE SUFFERED A BIT YOU'LL HAVE SOME IDEA OF HOW I FEEL .'

*

'G and T before dinner?'

'Please.' I pull my feet up on to the sofa and tuck the dressing gown over them.

'Do you want a rug?'

'No, I'm fine. Come and sit.'

As I lean my head against her breasts she strokes my hair. 'Well, my love, what have you got?'

'A young woman of twenty-three. She goes to a party. At eleven-thirty she leaves to pick something up from her locker. Three quarters of an hour later she's dead.'

'Principal stopped by with the results of the forensic report while you were asleep. Some alcohol; no drugs; death as the result of the fall. They've managed to contact her family.'

'I'm sorry you had to face her alone.' I fondle her nipple and it hardens under my fingertips.

'You can't always protect me.'

It's true I've tried; but equally true I haven't succeeded. 'How was our Betty?'

'She looked tired, though not as exhausted as you. She complimented me on my roses.'

'I sometimes dream about killing that woman.' I turn and kiss Ursula's beautiful throat.

'And she brought Caroline's bag and shoes back, to be packed with the rest of her things.'

'Fine, I'll take them in the morning.'

'What is it, love?'

I move my hand from her breast and propel an icecube around my glass. 'I don't know. Maybe it's just that it's not right for someone that young to die for no reason. And that's it I guess – no reason. There was no reason for her to be out there on that scaffolding. Nobody has come up with any reason for that – they just look bemused and say, "Well, she must have been drunk ..."'

'Love problems? Thesis despair?'

'No to both as far as I can make out. No special boyfriend. A thesis on Virginia Woolf that seemed to be going splendidly.'

'On Woolf? You didn't tell me she was an English student!'

'No.' I hadn't mentioned that on purpose and now I hurry past it before we get to the subject of Victor.

'And there's something else.' I reach into my pocket for the note. 'Read this.'

She catches her breath. 'Have the police seen it?'

'I don't think so. It was hidden under a box of file-cards on her desk. The silver writing looks like hers – of course it mightn't be anything to do with last night at all.'

'It does prove Mrs Thomas right though; they didn't like her.'

' "Ha! Ha!" It sounds like she was playing a practical joke on someone.'

'The someone doesn't seem to have been amused . . . Blast! I'll get it.'

She goes to answer the bell and a couple of minutes later calls softly round the door. 'David Murdoch, one of the students from the house, is here to see you – he's been away and has only just heard the news. He's in a dreadful state, Marjorie. He says he and Caroline were planning to get married . . .'

'I don't want to call in the police yet.' Dr Betty Slater leans back in her padded leather chair and looks at some invisible point on the ceiling. She and I are the same age but this morning she looks a lot older. I probably do too.

'All right. I'll talk to them again – but I think you're going to have to tell the police eventually.'

'I'm grateful, Marjorie. Very grateful. I'm glad to have you to deal with this – it's lucky that Victor's away. As head of the English Department he'd feel it was his job and I do think a woman will handle things better.'

What she means is that Victor is a malicious fool. I should probably feel gratified that she's finally realised it, but it's too late for anything like that.

'I'd better be off, I sent a note this morning apologising for any inconvenience, but saying it was urgent I talk to everyone again. By now they'll know something's up, though I did ask David not to say too much.'

'Yes, they'll have guessed by now.' She walks me to the door. 'And, please, do tell Ursula how much I enjoyed seeing her yesterday. You must both come round soon – I could do with her advice on the Principal's garden.'

'So you *didn't* like her, Matthew?'

'No.' He leans back in the kitchen chair and looks at me coolly. Yesterday he'd given the same polite answers as all the rest; today, however, things are different. 'But that doesn't mean I hated her. I didn't feel strongly enough to steal her thesis.'

'Some of the others say there was a lot of rivalry between you.'

'It wasn't academic rivalry, it was just that I wasn't going to be pushed into joining "Bloomsbury". Caroline seemed to think that because I was doing my thesis on Forster that somehow meant I should be anxious to belong to her group. The whole cult thing really pisses me off! What she really wanted was power over people – she queened it up there on the top floor.'

'They were all working on related topics?'

'Rachel's doing Lytton Strachey and Amanda's doing something on the painters – she's in Cambridge at the moment, which rules her out too.'

'Did you Caroline was involved with David?'

'I didn't think it was serious – she flirted with a number of people. But I'm not surprised to hear they were engaged.'

'Why not?'

He grins cynically. 'Well, a, he's got money, b, he's got a good body and c, – this is most important of all – he's American.'

'And why is 'c' a particular asset?'

He runs a hand through spiky brown hair. 'Jobs. There are no jobs here any more, but there are in the States. Every ambitious young academic needs an American spouse, it makes life a good deal simpler!'

'Coffee?' I pick up the nearest jar, past caring whose I'm using. David nods distractedly. He looks dreadful, though less so than last night.

'Did you see Amanda while you were in Cambridge?' I want to get him talking.

'For lunch on Monday.'

'She's doing research on art, is that right?'

'Mmm.' He nods without any interest. I've already rung the student counsellor and made an urgent appointment for him later this afternoon.

'Caro sounded so desperate, you know.' He wraps his fingers around the hot mug. 'It was awful being so far away and not being able to help.'

'Was she ringing from here or from College?'

'She said she was at College. She'd found her locker empty and didn't know what to do.'

David and I had checked last night; the locker door had been forced open, and the spare disks weren't in her bag either.

'It's the same as murder, isn't it?' His face is a mixture of anger and despair. 'Whoever stole them as good as pushed her!'

This morning Ursula's wearing a red silk dress and as I nibble a biscuit I wonder what it is about silk. Her lipstick is of the same colour and I'm reminded that she goes shopping for these things without me. Is she embarrassed by the way I look? Funny to think that I'd modelled myself on her. The trousers, white shirt and ribbon bow-tie are what she wore too until three years ago. I must admit the dresses look good but they didn't save her when the knives were out and I often wonder why she keeps them up. For some reason I've never felt able to ask.

'Do you remember hiding my conference notes that time?'

'No!' I'm genuinely taken aback. 'Ursula, I never did any such thing!'

She laughs and smoothes her skirt out over the grass. 'You did, you know. Remember that Easter when you thought I was getting tired of you?'

All I can remember is agony and blinding grief. She hadn't phoned for three days and there was no answer when I rang her.

'I wasn't answering the phone because I had to get that lecture written – surely you remember that? You arrived sobbing on the doorstep, and then dashed off again with my notes!'

A faint memory lurches unwelcomely into life and I wince. 'I think I remember something about some notes . . .'

'And you locked yourself into Adèle's room and threatened to burn them! I had to beg through the door . . .'

Christ, what we go through. 'Making love that night was wonderful; like shooting to the moon.'

I've arranged to talk to Sean in the computer room, where I warily push a hard square of blue plastic across the table. 'A *floppy* disk?'

'Yeah.' He's a pretty boy and I can't help trying to guess which of the others it was who'd paid to see him climbing naked. Matthew, perhaps, who's working on Forster. People say you can always tell but I've never been able to.

He grins. 'I know it's not floppy, but that's what it's called.'

'And there are just these three computers?' I've heard numerous references to them at various committee meetings. Colleges now have to compete for graduate students and apparently the high-paying ones from overseas won't consider applying to a college that doesn't have computers.

'Only one's actually a computer – these two are dedicated word processors.'

I don't pursue that; I'm just grateful that because of my administrative duties I only take on undergraduates these days – they still write in ink.

'And you all do your theses on these?'

'A couple of people use electronic typewriters. And a few have their own word processors of course.'

Of course. We pretend otherwise but they have to have money to get here in the first place. 'Is it usual to have two lots of disks?'

'Yes. But what was unusual about Caroline was that she kept her back-ups at College. People thought she was being paranoid – though in fact it was pretty good sense. It should have been fool-proof.' The smile's disappeared. 'It was a dirty trick,' he says, 'doing something like that.'

'What do you think you'd do if someone stole your thesis?'

He shakes his head. 'After all that work you'd feel like topping yourself. You would, wouldn't you?'

When the telephone rings I take the call in the scouts' room.

'Victor is back,' Betty announces. 'He feels that as head of the department he should be up there talking to the students too.' Her voice is uneasy. Victor is a fool, but a dangerous one; he's got the votes on more than one committee.

'Fuck him,' I surprise myself. 'If he comes anywhere near I'm not staying. You can tell him that. And if he wants to know why, it's not only because he's an idiot but also because he has no tact and no sympathy – the students here are all in shock and he'll make them worse. You know that as well as I do.'

There's silence as she weighs things up. I have allies of my own and there's still a guilty feeling in the Senior Common Room about what Victor was allowed to do to Ursula. Which is why I was made Senior Tutor, after all. Out of guilt, and as a means of letting Victor know he can't have it all his own way. Ursula had given him the job at College and over the years he'd undermined her position completely. By the time he started the rumour about her having affairs with students, things had gone too far for me to do anything and her breakdown had provided them with a convenient excuse. She'd had another since, just nine months ago, and during the worst I'd actually contemplated leaving her. I'll never forgive him for doing that to us.

'I'll tell Victor that as Senior Tutor this is your responsibility and that you don't need any assistance at present.' She hesitates. 'You will keep me fully informed, won't you, Marjorie?'

The back gate is pink, to go with the doors and window frames. I painted the gate myself last summer but as I push the bike through I notice that it's peeling already. Domesticity – never-ending.

Lunch is ready and Ursula's waiting for me, glass in hand.

'Love you.'

'And you.'

'Well?'

'What a surprise – it turns out that not everyone liked Caroline after all. But no one seems to have had any reason to *hate* her . . .'

'What about the boy working on Forster?'

'At the time the disks disappeared Matthew was at a sherry party given by his supervisor.'

'You've checked?'

'I have.'

'And David – we've only got his word for it that he wasn't around. And that they were engaged, for that matter.'

'I rang the college he was staying at in Cambridge and made discreet enquiries. He checked in for dinner on Thursday.'

'Had they announced the engagement to anyone? Could someone have been jealous?'

'I don't get any feeling of that. The lads all seem to be happily involved elsewhere, or too busy worrying about their research to be bothered.'

'The girls too?' She sits down opposite.

'No one's hinted anyone else was seriously interested in David.'

'It's not him I'm thinking about, it's Caroline.'

I laugh and help myself to salad. 'Statistically speaking there should be at least one lesbian in the house, but I seem to be the only one stalking the halls at present. Vinaigrette?'

She passes it over. 'I had another talk with Mrs Thomas this morning. It's feudal you know, the way College exploits those women. Can't you do anything about it, get their pay improved or something?'

'You know I've tried.' Recently I've found myself doubting whether my working-class Quaker grandmother would really have been all that proud of her successful middle-class granddaughter. Ursula's right, I should tackle the Bursar again.

Sensing gloom, she changes the topic. 'Mrs Thomas said that Caroline did sometimes have someone with her in the mornings.'

'I expect she did! David for one.'

'She emphasised the "someone" and gave me one of those little looks, you know. She didn't say "some bloke".'

I sip my wine, unconvinced. I don't see why sexual jealousy has to be a motive here. Anyway, I've already made up my mind to tell Principal she has no choice but to call in the police again. I'm conscious that David and I smeared our fingerprints all over the locker last night and probably destroyed any useful evidence: they're not going to thank College for any of this. We'll undoubtedly be given difficulties with the liquor licence again.

'It's something to keep in mind, though. Who else do you have to talk to?'

'Second floor, room 18 – Fadia, a thirty-year-old anthropology student from Egypt. She's been very upset by the whole business, and obviously bewildered by all this apparently callous questioning. She must think the English are completely mad!'

'Who else?'

'John, a physicist from Dundee. Earnest and worried about whether or not he's going to be offered a job as a stockbroker next year. I would have talked to him first thing with the rest of the ground-floor lot but he had to be present for some vital experiment in the lab. The last is Rachel, Caroline's closest neighbour. She was in that night but didn't hear anything; the police talked to her at length.'

'She didn't hear anything at all? Surely she must have heard her out on the scaffolding!'

'She says no. She had a headache and went to bed with some strong painkillers and hot milk.' Rachel's the only one I feel at all uneasy about and I suspect that's mainly because she's the only other member of 'Bloomsbury' who's around.

Ursula leans forward to fiddle with some greenery that's threatening to tip out of its vase. 'What is it?' she asks.

I sigh. 'Something was nagging at me yesterday, and I only worked out this morning what it was.'

She raises arched eyebrows. 'Well?'

'Well, Rachel says she was talking to Caroline in the kitchen at about seven o'clock, but that Caroline didn't say anything about planning to collect her disks from College. However, one of the other girls, Celia, mentioned that she passed the kitchen about that time on her way to the shower and she heard Caroline telling someone she was going to go to her locker after the party. So if it wasn't Rachel Caroline was talking to, who was it? She also told Paul and Zoë, but that was as they were all going out the front door together an hour later.'

'Holmes, you never cease to amaze me!'

I look at her over my glass. 'Not much, is it, for two days' work? In fact it's absolutely nothing.'

'Don't forget the note. What's this Rachel reading?'

'English – she's doing a thesis on Lytton Strachey. By the way, will you be bringing afternoon tea? I know you should be working on your book and that you've done more than your share of the cooking but . . .' I'm suddenly immensely sorry for myself; the position I've been put in is ridiculous and I'm making a mess of it.

'But of course!' She reaches across and squeezes my hand.

Meeting Rachel again I have no doubts at all – the girl's as innocent as the rest of them.

'Did you see anyone else in the house on Thursday afternoon, Rachel?' This is something I've drawn a complete negative on so far. 'Were there any visitors who could have gone into the computer room?'

'I didn't see anybody.'

I look out of the window again, hoping to catch sight of Ursula, and this time am rewarded with a splash of red under the copper beech.

'Did Caroline have any special friends, Rachel?'

She looks at me blankly and I curse myself for feeling so old and out of touch.

'What I mean is, did she have any lovers?'

'Like I said yesterday, there was David. He says they were engaged.'

The light catches her cheekbones: she really is lovely. But she didn't say anything about David yesterday. 'Anyone else?'

She shakes her head and when I try to catch her eye glances away. 'Bloomsbury acted as a hot-house . . .' Is there any point in risking it? By tonight it could be all over College, Dr Stevenson making lewd suggestions to the women students . . . one can't be too careful these days. Victor would love to get his teeth into something like that. A flash of red catches my eye again and I take a deep breath.

'No one else at all, Rachel? What about women friends? Did any women ever stay the night?'

'What a fucking filthy thing to say!'

She almost tips her chair over as she jumps up and I'm taken completely by surprise. This is it, I can't let her just disappear.

'I'm terribly sorry, I didn't mean to upset you. Could you do me a favour, Rachel?' She hesitates in the doorway. 'Dr Myers is waiting for me in the garden – could you go and keep her company till I get down there? I'll only be a few minutes.' I want us both to have the chance to calm down; and I don't feel I can handle this alone. I manage to smile. The look I get back is either pure hate or terror, I don't know which.

As I stroll towards them my attention is caught by two clouds playing lions above. They are so obviously lions, stretching long paws out at each other . . .

'Hello there!'

My gaze reluctantly returns earthward and I salute Ursula back as if the three of us meeting here is some happy coincidence.

'Rachel's been telling me about her thesis. She's working on Lytton Strachey, you know.'

'I know. Is the grass damp?'

Rachel scrambles to her knees. 'I have to do some work in the library.'

'Oh my dear, not so quickly!' Ursula puts a hand on her arm. 'It's funny you should be talking to me about Strachey because I was reading about him just this afternoon.' She gives me an odd look. ' "Synchronicity" – that's the term Jung uses isn't it, Marjorie? When the same topic, or words, keep coming up?'

Rachel looks close to tears. 'Please,' she almost whispers. 'I really have to go!'

I'd let her if I could. Ursula's doing a wonderful job, but I'll have to take over soon.

'This is what I was reading.' She pulls a book from the basket. 'You've read this, of course?'

Rachel stares rigidly at the cover and I'm suddenly aware that something's happening.

Ursula turns a few pages then points with her finger. 'This is the bit that caught my eye – right here, on page one . . .'

'No!' The book flies into the air and for a moment I think she's going to hit Ursula too. 'Leave me alone!' She starts up and runs across the lawn toward the house.

As the girl climbs her dress flutters happily like a soft, white flag.

'Rachel, stop!' I'd started yelling but then got frightened I'd distract her and make her fall. Now that she's made it to the second floor and is standing I can try once more. 'I just want to talk to you!'

She's not holding on to anything and I ask myself crazily if it would be possible to catch her. Could we bring cushions out from the living room to break her fall?

'Rachel!' Ursula calls from next to me. 'We know you were hurt and you wanted Caroline to understand that – I'm sure you didn't want anything terrible to happen!'

Her legs are long and brown under the dress and it's as if she's up there just to enjoy the breeze. I'm about to yell again, to tell her to stay still, when I notice a movement at one of the windows.

'Rachel!' Ursula manages to keep her attention on us. 'What you were going through was awful – we know that! You didn't . . .'

'Got her!' Matthew's arms are around her waist and as he hauls her in I catch sight of David standing behind him.

His face is grey. 'Did the two of you . . . did you go to bed together?'

'We were lovers all last year,' she says dully. 'Caroline didn't want people to know. She said we'd never get teaching jobs if people knew.'

'What about this year?' He looks pleading. 'When did you break up?'

'She said she needed men too – that she wasn't like me. The last time she let me sleep with her was about a month ago.' Her voice breaks and she looks across at me.

'I loved her. I didn't mean for her to fall! She hurt me so much and when I cried she just laughed! I felt the only thing she really cared about was her thesis and that if I took that away from her she'd know what I felt like.'

'But you were going to give the disks back?'

She nods. 'I put them out on the scaffolding. I wrote my own message on the bottom of the note she'd given me and left it on her desk. Then I opened her window so she'd see the disks when she came in . . .'

'Did you talk to her then?'

'No.' She wipes her eyes with the back of one hand. 'I didn't think she'd have any real problem reaching the disks. But, you see, I'm taller than her, and she mustn't have been able to reach – so she climbed out.'

'Shit.' Matthew leans back and closes his eyes. He's obviously wishing he was out of all this.

'It was like a nightmare! I heard her fall but she didn't even scream . . .'

'Did you go down?' Ursula asks.

'She'd hit her head – I could see she was dead. I felt numb and did things without even thinking. It took me ages to find all four disks – I was sure someone would come along.'

'Why didn't you take the note too?'

'I went back to her room and picked it up, but then I heard something and panicked: I just shoved it under a box on the desk. In the morning, when the police were searching her room, I was certain they'd find it.' She stops and for a few moments there's silence. 'I'll go to gaol, won't I?'

I look enquiringly at David who's studying Ursula's new Indian rug. I'd piled them all into the car, instinctively feeling it would be better to discuss things at home. After hearing her story I'm thankful for that. 'David?'

He lifts his head. 'Do you have to tell College?'

I choose my words carefully. 'Everyone would be relieved to be assured it was a simple accident. Do you know if anyone else heard what happened this afternoon?'

He shakes his head and looks at Matthew. 'I think the place was empty except for us.'

'What about you, Matthew?' I ask. 'How do you feel?'

He shrugs. 'I can't see what good it would do to hand Rachel over to the cops. I'm happy not to say anything about it.' I can see from his eyes that he thinks Caroline had it coming. One will keep silent because he loved her; the other because he didn't. There is some relentless logic in that.

'I'm disappointed in you, Marjorie.'
I stop stroking her shoulders and poke her in the ribs instead. 'Well, thank you! I think I handled today fairly well, considering. Or maybe it's not the events of the day you're referring to?' I turn her over on to her back. 'The sex left something to be desired, madam?' She nuzzles into my shoulder then struggles to sit up. 'What are you doing?'
'Looking for my glasses. And this.' She gropes on the floor and surfaces with a book. 'I'm disappointed because you haven't enquired about this at all!'
I blink at her. In the drama that had followed I'd forgotten all about the business with the book. She holds it up and I reach behind me to direct the bedside lamp on to its cover.
'*Virginia Woolf* by Quentin Bell.' The woman wearing a squashed black hat doesn't look anything like Woolf to me. 'You'll have to explain.'
She opens it at page one. 'See?'

Ha! Ha!
Virginia Stephen
Leonard Woolf

'Listen to this. "For their friends the marriage had the double advantage of keeping him in England while giving her a husband whom they liked. Of these, one, Lytton, received the news in the form of a postcard bearing the words, Ha! Ha! . . ." ' She glances up. 'I remembered this after lunch. So I went to the library and did some research. It says here, "One may suppose that he" – that's Lytton – "was both amused and relieved." Cruel of her, wasn't it?'
'Woolf or Caroline?'
'Caroline.'
'Yes. Very.' I raise the duvet and she slides back down, close against my side.

ANNE STANESBY

Non-Custodial Sentence

Monday, hangover, headache, depression. Same old story. Despite the unwillingness of the soul the body moved inexorably in the direction of the office. At the first traffic light I lit a cigarette. At the second I swallowed an aspirin. At the third I sighed deeply.

As I pushed open the door to the premises of Stewart and Co., solicitors, I could see that nothing had changed since Friday. Same old litter on the floor. Same old full ashtray in my room.

'What happened to Sadie?' Sadie was our cleaner.

'Off sick.'

I sighed again. Off with a hangover more like, which is what I wanted for myself at that very moment. I couldn't grudge it to her, though. I always told myself that when I got old I wanted to be like Sadie, except I didn't want to be a cleaner. She was a big woman like me but with a mop of lurid (dyed) red hair. She drank like a fish and smoked like a chimney, as I do. What I couldn't match was her line in repartee. She would stand in the office on those evenings when I worked late enough to catch her, fag in one hand, hoover in the other, and hold forth.

'I've said it before, and I'll say it again. The sight of a man's prick is the biggest disappointment a young girl can have. You take one look and you think, they sell things like that on the meat stall at the market and I wouldn't buy one to put in the curry.'

I sat down heavily. Out of the corner of my eye I had spotted a client sitting patiently in the waiting room, suffering no doubt from the illusion that someone was going to leap to it and offer some brilliant solution to whatever the problem was. Luckily I could tell even at a glance that she wasn't for me. I did the criminal cases and this one had definitely come in about something else. She

was too old and too respectably dressed to want advice from me.
My telephone buzzed.
'Client to see you.'
'Not me.'
'Yes, you. It's a criminal matter. Shoplifting.'
'She won't get legal aid, tell her I can't help.'
'But there's loads of charges and she's in court this morning.'
I groaned. There was to be no escape. Reluctantly I let the
woman in. She perched on the edge of a chair clutching her
handbag nervously. I looked her up and down. Not my style at all.
Natty blue hat, grey suit with brooch, chintzy white blouse, sheer
stockings, shiny black shoes. Her grey hair was tied back in a bun.
    Her name was Mary Lavender. She was born on 3 March 1923
and lived on social security. This, with her address, was all I
needed for now. We filled out the first legal aid form.
'How can I help you?'
    She produced a charge sheet. 'I'm sorry to trouble you so early
but I was only arrested on Saturday and I have to go to court this
morning – and – and –' She started to cry. 'I'm so, so, terribly
ashamed.'
'Don't be. People do far worse things than this.'
    The charges were shoplifting and our receptionist was right:
there were a lot of them. While Miss Lavender sobbed I scanned
the list. You name it, she'd taken it. Underwear, perfume,
knitwear, scarves, sheets, blankets, cutlery and all from stylish
shops.
'Where were you arrested?'
'In —–' (She named the only upmarket shop in our district.)
'I'd taken some perfume, and before that I'd taken a silk scarf and
before that a mackintosh. They found everything, of course, and I
admitted the other thefts at once.' Lifted a mackintosh – quite a
big item; I was impressed.
    'After my arrest the police went to my flat and found the rest. It
was all piled up together. I hadn't used any of it. The police were
really very kind, only they took my fingerprints, so humiliating.
Then –'
    I cut her off, time was getting short. I had other clients to think
of, some of whom would even now be dragging their unwilling
selves to the local magistrates' court, there to receive their just (or
unjust) deserts. I hurried Miss Lavender through the usual routine.

Another set of legal aid forms to be completed.

Had she taken all the things? Yes.

Did she realise it was dishonest? Yes.

Did she mean to deprive the owners permanently of them? Oh, yes.

Why did she do it? Nothing but sobs and I had to leave.

I said I'd get the case put off till legal aid had been considered and we could talk some more. Then, promising to meet her later, I careered off clutching a big pile of files.

The morning shot by as usual. First a visit to the little room occupied by the crown prosecution service. The unlucky inmates were being harassed by a large and impatient crowd of defence advocates all wanting information about the cases they were dealing with that morning. In the end I found out what I needed to know: whose case was ready to go and whose wasn't, whose bail application they'd object to and whose they wouldn't, who had extra charges to face and who was getting away with a few. They weren't ready for Miss Lavender. There were numerous additional items which they suspected her of stealing.

'Like a bloody Aladdin's cave, that flat, that's what the officer said.'

'But it can all be returned. She didn't use any of it.'

The prosecutor snorted in suspicious fashion. 'Must be potty.' I didn't argue with him.

Later, when Miss Lavender appeared in the dock, she looked so out of place that a few people in the public gallery tittered, whilst the magistrate raised his eyebrows and looked quizzical. Miss Lavender affected not to notice. I told her to come and see me soon.

By the end of the morning I had only one person left in the cells and I felt moderately smug. I persuaded Janine, the other solicitor who worked for Stewart and Co., to come for a greasy nosh. Janine did very different work from me. She was a women's lawyer. She represented women who'd been beaten, women who wanted maintenance from their husbands (usually a fruitless quest) and women who wanted to hang on to their children. She didn't like what I did at all. I didn't blame her; I didn't like it myself a lot of the time.

She didn't like our employer very much either. Janine was earnest and steady where Peter Stewart was unstable and erratic, with his causes, his manic energy and dubious financial deals. Janine kept assuring me that the Law Society were about to get him.

'Look at his lifestyle! Don't tell me he makes all that out of our practice. No way.'

It was true Peter had two houses, one in London, one in the country, and rather a nauseating number of fast cars and fast suits to match. I wasn't terribly interested though: so long as the Law Society didn't get me too.

As we exchanged the usual gossip a number of voices floated by. Their conversation was every bit as trivial as ours but then a voice I recognised intruded upon my consciousness. We were sitting in an old-fashioned cubicle with high-backed benches. Just as well, because the last thing I wanted was for the voice to discover we were there.

'Ssshh, Jack Prentice is here, just behind us.'

Janine made a face. Jack drove us both up the pole. He was a left-wing holy joe type who always made us feel guilty for not doing enough. He was very thick with Peter who was a sucker for causes, despite the fast suits. 'Free so and so.' 'So and so is innocent.' 'Compensation for so and so.'

True to form, Jack was harassing his unfortunate companion. 'I want you round my place eight o'clock sharp. If you're late I will not be pleased. I'm not interested in people who are unreliable. Is that clear?'

Apparently it was, because to our great relief Jack left soon after without spotting us. I caught a glimpse of his red hair and weasly face, with its angry red nose sticking out as if ready for combat. I noticed the young man with him, slight with spiky blond hair and stylishly dressed. He didn't seem the type to spend his time giving out leaflets or whatever boring task Jack had lined up for him.

The week rolled by and Friday saw me interviewing Miss Lavender. I had already built up a mental image of her that I would sell to the magistrates.

'My client, your worships, like so many single women of her generation cared for many years for her ailing mother, giving up all chance of marriage and a career. Now she is alone and totally dependent on social security.'

I asked Miss Lavender if she had in fact cared for an ailing mother for years and conveniently she had. Was she lonely? Oh yes. Did she need help? Oh definitely yes. Would she be prepared to talk to a probation officer? Oh certainly.

So it was all fixed. Guilty to everything next time (with a massive list of other matters to be 'taken into consideration' no doubt), and the case to be adjourned for a social enquiry report.

I then had to deal with the fact that Miss Lavender had convinced herself that she was going to prison. She seemed totally unable to accept that there were far worse people in the world than herself and that therefore she was not going to get locked up. I told her that today I'd represented or seen two alleged knife-point street robbers, one alleged manslaughterer, three self-confessed burglars and one car thief. She began to relax a bit. All the same she insisted on leaving her will with me for safe keeping, and her mother's brooch.

'I'm so afraid that if they lock me up I might not be able to stand the strain and I should hate not to leave my affairs in order.'

I told her that we weren't insured for jewellery but she said it didn't matter, the brooch was of sentimental value only and worth nothing.

For the next hour I talked to the burglars. I had the opposite problem with them. I could tell they were likely to get locked up but they wouldn't believe me either. I pointed out that if they could only stir themselves to be nice to their probation officers or make some show of offering compensation to the loser maybe I could wring the heartstrings of the meanest of magistrates. I knew I was good at wringing heartstrings. The burglars knew it too, which is why they had come to me. But even I had to have something to say. The interview went badly, with my clients in surly mood.

'You're supposed to be my brief, why can't you get me off?' said one.

'Compensation, you're joking. Silly fucker should have been insured,' said another.

'Well, he wasn't.'

'Oh well then, tough shit.'

'It's you who are going to get the tough shit.' I was beginning to get impatient. They sensed it and sloped off resentfully. As they got to my door they hesitated and started whispering and sniggering together. Then one of them turned. 'We'll get the compensation, don't worry.' Laughing nastily, they went away, creating a great deal of disturbance in the process.

The weekend passed, then another week. Another weekend and here we go, another Monday. I walked to the office in reflective mood. I was thinking about the meaning of life. Who am I? What is it all about? Why are we here? I'd had a whole twenty-four hours without alcohol. This was the result.

You are thirty-five years old, I thought to myself. Half your life over and what have you done? The answer was not much.

I had, of course, managed to qualify as a solicitor, eventually. I didn't know anyone who'd failed the exams as often as I had. Now I was stuck working for Peter for want of any better ideas. Apart from that I did nothing that could be described as remotely constructive. All I did in my spare time was go to pubs, restaurants, cinemas and various other places of entertainment. I visited friends or watched TV. Sometimes I cleaned my flat but not often. That's why I visited my friends but they rarely visited me. 'Louise Compton, you're disgusting.' The words of the most important person in my life rang in my ears as I plodded desolately down the litter-riddled street.

'I'm sorry, but you are. Just look at yourself, you are going downhill.'

I had looked in the mirror. She was right. I saw a fat woman with straggly brown hair, glasses (one lens cracked), shapeless black jumper (with cigarette ash on it), baggy skirt, stockings (holes), shoes (scuffed). She was slim, neat, fit and beautiful. I wanted to be like her.

'Let's go to the pub.'

'Louise, will you stop changing the subject. I want to have this out. I am worried about you. You are not looking after yourself. You look terrible.'

She was right. I had to do something. We didn't go to the pub. I promised her that I would give up alcohol, stop smoking, eat less and take more exercise.

I promised myself as I walked to the office that I would lead a more meaningful life. I would do voluntary work, get involved in good causes, go to art classes.

A curious sight brought this unrealistic reverie to an abrupt halt. There was a crowd of people outside the office, and a load of cops.

My footsteps, already heavy, became positively cement-like.
'Excuse me, may I come through? I work here.'
'Someone's been murdered, love.'
'Do you know who?'
'No, but it were burglars who did it.'
A policeman stopped me at the door. I started to explain who I was when he let on he'd recognised me anyway. Grudgingly he allowed me to advance a few inches, and then told me the news. Every evening Sadie went to the office, usually after we'd left. Each night she faithfully cleaned up the squalid debris of a day in a busy legal aid solicitors' practice. Last night she'd walked in on a burglary and one of the burglars had smashed in her skull. They'd also stolen all the cash they could find, the hand dictaphones and any other small, easily portable and sellable objects. Later we found they'd taken our dope as well.

The office had been ransacked. The desks and chairs upturned, the drawers emptied. The safe had been broken into, of course. They'd smeared excreta on the walls and left a few messages for curious eyes. 'Commie bastards'. 'Nigger lovers.' 'Shit eaters.'

The police were dusting for fingerprints but were not optimistic. No one had seen anything. No one had heard anything either. They'd broken in through the back, as usual. Our receptionist had found the body, she was at home being comforted. Peter was with Sadie's daughter, the only relative we knew of.

It was obvious the police wanted me out of the way. There seemed to be nothing to do but go off to court. I retrieved my files and left. On the way I tried to think about Sadie. The fact that she was dead had not sunk in, I could not absorb it. I thought about her killers instead. I knew what they'd be like. Thoughtless, thuggy young men, macho freaks. They were probably laughing about it now. I knew the type. I wished I didn't.

That afternoon we closed the office, or tried to. Constant interruptions prevented us from getting together and talking about what had happened, remembering Sadie, facing up to it. I nearly strangled Miss Lavender. She came in fussing just after I got back, wanting her will and her brooch. I tried to fob her off, saying I would look later, but she persisted. In the end I found the envelope, ripped open like everything else in the safe, and of course, no brooch. She became quite distraught. In the end I lost my temper.

'Someone I valued very much has been murdered and I'm very upset, and I don't give a stuff about your stupid jewellery!' She crawled out. I didn't expect to see her again.

Peter was understandably upset. He told me Sadie's daughter was inconsolable when the news was broken. She was on her own with a small kid. Peter wasn't sure she could handle it. A neighbour was with her at the moment. All the while he was relating these facts I could tell his mind wasn't on what he was saying. He kept poking around in a distracted fashion as if desperately searching for something.

'What are you looking for?'

'Oh, nothing, nothing.'

I knew it wasn't true. I'd heard from the others he'd been scrabbling around like that for hours. Something he didn't want to lose had gone missing, but he wouldn't say what. I looked at him sadly. He was going bald but what was left of his hair stuck up like a bottle brush and his brown eyes were red-rimmed with grief or worry, I couldn't tell which. His little-boy-lost look was working overtime. Janine came over and stood in front of me. She looked at me with disgust.

'I knew this would happen. It's those damn creeps you represent.'

'You can't be sure of that.'

'Oh can't I just? Who else would do a thing like this?'

I was rescued by Peter, who darted up to us like a frightened rabbit.

'Louise, please, it's Jack. Please tell him I'm not here. I can't face him, not now.'

'I'm surprised you can ever face him.'

Peter glared at me and darted into the room where we kept the stationery. I had a hard time getting rid of Jack. He was pretty determined to see Peter. When I convinced him Peter wasn't there he started grilling me about what had gone missing. He was as bad as Miss Lavender. He too had left something of vital importance in our safe. It seemed that no one cared about the loss of Sadie at all; the loss of their damned possessions was all that concerned them. I lost my temper with him as well. He lost his back. We shouted inelegantly at each other. In the end Janine calmed him down and made him go. She calmed herself down too in the process.

'I'm sorry I said what I did. I'm just overwrought. I know really

that to blame your clients is much too easy, much too simplistic.'
'Why? If it wasn't them, it was someone like them.'

The nasty little thought which had been waiting in the wings of my consciousness now walked out centrestage. The three burglars and their compensation, or the lack of it. Their remarks to me could be taken as a direct threat to break into the office and rip off what they could. They had probably never intended to murder anyone, but Sadie just got in the way. That's how a lot of people were murdered: their only crime being situated in the wrong place at the wrong time. But would they really have killed her? The average burglar runs away when disturbed and they were about as average as you could get. I tried to bring their features to mind; it was quite difficult.

Jason, small, wiry and energetic; such brains as existed behind their operations undoubtedly belonged to him. Ted, large and lumbering. He was the brawn. Then there was Steve, with his innocent doe-like brown eyes, pretty face and appalling criminal record. He'd done some rather unpleasant things in his time; I wondered about him. I also wondered if I should go to the police and tell them what I suspected. What about my duty of confidentiality? What about Sadie? What if they were innocent anyway? I decided I had to talk to Peter about it all.

He wasn't much help. I took him out to the pub once I'd persuaded him to stop looking for whatever it was. He was, as they say, shitting bricks. He gulped down two double whiskies, no problem, even though I knew one of his smart shiny cars was standing outside. I decided it must be something to do with Jack. Peter was always ready to see Jack, however busy he was. He looked completely desperate, worse than I'd ever known him. Worse even than the day the office overdraft reached rock bottom. I decided to try and say something helpful. I told him I could tell he was scared of Jack right now and I thought I knew why. He'd been minding something of Jack's (some world-boggling item of revolutionary claptrap no doubt) and now the burglars had got it and Jack was mad. Peter was stupid to worry about it so much. The burglar had probably already thrown it away with a complete lack of interest.

'Whoever it was only wanted money. Nothing that belonged to Jack could interest them. Forget it.'

There was the possibility, of course, that if whatever it was fell into the wrong hands, in this case the wrong hands being the police, then the long-awaited Law Society might finally come Peter's way, but I was too nice to mention that.

I wasn't having much effect. I scrutinised him closely. The man was terrified, there was no doubt about it, and I got the feeling he hadn't listened to a word I'd said. Suddenly he reached across and clutched at my arm.

'Louise, will you do me a favour? Will you go straight off and give Jack a message for me? I daren't use the phone.'

I didn't feel I had much choice but to agree, and the conversation about the burglars never got off the ground.

Jack lived on the sort of estate where the tenants went in for burning their own flats down so as to get rehoused. I decided to chance the unlit stairs rather than the urine-soaked lifts. I knocked on his door. He answered, gazing at me with acute suspicion. My message was verbal.

'Peter says,' I whispered in sinister fashion suitable to this momentous occasion, 'he's afraid some property you jointly owned has gone missing in the burglary, so act accordingly.' His reply was less than gracious.

'The fucking stupid bastard! Can't trust him with anything. We've fucking had it now!' He banged the door in my face and I went away.

I went home and switched on the TV. When it came to the local news they mentioned the murder. There was a touching shot of Miss Lavender looking distressed outside our office door. The viewers would never know she was only upset about her missing jewellery.

The next few days I recall as an unpleasant blur. Sadie's body was released for cremation. The usual conveyor-belt ceremony was performed with the usual religious trappings which meant nothing to anyone present and would have meant nothing to Sadie. A surprisingly large number of mourners turned up. Some I felt had only come because she was murdered; heart attack victims don't attract the same degree of attention. Jack Prentice was a classic example of the bogus mourner. He had never had time for Sadie when she was alive. Cleaners don't count for some people.

After we'd emerged from the neat little modern chapelette we stood around uneasily while the next bunch filed in. I amused myself watching Peter try to manoeuvre himself out of Jack's way. It was neatly contrived but in the end it didn't work. Jack virtually pinned him up against a Ford Cortina. Fragments of an acrimonious conversation wafted across to me.

'You fucking told me you'd left it in . . .' Whisper, whisper, whisper.

'Who do you think it was?'

Peter shrugged his shoulders. The murder was for the time being unsolved. The forensic experts, so far as we knew, had found nothing. Enquiries in the neighbourhood had elicited nothing useful. I caught Janine's eye; she was glowering at me with an expression which bordered on hate. I went red. I'd bumped into the three burglars a few days ago. I'd decided to have things out with them, hoping that the ensuing discussion would ease my conscience. It hadn't.

'We heard about the murder.' They sniggered.

'And where were you that night?'

'Down me mum's, watching tele.' More sniggering. This didn't make me feel any better. They'd only come up with their favourite alibi, and one that had been shot down in flames many times before when 'Mum', not wishing to commit perjury, had refused to come to court and give evidence.

'Some people think one of my clients did it.' Momentarily they looked quite concerned. 'Well, you wanted your compensation, didn't you?'

Now they were angry. It was Jason of course who hit on the salient point. 'You can't tell the pigs what we said. That's confidential, that is. You're our brief.'

'Sadie was my friend.'

More protests. In the end I said, 'You just call by and tell me where you were: the truth, that is, and then I can put these ideas out of my head.'

They hadn't called by and I hadn't told anyone. But Janine had sensed that I was holding back on something and she didn't like it. I didn't blame her; I didn't like it myself. But I just felt that I had to be sure; it was as if I envisaged myself as a member of some kind of jury for defence solicitors. It was as if I had to be sure within myself, beyond all reasonable doubt, that Jason and Ted and Steve were guilty, before I shopped them to the police. That meant I had to turn detective: me, the most unobservant person in the world. I didn't know how to begin.

The morning of Miss Lavender's trial dawned. I fully expected that some other solicitor would have been instructed to appear in my place but nobody showed. I went up to the Crown Prosecution Office and collected a long list of further matters that were to be taken into consideration if Miss Lavender agreed. They had a surprise for me. There was another long list. Miss Lavender's criminal record.

'And her name isn't Lavender's blue, dilly, dilly. It's Slater.'

I looked at the list. They were all nice little crimes, nothing violent or distasteful. Theft, forgery, obtaining by deception. It appeared that Miss Lavender was on probation already for doing the books at her last place of employment. As if wanting to place the final nail in the coffin of my prepared speech, the prosecution told me there was a warrant out for Miss Lavender's arrest. She'd failed to keep in touch with her probation officer and had been summoned to court to explain why. There'd been no sign of her and the warrant had been lying on file waiting for her re-appearance.

I went down to the court rooms. In the hurly-burly of an average morning it gradually became apparent that Miss Lavender was not going to turn up. I was not exactly surprised. In fact I wondered why she'd troubled to attend last time. Then I reflected that as an old pro, she'd probably worked out that in the short space of time that had elapsed between her arrest and first appearance, no one would yet have worked out who she was. She probably knew damn well that the case would be remanded as well, thus giving her time to sort out alternative accommodation and move in style. I didn't expect to see her again.

When the case was called the prosecution asked for another warrant, not backed for bail. This would ensure that the police did not have to let Miss Lavender go again, if they caught her. It was the same magistrate as before. He remembered Miss Lavender and expressed concern.

'It occurs to me, Miss Compton, that she is in need of some help. How was she when you last saw her?'

Silly old fool, I thought, for I had placed Miss Lavender amongst the ranks of the well-sussed and able to look after themselves. I confessed that when I last saw Miss Lavender she was upset because some jewellery of hers had been taken at our burglary, and I had been too upset about the murder to offer much sympathy. He looked genuinely sorry.

'What a terrible business that was! But you see, Miss Compton, the defendant can hardly have been planning to abscond if she'd left something with you for safe keeping, could she?'

Silly old fool again; he ought to have known that the Miss Lavenders of this world are well aware of the fact that even if the police are looking for them, they can turn up at their solicitors' office at any time to reclaim their property or seek advice, secure in the knowledge that for ethical reasons the solicitor will not inform the authorities. However, the magistrate had not worked any of this out and I owed it to Miss Lavender to do my best.

'I feel some degree of responsibility for her non-appearance,' I said. 'If I had not spoken to her as I did, maybe she would have come to see me again and told me everything.'

The prosecution made a face at me, but the magistrate was impressed. 'Oh, Miss Compton, please don't distress yourself. We all know what patience you display normally.'

The prosecution made an even worse face at that and at what followed. A warrant was granted but it was backed for bail provided someone could be found to stand surety to secure Miss Lavender's attendance at court at a future date. I doubted there was anyone in the world silly enough to risk it.

One week later I had a call from the duty solicitor. Miss Lavender had been arrested. The police couldn't let her go because she had no one to stand surety for her. She'd appeared in court next morning. I wasn't too surprised to hear that she'd not exactly insisted I be called and no one could get hold of me anyway. I was at home in bed with a hangover and the phone off the hook. The magistrate, I was told (not the nice kind one from before), had refused to drop the surety requirement, in view of Miss Lavender's record.

'But she didn't seem to mind. She said she's got nowhere to live at the moment anyway and she's been in prison before. She's pleaded guilty to everything and has been remanded for reports. She said could you go and see her in Holloway? She wants to apologise to you about something.'

I rang Holloway and booked in to see Miss Lavender. In a funny way I was quite looking forward to seeing her again.

That afternoon Steve, one of the three burglars, turned up. Slightly to my surprise he was accompanied by the stylish young man I'd seen in the café with Jack. The latter introduced himself as Rob and said he'd come in with his friend to clear something up. The something in question turned out to be Sadie's murder. Rob wanted to tell me that he and Steve had been out together that evening, into the small hours of the morning, when they had returned to Rob's place, got blasted on vodka and ultimately fallen asleep. Rob's acquaintance with Jack Prentice was put forward as a sort of reference as to his credibility.

'What about the other two? Where were they, do you know?'

They couldn't help me there. They didn't know why they hadn't been in to see me either. However, one thing they were sure of, it wasn't them who'd done it. I questioned how they could be so sure, if they didn't even know where the others were when it happened? They looked decidedly uneasy, frightened even. In the end Rob said, 'Don't tell Jack I said anything, but he knows it wasn't them. So does Mr Stewart. I bet if you asked Mr Stewart, he'd tell you.' That was all I could get out of them.

The day I was due to visit Miss Lavender I returned from court in a flustered state. I'd tried to do one case too many and I wasn't sure it had come off. The burglars' case had come up and now they were all in the cells, on their way to a youth custody sentence. They'd made me feel pretty bad about it, and Jason and Ted made accusations that I'd stitched them up and hadn't tried hard enough. This wasn't fair. They'd just left me with nothing to say; they'd even failed an offered appointment with the community service people. In their annoyance they seemed to forget where they were.

'Yeah, we done her,' they shouted derisively. 'We broke in, we smashed her old skull in.' Steve tried to shut them up.

'She knows it wasn't us, don't you, love?'

I didn't, in fact. Peter had not responded to my enquiry in a very positive fashion. 'Why should I know who did it?' he had demanded furiously. 'Stop trying to lay this on me, Louise, you've got to make up your own mind.'

Meanwhile the shouting continued and in the end the gaoler overheard them. He knew about the murder too.

'Are you going to tell the CID about this?'
'I'm not sure it's really them, and anyway it's difficult, I'm their solicitor.'
'Well, I'm not their bloody solicitor. I'm going to make sure this gets passed on.' He gave me the same contemptuous look I'd got from Janine. I was beginning to feel pretty worthless. Well, at least it was out of my hands now, which was a relief in a way.

I was too tired to notice that someone was sitting in our waiting room, but the receptionist drew him to my attention.
'He's a friend of Miss Lavender.'
He looked the part too. A man of about her age, smartly dressed, with a cravat, tweed jacket and grey trousers. He had a stylish head of white hair and a sun tan which set off his attractive green eyes.
'Could I possibly trouble you for a few moments? I know you are very busy so I promise it won't take long.'
What a relief after the burglars. The man introduced himself as John Porter. He was Miss Lavender's second cousin. I registered a bit of surprise as I'd already discussed Miss Lavender with her probation officer and had been told she hadn't a friend or relation in the entire world. He noticed my reaction.
'I can tell you are bewildered. I know my poor cousin has denied all knowledge of her family. It's a sad case.'
Miss Lavender, according to him, came from a wealthy and respectable background. However, she suffered from kleptomania and was quite unable to stop herself stealing. All sorts of therapies and treatments had been tried but to no avail. To the acute embarrassment and distress of her family she'd lurched in and out of prison. In recent years she'd avoided her relatives completely and they'd had no idea where she was. No doubt she had told everyone she met that all her family were dead. But Mr Porter had had the good fortune to be watching television the night Sadie was murdered and had seen the clip of Miss Lavender.
'I was relieved to see her, but of course I still didn't know how to trace her. Then I suddenly thought that as she'd been filmed outside a solicitors' office then maybe, regretfully, she was in some kind of trouble again. So I came in here and described her to your receptionist who was able to identify her as your client Miss Lavender. That isn't her real name of course.'

He leaned forward. 'But I hear she's in prison and only for lack of a £500 surety. I wish she'd let me stand for her. But she'll deny she knows me, I'm sure she will. I don't know if the police will accept me if she denies knowing me.'

I wasn't sure they would either.

'Oh dear,' he said. 'I do so want to help her. She looked so terribly unhappy on television, so distressed.'

I decided to put him out of his misery and told him the real cause of Miss Lavender's despair. Then the phone rang. It was the CID about the burglars. I didn't feel I could discuss this in front of Mr Porter. He got the hint.

'I'll leave my address with your receptionist. Please do try and persuade my poor cousin to accept help.'

I said I would, and as soon as he'd left the room I turned my attention to Detective Inspector Francis of the CID. He seemed not to understand my problem.

'So what if you're their solicitor? One of your staff has been murdered. If you know anything you've a duty to tell us.'

'I'm not sure that's correct – anyway I don't know anything specific, no more than you.'

He wasn't convinced. He wanted a statement, wanted me to come in that evening. I had no time to talk to Peter. I was going to be late for my appointment at Holloway.

Miss Lavender seemed pleased to see me. We sat in the claustrophobic little cubicle provided and smoked my cigarettes.

'It is so good of you to come.'

'I get paid for it.'

'But not very much. You could earn so much more in the city. Be honest, you know you could.'

'No one would give me a job in the city.'

'Oh, don't be so modest. They would, I'm sure.'

We got on to the nitty gritty of why Miss Lavender had not turned up at court, which was an extra offence to be added to all the others. She gave me the old chestnut about getting the date wrong and then being frightened to surface because she knew there'd be a warrant out for her arrest. That brought me on to the subject of Mr Porter.

'You could have bail now. All you need is £500 surety.'

'But I know no one.'

'You do. Your cousin Mr Porter. He came to see me. He wants to help.'

Her reaction was extraordinary. Anyone would think I'd said he called in with a letter bomb addressed to her and had asked me to deliver it.

'I want nothing to do with him, nothing at all! You've got to keep him from me, you must. How did he find me?'

I explained about the television programme and Mr Porter's subsequent act of detection.

'He's very concerned, he thought you looked so unhappy.'

'But that was only because of my jewellery. Did you tell him that?'

'I did, as a matter of fact.'

'I don't need him, I don't need him at all! Tell him to keep away.'

Nothing I could say would persuade her to let Mr Porter stand surety.

'I shall tell the police he's a fraud and I shall insist on remaining here. Does he know what court I'm appearing in and when?'

I assured her he didn't. We passed on to the subject of what the court was likely to do to her. The probation officer was not suggesting an immediate custodial sentence but a suspended one. She seemed quite happy with that.

'In the old days, my dear, they were much stricter than they are now. When I first started getting into trouble you just went straight inside, none of this community service and so on.'

I asked why she did it. She smiled at me and clasped my hand.

'You're so kind but don't get involved. I'm a hopeless case, I'm sure Mr Porter told you that. I can't stop myself and I'm too old to change now.' We parted on good terms.

I went back to the office and thought gloomily of the interview with DI Francis. Peter was not around: typical. I rang the Law Society who told me to look at their guide to the professional conduct of solicitors which, they said somewhat snootily, I should possess. I knew we had one somewhere and I began to poke around in the forlorn hope that it might surface. We still hadn't really tidied up properly since the burglary; there was rubbish everywhere. I squinted behind my filing cabinet, often a good place to locate missing objects. There did indeed seem to be quite a lot of debris behind it. With difficulty I shoved the cabinet back sufficiently to enable me to fish out assorted dusty books, files and papers. No guide. I lost my temper and swept everything to the floor. Then I stopped and stared around malevolently. What was I going to do? I had no idea.

Amongst the debris I could see a roll of negatives. I wondered idly what they were of. For the want of anything better to do at this moment of crisis in my professional life, I picked the roll up and held one of the pictures up to the light. The photographs were of men. First I thought they were male contortionists; then I changed my diagnosis to wrestlers. It took a very long time for the penny to drop. These men were performing wild sexual acts with each other and pretty silly they looked too. There was no way I'd let anyone photograph me in such a compromising position, particularly with a figure like mine. Some of the men in the photographs should have known better too. Their pot-bellied figures contrasted with those of their partners, slim and youthful. I wondered who would be stupid enough to have themselves photographed in such a way. I had another squint at the negatives. There was something familiar about that lithe frame and the spiky blond hair. Yes, I was almost positive I knew who that was. And one of the older men: surely I recognised that balding head, with strands of hair drawn carefully across? It looked a lot like Gerald Jenkins, a small-time local businessman who was in the habit of consulting Peter about a variety of small-time problems.

I looked at the negatives and one thought led to another. I wondered if the men realised they were being photographed. I wondered whether once they had realised, they would have wanted the negatives. Maybe they would have wanted them very much: enough to break into our office, if they thought that's where they were. And if Sadie caught them at it, well you could see why they'd disposed of her.

I thought about Gerald Jenkins. Sadie undoubtedly would have recognised him if she'd caught him in the act, so he'd have been in a bit of a spot. If my theory was correct then I felt sorry for him but not sufficiently to keep my mouth shut. There again, if I gave these photographs to the police and they were nothing to do with anything, just a few guys having a harmless frolic, how would I feel? Like the burglars, Mr Jenkins was one of our clients. How would I explain what I'd done to him? I decided that I didn't get paid enough to suffer these moral dilemmas. I poured myself out a very large glass of whisky and then, in a pleasant alcoholic haze, I put the roll of film in my pocket and went to see DI Francis. Helped by the whisky, I had made the momentous decision to play things by ear.

Staring him straight in the eye, which seemed a good tactic, I said, 'Can we have a discussion off the record?'

'Certainly.'

I knew nothing was really off the record with the police but at least he wouldn't get the tape recorder out.

'I've no evidence that those lads did it. They made some remark because I told them I couldn't keep them out of clink, but I didn't take it seriously at the time. All that shouting the gaoler heard – I think they just lost their tempers and said things they didn't mean. If they'd really done it they'd be in a right state and the last thing they'd do is boast about it so publicly. At least one of them has given me an alibi, but it'll be up to you to check that out.' DI Francis gave me a very suspicious look.

'So you've no ideas at all? Your colleague is quite convinced one of your clients is responsible. She says she can't think who else would do it. I don't think you are being as helpful to the police as you might be, Miss Compton.' I was glad I'd brought the roll of film. I got it out.

'I have no intention of being other than helpful to the police,' I said very sincerely. 'That's why I've brought this with me. I found it in our office. Behind my filing cabinet.' I passed it over to him.

'What are they of?' he demanded.

'You tell me.'

'No, Miss Compton,' he said patiently, 'you tell me what they are.'

Just as patiently I explained that I knew nothing about the photographs at all and had only brought them along in case they might assist the police in their enquiries. If I was wrong about that, then in view of the personal nature of what had been photographed I thought the best course would be to destroy them. If they were of assistance to the police I hoped he would proceed in a sensitive fashion. He sighed, picked up the roll and had a good look for himself. There was a pause while he thought about it all.

'They look like the sort of pictures someone might take for the purpose of blackmail, Miss Compton,' he said finally.

'That did occur to me.' There was another pause.

'Mr Stewart is a chap with a lot of money, isn't he? Two houses, expensive car, expensive suits. I wouldn't have thought he'd make that sort of money out of his little practice.'

My stomach was churning but somehow I kept my voice calm. 'I can't help you,' I said. 'Except, if you make prints from those negatives, I have reason to suspect I might be able to identify a couple of the young men in the photographs for you. Maybe they could assist further.' Rob and his buddy Steve would have some fast talking to do.

'Thank you, Miss Compton. I shall be in touch.'

Gerald Jenkins lived in a small flat above his small business. I went straight round there. I wanted him to know why I'd handed in those photographs. He answered the door in a dirty sweater, scruffy trousers and slippers. His eyes were bleary. I got straight to the point. I told him what I had found in our office and what I had done with them. He didn't react. Egged on by the whisky, I voiced my suspicions. I said for all I knew, he could have broken in to look for the negatives. At this point he became quite upset.

'If you repeat this conversation to anyone,' he said, 'I'll just deny it took place. If the police question me about the burglary I can assure you I have an unshakeable alibi and there won't be any forensic evidence against me either. But I don't want you to think I murdered Sadie, Louise; I'd met her and liked her too. I'm going to tell you the truth even though I daren't tell the police.

'Your precious employer and that damned Jack Prentice have been squeezing money out of me for ages on account of those negatives.' Beads of sweat broke out on his forehead. 'I didn't even know they were taking photographs. I just wanted a bit of the other and I was prepared to pay for it. Those young lads they got in: they knew what Prentice and Stewart were doing. I bet the whole damn lot of them are living pretty well off it. They've probably got loads of suckers like me in their clutches.

'The night Sadie was murdered I did call by Stewart's office. I hoped to catch him working late. I was going to grovel for more time to pay the next instalment: things were going badly for me and I couldn't afford to pay. I saw someone had broken in. I presumed they were after cash; I thought maybe I'd be lucky, maybe those damned photos were in there. So I got in. Then I realised the burglar was still there. He was making an awful noise;

I hid and peeped out to see if I could identify him. I couldn't see much, he had a long coat on and was standing with his back to me, writing all sorts of graffiti on the walls. He seemed to be small, though, and I thought I saw grey hair above the collar of his coat. I should have reported it when I heard about Sadie, but I was frightened. After all, how would I explain what I was doing there?'

'You just have,' I said. 'And I'm leaving now.'

He looked at me desperately. 'Louise, you do believe me, about Sadie, don't you?'

'I don't know,' I said. 'I'll have to think about it.'

'I'm going to tell the police,' he said with determination. 'I'm going to give evidence against Prentice and Stewart. They can go to prison and suffer for what they've done to me. I'm about to go bankrupt now and it's all their bloody fault.' His voice took on a pleading tone. 'But I can't tell the police about the burglary, Louise. They just wouldn't believe me.'

I went home, got drunk and was very, very sick. I didn't know what to think. I felt sorry for Gerald Jenkins but if he had murdered Sadie he would have to pay for it. And if it wasn't him then somebody else would.

Next morning, feeling hungover and depressed, I went to court for Miss Lavender's big day. To my surprise Mr Porter was there with a male friend. I had written to him to say Miss Lavender wanted him to keep well clear but the letter had been returned, 'Not known at this address.'

'Good morning, Miss Compton.'

'Good morning, Mr Porter. I'm afraid Miss Lavender turned your offer down.'

'I know, Miss Compton, I know. I took the liberty of phoning my cousin's probation officer. She was concerned about where my cousin is going to live and I explained that there is no need to worry about it, as myself and Miss Lavender's brother here, Mr Slater, will undertake to the court to look after her. She's putting a bit in the report about it, I believe. I hope you don't mind. We all tried to phone you but you're always out at court or engaged.'

'I'm afraid Miss Lavender may refuse to go and live with her brother, but I'll go and talk to her.'

'Oh, thank you, Miss Compton. You are so kind.'

Miss Lavender was predictably furious when I broke the news

that her family had come to her rescue.
'How did they get here? Who told them?'
'I'm afraid it was your probation officer.'
'How dare she! I never gave her authority to tell them anything.'
'Well, she's done it now. What do you want me to do?'
She was thinking. There was a look on her face that I had not
seen before. A calculating look. The sweet little Miss Lavender of
old vanished for a moment and then returned.
'I don't understand,' she said at last.' I don't understand why
they are here. Mr Porter only came to see you because I looked
unhappy on the television, but the sole source of my distress was
the fact that the jewellery which I left with you for safe keeping was
stolen from your office in a burglary. You told him that, didn't
you?' I assured her I had. She wanted me to go and repeat it all to
them and then order them to leave the building.
'I can't do that,' I said. 'The public have a right to be here.
They've done nothing wrong.' She became frantic.
'I will not go with them! I will not! You must make sure I get sent
to prison.'
'Don't be daft. You don't have to go and live with them if you
don't want to. You can apply to the Council for help with your
housing.'
She turned on me.
'Don't give me that! You're here to do what I tell you and I'm
telling you to secure me an immediate prison sentence.'
'There's no need to be like that. If you want me to help you
you'll have to be straight with me, which I can tell you haven't been
up till now. I can't just walk into court and ask them to lock you
up. They'll think I've gone bonkers, take me off the case and give
you another solicitor.'
The point had sunk in.
'All right,' she said. 'I'll have to trust you. I have no choice. I'll
pay you well. There will be a lot of money in this for you. You'd
like that, wouldn't you? I can tell you're down on your luck, just by
the way you look and the way you dress. I'm never wrong about
things like that. Is it a deal?' I didn't answer. She took my silence as
assent.
She didn't beat about the bush. She told me everything. Apart
from the criminal activities I knew about already she also went in
for stealing jewellery. Mr Porter and Mr Slater were not her

relatives but her partners in crime. Relying on their respectable appearance and good diction, they had managed to insinuate themselves into close quarters with the rich and, once there, the jewellery had been stolen by various means. The profits of these enterprises had always been shared equally. One day, though, Miss Lavender had had a particular piece of good luck: she had managed to pull off an unscheduled theft in the ladies' toilet. She'd taken a brooch, the brooch she had left with me. She wouldn't have told the men at all but the theft had been discovered quite quickly and she'd nearly been caught. Had it not been for them creating a handy diversion she definitely would have been. Then she'd found out that this brooch was particularly valuable. She wouldn't say how much but indicated it was a great deal. She decided that now was a good time to part company with Mr Porter and Mr Slater, so she did a moonlight flit from her lodgings. She hoped never to see them again and planned a happy retirement for herself living on the proceeds of the brooch.

But it hadn't worked out like that. She'd reckoned without the tenacity of her two former partners. They took great exception to Miss Lavender's decision to dissolve the partnership and even greater exception to her attempt not to share the loot with them. The theft had been highly publicised and they knew exactly how much she was going to make out of it. They pursued her from pillar to post. No matter what she tried she could not shake them off. In the end she decided that the only thing to do was to kid them into thinking that she'd lost the brooch. That's when she thought of faking a burglary. She knew it would have to take place on someone else's premises or the men would never fall for it. After her unfortunate arrest for shoplifting she saw her opportunity: she could leave the brooch with me and then break in and take it herself. It seemed perfect, only something had gone wrong. The men obviously suspected she still had the brooch, and they were waiting for her outside. They were nasty characters. There were no means they would not use to extract the details of the brooch's whereabouts from her, and they wouldn't be keen to leave a potential witness in circulation afterwards.

'This is where you come in. I'll be safe in prison and I want you to make sure that's where I go.'

'They'll still know where you are and you'll have to come out some time.'

'Time is everything,' she said. 'If I have time I can work something out. I'll get the better of them in the end. Now can you do this for me?'

I didn't answer.

'You can make sure I go to prison. Surely you can.'

'I could do. Yes.'

'Could? What do you want? I've told you I'll pay you. But you'll have to wait.'

'Would you wait if you were me?' She thought for a while and then started to rummage through her pockets. She handed a key through the bars on the cell door. She told me it was a key to a locker at a terminus somewhere in the world. But she wouldn't say where.

'The brooch is inside the locker. This way we have to trust each other,' she said. 'Neither of us can have the brooch without the other's help.'

Matron came over.

'Are you ready with this one? They're calling for you. It's the only case they've got left.' I nodded.

As we went up the steps which led from the cells to the court I said, 'By the way. Why did you kill our cleaner? Was that really necessary?'

'You're not going to worry about that now. Surely.'

'I'd just like to know, that's all. In fact, I insist on knowing. Otherwise the deal is off.' I played with the key for a bit to upset her.

She looked around to make sure no one else could hear. Then she whispered, 'She wasn't sensible like you. I offered her money to keep her mouth shut, but she wouldn't listen. She said she was going to phone the police. I couldn't have that! She was silly enough to turn her back on me. I suppose she thought someone of my age couldn't possibly be dangerous.'

The case was called. Miss Lavender went into the dock and I sat in the solicitors' section. Mr Porter and Mr Slater came into court to listen. They smiled benignly at me from the back of the court where they sat in the part reserved for members of the public. The justices were sitting that day. There were two men, one chairing, and one woman. Unfortunately for Miss Lavender they looked rather kind. The prosecution gave the brief facts and I then invited the magistrates to read the social enquiry report before I addressed them. They went out with it, which was just as well because I needed some time to plan my speech.

When they came back in I could have sworn I saw the chairman give a wink in the direction of Mr Porter and Mr Slater. He wouldn't have had any trouble picking them out. There was no one else remotely like them in the public section. I got to my feet. I stared intently into the face of the chairman and took a deep breath.

'Your worships,' I said. 'Despite the serious nature of these charges and despite the long criminal record of my client, I urge you to pass a non-custodial sentence in this case.' I started to lay it on thick although it probably wasn't necessary; I just didn't want to leave anything to chance.

Meanwhile Miss Lavender shouted and raved from the dock. 'Send me to prison! I will not live with my family. I will steal again!'

The magistrate winked again, this time at me. This meant I didn't have to go on. They weren't going to lock her up. At least not this time.

'Stand up, Miss Lavender, please,' said the chairman. I turned to look at her. She shot me a look of venom.

'I want to dismiss my solicitor,' she said.

'Now there's no need for that,' said the chairman patiently. 'We're not going to send you to prison. In fact we're going to give you a conditional discharge. We've read this report and we've tried to listen to your solicitor and despite what you've been saying, or shouting rather, we know your family are going to look after you. We hope we won't see you back in this court again.'

'But I want to go to prison! Please! Send me to prison!' Her pleading fell on deaf ears. She left the court flanked by her 'relations'. As they took her out she gave one last desperate look in my direction. I smiled at her as I tossed her key to the floor.

SARA PARETSKY

A Taste of Life

Daphne Raydor worked in the bookkeeping department at
Rapelec, Inc. Her capacity for work – her appetite for it – was
insatiable. In January when accountants go mad closing previous
years' books, Daphne flourished. She worked best in the night's
dark hours, comparing ledgers and totting up columns with greedy
delight.

Everyone at Rapelec loved Daphne in January. Helen Ellis, the
petite, arrogant assistant controller, stopped to flatter Daphne on
her plant arrangements or her perfume. Carlos Francetta, the
budget director, lavished Latin compliments on her. Flowers
appeared on her desk, and chocolates.

In February, these blandishments disappeared and Daphne
lived alone behind her barricade of ferns for another eleven
months. She was smart, she was willing, she was capable. But she
was also very fat. She was so fat that she had to make all her own
clothes: no store carried garments in her size. Her walk was slow.
She gasped for breath after climbing a short flight of stairs.
Daphne lived on the first floor of a three-storey walk-up. By the
time she carried her groceries up one staircase and into her
kitchen, she had to collapse for forty-five minutes to recover her
breath.

Daphne was an excellent cook. She could make elaborate
French dinners, including elegantly decorated pastries. Food and
wine were both so outstanding that Helen, Carlos and other staff
members would accept her dinner invitations. They would exclaim
at their hostess, who barely touched her food: how could she be so
fat, when she scarcely ate? After they left, Daphne would pull
another four portions from the oven and devour them.

Daphne ate constantly. Elegant French dinners she reserved for company. She shopped almost daily, at five different supermarkets so that no one would see the volume of food she purchased. She had chocolate cookies tucked into a corner of the couch, bags of potato chips at her bedside and in the bathroom. The freezer and refrigerator were always overloaded. Some food rotted and had to be thrown out, but Daphne consumed a lot more. She brought home packages of frozen hors d'oevres and ate them while they thawed. She kept frozen pizzas under her bed and ate them raw. She slipped chocolate into drawers and closets. She was never more than three steps from some nourishing little snack.

Daphne's present condition was especially sad to those who knew her as an elfin child. What had happened to her? Family friends blamed Sylvia Raydor.

Twenty years ago, Sylvia's face appeared regularly on the covers of *Harper's Bazaar* and *Vogue*. She was one of the top ten models in the country and could pick her jobs. When Daphne was born, Sylvia delighted in the photographs – hovering sentimentally over a white-clad infant, blowing a sad kiss to baby and nurse from the railing of the *QE II* – which only enhanced her popularity.

But as Daphne moved from infant seats to kindergarten, she became an encumbrance to Sylvia. If the child was growing up, the mother must be ageing. And worse, friends – former friends – commented often on Daphne's angelic beauty. Photographers tried to bring her into the child-model business. Others prophesied a beauty that would far outshine Sylvia's, for it had a sweetness to it lacking in the mother.

Sylvia began force-feeding her daughter ('Mummy won't love you if you don't eat all of this.' 'But Mummy, I'm not hungry!' 'Then Mummy will have to shut you in your room and leave you by yourself. She can't be with you if you hurt her feelings.') until Daphne weighed close to 300 pounds.

As for Sylvia, she hardened into a still-beautiful, if somewhat lacquered, jet-setter. She did a good business in television commercials (the housewife in the wildly successful *Greazout* detergent campaign) but was considered too brittle for magazines. She jetted to Minorca for the winter, spent spring in Paris, summered in the temperate zones off La Jolla, and generally alighted on Daphne's Chicago doorstep for a fleeting display of maternity in mid October. ('Daphne, my pet! Darling, how *do* you

manage to stay so fat! I eat and eat and can't put on an *ounce!*')
Usually she had a young escort in tow, flattered by Sylvia's beauty
and sophistication, yet contriving to make her appear a trifle old.
Daphne longed for love. She tried to satisfy her dreams with
novels, beauty magazines (carefully cutting out Sylvia's face the
few times it still appeared) and daydreams of an impossibly
romantic character. And while she read, or dreamed of herself slim
and desirable, she ate: a pound of pork chops with French fries, a
chocolate layer cake and a quart of ice cream. And later a few
pretzels and potąto chips with beer. And so to bed.

One winter a young man joined Rapelec's accounting department.
He had a type of serious youthful beauty and was very shy.
Daphne's fat, and her vulnerability, struck a responsive chord in
Jerry. After thinking the matter over for several weeks, he waited
until they were both alone at the end of the day and asked her to go
to a movie with him. Daphne, whose dreams had been filled with
Jerry's fine-etched features, at first thought he was making fun of
her. But he persisted and she finally agreed to go.
    The first terrifying date took place in March. By May, Jerry and
Daphne were lovers and Daphne had lost thirty-seven pounds. In
September, she bought her first shop-made garment in eight years.
A size twenty, to be sure, but a delirious occasion for her. In
October, she and Jerry signed a lease together on Chicago's north
side. That was where Sylvia found them some ten days later.
    'Daphne, darling! Why·didn't you let me know you were
moving? I've searched everywhere for you, and finally! Your
genius of a secretary dug up your address for me!'
    Daphne muttered something which a charitable listener could
interpret as delight at seeing her mother. Sylvia eyed Jerry in a way
which made him blush uncomfortably. 'Introduce me to your
friend, darling,' she cried reproachfully. Daphne did so, reluctantly, and then muttered that they were going to paint cabinets,
and didn't paint always make Sylvia sick?
    'You don't want to paint the first night your mother is in town,'
Sylvia said archly, inviting Jerry to compare mother with daughter,
indeed pausing for the expected remark ('You can't be her mother
– if anything she looks older that you!'). Jerry said nothing, but
blushed more than ever.
    'Why, you two babies,' Sylvia finally said. 'Anyone would think

I'd found you out in some guilty secret. Instead, here you are setting up house in the most delightful way. Let's go over to Perroquet to celebrate!'

'Thanks, Sylvia, but I – I guess I'm not hungry and these cabinets do need painting.'

Sylvia cried out some more, drew the embarrassed Jerry into the conversation – 'You must be making this goose of a daughter perfectly *miserable*, Jerry: she's never lost her appetite in all the years I've known her' – and finally dragged them off to Perroquet where she ordered for all of them and pouted when Daphne refused several courses. 'If you were a model, darling, one could understand. But you can eat whatever you feel like.'

Back home, Daphne burst into tears. How could Jerry love her, as fat as she was, and why didn't Sylvia drop dead? Jerry consoled her, but uneasily. And back in her suite, Sylvia could not rest. Daphne happy and in love? Impossible. Daphne thin? Never!

Sylvia's courtship of Jerry was long and difficult. She postponed her winter plans and stayed in Chicago, hosting parties, making a splash at all the society events, getting Jerry to escort her when Prince Philip hosted a dress ball at the British consulate.

Daphne watched wretchedly, hopeless and unable to act. She began eating again, not at her previous levels, but enough to put ten pounds back on by Thanksgiving.

Jerry, too, was miserable and unable to cope with Sylvia. He dreaded her summons, yet could not refuse it. The night finally came when he did not return to the apartment.

Desolate, Daphne sat up in bed waiting for him. By three, it was clear that he wasn't coming home. She began to eat, consuming the roast she had prepared for their dinner and what little other food they had – for her sake they didn't stock much.

As soon as the stores were open, Daphne went to the nearest grocery and bought as much as she could carry. Returning home, she dropped two heavy bags in the middle of the living room and sat down to eat. She did not take off her coat, nor bother to call her office. She ate a dozen sweet rolls, a cherry pie, and two pizzas. She was working her way through a box of chips with dip when Sylvia appeared.

Sylvia stopped in the middle of the room. 'What on earth are you doing here? I was sure you would be at work!'

Daphne got clumsily to her feet. She looked at Sylvia, furiously angry, yet feeling passive and remote. She wanted to cry, to eat a pound of chocolates, to throw Sylvia out the window, yet she only stood. Finally she spoke. Her voice sounded so far away that she wondered if she'd said the words aloud and repeated herself. 'What are you doing here, Sylvia? Get out.'

Sylvia laughed. 'Oh, I came to get Jerry's clothes – he didn't want to come himself – felt awkward, poor thing.'

Daphne followed her into the bedroom. 'You can't have Jerry's clothes,' she whispered. 'I want them myself.'

'Oh, do be reasonable, Daphne: Jerry won't be coming back. Why he ever wanted a fat lump like you I don't know, but at least it gave me a chance to meet him, so I suppose it was all to the good.' As she spoke, Sylvia began pulling drawers open, impatiently pawing through jeans and T-shirts.

'You can't take his clothes,' Daphne whispered hoarsely, pulling at Sylvia's arm.

'Buzz off now, Daphne, and finish your cookies,' Sylvia snapped, slapping her across the face.

Daphne screamed in rage. Scarcely knowing what she was doing, she picked up the dressing-table lamp and began pounding Sylvia's head with it. Sylvia fell against the dressing-table and at last lay crumpled on the floor, dead long before Daphne stopped screaming and hitting her.

Finally Daphne's rage subsided. She collapsed on the floor by Sylvia's body and began to cry. Jerry would never come back to her. No one would ever love her again. She wanted to die herself, to eat and eat until she was engulfed by food. Mechanically, methodically, still weeping, she lifted Sylvia's left arm to her mouth.

SUE WARD

Teddy

As she came down the church steps after the funeral, Mary saw the
cameras and paused, bracing herself. Instinctively she expected to
feel Teddy's restraining hand on her shoulder. He had always told
her not to be shy of photographers, and she'd been there in the
pictures beside him time and again. He'd stood with his arm round
her, far taller and with a personality that you could tell even from a
photograph was towering over all the rest.

But then she realised that he would not, ever, do that again. He
was dead, and the photographers were interested in all the
politicians and churchmen who had come to the funeral, not in
her. She would never again see his face staring out of a newspaper
at breakfast after they'd been somewhere together the day before.
There would only be herself, a small inconspicuous woman with
greying hair, just like any other housewife in her early sixties, of no
interest to anyone.

Her daughter saw that she had stopped, and took her arm.

'Come on, Mum,' she said, 'the car's waiting. It was a lovely
service, wasn't it? And so many people. Dad had so many friends
and admirers. It must make you feel proud.'

'Yes, indeed,' said Mary. 'Some people there I hadn't seen in
years, and others I didn't know at all.'

'Well, there'll only be people you do know at lunch now,' her
daughter said reassuringly, 'Bill and I have asked those you'll be at
ease with, and there's only about twenty of them. When we get
back you must sit down with a drink and not do a thing. Today
must have been a terrific strain on you.'

Mary was glad to do as she was told. The last week had been
bewildering, ever since the phone call which told her Teddy had

been rushed to hospital with a heart attack; could she get there immediately? It had not seemed strange that Teddy's last hours had been lived out with television crews outside the hospital gates and reporters crowding round the doctors asking for news. After all, that was how his life had been.

The strangeness came after Teddy's death had been announced. Her daughter and son-in-law had insisted she come and stay with them, and there had been no cameras at all. Long, long obituaries which she hadn't read, but she had made them keep all the papers so that she could cut them out soon, when she felt able to. She'd always kept Teddy's press cuttings carefully in scrapbooks; it was something to do on the many occasions when he was away. There had been special programmes on the television, but no one had wanted to interview her about Teddy. She understood entirely, of course – without Teddy there, why should the newsmen be interested in her? But she just felt strange. She had better get used to it, she supposed dully.

Back home, Janet helped Mary out of the car, and put her in a comfortable chair with a glass of sherry. Mary tried to refuse, but Janet insisted. 'Think of yourself for once, Mum,' she said. 'Drink up and don't worry what people think. You need it.'

People who had come on from the funeral began arriving, and each one came up to her and murmured solicitous words about her great loss. They were asking what she would do now, but she couldn't tell them. 'I'll be staying here for a few days longer, I think,' she said. 'Then I will have to go home and start sorting things out. There are piles of papers going back years. I'll have to decide what to do with them, and all Teddy's possessions.'

'Are you going to have an official biography written?' asked an MP who had sat on dozens of committees with Teddy.

'I suppose so,' Mary said. 'But I wouldn't know how to go about finding a biographer. I'll have to find out about that.'

Janet was standing beside her, and said quickly, 'There's plenty of time for that, Mum. Don't even think about it. You ought to go away on holiday before you go home.'

'No, dear, I don't think so,' Mary said sadly. 'I wouldn't know what to do with myself, without Teddy there. Better to go home and get busy, rather than mope in some hotel.'

A week later she was back home, in the neat suburban house where she and Teddy had lived for the last twenty years. It smelt musty and uncared for when she got back; there was dust on the ornaments. She had always boasted that she had kept it clean and tidy, that any of Teddy's friends and colleagues would find a welcome there; the spare bed was always made up, with flowers in the room. All sorts of people, from chance acquaintances, hitchhikers Teddy gave lifts to on the road, eminent foreigners, other churchmen, had stayed there. Sometimes, if he'd got home after she was in bed, she didn't even know that there was anyone staying. They'd just appeared at breakfast next morning and she'd had to fry another egg. Teddy never thought to mention it when she was getting up.

Her son-in-law Bill, who had brought her over, took her case up to her bedroom. He kissed her briefly on the cheek, and made her promise to come to Sunday lunch. As he left he asked anxiously, 'You're sure you'll be all right, then?'

'Yes, I'm sure,' Mary said. 'I'll give the house a good clean up first, and then get down to answering some of the letters that have piled up. Don't worry about me.'

After Bill had gone Mary stood lost in thought. She seemed so much slower at doing everything now. But she'd seen grief do that to other people; it was natural.

No reason to let my standards go, though, she supposed, just because I'm on my own. She unpacked carefully, putting things in the half of the wardrobe and chest of drawers that were hers, averting her eyes from the suits and shirts in the other half. She went and made herself a pot of tea, carefully putting it on the little tray with the white lace cloth, together with a cup and saucer, milk, sugar. Then she realised she had never taken sugar, and put the bowl back again. She went and sat in her usual chair in the sitting room, and looked at the letters stacked neatly in the bureau by the neighbour who had been looking after the house. I'll have to answer them all, she thought. But where shall I do the writing? I've not got a desk, I've never needed one. I could use the kitchen table. Or the dining table. But I'll need files and things. They're all in Teddy's study.

She got up and peered doubtfully in the door of his room, which she had entered in the past only to clean. She had never, ever, touched things on his desk. He'd been furious once when they were first married because she'd moved things to dust, and had lost a page of his sermon for that week. He had been as kind as anything, she thought, but he did have a biting tongue when he wanted.

No, I can't possibly use his desk, she decided. I'll have to sort it out sooner or later, but I couldn't possibly sit at it. Anyway, I'll give the house a good clean before I start opening the letters.

Denise was Teddy's secretary. She'd worked for him for years, moving around from one appointment to another with him. At first she'd been part-time, and then as Teddy became more important she'd gone full-time. By the time of his death she was supervising a typist and clerical assistant as well. She was a big friendly woman in her late fifties, rather plump with a broad, homely face. No one could say she was anything but plain, and she knew it. She'd never married, but had given much of her life to ensuring that Teddy answered his letters, kept his commitments and remembered what he had promised to do and for whom. She and Mary had often had to speak to each other, to sort out the various problems Teddy left in his wake. Only a day before Teddy's heart attack, Denise had phoned to say that Teddy had invited a bishop and his wife for dinner that weekend. Mary had exclaimed in horror; she'd agreed to babysit for a neighbour, and she was sure she'd told Teddy about it. But there was nothing to be done, and she just had to go round and apologise.

But Mary and Denise had rarely met face to face before the funeral. They were both on edge, neither knowing quite what to say to the other woman in Teddy's life, but each wanting to be friendly. 'What will you do now?' Mary had asked.

'They've asked me to stay on for a few months,' said Denise, 'to get everything straight. Then I think I'll probably retire. I'm too old to start again, and no boss could ever be like Teddy.'

They'd spoken on the phone a couple of times since then, about addresses of people who had to be written to, pieces of paper that had to be matched to files at home or in the office, arrangements for getting the piles of sorted papers to Mary at home. One of these conversations was going on a long time, with several points to clear up, when Mary took a step she'd been thinking about for a while, and said suddenly, 'Why don't we meet up to sort this out? Much easier than on the phone.'

'No, why don't we go out somewhere for lunch?' Denise said. 'We've neither of us been seeing people much. It would do us good to go out. Or even better, why don't we meet in the evening, so that I don't have to rush back?'

'But I don't ever go out in the evening,' Mary said. 'I wouldn't know where to go or anything. Teddy never liked me tó go out without him.'

'You'll have to learn, dear,' Denise said gently. 'Let's meet under the clock at Waterloo. I'd suggest meeting in a pub, but you'd probably not be happy about that.'

'No, I wouldn't. Very well, under the clock at Waterloo. How about tomorrow at seven o'clock? I suppose that will be all right. I can always get a taxi home, after all.'

The two women went the next evening to a small quiet restaurant that Denise knew. Most of the people there were young, and looked oddly at the two elderly ladies drinking sherry and eating a modest meal. Denise and Mary were too absorbed in their conversation to notice. They were reminiscing about old times, about problems they'd jointly solved as to where Teddy had to be, when, and who was meeting him.

'If it hadn't been for us,' Denise said, 'he'd have been in chaos. Never could organise his own life. A wonderful man, but he did need looking after.'

'Well, you couldn't expect him to think about ordinary things,' Mary said loyally. 'That's why I went with him so often – that, and not liking to be alone too much. I could remind him we hadn't eaten yet and make sure he caught the right train. Do you remember that time he went up to Northumberland to see some housing group, left the file on the train, and had to bluff his way through a whole day's meeting?'

'No,' Denise said, 'I don't remember hearing about that. When was it?'

'A couple of years ago, I suppose. I'm surprised you don't remember. He came back very angry with British Rail, because they never did find the file. Perhaps you were on holiday.'

'I could have been, I suppose, or my memory is going. How odd.'

They talked about other things, but as they were leaving Denise said, 'Mary, could you do something for me? I'm bothered about that Northumberland story. Could you look up in Teddy's old appointments diary to see when it was? I'd like to be sure I'm not going mad. So far as I can remember Teddy hasn't been to Northumberland for years.'

'Yes, of course,' Mary said. 'Don't worry about it, though. Either you were on holiday or I've got the story wrong.'

It was too late to do anything about Teddy's diaries that night, but next day she went into his study and opened the drawer where he kept them. She found the small pocket diary for two years ago, and began flipping through it, going slower and slower as the entries brought back different memories. That was the time they'd forgotten to give her a place at the dinner . . . that was when that charming man had stayed talking to her for hours after the service, until Teddy had come to find her . . . that was when Teddy had lost his voice and she'd had to read his speech, in fear and trembling, which he'd said was ridiculous.

At last she found what she thought must be the entry, and phoned Denise.

'It was May 4th, two years ago,' she said. 'He must have gone up the night before and come back on the sleeper. Morpeth is in Northumberland, isn't it? The entry says "Morpeth", with "Housing" in brackets after it.'

After a long pause Denise replied, sounding more troubled than she had last night, 'Are you sure? I've been looking in the big appointments diary too. I'd forgotten I still had those, that they hadn't yet come over to you. I've got it in front of me, and May 4th says "No appointments. Retreat". I thought he'd gone down to that place in Surrey, you know, that he used to go to when he was feeling very harassed and wanted some peace.'

'What place?' Mary asked blankly. 'Teddy used to laugh at retreats, and say they were only for people who couldn't stand the pace.'

'Yes, I know, but he still went there. Every few months, for a day or so. Mary, surely you must know about it?'

Mary sat down carefully in Teddy's big chair, and said slowly, 'Denise, I know nothing about it whatsoever. Let's take it more slowly. We must both be making some silly mistake. Are you looking at the right year?'

'I'm certain. Look, I'll find the next time he's down as going to the retreat. Hang on a minute – yes, July 11th. What's in his pocket diary for that?'

'Carlisle. Meet the Bishop.'

'I can't believe that he'd been telling us different things. He wouldn't do such a thing. Other people maybe, but not Teddy. He wasn't above the odd white lie in a good cause, but not to us. Look, why don't you come to the office with the diaries right now, and we can go through them together and work out a sensible explanation?'

Mary agreed, scooped up the pile of pocket diaries going back years, and caught the bus down to Westminster. Since Teddy's death she had forced herself to go to different places, but was usually sick with worry until she got to her destination. Today, though, she felt a different sort of sickness – a knot in her stomach, a feeling like one has after missing a step in the dark, she thought.

She'd never been in Teddy's inner office; at most she had waited for him a few times on one of the comfortable chairs in the outer lobby. Usually, though, he arranged to meet her in a café or at a station. As she went up in the lift she began to wonder whether he had done it deliberately in order to keep Denise and herself from meeting.

Denise, with a pile of diaries in front of her, was methodically listing dates. 'These are all the dates in the last five years when he's told me he was at the retreat,' she said. 'Let's go through the pocket diaries and put down what it says in each of them.'

Half an hour later they sat staring at the list. It seemed to Mary to make no sense. Twenty or so dates over the five years, 'Retreat' in one diary, an appointment indistinguishable from all the others in his busy life in the other. 'I'm sure I remember him telling me about some of these,' Mary said. 'That dinner in Oxted, he said the food was terrible. How could he possibly have been making it up? You don't think he was . . . well, not quite right in the head, do you?'

'Teddy? He was perfectly sane,' Denise said. 'There is another explanation, of course.'

'What's that?' asked Mary.

'Well, he could have . . . oh, I shouldn't say this to you – but he could have been having an affair with someone else.'

Mary stared at her, horrified at the suggestion. 'How can you say that about my husband?' she burst out. 'You're forgetting who he was. This wasn't some sordid little businessman, but a highly respected churchman. He was no hypocrite. How could he have been leading that sort of double life?'

'I'm sorry,' Denise said. 'I didn't mean to upset you.'

'You haven't. You've made me angry. You knew him a long time, but not as long as I have or in the same way, or you could never have made the suggestion. There's got to be another explanation. But how can we find out what it is? We can't go round asking people – we can't even ring up the retreat. Teddy was such a well-known person that it would be bound to get out. What else can we check? Did you book him in there each time?'

'No, it was the one thing he always kept to himself. Said it was his private place and he'd deal with it. I know where they are, but I had instructions never to ring him there under any circumstances. Could we find some excuse to get them to check their records?'

'I can't think of one,' Mary said. 'What about the bills? Did they go through the office?'

'No, I never saw them. He had them sent home – again because he said it was his private place.'

'I could look for them there, then,' said Mary. 'He never threw a bill out, and I haven't started on them, or his old cheque stubs, yet. They're all in a big box in the cupboard. It will take me a couple of days at least to go through them, they're all in a mess. Let's meet on Saturday.'

'Yes, let's. Look, I'm sorry I made you angry, but I would like us still to be friends. Would you like to go to the theatre or a cinema on Saturday? We could go to a matinée, forget our troubles for a couple of hours, and then talk it over afterwards.'

'I'd like that,' Mary said. 'I haven't been to the pictures for years. Teddy didn't like them.'

Back home, she pulled out the box into which Teddy had thrown all his bills. She'd never had anything to do with the money – he'd looked after it all and then her son-in-law had taken it on. Now she felt that she was moving into foreign territory, and the knot came back into her stomach.

She started spreading things out on the floor, then thought, No, this is silly, and sat down in Teddy's chair at the big desk.

She began to put things into piles – gas bills, electric, cheque stubs, bank statements – and sorted methodically through. She couldn't find anything resembling a bill from the retreat, though. All the bank statements were going in one pile, when she suddenly noticed that some of them did not have Teddy's name on them. There was a foreign one instead. It took a few moments to sink in that it was Tadeusz Winzitski, the name Teddy had been born with and his mother had changed when they came to England over fifty years ago, when he was a child. The address was not their home; it was that of his friend Jerry, a social worker who lived round the corner.

She put those statements in a separate pile, and went on sorting. Deliberately she didn't study the figures. He must be keeping the money for someone else, she thought. There's bound to be a good reason for this, and for his mysterious absences. He must have been doing good by stealth – going to see people, paying the money out for charity, making arrangements he didn't want the world to know about.

When did he ever do that? another part of her mind demanded. He was always looking for publicity. If he did something in secret, he made very sure someone leaked it to the press.

She stopped, horrified. What was she thinking? How could she be so disloyal? Her Teddy had been a saint, whom people revered and respected.

But he deceived me, the other half of her mind said stubbornly. She swallowed back tears, and thought of all the evenings she had spent with him at long dull dinners, the other evenings when she had sat at home with his dinner ready to be heated up at a moment's notice. She'd done washing and ironing to ensure he always had clean clothes for his engagements. Janet had had to tiptoe round the house while he was working. I trusted him and believed in him, she thought. That's why I gave up my life to looking after him. He was a great man. If I wasted my life, I shall never forgive him.

She waited until she was calmer, then picked up the phone and dialled Jerry.

'Mary, I've been waiting for you to phone,' he said. 'I didn't want to disturb you too soon, but I've been wondering what to do with the letters Teddy had delivered here.'

'Yes, that's what I'm ringing about, Jerry. Can I come round and sort everything out? Would some time on Sunday be all right? And can I bring Denise, Teddy's old secretary, with me?' she asked. 'We're sorting out Teddy's affairs together.'

She was startled by the double meaning of that word, but Jerry did not notice. 'Yes, come about four o'clock,' he agreed.

*

Denise was looking strained when they met on Saturday, and
Mary knew she looked the same. They both laughed a lot at the
low-brow comedy Denise had chosen, even at some of the really
blue jokes.

In the pub Mary was silent until they'd ordered their drinks and
found a quiet corner. Then carefully, her voice low and
unemotional, she began explaining what she'd found out.

'I looked at the statements in the end,' she said. 'There's
thousands of pounds in there. I don't have any idea what one does
about it now. And I don't know where the money comes from,
either. I've tried to tie up the statements with the other account
which he used to pay the household bills, but it doesn't fit at all. It
looks as if he was drawing out small amounts of cash every couple
of months, and paying in large sums. The dates link in with the
mystery trips in his diary, though. So the whole thing's connected,
somehow. I only hope Jerry can throw some light on it.'

'Well, at least it doesn't seem to fit my first idea,' Denise said. 'If
he were seeing someone else he'd have been paying out a lot more
money.'

'That's right!' Mary said eagerly. 'I've spent a miserable few
days and never thought of that. Of course, he wouldn't be getting
large sums of money *in*, would he? Oh, what a relief!'

'I'm not sure that it is, to be honest,' Denise said. 'One possible
reason for getting large amounts of money in like that seems to me
even worse. How could he have been getting it honestly?'

Mary was downcast again. 'You mean he could have been
stealing from someone?' She drank her lager slowly, miserably.
'But who? I can't think of any source of large sums of cash. I wish I
knew more about things. Surely, if it was any sort of fraud, it
would be cheques, or direct payment into the account. His face
was so well known it must have been something very secret, to get
away with it. And I don't see how he'd have been able to organise
the time, either. He was always dashing around so much.'

'Oh, he always thought he had time to do anything he wanted,'
Denise remembered. 'The number of times he was late for things.
He'd rush into one meeting, stay half an hour and rush off to the
next. I think if he hadn't had such a reputation as a good man,
people would have been very irritated by it. It was as if no one was
important enough to take up all his time.'

'Do you know,' Mary said slowly, 'I think he often behaved very badly. He was assuming everyone else was at his beck and call. Not only you and me – one person looking after him full time at home and another in the office – but lots of others. He'd just tell people "this can be done, that should be done" and then others went round picking up the pieces and actually *doing* it all.'

'Yes,' said Denise. 'There were several people who used to ring me up nearly in tears because he'd piled so many commitments on them. If they said something was impossible, he'd appeal to their Christianity in his high-minded way. "But don't you *care* about it?" he'd say. He did it to me so often, and I always fell for it. And then he'd take all the credit afterwards. It was a sort of blackmail really . . .'

Mary interrupted her. 'That's it! That's what he's been up to. It's where all the money's from – that's the explanation.'

Denise drank slowly. 'No, surely not. Blackmail's a horrible crime.'

'I know,' Mary said, 'but don't you see how it all fits together? The small amounts of money are for travelling to meet the person he's blackmailing; the large sums are what is being paid to him.'

'But why hasn't that person come forward since Teddy's death?'

'Well, if they did, it would mean revealing their secret, wouldn't it? They must be counting their blessings now, being rid of a burden at last. I wish I knew who it was. I'd pay all that money back to them, whoever they are.'

When they went round on Sunday, Jerry had a lavish tea laid out for them, and it was only polite to chat to him for a while. He was surprised at Mary's buoyancy.

'I thought you'd be absolutely lost, Mary,' he said. 'Don't be offended, but I never thought you had much of a life of your own. You always seemed to live so much . . . well, in Teddy's shadow.'

'Yes,' Mary said. 'But I must learn to come out of that shadow if I'm to live on my own, perhaps for years.'

After tea they took the letters away, asking Jerry to send on any more that came. He couldn't tell them much about them; Teddy had simply asked him to act as a correspondence address, years ago, giving no real reason. 'Just one of my less well-publicised activities, dear boy,' he'd said. 'I do like to keep some things out of the papers.'

The women walked quickly back to Mary's house with four

letters; two with handwritten envelopes postmarked Mitcham,
and two more bank statements.

The first letter finished all the doubts about what Teddy had
been up to. Scrawled on plain paper, no address and no signature,
it read simply, 'Leave me alone, damn you. I've no more money.
Expose me if you dare. I'll drag you down too.'

The other one was postmarked a fortnight later, the day after
Teddy's death. It said, 'I waited under the tree. You didn't come.
Why not? *Please* don't do it. I'll pay whatever you like. Just don't
tell anyone.'

'Well,' said Mary. 'That's it. Something pretty nasty that Teddy
was involved in. They've realised now that he is dead, or they
would have kept on writing. But it looks as if he was due to see
them on the very day he died.'

'Yes,' said Denise, 'but it doesn't get us very far. We know he
had his heart attack on the way across Parliament Square. He
could have been going anywhere. So it looks as if we've come to a
dead end, unless this person contacts you, and that's hardly likely.'

'I'm not giving up,' Mary said firmly. 'If we can't find anything
at this end, the alternative is to look into Teddy's past and see
whether we can work out what he was up to.'

'How can we do that?' Denise asked.

'People keep asking me if I'm going to authorise a biography. I
keep telling them I haven't yet made up my mind. But I have now.
I'll do it myself. That gives me the opportunity to do all the
research, to ask as many nosey questions as I want. I can go and
talk to all sorts of people.'

'Will people let you?' Denise asked doubtfully. 'He was quite an
important figure. Won't they insist on someone qualified, who
knows about doing research?'

'I don't think they could insist. He hasn't got a literary executor
or anything. Anyway, I am qualified. I've got a history degree.'

'Have you?' Denise asked in surprise. 'When?'

'Oh, way back. I first met Teddy when we were both at
university. I was going to be a lecturer. Then we got married and I
taught children instead for a bit. He said he needed me at home,
but I thought we needed the money; we had some arguments about
it, but then I got pregnant. It was during the war, and we had
evacuees in the house – it was a vicarage down in Devon. Then
after the war he went on saying he needed me at home, even when

Janet was older. So I've barely used my history, but I'd like to do so again; it'd be fun. One of the people I was at college with is a professor now. I could go and talk to her about it. I could get some sort of research grant, and employ you as my assistant when the money from the Church runs out. It could probably only be part-time, but it would be better than nothing.'

It all worked out surprisingly easily. Mary phoned her old college friend, and got all the help she needed with sorting out research methods. Even getting a grant was fairly straightforward; the university couldn't help, but when the Church heard what Mary was doing, a few donations were forthcoming. It was no more than a month before Denise was told her salary was guaranteed for twenty hours a week, for as long as Mary needed her. She moved her typewriter and a filing cabinet to Mary's house.

Mary took over Teddy's study as an office. Denise was surprised, the first day she worked there. 'Wouldn't it be better to leave it undisturbed, and use the spare bedroom?'

But Mary was definite. 'No, I've spent too long trying to write on the kitchen table, or with a pad on my knee in the sitting room. I'm going to have a proper workroom at last, and it's not going to be the spare bedroom because I'll want to have friends and relatives to stay. I've always wanted to write, and now I've got the chance I'm going to do it properly.'

'Did you ever try before?' Denise asked curiously.

'Once or twice,' Mary said, rather embarrassed. 'Odd poems and descriptions of things I'd seen. Teddy knew, and he always praised them, if I showed them to him. But somehow, once I'd shown him, they were different. He sort of . . . took them over. He'd say it was wonderful, but suggest all sorts of other things to go in. And then it wasn't my idea any longer, it was his, so there wasn't much point in carrying on with it. I did go to a writers' group a few times, mostly women like myself who were just getting into it, and I really enjoyed that. But then it seemed as if every time the group was on, it clashed with something important Teddy wanted me to do, so I never got there. After a while I got embarrassed ringing up and giving my apologies each time, and just dropped it. I wonder if they're still going? If they are, I might go back again.'

'Won't you mind going out at night?' Denise asked.

'No,' Mary said, 'I'm getting used to it. I've got to, after all. I can always ask my neighbours to run me down there and pick me up again afterwards, if the weather's bad. I've started baby-sitting for them quite a lot. Ellen – that's the wife – is wearing herself out trying to be a good mother and a career woman as well. But at least she's got a choice – I wish I'd had it when I was young. And she insists on her husband doing his share – says her work is as important as his. I wish I'd stood up for myself in that way, at her age.'

Denise looked at her curiously. 'How you've changed, Mary.'

'Yes, I have,' Mary said, suddenly looking very sad. 'I've got to. I can't go on worshipping a man who's turned out to be a rogue. I wasted most of my life looking after him. Now I've got to find a life of my own instead.'

The two of them stayed busy for several months. Mary had advertised in all the likely magazines for letters and reminiscences of her husband, and they flooded in. Days were spent sorting, filing, cataloguing on card-indexes. They drew up a rough outline of Teddy's life, and slowly pieces were filled in.

They followed one or two false leads, but in the end it was Denise who picked up the trail. They were working on the papers for twenty-five years ago, when Teddy was just becoming a national figure and was being invited to sit on all sorts of boards and committees. They had thought it was too early to be interesting; the bank statements started only twelve years back.

But Denise noticed a curiously brief appearance of a housing association committee in the files. It looked as if Teddy had been appointed, and then resigned, all within three months.

'That was unlike him,' she commented to Mary. 'And two months later it was taken over by another one. Doesn't that happen when housing associations get their affairs into a mess?'

'Yes, I think so,' Mary said. 'It might be worth investigating. We'll have to try to track down the records, and see who we can interview.'

Tracking them down took longer than she'd expected, and she gradually became suspicious that there was some evasion. The minutes of those three months' meetings were missing from the files; people became vague and their memory was bad when she questioned them. She tried the former chairman, then a pushy young lawyer, now a judge; then a couple of the committee members. The person she couldn't find was the secretary. He had an unusual name, Casarin. Mary was almost giving up in despair when she thought of a very obvious source, the telephone directory. There were two people in south-west London, though the initials were different from those in the housing association minutes.

Phoning up strangers, though, was something she'd always hated. Before she nerved herself to do it, she thought she'd take a look at the streets themselves.

Coming out of the tube at Morden Mary realised it was ridiculous; how could she learn anything by wandering round suburban streets and looking at an anonymous front door? However, doggedly, she took out her *London A–Z* and made her way towards the first address, 42 Abset Road. She'd found she was walking on the side of the road opposite the house. It was a cold day, and there were few people about. She stopped for a minute, looking at the house, wondering whether to go and knock, but couldn't bring herself to do so. It was too cold to stand still for long, so she walked on, and then turned at the end of the street and came back past number 42. A small shabby terraced house, net curtains at the windows, dark brown door, just like the thousands of others all round her. She realised that one of the net curtains was moving, and started walking again, afraid she had made herself conspicuous.

To reach the other address, she needed to get a bus from near the tube station. She walked back that way and after a while there were footsteps behind her. She fought down her usual instinct to walk faster, and stopped to look in the next shop window. The footsteps stopped too. She pretended to take an interest in the tired vegetables inside the window, and saw reflected in the glass a seedy middle-aged man leaning against a lamppost. She couldn't make out his face very well, but it didn't seem familiar. Could he know me, if I don't know him? she thought. I suppose so, I sat on so many platforms with Teddy, I was in so many newspaper photographs. Has he recognised me? Is this it?

She felt exhilarated rather than frightened, and started walking again, turning at random down a street that looked quiet. The man followed. Suddenly, she turned to face him.

'Mr Casarin,' she said calmly. 'You know who I am.'

She'd never provoked that sort of terror in anyone before. He backed away, hands held out, pleadingly.

'I . . . I thought I was free. I thought if you were going to come after me you would have done so by now. What do you want, after so long? Why can't you leave me alone? Isn't it enough that he bled me white, without you starting?'

'I think we'd better talk,' Mary said pleasantly. 'We'll find a café and get a cup of tea.'

She turned back towards the tube station, and went into a café, empty except for the man behind the counter. Mr Casarin followed as if mesmerised. She bought two cups of tea, and a couple of stale-looking cakes. His hands were shaking so much he could hardly hold his cup. She'd formed no very definite plan, but had thought she needed to be stern and uncompromising; suddenly, all she felt was pity for this sorry specimen. This was the man her husband had persecuted for years. Whatever he had done, it surely did not deserve that constant pressure.

'Mr Casarin,' she said, 'I wasn't in my husband's confidence about what he was doing to you. I only pieced it together after his death. I still don't know the full story, and I need to. Tell me what it was that Teddy knew.'

The terror on the man's face was replaced by relief, and then a furtive look. 'I don't see why I should tell you,' he said quite aggressively. 'Let the secret die with him. Why should I let you in on it?'

'Because I want to help you. I'd rather not go to the police, but I could if I need to.'

Her sympathy seemed to mean something to him. 'Very well, I'll tell you,' he said after a pause. 'A long time ago I stole some money from a housing association account your husband was involved with. The committee suspected it was me, but they couldn't prove it. They'd been very careless and wanted to hush it all up, so they decided to dismiss me. Your husband was appalled. They persuaded him it would do more harm than good to go to the police. He accepted it, but resigned from the committee. They'd ruined my career. I got a job as a clerk, and I thought I could claw my way back up, get a responsible position.

'Then seven years later we came face to face in an office. If I'd known he was coming I would have made myself scarce, but he just walked in, after having lunch with the boss. He managed to have a few words with me and got my address. I thought he was going to pray over me or something. I think that was all he intended to do at first, but the second time he came he asked for money. There was a sort of implication that it was going to charity, but he didn't actually say so – I don't think he ever really gave it away.

'I couldn't afford to be dismissed again, so I got it for him. I thought that was the end of it, but it went on and on.'

'How did you get the money?' Mary asked.

He looked round the café to make sure no one was in earshot. 'I stole it,' he muttered. 'I deal with the computer payroll. I invented an extra account. When he found out about that, it gave him an extra hold over me.'

'What have you been doing with the money since Teddy's death?' Mary asked.

'Well,' he said, 'it was a problem. I couldn't just kill it off, I would have been caught for certain, so at present it's being paid into another bank account. I haven't spent it, I was afraid to.' He lowered his voice again. 'You could have some of it – if you like, if you'll keep quiet.'

'I wouldn't dream of it,' said Mary. 'You must pay that money back.'

'I can't,' he said. 'They'll find out if there's any alteration. I'll give it to a charity if you want – all I ask is that you don't go to the police over it.'

'You found a way to get it out, you can find a way to get it back,' Mary said firmly. 'If you do that, I won't go to the police about it. But if you start using if for your own ends, I will. Now I want you to go away and think about it, and I'll meet you here again to discuss it.'

'What if I leave the country?' Casarin asked.

'I don't think you will,' Mary said. 'If you were the sort to take the risk of starting a new life elsewhere, you'd have done so long ago.'

She arranged a time to meet and Casarin agreed. She wasn't really afraid he wouldn't turn up; she could feel the power she had over him. She watched him go out of the café, and then asked at the counter if she could use the phone to call a taxi. When the taxi arrived, she gave the driver Denise's address.

She'd been reasonably sure Denise would be in, but still felt relieved when she answered the bell.

'What's wrong?' Denise asked as soon as she was inside the door. Clearly the strain which had gradually replaced the exhilaration during the long taxi ride was showing. Mary told her, briefly.

'You've got to go to the police,' Denise said immediately.

'No, I don't want to,' Mary said. 'I feel too sorry for the man. He's so small and insignificant and Teddy was such an over-whelming personality – he simply browbeat him into it. Besides . . .'

She hesitated, not quite sure how to go on, and then said, 'He's done me good. Without finding out about all this I'd still be a loyal widow trailing round wrapped in Teddy's memory and only doing things I thought he'd want. Today I coped with a really tough situation. I was up to it. I could have been tougher still, if I'd wanted. In any case, a lot of people rely on their image of Teddy. They think he's a saint. Have I a right to break that image up?'

'If the image is a lie? You and I have had our props knocked away, and survived.'

'Yes, but others wouldn't. I can't simply let Casarin go on stealing, but I don't think I should do anything else to him.'

'What about the biography?' Denise asked.

'I can't go on with that,' Mary said. 'I'd be lying in it, and I'm not going to do so. I've been deceived for too long – I'm not going to deceive anyone else.'

'But all that work will be wasted then!' Denise cried out.

'No, it won't,' said Mary, smiling suddenly. 'I'm going to write *my* autobiography instead. Maybe it won't get published, maybe no one will even read it. But it will be about me and no one else, and I won't be in anyone's shadow any more.'

SHEILA RADLEY

All in the Family

'Here, Mum – catch!'
But to Moya a ball was a missile, not a plaything. She dreaded being on the receiving end. Her sons, their eye and agility inherited from their father, were always kicking and throwing balls or hitting them with a variety of implements, solid or stringed. Usually she could leave it to Francis to share their games, but on a midsummer half-term family picnic she could not avoid participation. William's bright fair head had turned towards her, his hand was lifted to shoulder height . . .
'No,' she called back, trying to sound casual instead of anxiously self-conscious, 'count me out. It's too hot.'
Fourteen-year-old William ignored her appeal. His strong wrist flicked. She saw the small hard squash ball leave his hand and come at her, a black blur against the grass; she flinched and blinked and grabbed, the ball smacked against her fingers, bending them painfully backwards, and she dropped it, as she had known she would. As they all knew she would.
'Butterfingers!' jeered Matthew, two years younger than his brother. Hot with sun and mortification, she could sense rather than see all their beautiful, superior Lexham faces turned towards her, some pitying, some exasperated.
'Jane's ten times better than you are,' pointed out William, 'and she's in a *wheelchair*. Here, Jane.'
His brother had retrieved the ball for him, and now William turned to throw it to the young woman whose chair was being manoeuvred by his father into the shade of a tall hedge. His throw made no concession to her disability. The ball he had sent at his mother had been a contemptuous toss, but this one went straight

and hard, wide of Jane Lexham's chair. And despite the fact that she was being wheeled backwards on rough ground at the time, she laughed and leaned over and stretched out her hand to pluck the ball from the air as easily as though it were made of steel and she held a magnet in her palm.

'What did I tell you?' said William. 'Good old Jane.'

'*Aunt* Jane,' corrected Moya crossly, busying herself with the picnic basket. 'She's your aunt.'

'Aunts are ordinary,' said Matthew, thinking with disdain of his mother's sisters. 'Jane's special.'

Jane Lexham was indeed so special that Moya could hardly bring herself to look at her. She was so like her handsome fair-haired Greek god of a brother that they might have been twins; and because the boys took after their father in appearance as well as in sporting ability, the four of them gave the impression of being sole members of a club to which Moya, dark and ungainly, could never be admitted.

The Lexhams were talented, as well as athletic and attractive. Jane, confined to a wheelchair as a result of a riding accident at the age of eighteen, had occupied her enforced leisure by reading widely, learning to play the classical guitar and teaching herself to paint. She had also taught herself to type well enough to be able to earn a living. She was as independent as she could be, bright and positive, amusing despite the fact that she was frequently in pain. Everyone who met Jane was attracted as much by her character as her appearance, and drew inspiration from her; everyone, except her sister-in-law.

Moya, mixing a salad, glanced dourly at the happy quartet. Jane was teasing the boys, tossing their ball from hand to hand while keeping it out of their reach; and Francis stood by laughing, so pleased with his sister and his sons that he gave every appearance of having forgotten his wife.

Jealousy affected Moya physically, contracting her stomach so that bile rose in her throat. She hurriedly capped the pot of oil and vinegar dressing, trying to pretend to herself that it had gone off and that the smell had caused her nausea; but she recognised her emotion well enough. She had lived with it for ten months, ever since she and Francis and the boys had moved to Underwood Lodge to be near Jane.

She had tried hard to be sensible about her sister-in-law. She ought to be sorry for her, she knew that. But how could she pity someone who never seemed sorry for herself?

What Moya minded most was that Jane was always the centre of attention, not because she demanded it but because she attracted it. Her sister-in-law's physical attractiveness ate at Moya like an ulcer. It was true that Jane's disability had marred her Lexham looks: the thick fair hair, so bright on Francis and the boys, had become dulled; pain-killing drugs had made the fine complexion sallow; the long legs were wasted, useless. But all Moya could see was the noble head, the beauty of the smile, the elegance of the long-fingered hands that tossed and caught the boys' ball so casually.

'Fetch it, if you want it,' Jane cried to them as the onset of pain forced her to drop out of the game. She lifted her arm, its muscles strongly developed by the task of wheeling herself about, flicked her wrist and sent the ball spinning into the air. It curved, black against the oppressive grey-blue haze of the sky, and made a bouncing fall on a distant part of the grassy field that sloped sharply out of sight.

'You don't know your own strength,' said Francis admiringly. 'That'll roll into the quarry.'

The boys had hared after the ball, whooping. At the bottom of the slope they suddenly stopped short, bending forward from the waist like swimmers fooling on the edge of a pool, their outspread arms flailing. Then they overbalanced, shrieked, and disappeared from view.

Moya stood up, anguished, clutching a cracked hard-boiled egg so tightly that the shell shattered. 'The quarry! Oh no – Francis, Francis, they've fallen!'

'Not them,' said her husband easily, pouring his sister a glass of white wine. 'They know it as well by now as we did when we were children, eh Jane? They were just showing off – they'll have run down one of the paths. Don't fuss, Moya, they're all right.'

But Moya had not waited to hear his reassurances. She dropped the egg and ran, awkwardly, inelegantly, pumping her arms and throwing out her feet at a ludicrous knock-kneed angle. The sun bore down on her head and shoulders. Soon she was gasping for breath. Her ribs ached, assaulted from within by the unaccustomed demand on her lungs and heart, and from without by the bouncing of her heavy breasts. By the time she approached the lip of the quarry, she was near to collapse.

She peered over fearfully, expecting to see a sheer drop to a barren floor at least a hundred feet below. And then she recalled what her husband had told the boys as he drove them all to their new home. There was a marvellous wild place, he had said, not far from Underwood Lodge: an old ironstone quarry that had been abandoned about fifty years ago. The excavated soil had been piled in great heaps and planted with conifers, so that it became a miniature Switzerland. The quarry face had crumbled and slipped, and was overgrown with grass and bushes – and, would they believe, wild strawberries?

That was what the boys were gathering, she supposed dully, as her breathing eased and her vision cleared. She could see William and Matthew, their hands scrabbling among the grasses, standing twenty feet below her, about halfway down the steep slope. It was still a considerable drop, sharp enough to make her afraid to venture down the narrow path that the boys had taken; the occasional outcrops of rich brown ironstone formed fierce-looking sheer crags. But much of the quarry face was hung with a lush tangle of dog rose bushes and brambles, and the tall red spikes of willowherb.

Moya pressed her hand against her side to ease its ache. 'William!' she called, her voice sharpened by the combination of recent fright and the knowledge that she had made a spectacle of herself in front of Jane. 'Matthew! Come up at once – we're waiting to start lunch.'

'Yes, Mother,' called back William, in the weary, dutiful voice that she hated. She knew quite well that the words were a euphemism for 'Drop dead'; or something even cruder. The vocabulary that he brought home from his public school appalled her.

She trudged back to their picnic spot, this time on the footpath that ran along the edge of the quarry and then went by an easy gradient to the top of the field. She was in no great hurry to rejoin Francis and Jane; she felt hot and sticky as well as humiliated. Besides, they were no doubt getting on perfectly well without her.

She lifted her hand to shade her eyes against the sun so that she could see them more clearly. Francis was sitting on the felled trunk of a dead hedgerow elm, close to his sister's wheelchair. So close that she could see that he had his arm round her shoulders. Moya's hand shook, and the sunlight splintered through her fingers, blinding her. Bile soured the back of her tongue. She crouched and bent her head, her chest heaving as she let the sparse, bitter fluid run from her mouth and fall to form globules in the dust. She knew then that she hated Jane infinitely more than she had hated any of Francis' extra-marital girlfriends. They had all been temporary; he would never leave her for them, if only because of her money and the boys. But Jane was permanent.

She stumbled to her feet, pushed her hair away from her flushed face and plodded towards them, meditating blackly. Then her spirits lifted a little. The boys had appeared, scrambling over the lip of the quarry and running straight up the field the way they had come. They were holding their cupped hands out in front of them, bearing gifts, and they looked so happy and healthy that Moya felt able to forgive them anything. After all, there wasn't a mother of her acquaintance who didn't admit that there were times when she found her children's behaviour abominable; and these boys, tall and strong for their age, were far more beautiful than most. Moya's heart was buoyant with pride at the thought that, unlike her as they were, she was the one who had produced them.

They passed within a few yards of her, their hands heaped with tiny scarlet berries. 'Wild strawberries?' she called out gaily, but they ignored her.

'Jane, hey, Jane,' they cried. 'We lost the ball, but look what we've found instead!'

And now there were four fair heads close together, the Lexham club in committee. Moya was totally excluded. She turned away, but this time she had no sensation of sickness; having expelled the bile, she felt stronger. Her jealousy had been replaced by a calculating anger.

I hate Jane, she thought, relishing the admission. She's trying to take my place, and I can't be expected to put up with that. I won't put up with it. She nodded to herself sagely, standing there with her feet planted apart, her hair disordered, her face red and streaked with dust, her eyes glittering with resolve. Something, she told herself, will have to be done about it.

Their move from outer suburban Surrey to rural Northamptonshire, after the death of Francis' widower father, had been as much

Moya's wish as her husband's. She knew that Francis was very fond of his sister, and felt a responsibility towards her, and her own feeling towards Jane at the time was a compound of pity and patronage.

Underwood Lodge, the family home, had been left equally to Francis and Jane. It was a substantial house, built of local ironstone and Collyweston slate. Adaptations had been made after Jane's accident so that she could live in the ground-floor rooms, and their father assumed that after his death, Francis and his family would move in with her.

This was not, they agreed at a family conference after the funeral, a good idea. Jane was an independent person and very mobile in her wheelchair. She had been used to cooking for herself and her father, and she couldn't be expected to share her kitchen with Moya any more than Moya with her. On the other hand, Jane had no wish to live in such a large house on her own. She looked forward to seeing far more of her brother and his family and she offered – if Francis would buy out her share in the Lodge and so provide her with enough money – to buy and adapt for her own use one of the small but equally attractive houses in the village.

It was Moya who provided Francis with the necessary money. Neither he nor his sister had capital of their own; Underwood Lodge was their sole inheritance. But Moya was modestly affluent. She, not Francis, had bought their house in Weybridge; she paid the boys' school fees. The move to Underwood Lodge would have been impossible without her agreement and financial backing, and so when the arrangement turned sour she had only herself to blame.

At the time, it had seemed an excellent plan. She knew that Francis loved the house, and wanted to bring up the children there. She herself liked the house well enough; she was also conscious that Mrs Francis Lexham carried greater social weight in Northamptonshire than she could ever hope to do in Weybridge. But the chief attraction of the place for her was its distance from London and Francis' girlfriends. Commuting, she calculated, would take up most of his time and energy, and the after-work drinks and suppers with his secretary would have to stop.

She was right. But what she had not bargained for was that much of what little spare time her husband had would be spent with his sister. Independent as she was in her newly adapted house,

Jane still needed someone to do what her father had always taken care of: the high and low tasks that could not be solved by adaptation.

Not that Jane made excessive demands upon her brother. She had learned to endure frustration as well as pain, and she took it for granted when they first arrived that Francis would always put his wife's needs before hers. But Jane was not a saint. She had never much cared for Moya, or thought her good enough for Francis, whom she adored, and she rejoiced in the fact that he so obviously preferred her company to his wife's.

For his part, Francis was delighted to be able to re-establish the intimacy they had enjoyed as children. He was not in the least sorry to have moved away from his girlfriends; his sex drive had never been very strong, and each girl in succession had soon become a complication and a nuisance. What he most enjoyed was the company of attractive and intelligent women, and he knew no one more attractive and intellegent than Jane. He was reasonably fond of Moya, appreciative of her household management and culinary skills, and grateful to her for providing him with his sons; but he much preferred being with Jane. Besides, she needed him. Moya didn't.

He was right: Moya didn't. She could manage perfectly well without him. What made her sick with envy in the months after they settled in at Underwood Lodge was not rejected love but damaged pride. Francis was her husband. The major part of his attention was, she thought, her due.

She tried at first to demand it: 'Surely you're not going there again this evening? That'll be five times this week! What about me, stuck here on my own all day? What about the jobs that *I* need doing?'

'For heaven's sake, Moya – you're not stuck here, you've got your own car and you're free to go where you like. As for jobs about the house, you know perfectly well that you're better at most of them than I am. Jane's *disabled*. How can you possibly be jealous of her?'

'I'm not jealous. Don't be ridiculous.'

'It looks remarkably like jealousy to me.'

'Is it unreasonable of me to expect to have my husband to myself occasionally? When you *are* at home, she's usually round here.'

'But we're a family. We're the only family Jane will ever have.

Good God, haven't you any compassion for someone in her situation?'

But as the months went by, and her husband and sons devoted more and more of their attention to Jane – and, worse, so obviously enjoyed it – Moya's capacity for compassion shrivelled completely. At the summer half-term picnic, she knew that she could endure the situation no longer.

Walking up the field from the quarry, she rejoined the others quietly, saying nothing; but smiling a little to herself. She served the picnic lunch, making sure that Jane's plate of salad looked as attractive and appetizing as possible; and afterwards she settled down with her back against the fallen tree for a doze, while Jane wheeled her chair, with help from Francis on the rougher ground, down to the edge of the quarry so that she could watch the boys gather more strawberries.

When they returned, Moya was sitting up rubbing her right leg. No one took any notice of her at first, but eventually Francis said, 'What's the matter?'

'I don't really know. I've had a terrible attack of pins and needles, and now I don't seem able to get up. Lend me a hand, Francis.'

He hauled her to her feet. She could hardly bear to put the right foot on the ground, and her husband had to hold her up.

The picnic was over. The boys repacked the basket, under their mother's direction, and they turned for home; William with Jane, Matthew carrying the basket, and Francis supporting Moya.

'Isn't this stupid?' she apologised as she hobbled slowly along, wincing every now and then. 'I'm so sorry to spoil the afternoon for everyone.'

'Don't worry about that,' said Francis. 'How does the leg feel now?'

'A little better, I th–'

'Take it slowly,' he advised. 'Tell you what, when we get to the road you can rest on the bank and I'll go ahead and bring back the car for you.'

'Thank you, dear,' she said.

It was usually their mother who collected William and Matthew from school at the end of each term, but that summer it was their father. The boys worshipped him, but they were too excited to notice that he was harassed, grey-faced with worry.

After ten minutes of chatter, including affectionate enquiries about Jane, Matthew thought to say, 'Where's Mum?'

"She's not very well, I'm afraid,' said Francis, choosing his words carefully. 'You remember that she had a bit of trouble with one of her legs at half term? Well, it got worse. It's both legs now.'

'Has she been to the doctor?' asked William.

'Yes, of course. Her own doctor, and a specialist too, but they haven't yet been able to find out what's wrong. She's just been to a London clinic for tests, so we may know more when the results come through.'

'Can she walk?'

'A little, sometimes. The numbness comes and goes, you see. At first she managed to get about with the help of sticks, and she can still do that occasionally. But mostly she's in a wheelchair.'

'Christ . . .' said William. His mother would have reproved him for that, but Francis let it go.

Matthew, who had been very quiet in the back seat, began to whimper. 'What about us?' he said. 'How can she look after us now?'

'Oh, we shall manage,' said Francis with forced brightness. 'Actually, you'll be surprised at what she can do from her wheelchair. She can't get upstairs, of course, but fortunately the ground floor is adapted for wheelchair living. Mrs Howe comes in more often now to do the cleaning, and you'll have to make your own beds and try to be tidier than usual, but your mother still does all the cooking and household organising. And she's had her car controls changed to hand operation, so she can still get about.'

'She's not ill, then?' said William. 'I mean, she doesn't *feel* ill?'

'She has quite a bit of pain,' said Francis, careful again. 'You must bear that in mind. We've all got to be considerate and helpful towards her. But on the whole she's fairly well in herself. She's taking it very bravely and cheerfully.'

William turned in his seat to look hard at his father. 'She's not putting it on, is she?' he asked suspiciously. 'I mean, it's a bit of a weird coincidence, isn't it, to have her in a wheelchair as well as Jane?'

Francis affected to be so preoccupied by overtaking a combine harvester that he didn't hear.

*

As Francis had told the boys, Moya was taking her disability very well indeed. Jane had provided her with a perfectly splendid example of cheerfulness in adversity, and she did her best to live up to it. As she explained to her husband and his sister, that was the least she could do.

Francis and Jane, in their turn, were usually most helpful and attentive. The only thing that distressed her, about them and about her sons when they came home from school, was that their attentiveness was sometimes grudging and their attitude suspicious.

To some extent this was understandable, Moya felt. After all, the coincidence was extraordinary. And then, the boys were upset by having to do more for themselves than usual. Jane resented the fact that she saw considerably less of her brother, and Francis was torn apart, poor dear, by his increased responsibilities. Moya understood, and bore his occasional ill humour with exemplary patience; until the day when she received a letter from her doctor about the tests that had been made on her at the clinic.

Francis had been awaiting the report with anxiety. As soon as he reached home, after a trying day at his City office and the long commuter journey, he made his usual enquiry about whether she had had any news. She showed him the letter. In the ensuing quarrel – fortunately the boys were out at the time – they said unforgivable things to each other, and Francis slammed out of the house.

He went straight to Jane. 'Nothing,' he reported to her, almost incoherent with anger. 'The best specialist money can buy has found nothing physically wrong, except some muscular deterioration in her legs – and as I pointed out to her, that could be accounted for by lack of use. He suggests that she should be admitted to the clinic for a further series of tests, but she's making excuses. Naturally. What'd be the point, if she knows there's nothing wrong? As long as she goes on saying that she's in pain and her legs give way when she tries to walk, no one can disprove her.'

Jane struck the arms of her wheelchair with impotent fury. Her blue Lexham eyes, darkened by pain, had sunk further into their sockets during the past few weeks; her cheerful veneer had gone. She felt that her sister-in-law was mocking her disability, insulting its reality. 'What that woman is doing is obscene! It's grotesque! My God, how could anyone voluntarily submit to being trapped, as I am – to being dependent on other people. How can any sane person *choose* never to walk again?'

Francis was grim. Like his sister, he had changed since half term. Instead of being charmingly indolent, always ready to take the easiest way, he had become tense with worry and suspicion. Like Jane's, his character had hardened.

'How do we know that's what she's chosen?' he pointed out. 'How do we know that she *doesn't* walk, when she's in the house alone or when she goes out of the district in her car?'

'Damn her,' said Jane through her teeth. 'Damn her, damn her, damn her . . .' She looked up at her brother. 'You know, I've never wished ill on anyone, not since my accident. I've suffered too much to want anyone else to suffer, however much I might have disliked them. But by God, I hope the medical staff put Moya through it while she was at that clinic . . . She doesn't need any more medical tests, Francis, she needs to see a psychiatrist.'

'I know,' he said harshly. 'I told her that this evening. We had a blistering row. You know all that phoney gentleness and calm she's been exuding? Well, that's vanished now. As soon as I suggested a psychiatrist – and I'm afraid I didn't do it tactfully, I was too furious – she began spitting evil. She hates you, Jane. She's riddled with jealousy because of our closeness to each other. She even implied incest –'

Jane's sallow skin darkened with fury. 'How dare she? How bloody *dare* she?' She caught urgently at her brother's hand. 'Francis! We can't let her go on like this. We'll have to do something about her.'

His staring eyes avoided his sister's, but his hand returned her strong grip. 'I know, my dear. I've come to the same conclusion.'

William and Matthew had been cutting the grass in Jane's back garden when their father arrived and, sensing from the look on his face that something was badly wrong, they had contrived to eavesdrop from underneath the sitting-room window. Now, having stared at each other with mounting alarm, they scuttled away for a conference in the toolshed.

'What's incest?' asked Matthew.

William enlightened his younger brother in basic English. Matthew was shaken.

'Is it true?' he asked wretchedly. 'Dad and Jane – do they?'

'How could they?' said William, who was less knowledgeable than he thought. 'Not with Jane in a wheelchair.'

Matthew was partially comforted. 'But why did Mum say so, then?'

'Because she's cuckoo,' said William. 'Bonkers. Bananas. Mad.' He tried to sound nonchalant, but his complacently secure world had been turned upside down and he was as distressed and frightened as his brother.

Matthew was trying hard not to cry. 'What are we going to do?' he whispered, his eyes as big as damp blue saucers.

William was frowning, thinking hard. 'I don't know yet,' he said slowly. Then he squeezed his brother's shoulder. 'Don't worry, Matt, we'll think of something.'

Moya wasn't sure which of the Lexhams suggested a family picnic in the quarry field, not long after the boys came home from school. The plan simply evolved, and she was content to go along with it.

Her relationship with Francis had been strained by their quarrel, during which he had made intolerable insinuations about her mental health. But he had given her an apology later that evening, and they had subsequently treated each other with a wary, dignified courtesy. Her relationship with the others was more difficult: Jane avoided her, and the boys had become resentful and sullen. All of them were less considerate than they had been, but lack of consideration was, Moya supposed, one of the crosses that she must expect to have to bear. A family picnic seemed to her a good opportunity for easing some of the tensions.

It was early August, too soon for the blackberries in the quarry to be ripe, but it was generally agreed that it would be worth going to inspect their progress. Accordingly, instead of making their way straight to the picnic spot by the hedge, they all – Moya and Jane in their wheelchairs, Jane wheeling herself and Moya pushed variously by Francis, William and Matthew – took the path that curved down the field and then ran parallel with the quarry, several yards from the edge.

No one felt very communicative that day. It was hot, even hotter than it had been for their half-term picnic, and nearly all of them had occasion to wipe sweat from their faces.

There was no one else about. They could hear the distant growl of combine harvesters gulping through fields of ripe corn, and an occasional ear-splitting roar as combat aircraft flew low-level sorties overhead, but the quarry field was completely secluded, shut in on three sides by high hedges. The only movement came from butterflies, grasshoppers and their myriad distant relations, and the drifting skeins of down from the willowherb flowers that had gone to seed in the quarry.

The slow procession paused and bunched as it drew level with the edge, from which some blackberry bushes protruded. Moya, whose chair was in the forefront, leaned forward so that she could see the state of the berries.

'They're not nearly –' she began; and then someone tilted her wheelchair sharply backwards, swivelled it violently and propelled it towards the quarry. She screamed, and tried to leap out, but her chair shot over the edge. Then its wheels caught in a bush. It tipped, and sent Moya sprawling down the forty foot drop, bumping and sliding through the grasses and over the ironstone outcrops until she came to rest near the bottom.

Moya could never be sure which of the Lexhams tried to kill her. She had plenty of time to speculate about it, confined as she was to a wheelchair, her back broken by the fall.

She had not known which of them was pushing her chair at the time, but perhaps that wasn't significant. Any one of them might have done it. Any one of their fair heads might have bent over the back of her chair, and any of their strong arms and supple wrists could have given the necessary push. Sometimes she thought it was Francis, and sometimes she suspected Jane; sometimes she thought it could have been William; or William and Matthew together. It didn't matter. Their abject, horrified silence made them all culpable.

Moya laid no charges. There was no need. Vindictiveness was pointless, because she knew that she was now assured of what she wanted: the unswerving, ungrudging attention of all four members of her family for the rest of her natural life.

MARGARET YORKE

The Liberator

My mercy mission began in Italy. I noticed him first on the plane: a coarse-featured, stout man with wide pores and purple thread veins on his face. He sat across the aisle from a still-pretty, faded middle-aged woman who seemed to be, as I was, travelling alone. When the stewardess with the drinks had passed, he leaned across with his glass in his hand and made some remark to the woman, who was reading. She looked surprised, but answered pleasantly. Thereafter, she was unable to return to her book for the rest of the journey, for he continued to talk, and when we boarded the bus at Genoa there he was, assiduous, by her side, helping with her hand luggage.

The hotel, in a small resort about forty miles north of Genoa, was across the road from the sea, a modern concrete block with balconied rooms at the front, and behind, single cells with the railway below. I had forgotten that: the railway line that runs along the coast, sometimes in front of the towns, sometimes to the rear, but always with express trains thundering through during the night, blowing their whistles piercingly at level-crossings.

With machine-like efficiency the hotel staff and the tour courier sorted the travellers, collected passports, and allocated rooms. The faded woman, the red-faced man and I all had rear-facing single cells. Off to the front, to their airy balconies, went the fortunate married, or anyway the twosomes.

Because of the trains I slept badly, and was angered at my own stupidity: I, usually so careful in my research, had slipped up over this booking which I had made in some haste after my sudden, premature retirement. I had felt the need for a change of scene and had quickly arranged a modestly priced package tour instead of the well-planned journey of some cultural interest I usually took later in the year. Now I had a bedroom which was no haven wherein to retreat in the heat of the day, nor a place of repose at night.

I went down early to breakfast and saw the faded woman at a corner table with her *prima colazione* of rolls and coffee. She glanced up and murmured 'good morning' as I passed, and her sigh of relief as I went on to sit some distance away was almost audible. She sought company no more than I did.

The pairs in their better rooms were sleeping late or having breakfast upstairs; few people were in the restaurant so early, but George was: I learned his name later. He came breezing in, sparse grey hair on end and colour high. He had been for a walk and already he glistened with sweat. He wore a bright yellow towelling shirt, crumpled cotton slacks, orange socks and leather sandals.

'Good morning,' he cried, walking up to the faded woman and pulling out a chair at her table. 'I'll join you,' he announced. 'Who wants to be alone?'

Plenty of people, I thought grimly, if the only company available is uncongenial. I felt sorry for the woman, whom I judged to be recently widowed, observing her ring and her faint air of defeat. Most divorcees, I have noticed, soon develop a certain toughness; the widows who do acquire it take longer, softened as they are by sympathy.

He talked at her all through breakfast, and when various couples who had been with us on the plane came into the room he greeted them all jovially. Most responded with reserved cordiality. He was all set to be the life and soul of the fortnight and to wreck it for other people, particularly the faded widow who would find escape difficult. I had seen this sort of thing happen before but had done nothing about it beyond protecting myself.

On the beach, later, I saw them among the rows of deck-chairs. He had accompanied her to book them; thus they were allotted neighbouring chairs and would remain together for the fortnight. I saw dawning realisation of this on her face as they trudged over the sand to their shared umbrella, and for a moment our eyes met.

She tried to get away. She was a good swimmer, and struck out boldly while he floundered in the shallows. I first spoke to her out there, in the water, clinging to a raft, and in the same way she made friends with a retired colonel and his wife and two more couples.

These people, all aware of her predicament, would sometimes invite her to join them in the bar or to go out in the evening for coffee. I, keeping my own company rigidly, a book held before me, would see her with her other friends drinking *strega* with her *cappucino*, briefly happy. Sooner or later, however, along would come George.

'Mind if I join you?' he'd blithely say, and would do it.

The couples were civil. They talked to him for a while but finished their drinks and then left, abandoning meek Emily, as I christened her, to her fate.

Meal times were the worst. Because he had adopted her at breakfast, the head waiter had assumed them to be together and had allotted them a shared table for all meals. I had had to assert myself to be left alone. It was easier for the staff to seat people in groups and it took strength of will to stand against the system: as it always does. George spoke a bastard Italian, very loudly, expecting to be understood and becoming heated when he was not. The waiters, whose English vocabulary was limited to phrases connected with food, drink and cutlery, were at a loss to respond courteously to these aggressive attempts at dialogue. Emily would intervene when George paused for breath, speaking in a soft voice; her limited Italian was precise. George, however, soon shouted her down, like a dominant husband, so that her little attempts to improve understanding withered and died. He ate grossly, too, demanding extra portions and shovelling the food into his mouth, even belching. Afterwards, he complained of indigestion.

Emily tanned, under the sun; she even bloomed a little as a result of the food, which was very good; but she grew edgy, was restless, twitched her hands. And she was not sleeping. I could see her light on, late at night, when I leaned out of my own window to watch one of the trains rush past in the darkness.

She had paid good money for this holiday and it was being ruined by an obtrusive boor.

I often walked round the town in the evening buying fruit and mineral water to consume in my room, and I enjoyed these expeditions. Once I met Emily, scurrying along, head down, arms full of packages. George was not in sight. I did not detain her by speaking, for he might be in pursuit – and he was: I saw him approaching, large belly bulging over his stained slacks, searching about for her.

'Have you seen Mary Jolly?' he asked. 'I've lost her.'

So that was, in fact, Emily's unlikely name.

'She's gone that way,' I said, pointing to a narrow alley between chrome-painted houses, where children played and cats skulked. 'You'll catch her if you hurry,' and I had the satisfaction of seeing him depart in the opposite direction from that taken by his quarry.

I caught her up myself. She was buying postcards, in a shifty, worried manner, peering over her shoulder as she made her choice in case he was on her trail.

'It's all right,' I told her. 'He's gone in the other direction. You can take your time.'

She looked startled for a moment; then she smiled, and I saw how pretty she must once have been.

'He means well,' she said.

Fatal words. I wondered how many other people's holidays George had wrecked over the years, and indeed, how his good intentions affected those he met in daily life at home.

'I never manage to miss him at breakfast, no matter what time I come down,' Mary-Emily confessed as we walked on together. 'Early or late, he's always there. And my room is too dark and dismal to stay in for breakfast. The trains in the night are so awful, too. Don't they wake you?'

I agreed that they did.

Mary-Emily had tried ear plugs, but could not sleep at all with them in her ears.

A morning glory trailed over the railing above a culvert alongside the pedestrian tunnel under the railway line. It was a dark, eerie passage, where sounds echoed in the vaulted concrete cavern, but above it the blue flowers were brilliant.

'It's so pretty here,' said Mary-Emily. 'The town, I mean, with the oleanders and the palm trees. And all the buildings. Look at that lovely wrought-iron balcony.'

I admired it, but I was thinking. An accident would be impossible to arrange, for George did not swim out far enough to drown, nor were there any cliffs, and there were people about most of the time. It would have to be done here, near the railway. Timed well, the sound of a train would mask any noise. No one would suspect an elderly spinster, a retired schoolmistress of modest demeanour. No one here would know that the elderly spinster had once worked with the French Resistance and was no stranger to violence. It was too late to save Mary-Emily's holiday this year, but no one else would have to suffer George in future.

I went on the organised coach trip to Monte Carlo, which I had not originally planned to do, but I bought the knife there: for my nephew, I said in my excellent French. The shopkeeper never suspected that I was English, just as no one had all those years ago when, after the German advance, I was caught in Paris.

George and Mary-Emily had booked to go on the outing too, but when the coach was due to leave she had not turned up. George made the driver wait and went to find her, returning to say she had a headache and was not coming. He almost decided to stay behind in case she needed anything, but I persuaded him to come; she should have this one day off, I resolved, silently commending her resource, and I invited him to sit with me in the coach. He talked without pause throughout the journey, and I learned he was a widower who lived alone in Leeds and sold insurance; he had one son whom he almost never saw. Since his wife died, he told me, he had learned about loneliness and that was why he befriended the solitary. The effrontery of it! He supposed, by accompanying me now, that he was benefiting me! No wonder his wife had been unable to survive such insensitivity, I thought. When we reached Monte Carlo I managed to elude him among the crowds, to make my purchase unobserved.

At dinner that night Mary-Emily looked tranquil after her undisturbed day. After the meal she went into the town with the army couple, and when George followed them, I followed him.

But there was no chance for action that night. I joined the group at a café and we talked late, sheer numbers wearing George down so that others might speak; because I was there to dilute the mixture the couple lingered. Mary-Emily was secretary-receptionist to a doctor in Putney, I learned. I described my years of teaching in a girls' school but did not mention the war. We walked back to the hotel together, and Mary-Emily went up to bed ahead of everyone else.

In the end, I did it in daylight. At least, it was light above ground. I found George, one afternoon, pacing up and down the hotel garden wondering where Mary-Emily was. It was a shame to waste a minute of such weather indoors, he said.

She was sure to be skulking in her room; when he had given her up and gone down to the beach she would appear in a shady corner of the hotel garden with a book, and remain there, as I did, until she went down for a swim. This was her latest tactic.

'She's gone to have her hair done,' I lied. 'And I'm just going – I have an appointment after hers. Shall we go together? You could walk back with her.'

'She hasn't left her key,' he grumbled.

'I expect she didn't bother – I don't always leave mine – see, I have it now,' I said, showing him the large, brass-tagged hotel key.

He was so stupid that he did not know the hairdresser, like all the shops, closed in the afternoons. If he did query it as we proceeded, I would say the hairdresser was an exception. If necessary, I would walk him round the town, always quiet at this hour, until I found a deserted spot where I could do it, but first we had to go through the tunnel. At that time of day the chance of its being deserted was good.

My luck was in. Not a soul was in sight as we entered the subway, and a goods train even rumbled obligingly over our heads as I plunged the knife in so that he died silently, and at once. There was just an instant when he gave me a startled, incredulous stare before his life gurgled away.

I withdrew the knife, slipped it into my pocket wrapped in a handkerchief, and walked unhurriedly back to the hotel. George would be found very soon. I must hope no one had seen us depart together, but it was a risk I had to take. If I had been noticed, I could say that I had felt unwell and had turned back, leaving him to continue his walk alone. Suspicion would never fall on me, an inoffensive, elderly woman.

Back in my room, I washed the knife and wiped it carefully, then rinsed the handkerchief in which it had been wrapped. That afternoon, when I bathed, I would have the knife strapped to my body with sticking plaster, and I would sink it out there, deep in the Mediterranean. I had not felt such satisfaction in a job well done for years. In those long-ago days I had swum rivers with a knife in my belt. People forget that the elderly have all been young once, and some have done remarkable things.

The murder was a nine days' wonder: various drop-out youngsters were questioned and grilled by the police, and known local ne'er-do-wells, but the tourists were never suspected. I said that I had walked with George to the mouth of the tunnel and had left him there; it is always wise to tell the truth.

Two days later we went home, as planned. Oddly, Mary-Emily wept at the news of George's death. She was tender-hearted: one of life's victims. That was why she had not been able to protect herself from him.

The next year, on Aegina, where I had gone after a week in Athens, I met a couple who, morning and afternoon, carried airbeds down to the beach, to roast. Or rather, the wife carried them, trudging behind her empty-handed mate. She bore also, slung round an arm, a carrier holding towels and suncream. Her skin grew scarlet; she panted; her eyes had the dulled look of a cowed beast. She was beyond protest – long past hope – but she should have her chance.

Disposing of him was easier than getting rid of George. Daily he paddled far out to sea on his mattress, then dozed, floating in the sun. People commented on his foolhardiness, lest the *meltemi* blew up suddenly. I never saw him swim, and guessed he could not; real swimmers show respect for the sea. I merely pierced his mattress with a penknife, swimming close to him on my back as if I had not seen him, ready to apologise when I gently thumped against him. Drowsing, he scarcely noticed me. I had entered the water from some rocks, away from the hotel beach, and I left it the same way before the air bed began to sink, dropping the penknife in deep water. He had been floundering for some minutes before a water-skier's boatman noticed his predicament and turned. I had guessed that his blood pressure was high; he drank a lot, and looked a likely coronary candidate, so that if he did not drown, heart failure might account for him.

I was never sure, in fact, exactly what he died of; it was a tragic accident, everyone said, and the formalities were soon over. It was thought that the mattress must have been punctured on a rock. I hoped he was well insured.

Next year I pushed a woman from a cliff top near Nissaki. Daily I had watched her humiliate both husband and teenage daughter as she dictated their plans for the day in a hectoring voice which caused all heads to turn. She spoke to me with gracious condescension, and was at her most odious when ordering the Greek waiters about in her loud voice as if they were deaf. Once, father and daughter slipped off along the cliff path to the next cove without letting her know where they were going, and she was furious when they returned, sheepish but happy, after eating shrimps at the little taverna and swimming from the rocks. They did it again another day, and then I told her where they had gone, adding that I was going to walk that way myself. No one else was in sight. Her horrified face when I lunged against her and pushed her over the cliff top remained in my mind for some hours. She screamed as she fell. I walked back quickly the way I had come, and after her disappearance was reported, agreed we had started out together. She was worried, I said, because she did not know where her husband and daughter were, and had set off to look for them. I had left her after a time as I found it too hot for walking. Her body was washed up the next day on rocks beneath the cliff.

The daughter seemed very upset and the husband was stunned. I hoped they would not blame themselves for long and that they would make good use of their freedom.

Then Mr Bradbury, next door to me in Little Wicton, bought his scooter.

For years we had been neighbours, and Mr Bradbury left the village daily for his London office, getting a lift to the station with a friend. The friend retired, and Mr Bradbury bought the scooter. Thereafter, he tooted his horn in farewell to his wife every morning at a quarter to seven as he rode off. It did not disturb me, for I was always awake then, but it woke others. Besides, blowing one's horn at that hour in a built-up area was against the law. He tooted again each evening when he returned, an announcement to his wife, just as his morning signal was a farewell. When I mentioned to Mr Bradbury that he was disturbing people, he was quite rude and said that what he did was his own business.

Reporting him to the police would cause a lot of unpleasantness; and a man capable of such thoughtlessness for others would not stop at merely blowing his horn; who knew what went on in the privacy of his home?

His journey to the station took him along a quiet lane, and one morning I was there ahead of him, with a wire across the road. Several cars passed, running over my wire as it lay on the tarmac, and I let them go, watching from my vantage point behind the hedge. It was like old times; I had enjoyed planning this and felt quite youthful again as I waited for Mr Bradbury. My acquaintances in Little Wicton thought I was in London for the night, but I had driven back at dawn and hidden my car some way off; I would return again to London for two nights when the deed was done.

Mr Bradbury never saw the wire spring taut before him. I braced myself to take the strain; I had wound it round a tree as a support, finding a place in the road where two elms faced each other on either side. He was travelling fast, the bike engine noisy in the morning air.

His ridiculous martian helmet saved his skull from shattering, and he lived for a week before the rest of his injuries killed him. I remembered to remove the wire, not losing my head as he hurtled through the air, and I got away before the next car came along. Such a shock, I said to his wife later, when I came home to hear the news.

She grieved a lot.

'He loved that silly bike. Would blow the horn like that, saying good-bye, though I know he shouldn't have. I'd have got him to stop it, in a bit,' she said, looking bleak. She'd soon get over it, and find a way to use her life more profitably than spending it cooking and cleaning for one selfish man.

Mr Bradbury had an invalid mother, it seemed, whose fees in a private home used up much of his salary, and this was why they had never run a car. Mrs Bradbury seemed to think that she would now have to provide for the old lady though there was some sort of insurance.

It was a surprise, two months later, when the doorbell rang and I saw a woman whom at first I did not recognise on the step; her hair was quite grey and her face lined. It was Mary-Emily.

'Ah – you do remember me,' she said, as I struggled at first to place her among the generations of girls I had tried to ground in the rudiments of French grammar, and then realised who she was. 'I was passing and thought I'd see if you were at home.'

'Do come in,' I said, but I felt the first sense of unease. I was sure I had not told her where I lived. I don't give away detailed information about myself; old habits die hard. 'How are you?' I asked. 'Still living at – Putney, wasn't it?' I pretended to be uncertain.

'Yes. I need not enquire about you. You don't look a day older,' said Mary-Emily.

It was true. I took care to keep physically active, and though I missed my work, now I was on the alert at all times, looking for opportunities to free others from bondage, so that my perceptions were acute.

I made tea for Mary-Emily and offered her a home-made scone. She told me she had remarried.

'You've met my husband and stepdaughter,' she said. 'You were in Corfu when his first wife died in a fall from a cliff.'

She could suspect nothing, but I knew sudden fear.

'It was such a coincidence that poor George should have been killed like that in Italy, and then Betty in Corfu, and that you should have been there both times,' said Mary-Emily, and took a bite of her scone.

'But Betty wasn't killed,' I objected. 'She fell – either accidentally, or it was suicide.'

'She could have been pushed,' said Mary-Emily. 'And wasn't there a fatal accident on Aegina, too, when you happened to be there?'

How could she have found that out? Anyway, it didn't matter. Nothing could be proved.

'Accidents do happen,' I said, pouring out more tea.

'Rather often, in your company,' she said, looking at me steadily. She had changed in character as well as in appearance, I realised; she was bolder. I decided to attack.

'Well – things have improved for you, haven't they?' I remarked. 'You've remarried, and that man and his daughter are no longer bullied or humiliated. I'm sure you're good to them both, and no one could miss that dreadful woman, just as no one could miss George.'

'George meant to be kind, though he failed,' said Mary-Emily. 'And Betty was domineering because both Hugh and Jane are so weak that someone has to take charge of them. You never saw them at home – only their holiday face. They still blame themselves for causing Betty's death by slipping off on their own.' She put sugar in her tea and stirred it. 'Hugh and his family were patients of the doctor I worked for. After Betty's death someone had to marry Hugh to save him – drive him on – and to fend for Jane. Better me than someone who wouldn't understand him. I try to remain kind, but I'm getting quite aggressive myself,' she said, and took a sip from her cup.

I waited for her to disclose the reason for her call. Was it to blackmail me? How had she found me?

'I believe your neighbour, Mr Bradbury, was recently killed in a road accident,' she said.

'Yes,' I replied. 'The roads are so dangerous.'

'You shouldn't have done it,' she said. 'I can see that you've set yourself up as some sort of judge, deciding that certain people should be exterminated, like the Nazis during the war. But I don't know why you picked Mr Bradbury. He seemed harmless, from what I can discover, and he grew beautiful begonias.'

My hand, holding my teacup, remained quite steady as I said, 'Picked him? What do you mean?'

'He must have annoyed you in some way,' she said. 'It was people who annoyed you whom you despatched.'

She was wrong. It was people who made life intolerable for others, not me, whom I removed. But I did not fall into the trap of replying. I tried instead to think of a way to silence her. For the first time since the war it seemed that I would have to act for my own protection.

'It will make a sensational case when it comes to court,' she was saying. 'Wartime heroine turned murderer. You see, I know all about you now. I traced you through the travel agent Hugh booked with that time. And in case you're thinking of a way to dispose of me, save yourself the trouble. Detective Superintendent Filkin from the local CID knows everything, and he'll be here soon. He allowed me some time with you first, for my own satisfaction, as I was the one to uncover your trail. It's taken me a year, and at last I've got proof of something you've done. There are marks on the trees where you stretched the wire across the road to bring Mr Bradbury off his scooter, and even after this lapse of time there were shreds of clothing found in the hedge where you hid. I'm sure they'll match something upstairs in your room. It was your speciality during the war, wasn't it? Dealing with German despatch riders. Commendable then, but criminal now.'

How could she have found out so much? I could not ask, for to ask was to admit. But she told me a little.

'You were the last person to see Betty alive. Her death didn't make sense – she'd never commit suicide, and she was much too capable to fall accidentally. I enquired at newspaper offices about other accidental holiday deaths, and I followed up some of them, asking if you were there at the time. It wasn't easy, but I discovered that you were on Aegina when there was an accident. The woman whose husband died told me you were there. Poor thing, she had a mental breakdown and has been in and out of hospital ever since.'

'I'm not surprised. That man had destroyed her,' I said.

'She could have protested,' said Mary-Emily. 'Or left him. But she was one of those helpless women who are good only at running a home. She married him for material security, which he gave her. She didn't deserve more.'

'Now who's making a moral judgment?' I demanded.

Mary-Emily ignored my comment.

'It can be proved that you were present on those three occasions,' she said calmly. 'It adds up to just too many coincidences. Maybe there were more, which I haven't discovered, but if so the police will ferret them out. They're very thorough. However, there will be enough proof from the Bradbury case to put you in prison for the rest of your life. You won't like that, will you, being confined – shut up? You're paranoid, I suppose.' She set down her cup. 'I found out what happened at the school where you taught – how you started to bully girls who found their work difficult and eventually locked one up in a music practice room for three hours. The headmistress wanted no scandal because of your war record, so she asked for your immediate resignation.'

My mind was batting about like a rat in a trap seeking a way of escape. There must be one; there always had been before even from that cell I was once in, shut away from all light and freedom. I could never endure that again.

Mary-Emily got up.

'I'm going now,' she said. 'The superintendent will be here in a little while. There will be time for you to make some arrangements.'

I had the pills. I kept them, just in case. You never knew. Not cyanide, like we had then, but strong barbiturates obtained from a gullible doctor who thought I needed sleeping pills. When she had gone, I swallowed them down with tea – I made a fresh pot – and laced the cup with brandy to help them along. I could see no other way. This would protect my reputation for posterity, for my deeds were on record for anyone to read, and save me from confinement.

Mary-Emily had surprised me. I would never have thought she could possess so much initiative. And then I realised that it was through me she had discovered her own power; she had married a weak-willed man and had been forced to develop strength of her own. She would not be a victim again. My own ill luck lay in the coincidence that two people whom I had liberated had known one another.

The pills are working. I feel drowsy already. That superintendent should be here soon. He'll arrive in a police car. I won't open the door, and it may take him some time to decide to break in. Will he realise what I've done and take me to hospital – yes – of course – and they'll use a stomach pump. I hadn't thought of that. They may prevent my final escape. Why didn't I think of it? But Mary-Emily said there would be time to make arrangements. How long ago did she leave? I can't see the clock very well. Why, it's over an hour already – nearer two – the superintendent is late . . . very late . . .

What's that noise? The doorbell? No – it's the telephone . . Who can it be? Shall I answer it? I can't – my legs won't move – I can't reach it . . .

Mary-Emily let the telephone ring for a full five minutes. She had been right. The old woman had taken something which by now had begun to work. She walked away from the telephone box from which she had been able to watch the house and see that no one had left it. Her car was parked nearby and as she got in she glanced at her watch. It would take her about an hour and a half to get back to Putney, and by the time the old woman realised that there was no Detective Superintendent Filkin and that the police would not be calling, she would be beyond help. Mary-Emily hoped she would realise that, but she could not be certain if that part of her plan had worked. She had only one regret; that she had been too late to save Mr Bradbury. But his killer would despatch no one else, for whatever motive.

Mary-Emily, however, had learned that with some ingenuity and a lot of daring, such things could, if necessary, be accomplished.

JANE BURKE

The Permanent Personal
Secretary

Peggy always said she'd like to kill him. Of course, people are
always saying things like that, so I never took her seriously.
Perhaps there is too much I fail to take seriously – work, health,
relationships.

The Health Authority was my fifth job that year and I was
counting the days until my holiday – Skiathos, June, three weeks.
In any event I would have been counting the days till my contract
expired. The job was gloomy, the work tedious yet demanding, the
surroundings lugubrious. It was one of those bright, clean,
modern offices, full of shoulder-height partitions and computer
terminals and textured brushed nylon chairs and wall-to-wall
carpeting; also windows that wouldn't open, blinds that wouldn't
draw, an inconvenient little kitchen and toilets on a different floor.
All the office equipment was in garish plastic colours like orange
and apple and there was never enough stationery.

Peggy was permanent.

'God, how can you stand this place?' I'd argue. 'How do you put
up with him? It'd drive me spare.'

We would be loitering over a cup of coffee and a surreptitious
cigarette some dead hour of the afternoon when all the executive
officers were either still at lunch or else had gone home early.

'Oh, I shall be leaving soon. I'm not one to stay in the same job
for ever. I'll fancy a change soon,' Peggy would say.

To me it sounded as if she would be in the job for ever. One of
those people who complain and complain, who moan irritably at
every minor inconvenience but never actually do anything about
ending their discomfort. Life is very insecure and people have to

find their niche and stick with what they can bear. I am not putting the woman down, I suppose I can just bear different things. Perhaps my problem is that I won't stick to anything long enough – not jobs, not relationships, not even day-dreams. You need a lot of day-dreams to make a go of being a secretary.

What I realise now is, Peggy was older and wiser than me, to use a cliché. There I was, patronising her in my mind and mentally spending my wages on tsatsiki and Pamplemousse T-shirts, and all the time she was hatching a real solution to her situation. Or at least a real change. Not just exchanging one thing for another but actually jumping off the roundabout. Well, maybe. Perhaps she'll get away with it.

Peggy had day-dreams. She was quiet, didn't have a lot of chat, wasn't matey with the other women but was perfectly pleasant and amiable to work with: what she did do was read. Books were her way out. When I first arrived she was usually deep in her Mills & Boon, her Catherine Cookson or Maeve Binchey. She actually liked good, well-written books but would read whatever was put before her. Soon after I arrived she began a stream of thrillers and whodunnits – Dorothy L. Sayers, P.D. James, Agatha Christie – nothing very violent. 'What I like about these,' she would say, 'is that they make you wonder why more people aren't being bumped off every day. They make it all seem so easy.'

'That's what I hate about them,' said I, 'they're so unrealistic.'

'Oh, I don't think they're just *fantasy*,' she said.

Peggy was middle-aged, single, not plain, not pretty, big, shrewd, wore dullish clothes with an occasional splash into fashion. She had soft, fluffy brown hair and clever blue eyes, and sometimes a tight, ironical way of smiling that was quite striking. I liked her but was never close to her. I always used to find myself going home and thinking we'd talked about me again, what I was doing, who I was seeing, where I was going at the weekend. She fended off questions about herself, I decided, but not as if she had anything to hide. More as if she didn't think her life was of much interest to anyone but herself. Now this is not an unattractive characteristic, but it can become exasperating. It is as much an inter-species relational weapon as any other conversational gambit and can become as annoying.

'Tell me about yourself,' I'd try occasionally.

'Oh!' she would laugh. 'I go to the library a lot.'

She was not ill informed politically. She used to read the *Daily Mirror* but had her own opinions about everything. She was a union member to the extent of attending the one annual general meeting ordinary mortals were encouraged to attend, and used to fill in her ballot forms neatly. 'Oh, I'd go on strike like a shot,' she used to say. 'Anything to put Clarence to a little inconvenience.'

Clarence was Mr Clarkson, our district administrator. I was only the help but Peggy was saddled with the title of personal assistant to this bimbo.

If you've never worked in an office you might be tempted to think the worst type of boss would be the stereotype: upper class, sexually rampant to the point of assault, ignorant, superior, the sort who forgets your Christian name (should he ever have learnt it), who gets you to send his wife flowers when he manages to manoeuvre himself out of some domestic commitment at short notice. Actually, you would be right. However, Clarence Clarkson was not quite like this and in my experience he certainly took the biscuit when it came to making a secretary's life a misery.

Clarence always remembered everyone's name but insisted on abbreviating or lengthening it – Peg, Janey, Deb, Babs. Clarence treated us all as equals, which meant he got to stare at our tits a lot whilst subjecting us to his opinions. Clarence also liked to hear our opinions because he said he believed in liberated, thinking Woman, but it was really because he could then use his power to contradict us soundly and feel good for the rest of the day. Clarence liked to justify himself to us all the time because we didn't actually exist as real people and therefore couldn't criticise him effectually afterwards.

I knew quite a lot about Clarence because every so often I'd had to stand in for Peggy and take dictation. Dictation usually consisted of the communication of a spattering of work in amongst a large amount of irrelevant material.

The man was ex-working class, had been to a provincial university in the sixties and done well for himself. At that time, he confided to me, he had been a socialist: 'Wilson's whizz-kids, those were the days . . . now, of course, things are different. The Labour Party is no longer the party I gave my allegiance to all those years ago. I voted Tory myself in the last election, much as I hate that woman. But somebody had to put the country to rights, teach the unions a lesson. I could give you twenty reasons why a form of radical Toryism is what this country needs most now; I mean, look what's happened to the SDP. It's what the people want, Babs, you have to admit it.'

I had made the mistake once of confiding something of my own politics to him also and was still trying to live down the tinge of parlour radicalism.

The particular day in question was a fine, bright May morning. For once the office colours looked cheerful rather than post-modern and I started the morning feeling so good I even remembered to water the geraniums before settling down to type up a long report on increasing regional bed throughput. The geraniums, generally, were Peggy's responsibility; she was rather fond of plants. At ten o'clock I whisked out one thick, crisp, clean page and suggested coffee. Our usual routine.

'I'll get it,' she said, but we were both keen to get away from our desks for a moment and I got to the door first.

'My turn,' I insisted. 'Are you still on the diet?'

'I'm always on a diet,' she said gloomily.

'Only two sugars then.' This was our joke.

Over coffee I read the paper and she took out her latest Agatha Christie. We read companionably with comfortable comments to each other.

'Good God, that bloke's been acquitted for strangling his wife while he was asleep,' I told her. 'Now I've heard everything. I bet even Agatha wouldn't have fallen for that one.'

'Well,' said Peggy thoughtfully, 'it's not provable either way . . .'

'I'm not sure being able to prove something means that much. Surely you have to use your common sense. In those thrillers isn't the solution of the mystery usually dependent on all sorts of factors that the police could never accept as evidence, or whatever? I mean, in real life, knowing who did it isn't the difficult bit – it's being able to prove it in a court of law.'

'I suppose so.'

'So who's been murdering who in the latest effort?' I asked her.

'An Indian colonel's widow has retired to post-war Britain, set up a boarding house and invited all the people in the world she hates most to live with her.'

'And one by one they're all being murdered?'

'Slowly but surely.'

'Any stranglings in their sleep?'

'Nothing like that. It's mainly good clean poisoning.'

'Poisoning! Now that's what I call an old-fashioned murder method. You don't hear of it much nowadays . . .'

'I wonder why not,' mused Peggy. She sounded interested.

'Oh, I suppose it wouldn't work. Poisons are hard to get now – you can't just walk into a chemist's and procure arsenic for rat killing any more . . .'

'But think of hospitals. Why, I had to go down to St Margaret's last week to look up some old patients' files and the new pharmacy store was just wide open. It's still only half built. Anyone could have walked in.'

'Yes, but think of the knowledge you'd need – what to get and how much to give and how to disguise the taste . . . it can't be easy to persuade someone that their tea doesn't taste of strychnine.'

'Well, everyone reads all those medical articles in magazines these days; we're all very well read really.'

'It takes more than being well read to poison somebody effectually.'

'It takes,' averred Peggy judicially, 'being well read, having the opportunity and motive *and* being well organised.'

'You make it sound like choosing TV channels on a night in.'

She shrugged and laughed.

At this point Mr Clarkson breezed in. 'Morning, Peg, Babs.' He leaned over Peggy's desk so he could examine her book and read the title. 'Agatha Christie, eh, Peg? I didn't think women of today were interested in that kind of nonsense, murders and such like.' He paused by my desk to glance at my breasts. 'What about your socialism then? I wouldn't have thought this was ideologically correct. You'll be off to Siberia in no time and then who'll miss you, Babs? Well, I will at least.'

The morning leer and loiter being over, Clarence headed for his room and let the door swing shut behind him. I could imagine him up-ending his briefcase, flinging his overcoat over a hook and slumping into his executive swivel chair. I guessed he'd sigh, poke about at his mail and wish for the nth time that he'd got himself into a more glamorous and lucrative line of business than health service administration, a job where he'd be entitled to a real leather office suite, real parlour palms in the window instead of busy lizzies, a real expense account and a really smart permanent personal secretary.

We had just settled back into the typing again when Clarence put his head around the door and asked, 'Could someone bring me a cup of coffee, please?' He looked around with that pathetic, lost puppy-dog look that was supposed to be so endearing. Perhaps it would have been were it not attached to his rather greasy, nondescript, slightly pop-eyed face.

Peggy pursed her lips and started to get to her feet.

'No, my turn,' I said quickly.

'I hope you ladies aren't fighting over me again?' he cautioned before disappearing round the door again. We ignored him.

'You got them this morning, Barbara.'

'It's my turn for *his*,' I decided. As I clattered about the little kitchen I wondered why I bothered. When I'd started temping I used to make it an issue that I would not make coffee for anyone capable of making it themselves, unless as a mutual courtesy. But of course if I didn't do it someone else had to, and it hardly seemed fair to leave all of Clarence's domestic duties to Peggy.

The kitchen was a little cubbyhole just outside the outer office between us and the stairs. No one else used it much. It had just enough room for a small sink by the window, a cupboard beneath it full of cleaning equipment, and a couple of wall units in which were kept cups and saucers, mugs and plates, coffee, tea and, sometimes, biscuits. A small fridge held milk and occasionally our lunches. This little refuge was far enough out of everyone else's way to be safe to leave possessions not intrinsically of much value in.

When I returned Clarence was leaning over Peggy's desk in an overbearing manner and rambling on laconically in inimitable fashion. Peggy had her notebook out so he must be dictating. Sometimes it was hard to tell.

'About this circular re the new community health council at Shot End,' he was saying. 'We'll have to write to Blah, Blank and Blower to get their opinions. You know the sort of thing – "Dear Sir, etc., I enclose a circular for your information" – thanks, Babs – "would be interested in all comments." Mention the public meeting on the – you know what date it is, ask Blah to get up a few replies to questions on the premises problem. I hear someone's making waves. Of course we don't have the money for it anyway, but we won't get into that. That's not for the record, Peg. "Yours, etc." I leave you to dot the i's and cross the t's.'

One day I swear I'll write up letters exactly as he dictates them, I was thinking as he disappeared back into his office – grammatical omissions, sarkey asides and all.

He was back again before I could sit down, a thin sheaf of papers in one hand, obviously ripe for more communication. But before business, pleasure. He looked me up and down. I hurriedly retreated behind my desk.

'Good heavens, is that a mini skirt, Babs?'

I pointed out that mini skirts are generally thought of as ending above rather than below the knee, and also that it was no business of his what I wore. A few minutes of banter passed pleasantly.

'Well, I must say I remember the days of the first minis, wonderful days! We men all enjoyed them tremendously, a bit of fun if you know what I mean. Don't suppose you do though. Still, I expect Peg's old enough to remember mini skirts – or is that an indelicate assumption? Mind you, if women expect to be treated equally they have to be prepared to put up with questions like that. They have to be prepared for a bit of piss-taking nowadays. I prefer it. Not so much formality in the office as there used to be.'

Peggy reminded him that he was there to talk about the day's appointments.

'Oh, yes, of course, but there's no reason why we can't have a pleasant chat first . . . I bet you'd be the first ones to complain if we men stopped holding doors open for you. I know you all like those little attentions, that's why women's lib is very limited really. I mean, I'm all in favour of equality but I think it's got as far as it can now. I think those feminist extremists are in a fair way of ruining everything for the ordinary woman, the woman in the street!' He laughed, obviously thinking this a joke.

'You know,' he went on suddenly, turning to me, 'I know you'll think I'm being sexist but really that jumper quite suits you. I don't know, it seems to set off your figure very nicely, perhaps it's the colour. It's no use pretending you're not a pretty girl, Babs! I mean, a man can't help but notice, and you know it's a compliment, I'm not trying to put you down.' He changed tack slightly. 'And, Peg, you know, you're the most efficient secretary I've ever had. Has anyone ever told you that if you'd just lose a few pounds you'd be a very attractive girl? Don't your boyfriends tell you that? – I know you never talk about your boyfriends at work but I know you must have lots?'

It had taken me a long time to perfect my blank and impervious expression as I sat through tirades like this. Just when he seemed in full flood, Peggy stood up and said, 'I'm sorry, I thought you wanted to discuss the day's business.'

'Yes, yes, of course,' he grinned. He showed her into his office with an ironic flourish. Unfortunately he left the door open so I could hear them working through his agenda for the week. When I got up to photocopy some documents I could see Mr Clarkson running his hands through his undistinguished greying hair and sprawling casually backwards in his chair as he must have seen business moguls do in films.

One of the worst aspects of working there was the loudness of Clarence's voice. The fact that he rarely shut his office door during consultations and meetings was just another of his irritating mannerisms. For him it was a sign of office democracy; for us it meant you could always hear him rabbiting on at full tilt no matter now fast you clattered away at your typewriter.

On this particular day I couldn't help but overhear him giving Peggy a confidential report to type on how the district health services would cope should a thirty megaton bomb be dropped on the High Street. I heard Peggy laughing after a glance at it. 'That's all very well,' I heard him continue, suddenly sober, 'but the government want this information and I happen to think the issue of civil defence is extremely important.'

'But I typed the first draft,' Peggy pointed out, 'and it's full of nonsense like sandbagging the ground-floor windows of the hospitals and sending home all patients who can be moved for the duration so that the beds can be used for "casualties" . . . my God, if only people knew the effectiveness of all this *planning* . . .'

'I suppose you'd just like us to sit still and let the Russians run all over us?' Peggy was silent. I too have discovered that there is no answer to this as the sort of people who pose the question are emotionally incapable of trying to understand the complexities of international relations.

In the ensuing silence, Clarence managed to switch with his usual logic to another 'sensitive' subject. 'And in times like these,' he said, rustling his copy of the morning's paper, 'everyone has to be prepared to deal with terrorism at every level. I just thank God *we* didn't have to deal with the results of this yesterday.' He was presumably pointing to the glaring headlines I had already noticed, including words like 'carnage', 'bloodbath' and 'cowards'. And this was only the *Guardian*.

It occurred to me that you only had to catch sight of this particular group of lurid nouns to know that another Irish 'atrocity' was being panned by the neutral British press. Another car bomb had been set off outside a West London barracks the previous afternoon. 'Five men dead, twenty-seven more in hospital, fourteen with serious injuries,' Clarence mused.

'Thank God they didn't kill any horses this time,' Peggy could not resist saying, 'or they would really be in trouble.'

'You cannot possibly defend vicious murderers like these,' he began. I knew how Peggy would be feeling, wanting to kick herself for saying anything at all. I pounded fiercely away at my statistics. Obviously he was going to go on now for quite a while. 'How can you defend this type of crude violence? I agree, there *is* a problem in Northern Ireland, there *has* been injustice. But these savage acts only alienate people, moderate people like me, from their cause. They don't do themselves any good by indulging in this senseless slaughter.'

'Perhaps they're absolutely at the end of their tether,' I heard Peggy suggest. There was a certain amount of tension in her voice which seemed to indicate that Peggy herself might be feeling somewhat similarly stretched.

'And I can't understand how any intelligent person can condone such acts,' Clarence added poignantly. I could tell from the sounds that he was getting up, preparing to end the interview because it was no longer comfortable for him. 'I know you were brought up a Catholic yourself, but still . . .' Perhaps the thought of convent school girls helped to lead his mind back to pleasanter associations, because as they reached my desk, he smiled and drifted easily from one mode of offensiveness to another. 'Just think, eh, the mother superior's little angels growing up into feminists and terrorist sympathisers . . . I don't know what they teach girls in school now anyway.' Having reduced us in his own mind, if that was the correct term, to examples of modern feminine hysteria, we were dismissed with a pleasant smile. Clarence ambled away for a chat with one or two of his cronies elsewhere. Leaving us to get on with the work. Peggy sat down stony-faced at her desk, and said nothing.

*

Clarence had two meetings that morning, followed by a long working lunch. He returned, looking a little flushed, at three, which was fairly usual. As usual, also, before half past he stuck his head round the door and wondered aloud if anyone could possibly fetch him a cup of coffee. I was knee-deep in ordering but I reckoned it was Peggy's turn anyhow. I heard her getting to her feet and leaving the room but I was not paying much attention. We were not due for another break till four o'clock, so Peggy returned with only one mug on a tray and took it through into Clarence's office. On the way out she very gently shut the door. Peggy sat down and started to type rapidly, the old electric typewriter, which was all they offered us, fairly buzzing away.

A little later I heard a funny noise from Clarence's office.

'Did you hear something?' I asked, raising my head.

Peggy shook her head, and didn't even look up. 'Can't hear a thing over all this,' she said.

'I think Clarence has finally overdone the liquid lunch and fallen off his chair,' I scoffed.

She smiled briefly, concentrating.

Just after four o'clock I got a phone call for Mr Clarkson. 'Do you think Clarence is officially in?' I asked Peggy before putting it through.

'I think he'll have to be,' she said.

I tried to put the call through but Clarence's line seemed to be engaged. 'Oh God,' I muttered, 'the silly sod's left the phone off the hook again.' I got up reluctantly and knocked on his door, then, hearing no reply, I pushed it open. The phone was on the carpet and so was Mr Clarkson. My mind went completely blank and I backed away rapidly, feeling quite faint and trembly. 'Something's wrong,' I heard myself saying. 'I think he's ill . . .'

Ill was not actually the word for what I thought had happened to Clarence.

Within seconds Peggy was on the phone to the police. I could hear her saying, 'It's an emergency, please. Send an ambulance. There seems to have been an accident . . .'

A little later, when the fuss was at its height and no one was paying any attention to me, I began to stop feeling numb and decided a cup of tea would pick me up no end. By this time our office was a seething mass of police, ambulance men and on-lookers. But considering that this was a Health Authority and highly staffed with medical men there was remarkably little actual hysteria. Fragments of conversation floated by: 'Of course, he always looked as if he had a touch of blood pressure . . .' 'Worked too hard, always at it . . .' 'It's usually the heart –' 'My wife's uncle . . .' I wanted to get out of the way in case somebody suggested I call his wife. Cowardly as ever, I found myself thinking this was more of a job for Peggy, and suddenly realised she must have quietly absented herself some time before.

I found her in the kitchen doing the washing-up. Shock, I thought, takes strange forms. Coffee-pot, filter, mugs, saucers, spoons were all upended and glistening on the draining board.

'You could have left this till later,' I suggested sympathetically.

Peggy jumped, look around, and said, 'Oh, it's you.' Then she added, 'I don't like leaving a mess . . .'

After I switched on the kettle I began to wonder. 'Perhaps I'd better not – aren't you supposed to leave everything untouched?' I told you I was naive. It was only then that I noticed the very last thing that Peggy was carefully rinsing under the splashing taps – a small phial with an unmistakeable St Margaret's Hospital Pharmacy label on it. St Margaret's was only about a ten minutes' walk away. We exchanged a look. Peggy slipped the jar into her pocket. 'I'm just going to the toilet,' she said.

I made myself a cup of tea very slowly and rather thoughtfully. By the time I had drunk it amidst the clearing hubbub I had made my mind up. I was only glad they had removed the body quickly. Corpses tend to soften my resolve.

Peggy had returned to her desk and the police were ready to interview us. Peggy said nothing to me but I listened keenly to her story, a simple 'We were working. Mr Clarkson made his own cup of coffee' – and then heard myself confirming it. 'Oh, yes, Mr Clarkson was a sort of modern boss, he always made his own coffee.'

Peggy looked at me very hard before she smiled.

As I said, I'm counting the days till this assignment ends.

Biographical Notes on the Contributors

Abby Bardi is a lecturer in English for the University of Maryland's European Division. A singer/songwriter and Jazzercise instructor, she lives in Gloucestershire with her husband and two children, and has recently completed her second novel.

Diane Biondo is the author of four plays, *Slipstreaming, Hitting Home, Penance* and *Four Walls*. She has co-written a chapter for *Feminism and Censorship – the Current Debate* (Prism Press, 1988). Her short story 'Monopoly' has been accepted for the forthcoming Sheba anthology, *Serious Pleasure*. Since first coming to London from Brooklyn, New York, in 1981, she has earned her living working in the book trade.

Jane Burke was born in Birmingham and brought up in a mining village near Sheffield. She has worked as a research assistant and secretary within the National Health Service. She is currently working in London as a nurse at the Elizabeth Garrett Anderson Hospital for women, bringing up a baby son, and writing a novel.

Amanda Cross is the pseudonym of Carolyn Heilbrun, Avalon Foundation Professor in the Humanities at Columbia University, New York. Her mysteries are *In the Last Analysis, The James Joyce Murder, Poetic Justice, The Theban Mysteries, The Question of Max, Death in a Tenured Position, Sweet Death, Kind Death, No Word from Winifred* and *A Trap for Fools*.

Susan Dunlap is the author of nine mystery novels and a number of short stories. Her novels feature forensic pathologist turned private investigator Kiernan O'Shaughnessy (*Pious Deception*) Californian Police Detective Jill Smith (*A Dinner to Die For, Too Close to the Edge, Not Exactly a*

Brahmin, As a Favor, and *Karma*) and public utility meter reader Vejay Haskell (*The Last Annual Slugfest, The Bohemian Connection,* and *An Equal Opportunity Death*). She has been a social worker. Now, besides writing, she teaches Hatha Yoga.

Val McDermid has worked as a journalist since 1975 and currently works for the *People* in Manchester. She is active in the National Union of Journalists and has held several Branch Official posts. Her first mystery novel, *Report for Murder,* was published by The Women's Press in 1987. She has had two stage plays performed and her radio play *Like a Happy Ending* was the first publication of the Scottish Society of Playwrights.

Millie Murray was born in London in 1958, of Jamaican parentage. Her novel *Kiesha,* for teenagers, was published by Livewire in 1988. Her stories 'The Escape' and 'Changes' have appeared in *Watchers and Seekers* (The Women's Press, 1987) and *A Girl's Best Friend* (Livewire, 1987). She is currently writer-in-residence in the Borough of Newham.

Rebecca O'Rourke is a member of a small lesbian writers' group. She is also an active member of the Federation of Worker Writers and Community Publishers, in whose workshop publications much of her work appears. She has written a number of critical works as well as a novel, *Jumping the Cracks* (Virago, 1987). She lives in London and works as an adult education tutor.

Sara Paretsky is author of five mystery novels featuring Chicago-based private investigator V.I. Warshawski: *Indemnity Only, Deadlock, Killing Orders, Bitter Medicine* and *Toxic Shock.* She is president and co-founder of Sisters in Crime. She lives in Chicago.

Sheila Radley was born and brought up in a Northamptonshire village. She graduated from London University in 1951. After serving in the Women's Royal Air Force and then working as a teacher, a civil servant and in advertising, she moved to Norfolk to help run a village post office. The crime novels in her Chief Inspector Quantrill series are *Death and the Maiden, The Chief Inspector's Daughter, A Talent for Destruction, Blood on the Happy Highway, Fate Worse Than Death* and *Who Saw Him Die?*

Anne Stanesby is a solicitor who has worked in private practice, for a law centre, for the organisation Release and currently works for a local authority in London. She contributed to *Trouble with the Law* (Pluto Press, 1978) and wrote the *Consumer Rights Handbook* (Pluto, 1986). Previous publications have been in the field of legal advice, including handbooks on immigration law and on hallucinogenic fungi.

Penny Sumner was born in Australia in 1955. She came to England in 1979 to do a doctorate in English at Oxford. She tutored part-time at Oxford, was warden of a student house and assistant dean at one of the colleges. She is currently teaching at the University College of Wales, Aberystwyth. 'Caroline' is her first published story.

Sue Ward is a freelance journalist and researcher who specialises in pensions and financial questions. She has written a number of technical books, although 'Teddy' is her first published fiction. She has been a Londoner most of her life, but has recently moved to the North-East.

Lucy Anne Watt grew up in Hampshire and graduated from the University of Manchester. She has worked as a teacher at a village school and at the London Stage School, and as a secretary/editorial assistant for national newspapers and magazines. She currently runs a small business in Dorset. Her poetry has appeared in journals and anthologies, including *New Poetry 8* (Hutchinson, 1982) and *New Chatto Poets II* (1989).

Barbara Wilson is author of the two previous mysteries published by The Women's Press, *Murder in the Collective* and *Sisters of the Road*, and of the forthcoming *The Dog Collar Murders* (Virago). She lives in Seattle, where she is co-publisher of Seal Press.

Margaret Yorke lives in Buckinghamshire. She was a war-time driver in the WRNS; a school secretary, bookseller and Oxford college librarian before becoming a full-time writer. She wrote a number of problem novels before turning to crime with *Dead in the Morning* (1970). Her books include *No Medals for the Major, The Scent of Fear, The Hand of Death, Devil's Work, Find Me a Villain, The Smooth Face of Evil, Intimate Kill, Safely to the Grave, Evidence to Destroy*, and *Speak for the Dead*. She chaired the British Crime Writers Association (1979–80).